CIRCLE OF NINE
Beltany

Book One in the Circle of Nine Series

D1416865

VALERIE BIEL

Published by Lost Lake Press
www.LostLakePress.com

This book is a work of fiction. Any references to historical events, real people, or real places are used fictitiously. Other names, characters, places, and events are the product of the author's imagination, and any resemblance to actual events or places or persons, living or dead, is entirely coincidental.

Copyright ©2014 Valerie Biel

All rights reserved. No part of this book may be reproduced, scanned, or distributed in any printed or electronic form without permission.

Cover Art and Interior Art: Kelsey Curkeet

Library of Congress Control Number: 2014947210
Lost Lake Press, Randolph, WI

ISBN: 0990645002
ISBN 13: 9780990645009

ACKNOWLEDGEMENTS

I would like to thank my fantastic critique group, Silvia Acevedo, Christine Esser, and Keith Pitsch, for their astute editing capabilities and wisdom of all things writerly. Infinite thanks to Tillie Roth and Brenda Schaefer who read through more versions of this book than I care to admit. Thanks also to my many other test readers. Your early support made all the difference. And most of all, to my husband and kids, who give me the space to write because they know how much it means to me.

THE WHEEL OF THE YEAR

MABON SAMHAIN YULE IMBOLC OSTARA

LAMMAS SUMMER SOLSTICE BELTANE

SEPT. 20-23 OCT. 31 DEC. 20-23 FEB. 2 MAR. 20-23

AUG. 1 JUN. 20-23 APR. 30

LIFE DEATH

REBIRTH

◆

Magic stirs as fingers trace the sacred knot carved on my case.
Power swirls into my binding. The riddled spells begin unwinding.
It's time to learn what lies within I whisper gently to the Quinn.

◆

CHAPTER ONE

The grandmother clock chimed midnight in the hallway below my bedroom, and I whispered my first birthday wish, "No shoveling, no shoveling, no shoveling." The odd shadows cast by the yard light made it seem as though the snowflakes spiraled backward into the sky. Leaning closer to the frosty pane, I was relieved to see only a thin layer of snow on the ground – definitely not enough to shovel, but, thankfully, enough to hide the ashes that had once been our Yule tree.

The tree had been part of our winter solstice celebration on December 21. Twelve days later Mom always burned the tree on top of the herb garden. I was grateful she chose to perform this little ritual in the backyard instead of the front yard where everyone could see, and now at least the ash pile was covered with new snow. Our neighbors knew we didn't celebrate the same holidays as they did, but I didn't think there was any point in drawing attention to that fact.

With the exception of torching our tree – and yeah, I knew it was a big exception – I liked to imagine our Yule celebration was like everyone else's Christmas. It was one of the few times during the year when I felt like I fit in.

As my breath slowly fogged my view of the backyard, Mom popped her head into my room. "Happy Birthday, Brigit Blaise Quinn. It's getting late, but I'm glad you're still awake. I have a present I want to give you."

"What? Now?" My birthday was only a minute old.

Mom carried a wooden box into my room. Her cheeks were pink and her eyes sparkled with excitement. "I've waited years to give this to you. My mother gave it to me on my fifteenth birthday, and now it's my turn to pass it on to you." She sat on the edge of my bed, and I maneuvered out of my comforter to perch next to her.

"Obviously, you know we follow a different path than most people," Mom continued.

I nearly snorted at her understatement that the Pagan religion she followed (and I tolerated) was a simple life-style choice.

She paused and seemed to search for the right words. "You remember the story I told you about the Tuatha de Danann, the ancient Irish tribe?"

"Sure, I like that story." The magical tales about the mythological founding tribes of Ireland who built all the stone circles were my favorites.

"Right, but the thing is – the Tuatha aren't a myth. They really existed."

"It's not just a legend?"

"No, it's not. They ruled Ireland four thousand years ago, until they were defeated and banished to the mountains."

"Okay." I shrugged my shoulders, confused why this was important.

"There are some people who can still trace their lineage back to the Tuatha and that includes us. We're their descendants."

I didn't understand why she was making a big deal about this. "Everyone's descended from someone, right?" And then I had a neat thought. "Wait! Does this make me royalty? Are you going to tell me I'm a princess?" Now that would be a really great birthday present.

She smiled at my suggestion. "No, this doesn't make you a princess, but being a descendant of the Tuatha is exciting in a different way."

She shifted the box onto my lap and said, "We can learn a lot from our ancestors."

Curious, I ran my hand over the intricate carvings on the lid and grasped the heavy metal clasp. It was obviously very old. When I flipped it open, the hinges actually creaked. Inside was a thick book with a sturdy brown leather cover, worn around the edges. I took it out, but, before I could open it to see what was inside, Mom covered my hands with hers and said, "You're old enough to know. This is your history, where you are from, and who you could be if you choose it."

Puzzled by her strange message and sudden seriousness, I waited for her to pull her hands away, and when she did, I turned to the first page. Although the script was hard to read, I made out the name Onora Quinn and the date September 19, 1324.

"Someone really wrote in this book nearly 700 years ago? There's no way it could have lasted this long." I squinted hard at the old page.

"It has survived against all odds, so treat it gently. Onora was your twenty-fifth great-grandmother and the first of the Tuatha to record her story in written form. This book has been passed down to each generation, and now it's yours." She looked a little sad for a moment and then warned. "Don't stay up too late reading."

But, of course, I did.

CHAPTER TWO

Onora Quinn
The Nineteenth Day of September
In the Year Thirteen Hundred Twenty-four

I slowly deciphered the old writing as I began to read the verse written below the name and date. Part way through my fingers tingled and my room blurred away. I could see Onora. Her long red hair cascaded to her waist like a shawl as she bent over a table with a quill in her hand. She was writing in a book – this book! Then the scene changed abruptly, shifting like I was watching a movie.

O nora could not be late. Her presence and the sacred items she carried were essential for the ceremony. Her heart thudded rapidly, keeping time with the rhythm of her feet as she pounded down the path to the base of the hill. She'd been careful to slip out of the village unnoticed after hearing the severe warnings in the priest's Sunday sermon.

Father Banan's decree that the ancient ways were wicked and sinful had not made sense to Onora, but she was unable to challenge him without the risk of being labeled a witch. She did not blame the villagers who now followed Father Banan's teachings. His preaching was very persuasive, and to most people the old stories of the Tuatha were simply legends passed down to each generation. Only a few knew the truth that this founding tribe of Ireland had been real and its few remaining descendants still existed, quietly honoring Mother Earth as guardians of the ancient ways.

Onora chose to ignore the warning because tonight she and her fellow Tuatha decided they wouldn't hide in the shadows. It was Beltane Eve and the bonfire inside the stone circle at Beltany was a necessity to usher in the first day of May. Although it would surely be seen from the village, they felt safe from discovery because everyone knew the peril of interfering with the ritual blessing. She could not imagine that even the most devout of Father Banan's followers would risk a year of misfortune and poor crops by venturing out on this night to stop them.

Even so, Onora couldn't help scanning the path behind her for pursuers, letting out a little sigh of relief at its emptiness. With the last of the sun flickering orange light across her face, she hitched up her long skirt and started the steep climb to the stone circle.

She was breathing heavily when she finally reached the top of the hill where the tall stones cast long shadows across the grass. The others had already decorated the altar stone with blossoming hawthorn branches and wreaths of daffodils. She inhaled the flowers' fresh scent and quickly took the necessary items from her bundle. The silver goblet went in the place of honor at the center of the altar and beside it she placed a matching silver dagger. She set the leather flask of mead off to the side.

As the May Queen this year, Onora would lead the ceremony honoring the sun's growing warmth and blessing the year's crops. She walked through the stone circle and was handed a torch when she joined the other eight maidens next to the pile of brushwood in the center. They all turned to look at the sky, and when the sun dipped below the horizon, she touched the flame to the kindling. The fire caught and began to crackle. She watched it grow and tossed the torch into the flames before stepping back into her place and linking hands with the others.

Onora's steady voice began the chant and the others joined in.

"Within this circle of ancient stone
Years and years of flame have shone.
Guiding us each Beltane Eve
With the words we now weave.
Mother Earth, your power true
We honor you in all we do.
Bless us now as the season shifts
With the bounty of your gifts.
Goddess grant us health and love.
Embrace your children from above,
So we can live well and strong,
Today, tomorrow, all year long.
Show us now your endless power
As we fuel the fire 'til May's first hour."

The last word was barely out of their mouths when the flames flared and made the nine maidens jump back.

"She's heard our call," Onora said as the others murmured excitedly to each other.

They rejoined hands and continued circling the fire as they waited eagerly for the arrival of the Oak King and his fellow princes. With the eyes and ears of Father Banan's spies everywhere, the maidens had been careful to invite only young men they trusted. This year's Oak King was Onora's betrothed, Ian. They had promised themselves to each other in the hand-fasting ceremony in August of last year and, following tradition, they would take their official vows exactly one year and one day later.

Without warning, the young men jumped out of the darkness and scared the girls, their shrieks turning to laughter as they greeted each other. The couples joined hands and walked to the altar. Onora filled the goblet with mead and held it in her right hand and the dagger in her left. She dipped the blade into the golden liquid, lifted them high and began the sacred blessing.

"Goddess of summer, bless the fertile earth and all her creatures both male and female. Place the dark days of winter behind us and let the sun make our crops bountiful so that we may live well until Beltane next. Let us unite in love and harmony for all days."

Everyone responded together, "Make it so."

Onora took a drink of the mead, enjoying the taste of the sweet honey wine before passing the goblet around for all to share. The young men grabbed their partners and, in a swirl of skirts and boisterous voices, began a final dance around the fire. One by one each couple, their faces flushed from heat, mead, and anticipation, left the circle of stones for the privacy of the nearby woods. Onora stopped to gather the goblet and dagger before she and Ian did the same.

They were nearly to the trees, when the shouts of warning startled them. Only then did they notice the bobbing line of torches approaching from the village.

"Run, run! They've come for us!" cried a closer voice, and Onora and Ian fled deep into the woods with their pursuers close behind.

Ian whispered, "We must hide ourselves, or they'll catch us for certain."

He pointed to a space between two mossy logs, and they quickly climbed in, covering themselves with last year's fallen leaves. When Onora turned her head, she could see through a small opening and gasped when she glimpsed the light of the torches dangerously near. Ian squeezed her arm warning her to keep still. The voices were clear.

"I'm sure some of the heathens came this way, Father," said a male voice.

"Aye, they did, but I cannot hear them anymore. We may not catch them all tonight. I'm sure the ones we have will let us know who led this wickedness. Whoever led them astray must renounce their godlessness or burn in Hell. We cannot have this evil in our midst any longer." Father Banan's deep voice was unmistakable.

The searchers were standing so close that Onora could see the stitching on their shoes. She was sure that they would hear her breathing. Ian must have sensed her panic and his slight touch helped to calm her.

"Let's take the longer path to the village and see if we can round up more of them," Father said.

Ian and Onora heard the men leave but stayed hidden for a long time. When they finally felt it was safe to come out, they were stiff and covered with dirt. It was still dark in the woods, but dawn could not be far off.

"Ian, we cannot go back to the village," Onora said. "They will surely guess I led the ceremony even if the others keep quiet."

Onora waited for Ian's answer as he paced back and forth. Finally, he responded. "We have badly underestimated Father Banan's power. I never believed so many would see evil in the old ways. We would be foolish to return, but where shall we go?"

"We must go to Bressa. She will keep us safe until we can decide what to do." Onora spoke with confidence.

Ian sounded less sure. "Do you not believe someone will think to look for us there? It is known you visit her often."

"Yes, but where will they look? Only my mother could tell them exactly where to find Bressa after her banishment from the village. Not even you would know if I had not taken you to meet her. Please do not tell me you think my mother will betray us." Her voice rose at the implication.

Ian stared at Onora's frantic expression and gave in. "Let us go then. We waste the last of the darkness arguing."

They began walking and linked hands after a few paces. The sun was high in the sky when they reached the edge of Lough Dooras. Bressa lived on the island in the middle of the lake, but her home was well hidden by trees. The only visible signs of civilization were ancient ones. Two statues at least ten feet tall and carved from pillars of rock sat near the shore, one facing east and the other west. Their formidable expressions, combined with the superstitious legends told around the hearth, made the island a forbidding place. Most people believed bad luck would befall them if they dared to visit it.

"Will she know we have come, or will we have to swim?" Ian asked.

"She will come," Onora said confidently and sat down on the bank to wait.

Ian sat down, too. He knew better than to question how Bressa would know they were there.

It wasn't long before Bressa appeared through the trees. Although she was small and slightly bent from age, she was surprisingly strong. She easily pulled her boat out of its hiding place in the tall grass, slid it into the water, and rowed over to them, gracefully avoiding the rocks rising from the lake's surface. Her long, white hair blew in the breeze, and they could hear her singing as she got closer. When she bumped into the shore, Ian grabbed the edge of the boat.

Bressa turned and said, "If I am to believe the tea leaves at the bottom of my morning cup, there is danger all around you. Let us get back to safety, and you can tell me the tale."

They repeated the process quickly, rowing across and hiding the boat. A few steps into the trees Bressa's house appeared almost magically before them. It was as if one minute it wasn't there and the next it was.

Their eyes took a few moments to adjust to the dim light inside. The only window was covered with an oil cloth which was pulled back, but the nearby trees blocked most of the sunlight.

Her house was one big room with a fireplace in the middle. There was no chimney, but a hole in the roof allowed the smoke to escape. Under a loft on one side of the room, there was space for Bressa's bed and a large chest. The rest of the room was taken up with a rough table and chairs, and along the edges stood shelves containing a number of pottery jars and food items.

Bressa went over to the fire to make some more tea while Onora and Ian took seats at the table. The last time Onora had visited, she had explained how Father Banan said the ancient customs were wicked, and God would punish those who took part in the rituals honoring the earth's seasons.

"We knew he was gaining followers in the village, but we did not think the danger was so great," Onora exclaimed. "They came for us after the Beltane fire. We were in the woods and were able to hide, but I know many were caught. He said I must renounce my godlessness or I will burn in Hell." Onora's eyes brimmed with tears.

Bressa brought the tea and some bread to the table. She sat down with them but didn't say anything.

"Bressa, how can they think I am evil?" Onora asked with a trembling voice. "I am afraid my friends will be hurt."

"There, there," Bressa said patting Onora's hand. "I feel a growing ill-wind, but the time will come for action soon enough. Now, finish your tea and bread so you can rest. We will talk more later."

Ian and Onora climbed to the loft where they collapsed onto the blankets laid out for them. They were asleep within moments.

Bressa stirred the fire, sending sparks into the air. She stared at the embers to see what they would tell her of the future. Her eyes widened, and a stricken look came upon her face. The tears flowed down her cheeks, and she made no attempt to wipe them away.

⟶ ∞∞∞ ⟵

I was getting stiff from sitting so still. When I changed position, the lamplight flickered on the page, making it glow for a moment. I rubbed my eyes and checked the clock – two in the morning! No wonder my eyes were playing tricks on me. I began to close the cover and glanced back at the page so I could remember my place. I couldn't believe it. I was still at the beginning. Impossible! How could I read for three hours and still be on page one?

I read the words as if I were seeing them for the first time:

> *Here I now begin the spell.*
> *See the story I must tell.*
> *Read this page and I command*
> *You will begin to understand*
> *How everything has happened.*
> *If only words you see before ye*
> *Then alas you are not worthy.*

Had I somehow dreamt up Onora and Ian's story? My imagination wasn't normally that good, but it was equally hard to believe the alternative that the book had come to life somehow. I really needed to ask Mom about this, but it was the middle of the night and I couldn't ask her now. I set my alarm earlier than usual so I'd have time to talk to her before school. I was exhausted, but morning could not come soon enough.

CHAPTER THREE

I jolted awake at the first blast of my alarm. For a sleepy moment I was confused by the time on the clock. Then I remembered why I wanted to be up so early.

Getting ready for school took no time at all because I rarely fussed with my hair or make up. The only thing that took a little longer was brushing through my wavy, shoulder-length hair and pulling it into a messy bun. I thought my hair was my best feature, even if the dark blonde color was a little boring. A few minutes later, I ran into the kitchen, ducking through its low doorway as I entered. Our little house was very old, and even now the kitchen had most of its original colonial features, which wasn't rare for this part of Massachusetts. I loved the white walls, beamed ceiling, and the massive stone fireplace taking up the entire back wall.

"Hello, Birthday Girl! So how does it feel to be fifteen?" Mom asked when I came in.

I shrugged because I didn't know how to answer her. I hadn't expected to feel different at all, but the book had cast a cloud over any normal birthday excitement.

"I knew you'd want to talk before school. That's why I made breakfast early. Come and eat before everything gets cold."

I sat down but didn't touch the food. I needed answers but I wasn't sure I was going to like them. "That book is really strange – scary even. It felt like I was watching a movie. When I stopped I should have been dozens of pages into the book, but I was still on Onora's first page. I don't understand. Was I imagining things? Did I fall asleep and dream all of it?"

She took a deep breath before speaking. "You didn't dream or imagine any of it. I was very confused when Grandma gave me the book, too. There's nothing to be scared of. It is a wonderful, wonderful gift the women in our family seem to have, this special way of telling a story. You can see the events from the past each woman wants us to remember."

"Why didn't you tell me that was going to happen?"

"Would you have believed me without seeing it for yourself?"

I stared at her for a minute unable to process what she was saying. "I'm supposed to believe the book *showed* me the story when I read the first page?"

"It's hard to accept, I know, but isn't that exactly what happened?"

"I don't *know* what really happened." I shook my head in disbelief. "It doesn't make sense to me. People can't make books that tell stories that way."

"Some people can," she stated simply.

"Can you?" My voice cracked. It was an incredible thing she was trying to get me to believe, and I felt like I had entered another dimension.

She stalled by taking a drink of her tea and finally said, "Yes, I think I can. Grandma taught me how, but I haven't tried since before you were born when I put my story in the book."

I stared at her for a moment, incredulous. Finally, I asked, "Will I be able to do it?"

"Probably. If you can see the stories, you should have the power to record one, too."

"Oh, my God, Mom." What she was saying to me couldn't be true. Could it? If it was, then all the things everyone had ever thought about her – about us – all these years was true. My disbelief simmered into something else entirely.

"So what does this make us? Witches or something? I do not want to be a freak!" I was shouting across the kitchen table at her, and she cringed slightly at the force of my temper as I banged my fist on the table, making the dishes rattle. I couldn't remember ever being this angry. My pulse throbbed in my ears, and I felt the heat in my face. "Why didn't you explain this to me before now?"

She was unfailingly calm, which made me even angrier. I wanted her to shout back at me.

Instead, her voice was even and soft when she spoke. "Brigit, you need to take a deep breath. I know it seems unfair I've never mentioned this. Tradition dictates that our heritage isn't revealed until you are old enough to understand and not abuse your power. This is not a curse. It is a gift. The Tuatha have certain abilities, but . . ."

"Abilities?" I screeched. "What abilities?"

"It's too soon to know what yours will be. Each Tuatha has different gifts, and now that you are fifteen, we'll explore what yours might be. Maybe it will be something like my skill in botany. It's no different than anyone else's talent like musicians or mathematicians. It's nothing to be frightened of."

But I was afraid. No matter what she said, I knew this was nowhere near the same as being able to play the piano well or do Calculus. "We *are* witches," I whispered.

Mom shook her head forcefully. "No, we don't use that word. We are Tuatha." She finished very seriously with her eyes staring straight into mine and squeezed my hand in reassurance.

I wrenched my hand out of her grip and glared at her. I didn't want any part of this. I wanted to go back to being Normal Brigit like I was yesterday – well, almost normal anyway.

She ignored my simmering defiance and left the table to pour more tea. "You have a choice. You *always* have a choice to be whatever you want to be, but you owe it to yourself to know what you are choosing between."

Her cryptic answer only frustrated me and when my ride pulled up, I grabbed my backpack and stomped out the door without saying goodbye.

When I jumped into the back seat of the waiting car, my best friends Jess and Moriah nearly flattened me with their mega-decibel shout. "Happy Birthday!"

Their enthusiastic greeting made me grin and pushed a little of my anger and confusion away. I took a deep breath and pressed my sweaty palms against my thighs so my friends wouldn't notice my hands shaking.

"We can't wait to eat at Romano's tonight. I can-a taste-a the sauce-a already," Moriah said with her silly Italian accent.

Moriah always made me laugh. I was looking forward to eating at Romano's, too. It was the only really nice restaurant in town, meaning it actually had tablecloths.

We got to school as the first bell rang and snaked our way through the crowded front doors with the other students. At my locker, I was surprised by a bright blue envelope taped to the door with my name written in fancy calligraphy.

"When did you do this?" I shouted to Jess and Moriah as I removed the envelope and waved it in the air at them.

"It wasn't me," Jess yelled back.

"Not me either. I'm saving your presents for tonight," Moriah said.

They looked puzzled, before rushing off in different directions. I was positive they were just pretending they hadn't done it to tease me. I risked being late for class to open the envelope, and gasped in astonishment when I pulled out a sketch of myself. The message on the back said, "Have a Great Birthday!" There was no signature. I examined the drawing again and decided it had to be from Moriah. It didn't look like her work, but she was my only friend who could draw.

As I turned to walk down the rapidly emptying hall, I noticed another freshmen girl a few lockers down, staring at the card I was holding. I didn't really know her because she was part of the popular group. In an effort to be friendly, I was about to explain that it was my birthday when her words lashed out at me.

"I didn't know the witch girl had any other friends besides *those* two misfits."

I stared back at her in shock. This was the wrong day to mess with me, I thought as the bewilderment from my conversation with mom overwhelmed me again. An unfamiliar angry heat flushed down my arms, and I did something that surprised us both. I confronted her.

"What did you say?"

Her long, black hair whipped around in an arc as she pivoted toward me. "I didn't say anything." She gave me a look that let me know she thought I was a complete idiot, and then added, "Why would I talk to you, Freak?"

It wasn't weird to be called a freak, but what was weird is that I never saw her lips move when she said it. So unless Miss Hair Flip had suddenly taken up ventriloquism, my mind was playing tricks on me.

I was most definitely not Normal Brigit when my mouth opened and I hissed back, "Bitch." I froze to see what she would do. My mind was racing. I knew better than to pick a fight. Go along to get along – be inconspicuous – don't engage a bully, they're only looking for your reaction. My self-preservation tips circled my brain along with this new energy.

My adrenaline rush faded when she didn't even turn around. I was that inconsequential. But I did hear her mutter, "Witch," as she walked away.

You might be right, I thought and hurried to class. All morning I alternately worried about the Hallway Incident, Mom's Big Revelation, and the Mystery Artist.

At lunch I normally would have talked to Moriah and Jess about all three, except I felt stupid for how I had acted in the hallway, and I had no idea how to even begin to explain my legendary ancestry thing. Instead, I focused my attention on the anonymous gift. "Moriah, thanks for the sketch. You don't have to pretend any more. I appreciate the surprise."

"What are you talking about? I didn't give you a sketch. Is that what was in the envelope? Let me see it," she demanded.

I pulled the envelope out of my bag and handed it to her. "Besides you, who would have done it?"

"You must have a secret admirer," Jess said, nodding and leaning over to look at the drawing with Moriah.

"Not likely." I shrugged and picked at my lunch, pondering the possibilities in silence.

"Oh, oh, OH!" Moriah finally said, nearly choking on her food as she flapped her hands in the air. "Oh my God, I think I know. Yesterday, when I was in the art room after school, Tyler came in to work on a project. We were just talking about stuff, and I mentioned how we were going out to-night for your birthday. He asked me what you were really like, and I said how you were smart and fun and stuff like that."

"What? Tyler asked about me?" I gasped. "It doesn't make any sense. I've only talked to him a few times."

"Well, I have noticed him watching you a lot in art class lately. Maybe he was working on this sketch," Moriah suggested.

"Why didn't you tell me?" I wasn't sure what I would have done with the information, but it would have been nice to know a guy was paying attention to me – especially Tyler.

"Sorry. It didn't seem important until now," Moriah explained.

I didn't understand how she could think that was unimportant, but I knew it couldn't be him. "There's no way Senior Hottie and Athlete of the Year would be sketching me. Maybe it was Miss Sienna," I said.

"I think if she did it, she would have signed her name," Jess said.

I had to agree with her point about my art teacher, but there was no way it was Tyler McGrath. I would just have to see if he was acting suspicious in class. It would be easy to watch him because there were only twelve of us in Independent Art. Moriah and I usually kept to ourselves because we were the only freshmen who had been given permission to enroll.

The next two class periods went by as slow as homework on a sun-ny day. When I got to the art room everyone else was there except Tyler. Where was he? Keeping watch on the door, I pulled out my paints. We were working on portraits. I had painted Mom sitting on an old bench in our garden. I hoped to give it to her for a Mother's Day present. At the moment, though, I was having trouble getting the lighting on her face right. Finally, Tyler came in, looking upset. Miss Sienna simply raised her eyebrows when he roughly set up his supplies.

I kept glancing his way during class. His expression remained dark. I barely had the nerve to talk to him on a good day. I definitely wasn't going to approach him if he was in a bad mood. At the end of class, it took me a few minutes to clean up, and I was about to leave when Miss Sienna called Tyler into her office. They didn't shut the door, and I didn't mean to over-hear, but their words carried into the classroom.

"I can tell you're upset. Did you get a rejection letter?" Miss Sienna's voice was full of concern.

"No, that's not it. I got accepted, but my dad went nuts. He said over-his-dead-body would he allow me to go to art school. He wants me to take the full ride to play basketball instead. My mom wants me to do what I want to do, but my dad is definitely against it."

"Do you want me to talk to him? I could explain how prestigious this art school is and what this could mean for your future success. Maybe it would help?" Miss Sienna said kindly.

"I don't think it will matter. He says it's foolish to throw away the full basketball scholarship. He says art school is too expensive even with the partial scholarship and that my art will never generate enough income to live off of."

There was a moment of silence before Miss Sienna replied. "Don't do anything yet. You still have time to confirm with either school. Maybe he'll change his mind."

I was stunned. Tyler wanted to go to art school instead of play college basketball? No wonder his dad was going nuts. Tyler's big offer from Penn State was all anyone talked about lately.

I should have moved faster to get my butt into the hall, but Tyler stepped out of Miss Sienna's office and saw me standing there. The look on my face must have told him that I'd overheard the conversation.

"You heard all that?" he asked.

"Yes," I said, wishing I could disappear. His expression was more depressed than angry, so I risked saying more. "I think it's cool you want to go to art school."

"Well, you and Miss Sienna are the only ones who think it's a good idea."

I felt bad he hadn't gotten more encouragement from his family and tried to cheer him up. "I think you're a great artist and if you've been accepted, then the admissions committee believes you're talented, too. What school is it?"

"The Boston School of Fine Arts," he sighed.

"You're kidding! That's where I want to go. It's an awesome school."

We walked down the hall together while we talked about the college art program. When I got to my locker, Moriah and Jess stared at us in shock from a few feet away. The excitement of having an actual conversation with Tyler made me forget he might be the Mystery Artist.

I was too nervous to come right out and ask him if he'd done it, but while I picked the last of the tape from my locker door I managed to squeak out, "For my birthday someone surprised me with a sketch of myself. I'm not sure who it was, but it totally made my day."

I forced myself to remain calm as a guilty flush crept across his face. He dipped his head, and I thought he mumbled, "She's so awesome. Don't blow it McGrath." Clearly I was indulging in some wishful thinking.

He looked back up at me then and said, "I know I don't know you very well, but I thought you might like it."

I gaped at him in disbelief before finally uttering, "Thanks." Ugh! There were probably a million wonderfully witty things I could have said instead of that lame reply. I was an idiot – a polite one though.

He started to walk away but turned back. "I need to get to practice, but I wondered if you would go out with me after the game on Friday?"

I stared at him again, stunned. This can't be happening.

He broke the silence. "I mean, if you're not busy or anything."

For a moment I thought he might be playing a trick on me, but I saw worry flit across his face as if he were thinking, she's going to say no.

His insecurity spurred me into action. No way was I turning down this gorgeous, talented boy. "Sure, that – that'd be great," I stammered in my excitement.

"Excellent." He smiled and headed for the gym.

He was barely gone when Moriah and Jess skidded up to my locker. "Tell us. Tell us!"

"Oh my God! I can't believe this. He *is* the one who gave me the sketch and he asked me out." I was grinning like a fool, but I couldn't help it. My birthday was turning out better than I ever could have imagined!

Chapter Four

For the next few hours I obsessed about why Tyler had asked me out, pushing all thoughts of the Tuatha and my potential abilities aside. My earlier excitement had been tempered by my disbelief that he could really want to date me. I even called Jess for reassurance. She picked up on the first ring.

"Wow," I said, "that was fast."

She giggled and said, "Jason said he'd call when he got home."

She had a bad habit of giggling whenever she was talking about or talking to her boyfriend for all of two weeks. In fact, he was her first boyfriend ever. While this giggling thing was getting annoying, I could forgive her since she seemed so happy. I asked her if she thought it was odd that Tyler had asked me out.

"Brigit, why shouldn't someone awesome like Tyler ask you out? Don't you see how cool you are?"

"In case you haven't noticed, I'm not exactly the most popular girl in school. I don't think the word 'cool' applies to me."

"Well, I do. You are smart and funny and cute and talented. That's what really got his attention, right? Your artistic talent."

She was laying it on a bit thick. "You have to say that stuff – you're my friend."

"Hey, I'm not lying to you. You need to have more self-esteem . . ."

"Gee, thanks Dr. Phil," I said, talking over her and flopping backwards onto my bed.

". . . and it's so great because now we can double-date sometime." She giggled again, but was interrupted by the call-waiting beep. "Gotta go – it's Jason," she said and immediately hung up.

That evening when the four of us walked into the restaurant, Mr. Romano came up to us. "Welcome, welcome, your table is ready. This way please."

Mr. Romano continued in his lilting Italian accent, "Benvenuto! Bella, bella, you are all so lovely. Bree-jeet, I can't believe you are fifteen today." And to Mom, "The years have flown by, but you look as young as these girls, Cee-leste."

She laughed and teased right back. "And you are as handsome as ever."

Mr. Romano was always the same, sprinkling in Italian here and there and charming the female customers. With anyone else it would have been creepy, but he was so genuine we couldn't be offended.

I noticed some of the other diners watching the flirtatious exchange and cringed, wondering what they were thinking about my mom. Today she was wearing one of her many bright, flowing, long dresses, better suited to a summer day than the middle of January. This *interesting* fashion sense combined with her waist-length, blonde hair and drop-dead good looks, made it hard for people not to stare. She looked more like a goddess than a mom. It's no wonder people gossiped about her.

We sat down and ordered right away because we all had the menu memorized. After eating an enormous amount of pasta and garlic bread, we could barely move.

"Are we ready to go back to the house for cake?" Mom asked.

"I can't even think of eating anything else right now," Jess groaned and put her hands on her stomach. "Maybe Brigit should open her presents first."

Moriah and I seconded the idea.

"Okay, presents first it is," Mom answered, and we followed her out the door.

Back in our little living room there was exactly enough space for the four of us with two overstuffed chairs by the fireplace and a loveseat on the opposite wall. I looked eagerly at the presents on the coffee table. I did love presents – well, usually – I wasn't so sure about the book from last night though.

"Go ahead and start," Mom said, smiling. "But, I'm saving this one for last." She grabbed a fat green envelope from the table and put it on her lap.

I tore the paper off the first present. Moriah had gotten me much-needed art supplies. "Excellent, thank you," I said, examining the tubes of paint and the fine horse-hair brush that she'd obviously splurged on.

Jess had given me two CDs by groups I'd never heard of before. She knew I was hopeless at keeping up on new music. With her help, I could at least fake it when the topic came up.

"Thanks, these will be great to listen to when I'm painting," I said.

There was one more present left on the table. It was a jewelry box. I opened the lid and let out a long breath. "Oooh," I said, touching my fingers to the most amazing pendant. A large golden stone in the shape of a teardrop hung off a delicate silver Celtic knot.

"It was your grandmother's. I thought you might like," Mom explained.

"It's gorgeous," Moriah said when I passed her the box. "What's the stone called?"

"Amber," Mom answered.

"It's so cool it belonged to your grandmother. How old is it?" Jess questioned.

"I don't know exactly, but I'm quite sure it's been in our family for generations. I never saw Grandma wear it, but it was with her things when she passed," Mom answered.

My grandmother died when I was four, so I barely remembered her. When I was little, Mom liked to tell me stories about her, and I would listen while she worked in the garden. There were also stories of my great-grandmother and so on back until it blended into one long female history. I liked the stories although I didn't have much in common with these women, except for our last name. The Quinn women always kept their last name when they married and passed it on to their children. Before I could stop myself,

I felt a bubble of excitement at the thought of reading Grandma's story in the book I was given last night.

I hugged Mom tightly. "This means a lot to me." When I pulled away, there were tears in her eyes.

"Okay, enough of that." She blinked rapidly and wiped the corners of her eyes. "I've saved the best one for last." She handed me the green envelope.

I tore into it, unfolded the papers and couldn't believe what I read. It was a plane ticket – to Ireland!!

"I – I don't understand? You want me to go with you?"

"Yes. You're old enough now, and I'm sure you can make up the school work," Mom explained.

I really hadn't expected this! Every year Mom went to Ireland at the end of April in time to celebrate Beltane with her best friends. They called themselves the Circle of Nine. Beltane, or May Day, was one of our eight holidays and the only time of year the nine women got together. They lived far apart but wrote to each other frequently, preferring snail mail to email or the phone. I loved looking at the envelopes when they came with their strange postmarks, elegant writing, and old-fashioned wax seals. Although I'd always been curious and tried to snoop, I never could read what they wrote because Mom tucked the letters away in a locked box.

"That's so awesome – a trip to Ireland! I wish I could go with you!" Moriah and Jess said, talking over each other.

"Mom thanks. I really mean it. You know I've wanted to go forever."

"I think it will be really special for you to see where your ancestors came from," she replied and got up from her chair. "Now, do we have room for cake?"

"Yes!" We all said, looking forward to the mouth-watering German chocolate cake with its gooey coconut-pecan frosting.

After we took everyone home, Mom and I cleaned up the kitchen together.

"Did you have a good day?" she asked. "Well – I mean – after this morning anyway?"

"Yes, mostly." I decided not to share anything about the Hallway Incident with the snotty girl because that would lead to more questions than I felt like answering. I also didn't tell her about Tyler. I was still in disbelief that he'd asked me out, and I was afraid I might jinx something if I talked about him too much.

"Maybe next year, when you're turning 16, we can have a big party."

"A party?" I snorted "I don't think so." I was surprised she had suggested it. Even though five years had passed, I got upset thinking about my disastrous tenth birthday when the popular girls in my class made it their mission to keep everyone home – well, everyone except Moriah and Jess. Mom's strangeness never seemed to bother them. I was still ashamed at the terrible names I called her that day. She hadn't gotten mad. She just held me in her arms while I cried away my embarrassment and disappointment. I had desperately wanted to fit in, and her eccentric ways made that next to impossible.

The slightly frozen look on Mom's face made me think she was remembering that awful day, too. I didn't want her to feel bad and quickly added, "Mom, this was a great birthday. I don't need a huge party to celebrate – really."

Her expression relaxed, assuring me I had said the right thing. "Thanks for my presents, especially the plane ticket. I can't wait to go to Ireland!"

"Oh, that reminds me. Speaking of presents, you should finish reading our family's book before the trip."

I let out a groan. It was a huge book. Not only did my family inheritance include some Unspecified Ability, it also included homework. Great – just great.

CHAPTER FIVE

I woke up in a crappy mood which didn't get any better when I bent down to pack my book bag and noticed the bright orange sticky note on my folder. It said "Mr. Lintel 12:00." Damn it! On top of everything, I had to meet with Mr. Lintel at noon today about my term paper grade from the semester that had ended the week before. He'd given me a completely unfair C-, and I needed to make my case for a better grade, something I wasn't sure I was capable of doing.

I felt sick. Maybe I could crawl into bed and stay home. I thought about trying to get away with a sick day, but I knew it was impossible. Mom would know I was faking it. I grabbed my bag and trudged down the stairs. Mom misread my expression and launched into a smooth-things-over speech.

"Brigit, I know we didn't talk about – er – things – the way we should have yesterday because it was your birthday, but we can talk more when you get home. Okay? Try not be all stressed out at school today."

"It's not that, at least right now. I have to meet with Mr. Lintel about changing my term paper grade. I'm sure it's going to be a *super-great* day."

"Oh, I'm glad you decided to talk to him."

"I don't think it will do any good. He hates me. I knew I was asking for it by writing on 'The Contributions of Women during the Civil War,' but I didn't think he could argue with facts." I sighed and pulled on my coat.

Mom nodded sympathetically. "What do you have to lose? I'll bet you will be very persuasive."

I shrugged, not having the energy for more than that. Trying to lighten my mood, Mom wiggled her fingers in the air and said, "I can always put a spell on him for you."

I scowled at her. How could she make a joke like *that*?

"Hang on a second, I'll be right back." She went into the living room and returned with something in her hand "Here, wear this today for courage." She held up Grandma's amber necklace.

"Isn't it a little too much for school? I don't want lose it."

"You won't lose it. Trust me, and wear it today, okay?"

I lifted my hair up so she could fasten the clasp. I turned to the mirror by the door to see how it looked. I had to admit it was pretty. The amber matched the gold flecks that tinted my otherwise boring brown eyes.

"Perfect," Mom whispered, giving me a quick hug. "Brigit, I didn't say anything before," she hesitated before continuing, "but don't mention the Tuatha and the book to your friends, okay? It's something we don't talk about with other people."

"As if they'd believe me anyway," I muttered before slipping out the door.

The morning did not go as quickly as I wished. I'd been hoping to see Tyler before class, but we'd gotten to school a little late. And because he was a senior, and I was a freshman, we weren't in any classes together except for art. Our lunch periods weren't even at the same time, not that it would have mattered today because I had my meeting with Mr. Lintel.

I reached Mr. Lintel's room a few minutes before noon, but found the door locked and the lights off inside. I was hoping he had forgotten but decided it'd be best to wait for him to turn up. I leaned against the wall, fiddling with the necklace. Moriah and Jess gave me a thumbs-up when they passed me on the way to lunch. They knew I was worried. I'd been distracted all morning, missing a lot of the things they said. I used the meeting as my excuse even though I was preoccupied with more than that. My stomach gurgled, and I wasn't sure if I was hungry or sick. I kept thinking, I can do this, over and over again. Somewhere in the middle of my mantra, the pendant began to feel warm. I dropped it back against my skin. It was definitely warm, and the warmth spread across my chest to my shoulders and down my arms to my hands. It felt good.

"Daydreaming, Miss Quinn?" Mr. Lintel's voice seemed far away. He unlocked the door, and I followed him inside without speaking.

"You said you wanted to talk to me about your term paper. What seems to be the problem?" He asked as though he had far better places to be. He then added, "Let's see if this stupid girl can put together a coherent argument." I stared at him in disbelief, not because of *what* he said, but because I'd been looking right at him and never saw his lips move.

I was losing it. My heart rate sped up. My hands began to shake and sweat. My mind was obviously creating things that weren't happening. In my panic, I was about to flee to the bathroom when the calming warmth surged from the necklace again and loosened the lump in my throat.

I swallowed and said very evenly, "Mr. Lintel, I think there may have been a mistake. You took issue with many of the facts in my paper, but I was careful to footnote each of them."

"Miss Quinn, if I remember correctly, I believe some of your sources were questionable. Let me see."

I handed him the term paper.

"Ah, yes, the information from Sarah Mills' book on women and war is totally unreliable. She exaggerates the things women have done to make the case that women are as tough and dependable as men. I took points off each time you used her book as a source."

My panic was switching over to anger, and the pendant became almost uncomfortably hot.

"But, Mr. Lintel, all of her facts can be substantiated in other reference books. I simply used her book because it was the most comprehensive source on this topic." I couldn't believe it was me speaking. I didn't even sound like myself. Where were these words coming from?

"Miss Quinn, if you can show me these same facts in another location, I will raise your grade. You have until noon tomorrow. Grade changes have to be in to the office by then." He looked at me rather smugly, knowing I would have a hard time proving my case by then. "That ought to stop this futility." His last sentence reached me just as my brain processed that his lips were still pressed into a thin smile.

It was happening again – the voice in my head. I turned away and blinked back the tears I felt threatening. I would not cry in front of him. My eyes rested on the bookshelf at the side of the room for a moment. Suddenly, the heat flared in the necklace once more, and I knew with an odd kind of certainty what I needed to do.

Again, my voice was strangely confident. "Mr. Lintel, I can prove all of these facts to you right now." I marched over to the bookshelf and began pulling volume after volume out. I placed nine different books on his desk. Opening the first one, I flipped to the exact page I needed and handed it to him. "Here's the first one," I said, pointing to the correct paragraph.

"What in the . . . how did you . . . you can't expect me to believe you have these already researched?" He barely managed to stammer out his question.

Even though my hands shook as I grabbed the second book, I was again able to open to the page I needed. One after another, I placed the books on his desk, flipped to the correct page. The final book thumped down hard, making Mr. Lintel jump a bit as he stared incredulously at the pages. My heart continued to race, but I calmly said, "You will find confirmation of each of my 'questionable' facts on these pages. I trust that you will raise my grade appropriately."

"You can't . . . I don't . . ." Mr. Lintel's mouth opened and closed like a fish gasping for air.

"All the facts are there, believe me," I said and walked out of his room.

Once I was out in the hall, I touched the necklace again. It didn't feel hot at all. I couldn't believe what I'd just done. How did I have the guts to challenge him like that? How did I know which books to grab and how did I turn to the right pages every time? It was so crazy but exciting. He had to raise my grade now. Pushing aside my fears for my own sanity, I reveled in the moment. I felt like cartwheeling down the hall, but that would be dangerous for everyone, including myself. I'd taken a few appropriately sedate steps before noticing that Moriah and Jess were already coming toward me from the cafeteria.

Jess held out her hands. One had an apple and the other a brownie. "Take your pick," she said, "healthy choice, chocolate therapy or both. We weren't sure what you would need."

"Wow, you're looking a lot happier than I expected, though," Moriah said. "What happened?"

"You are never, ever going to believe it," I said, beaming. "But, I'm almost positive I'll be getting a better grade." The huge bite I took out of the apple prevented me from saying more.

CHAPTER SIX

I was excited and nervous to see Tyler outside our final class of the day. "Hi," I said, suddenly too jittery to say more.

"There you are. I've been looking for you between classes all day." His smile was genuine.

"You have?" I began to relax.

"Yeah, I wanted to ask if you needed a ride home. I don't have practice until six tonight."

"That'd be great." I smiled back. How did I get so lucky that this perfect guy likes me?

"Are you two coming in sometime today?" Miss Sienna called into the hall.

I hurried to set up my supplies in my usual spot next to Moriah. Tyler always sat on the other side of the room next to the seniors. I would have loved to sit next to him and talk while we worked, but it would have been really strange to switch places. Everyone would notice, and maybe he didn't really want everyone to know he asked me out.

I kept glancing his way, and each time I looked up, he was looking at me, too. He made a funny face, and I laughed out loud.

"What is *up* with you today?" Moriah asked without looking away from her drawing. "First, you are super spacey all morning. Then you are cryptic about the whole Mr. Lintel thing. Don't think you are going to get away with not telling me that story. Now, you are laughing to yourself. Are you going to let me in on the big joke or what?" She glanced up in time to see me staring at Tyler. "Oh. *Now* I get it." She laughed, and like a love-sick cartoon, rapidly blinked her lashes at me and teased, "Whatever has happened to my serious friend? Could it be love?"

"Shhhhh," I said, trying not to laugh at her ridiculous expression. I leaned closer and whispered to her. "He asked to drive me home from school today."

"Nice. So your mom's okay with you going out with him? My parents would flip if I asked to date a senior."

I'd never thought about Mom saying no to my date with Tyler – especially after I had already said yes. "I didn't ask her yet, but I'm sure she'll be fine with it," I said with more confidence than I was feeling.

"Why tell her at all? I have an idea," Moriah said. "We're going to the game together anyway. Tell her we're going to get pizza and hang at my house after. I'll cover for you."

"I guess it could work." My conscience twinged. I really wanted to tell Mom, but I couldn't risk her saying no. Moriah's plan was the perfect solution.

I turned back to the portrait of my mom, but now when I stared at her face on the canvas, I got the eerie feeling she already knew I was planning to lie to her.

Once class was over, I rushed to my locker. Barely focusing on what books I needed for homework, I randomly stuffed things in my bag, hoping I'd gotten it right. When I stood up, Tyler was walking toward me.

"Ready?" he asked.

"Yep, all set." I gave a little wave to Jess and Moriah and noticed a number of other freshmen girls staring at us. It wouldn't be long before everyone would know there was something going on between Tyler and me.

We headed for his car in the student parking lot. He drove an older jeep with fading red paint dotted with rust spots. I went to open the door, but he reached the handle first and our fingers touched.

"Here, let me," he said. "It sticks a little." He yanked it open and shut it for me once I was inside.

After he started the car, he turned toward me. "Do you have to get home right away or can we sit here for a few minutes?"

"It's no big deal if I'm not home right away." I stared at him. God, he was gorgeous. His dark brown hair was just messy enough to be perfect. I really wanted to touch it. I always thought his eyes were completely brown, but in the daylight you could see a hint of green in them.

"What are you thinking?" he asked.

I didn't have the time to come up with something witty, so I stuck with the truth. "Well – your eyes – I always thought they were brown. I never noticed the green in them."

"Yeah, my gran says it's the Irish in me coming out when the light makes them look green." He seemed uncomfortable talking about himself and changed the subject. "I can't wait for tomorrow night."

"Me, too," I said. "I was so surprised you asked me out. We hardly know each other."

"I've wanted to get to know you better ever since I saw your first project in art class. I know we haven't talked much, but when I look at your paintings I feel like I understand you."

"Really?"

"Yeah, you're an amazing artist."

With anyone else I wouldn't have believed a compliment like that, but Tyler was an artist, too. He understood what it was like to put a piece of yourself onto the canvas. He leaned closer to me, locking me into a deep gaze. His sudden intensity made me a little nervous, and I glanced away for a second right as he moved in for a kiss.

My timing was terrible, and his kiss missed its mark, grazing my cheek. Embarrassed, I looked back at him quickly and found him grinning as though he meant to kiss my cheek all along.

I tilted toward him, hoping our aim would be better this time. When I reached up to steady myself on his shoulder, I shivered, breaking the power of the moment. It was really cold inside the jeep, even though the engine had been running.

He pulled back and grabbed my hand, feeling its iciness. "Geez, I'm sorry the heater isn't working very well. Let me get you home before you freeze."

Trying to hide my disappointment, I sat back in my seat. "Do you know where I live?"

"The town isn't that big. Everyone knows where everyone else lives."

"True," I agreed and then panicked when I realized I'd have to explain things to Mom if she saw me get out of Tyler's jeep. "You don't have to go all the way down my street. You can drop me off on the corner."

"I don't mind."

I couldn't argue without telling him I hadn't told my mom about our date. I kept my fingers crossed that she wouldn't be looking out a window. When we pulled up, I wondered if he thought our house was weird like everyone else. I was glad that it looked more cheerful than usual with the red granite walls sparkling in the sunshine. It helped a lot that last year's creepy, overgrown garden was covered with snow. In the middle of summer when the plants were wild, our house looked sinister like a scary fairy-tale cottage where the vines might reach out and grab your leg when you walked by. It wasn't just me. Kids from the neighborhood crossed the street to avoid walking past our house.

I didn't see any sign of Mom. Just in case, I didn't linger. "Thanks for the ride," I said quickly and hopped out.

"See you tomorrow," Tyler called after me.

"I'm home," I shouted when I walked through the door. There was no answer, and I was relieved that she wasn't home. I grabbed a huge blueberry muffin before going to my room. The apple and brownie I ate in place of a regular lunch hadn't been enough to fill me up.

While I ate, I should have started my homework, instead, I opened the book for another episode of Quinn family history. The story I wanted to *read* more than any other was Mom's. I flipped forward until I found her name.

Celeste Quinn
June 25, 1992

How to do this, how to tell?
I write this now my fear to quell
Of how I fled into the night,
Away from what I thought was right,

33

To save me and one tiny other
From an evil, dark with hunger.
Beware the signs, learn the lesson.
You cannot trust every person.
Watch the scene unfold wholly
If your gift makes you worthy

The words "one tiny other" made my heart thud heavily. I rechecked the date before I began counting backwards rapidly in my head. Mom would have been nearly two months pregnant with me – she was talking about me.

My eyes automatically went to the photo I kept on my desk. Mom and Dad were grinning broadly with their arms around each other, obviously very happy on the day of their engagement.

My dad's name was Rowan Dunne, and Mom met him when she lived in Ireland for a year. Mom told me that they had loved each other very much but in the end staying together was impossible. I never knew why, and she wouldn't say, no matter how many different ways I asked. And the worst part was – he never knew she was pregnant with me. I learned this last fact about six years ago when I listened in on a phone conversation she was having with a friend. But I was absolutely sure that if he knew I existed, he would want to get to know me.

I had been desperate to learn more and waited for Mom's story to begin for me, but nothing happened. I wiped my blueberry muffin fingers on my jeans and tried placing my hands on the page. Still nothing. Come on book – work! Who had frightened her? Who was she protecting me from? I had to know.

I flung myself back onto my bed with my feet resting on the floor. Staring at the ceiling, I let out a frustrated sigh. Maybe I didn't have the gift Mom thought I had. Even though I hated the idea of being different, I wanted the book's magic to keep working for me.

Sometime later I was startled awake by movement on my bed. Mom was sitting next to me.

"Sorry. I didn't mean to scare you. It's so dark in here. Are you okay?"

"Yeah, I'm fine. It wasn't dark when I first came up."

She turned on the bedside lamp and noticed the book. "I know I should ask if you did your homework first, but I'm guessing the book was too much of a temptation."

"Mom, it didn't work for me today."

"What?" She narrowed her eyes at me. "Were you going in order? I told you that, right? The book only allows you to view the stories in the order they were written. You can't skip around."

"No, you didn't tell me that." I was so relieved and a little annoyed with her.

"Oh dear, that was important. I'm sorry I forgot that part." She glanced at the open page. "Let me guess. You wanted to read my story?"

I nodded. "I can tell from your verse that you were pregnant with me when you wrote this and that you were protecting me somehow. Who were you afraid of?"

"Oh, Brigit, I wish I could tell you everything, but I can't. You have to read the stories in order." Before I could protest, she held up her hand. "I didn't make the rules, but I can tell you that there's no danger to you – not anymore. C'mon, let's go make dinner, and you can tell me about your day." She pulled me off the bed and led me into the kitchen.

"I'm dying to hear about your meeting with Mr. Lintel. Did he agree to change your grade?" Mom asked as we chopped the vegetables for our salad.

"It was the strangest thing. He told me if I could show Sarah Mills' conclusions in other reference books he would raise my grade. He gave me an impossible deadline, and I was getting so upset. I could tell I was going to cry, but then the necklace seemed to heat up. It made me feel . . ." I shrugged as I searched for the right word, ". . . confident, I guess. Suddenly, I knew what to do. I pulled all the right books off his shelf. And the most amazing thing happened. I flipped to the page I needed to reference each time I opened a book. I don't understand how I could do that, but it was great. The look on his face was hilarious."

"Oh, I wish I could have been there." Mom clapped her hands like a little kid.

"You've got to tell me the truth, though. You wanted me to wear the necklace this morning, and I know I wasn't imagining things when I felt it heat up. How did I find the right books? Did the necklace help me some-how?" My question sounded crazy.

"Do you believe an inanimate object could have the power to do what you described?" There wasn't a hint of skepticism or sarcasm in her voice. She asked this as if she really wanted to know what I thought.

"Of course not," I answered quickly. Then I paused for moment and amended my answer. "I don't know. Maybe? It was such an odd coincidence – the heat of the necklace and my new confidence. I've never been able to speak so clearly in a situation like that. Plus, all of the books opened to the right page. Mom, what did you do? You've got to tell me what happened. All of this is really freaking me out!"

"I promise you will learn everything at the right time. My advice is to keep reading the book."

"That's completely unfair!" I shouted. "You can't just drop some crazy magical heritage in my lap and shrug your shoulders and tell me to read a book!" So far my Birthday Revelation was only clouding everything with confusion. I didn't even know what was real anymore. "You've got to tell me what's going on, Mom!"

"Calm down, Brigit. I guess this must seem impossibly strange to you – at least right now. I remember feeling a lot like that when Grandma first gave me the book. I've said all I can say for now. The book will show you the path – the path of the Tuatha and our role as guardians of the old ways. When you're done reading, you can make a decision about whether it's the right path for you."

She had said all she was going to say on the topic. I knew it didn't pay to ask any more questions. We ate in strained silence. When I was done I rinsed my plate and loudly jammed it into the dishwasher, not that Mom needed any reminders about how angry I was.

I was nearly to the doorway when I remembered to ask about going to the basketball game.

"Is it okay if I go out for pizza with Moriah and Jess after the basketball game tomorrow night?"

"Sure, that's fine, but when did you become such a big basketball fan? I think this is the fifth game you've been to this year."

"It's fun. The team is doing really well this season."

I left the kitchen, breathing a sigh of relief on the stairs and rationalizing that I had no choice but to lie. I was not missing my date with Tyler!

In my room the book drew me over, and I sat down to look at it again. I really, really wanted to continue Onora's story but knew I should do my homework. I tenderly turned the pages, admiring the fascinating artwork inserted between the stories. I recognized an intricately drawn Eightfold Wheel depicting our seasonal celebrations – Yule, Imbolc, Ostara, Beltane, Summer Solstice, Lammas, Mabon, and Samhain. The designs were beautiful, using gold leaf and gorgeous deep ink colors which had somehow remained vibrant through the years. I traced them lightly with my finger and with abnormal disobedience decided homework could wait.

CHAPTER SEVEN

Getting comfortable on my bed, I opened to Onora's page and read her verse again. The strange tingling in my fingers returned as my room blurred away.

Onora and Ian woke to the enticing smell of roasting meat. Peeking over the edge of the loft, Onora saw Bressa slowly turning the spit holding the fowl while the drippings spat and sizzled in the fire.

"What is the hour?" Onora asked when Bressa looked up.

"Tis late. The sun is an hour gone. I thought it best to let you sleep." Bressa beckoned with her free hand. "Come. I have much to tell you both."

Once down the ladder, Onora and Ian sat at the table. One end was set for a simple supper. The other end held items which Onora instantly recognized: a small iron pot, half full of water with marigold petals floating on top, sat next to a pewter saucer holding the ash of dried thyme leaves. Bressa had been gazing into the future.

"Please tell me, Bressa, what is going to happen?" Onora asked with a trembling voice.

"I saw something most alarming in the embers earlier. I needed a clearer picture." She gestured to the end of the table. "When I looked at the water's surface in the pot I saw what would happen in the village. Father Banan has worked the villagers into a rage with accusations of witchcraft and devil worship. By now, they have already taken your mother from her house."

Onora gasped. "Bressa . . . no . . . my poor mother. She cannot be drawn into this."

"For that it is too late, child. She has been in this from the beginning, from the first lesson I gave her in the ways of the Tuatha when I lived in the village. She was such an eager learner and loyal, too. I never expected her to continue our friendship after I was banished, but she was never afraid. Her courage will serve her well now. All of your friends from the Beltane fire have been captured as well."

"It is me they really want. I must go back. Maybe they will set everyone else free if I do." Onora was in tears.

"Let me finish," Bressa interrupted. "There's no need to return. They are coming here. They are on their way already."

"What? My mother told them the way? How could she betray us?" Onora wailed in disbelief, holding her head and bending in agony.

"Onora!" Bressa said sharply. "Do not judge your mother so harshly. She was tricked. What she did, she did out of love for you. Father Banan suspected you would come to me for help, so he pretended to have captured you and said you would be released if she showed him the way here. Your mother knows that I am safe on this island. She freely gave the information in order to save you."

"Maybe I can give myself up. Maybe Father Banan will be lenient, and I won't be punished too severely."

"I won't allow it," Ian shouted and slammed his fist on the table. "The risk is too great now that you have more to protect than yourself. You know what they are doing to those they believe are witches." Ian's words were angry, but his face showed stark fear.

"I have to agree with Ian," Bressa said and stirred the marigold petals in the pot once more. "Father Banan will not be appeased with an apology and some simple penance. Belief in the old ways challenges his authority. He will end this with violence. I can see it."

"I know I must be careful," Onora said, folding her arms over her still-flat abdomen protectively, "but, Ian, can we stand idle and watch our friends being hurt? How can a holy man do such things, foul trickery and lies, cruelty and even murder? What can we do?" Onora's voice trailed off to whisper. Ian moved to embrace her.

"Ahah, Ahah!" Bressa's cackling laugh startled them both and they watched in disbelief as she looked up from the pot with a smile. "We will trick them right back! I can see the plan. Let me tell you while we eat."

By the time they finished their late meal, Onora was thrilled with the simplicity of it all, but Ian's face wore a skeptical scowl.

While Onora was getting water from the lake, he said to Bressa, "It is too much of a risk. If this fails and they capture her, I will lose everything I love. When we were hand-fasted last year, I promised to protect her with my life and now that extends to the babe she carries. What is wrong with leaving here and never returning?"

"You must not flee this island, Ian!" Bressa said with a desperate intensity. "It will end badly if you do. Please trust me on this. The only path I can see that has any hope is the one we are on. Come now. We have much to do." Bressa turned and muttered, "Fate, fate you fickle foe. I must try to change what I now know."

They worked through the remaining hours of darkness and carried out a successful trial of their plan. As the faint light began to tinge the sky to the east, Bressa and Onora took their place between the stone statues where they could mind the shoreline. Ian built a small fire to warm Onora and dry her hair and clothing before sliding back into his position.

They waited and watched the bands of mist disappear in the warming air. The sun had now risen over the trees creating a near perfect reflection of a second forest on the calm surface of the lake. Then the peacefulness of the dawn was harshly broken by approaching voices. Onora and Bressa linked nervous hands as the wailing and shouting became more distinct and the mob finally appeared through the trees.

The captives, their hands bound tightly in front of them, were prodded and pushed to the shoreline. The nine women, Onora's friends plus her mother, stood huddled together with petrified expressions on their faces.

The villagers surged forward shouting, "Witch, witch, witch!"

Onora's stomach knotted with anxiety when she recognized her friends' families on the fringe of the crowd, clutching each other in fear.

Father Banan stepped to the shore, bringing with him the group of men from the Beltane festival. Onora exchanged a confused look with Bressa as they noticed the men walked freely, unbound behind the priest. Father Banan glared across the water at Onora and Bressa, holding a cross in his raised hand. The crowd quieted. He turned to the bound women and shouted, "You heathen women are known to be devil worshipers. Your spell-casting and sorcery has coerced the pure hearts of these young men into vile acts of godlessness. You shall be punished for these sins unless someone takes responsibility for your bewitching."

He turned to face Bressa and Onora across the lake. "Bressa Gormley and Onora Quinn, will you confess that, in the devil's name, you bewitched these women into doing your bidding? If you so confess and surrender, I will hold them harmless, and they shall be free to go."

While everyone waited for their answer, Onora scanned the faces of her friends, one by one, trying to send them a hopeful look. They stared back at her imploringly, and one of them shouted, "Onora, please." She looked at her mother last and saw her grim resolve. She wished she could explain everything and save them the suffering of the next few moments.

"No," Bressa and Onora shouted together loudly and clearly, with Onora adding, "We do not worship the devil and have never bewitched a soul."

Screams and cries erupted from the crowd, the accused, and their families. Onora feared that some of the enraged fathers might come across to the island to get them. Their panic for their daughters' lives outweighing their fear of the island, but there were no boats, and the large rocks were too far apart to use as stepping stones.

Father Banan held up his hand for silence, and once the crowd quieted down he spoke, "You have heard their denial." He walked up to the bound women holding out the cross. "We must now put the word of these women to the test. If they are not worshipers of Satan, they have nothing to fear. God will save them."

He knelt at the shore of the lake and crossed himself. He dipped the base of the cross in the water and prayed aloud, "Dear God imbue these waters with your holy spirit. May it be your will that any soul which is not pure be rejected from this lake and a permanent place in your kingdom."

Turning to the crowd, he again spoke. "To test their claims of goodness, we shall bind them, hands and feet together, and throw them in the water. If the water accepts them for a suitable time, we know them to be free from sin. If they float, we will know these waters are too pure for their dark souls."

Kira was the first – kind, beautiful Kira. She sank to the ground to avoid their reach as they came for her. They grabbed her long dark hair and dragged her to the water's edge where they tied her bound hands to her feet. She screamed over and over, "I am innocent!"

The crowd again shouted, "Witch, witch, witch," as two men carried her through the shallows and, with a great heave, threw her into deeper water. The piercing wail of Kira's mother echoed across the lake as all eyes watched the bubbles disappear from the surface.

Onora sank to her knees next to Bressa, with her hands over her ears. She could not bear the terror of her friends as they were thrown in one after the other – Trionna, Marin, Grania, Leannan, Orla, Arwen, and Cayleen.

Of course, none of them were rejected by the water.

The crowd was quiet. Their fervor for blood had disappeared. Only the weeping and low murmur of voices comforting one another could be heard from the families.

Onora's mother was last. Father Banan shouted across the water. "You can still save your mother. Onora, confess your sinful ways."

Onora and her mother locked gazes, and Onora held her arms wide as if to embrace her and said, "I am so sorry, Mother. I love you." And to Father Banan she said, "I cannot confess what is not true."

Father Banan addressed her mother directly. "Maureen Quinn may God save you."

Her mother did not make a sound as the men threw her in. The ripples vanished quickly, and all were left staring at the smooth surface of the lake.

Father Banan said at last, "This blessed water has accepted these women proving them true and good. They are now rewarded with a place in the kingdom of God. Let us retrieve their bodies so we may put them to rest in sanctified ground."

He turned back to face the island. "Onora Quinn you are now dead to us and banished from the presence of these God-fearing people. Never again shall you live within the walls of the village. If you come near, you will suffer the same fate."

The men who had assisted Father Banan waded into the water with ropes attached to them as none could swim.

"Brigit, are you okay?"

Mom's voice pulled me away from the story. She was standing in the doorway.

"You're crying."

I touched my cheeks and felt the tears of grief for Onora's friends and mother. "I can't believe Onora wasn't able to save everyone."

"Oh, you haven't finished her story. You really need to keep going. There's quite a bit more." She nearly left but then stopped for a moment. "I haven't seen these stories in years. Could I follow along with you for a little while?"

I answered her question by moving over on the bed to make space. I was glad for her company. We shared the book between our laps, and she read the verse out loud transporting us back into the story.

The men dove down again and again in search of bodies but came up empty handed. The crowd on the shore had partially dispersed. Father Banan, the searchers, and the grieving families remained. A cart and pony, stamping impatiently, stood ready to transport the bodies back to the village.

One of the searchers slogged from the lake and reported to Father Banan, "Father, we cannot find the bodies. I think they are lost to us. How long shall we go on?"

Before Father Banan could answer, one of the mothers screamed, "By God's good graces, it's a miracle!"

People fell to the ground, clutching their hands together in prayer and stared incredulously down the shore as one of the girls waded out of the lake. "It's Kira," they murmured with astonished voices. She walked slowly through the shallows, grabbing onto the large rocks to keep her balance on the slippery bottom. Her hair and clothes streamed water when she gave one last step onto the shore before laying down in exhaustion.

Onora was now on her feet and watched nervously from the island. "The plan is working Bressa." She gripped Bressa's hand tightly.

Kira's family and Father Banan rushed to her side. Her mother gathered Kira in her arms and rocked back and forth, crooning, "My dearest . . . my dearest . . . God has given us a miracle and returned you to us."

"A miracle . . ."

"The ropes . . . how did she . . ."

"How can it be?"

All the voices blended together with their declarations and questions. Kira, with the help of her father, was able to sit up. She took in the amazed expressions of the crowd and Father Banan's skeptical look. He narrowed his eyes and said, "Please tell us what happened, and we shall decide if this is truly the hand of God or the work of Satan."

"Father, it was a miracle to be sure. I felt the water close over me and prayed as hard as I've ever done to be saved. I heard a beautiful voice, the voice of an angel, telling me not to be afraid. A great peacefulness came over me. I don't remember any more until I began to walk out of the lake." Kira told her tale with conviction.

Father Banan deliberated. He looked back and forth between the penitent villagers and Kira. Those who witnessed the miracle appeared even more faithful than before and looked to him for his final word on the situation. He smiled at each of these devoted faces, seeming to count the growing number. His elation was evident in his booming voice. "Kira, God has saved you from the grips of the devil. We must rejoice that God has deemed us worthy to witness such a miracle. Let us pray." He knelt down as did any who had remained standing.

All joined in with the familiar prayer of thanks and were nearly finished when the sound of splashing had them lifting their heads to look at the lake. The villagers' voices switched from their prayerful intonation to shouts of true joy and awe. "It can't be . . . God has blessed us with a grand miracle . . . Blessed be God."

Emerging from the water holding hands were all seven of the other girls and Onora's mother. They trudged through the shallow water weighed down by their heavy skirts and stepped on shore like triumphant explorers discovering a new land.

Onora and Bressa smiled at each other. Onora said in relief, "Ian did it. The plan really worked. Everyone is safe."

"Did you doubt me so much, Onora?" Bressa chuckled and gave her a big hug.

They watched the euphoric scene across the water as families greeted their daughters. Onora's mother turned to the island and raised her arm waving happily at them.

Father Banan noticed and stared at her with a look of hatred. He pivoted to face Onora and Bressa and shared this same fierce look with them. His façade of pleasantness returned like a mask as he addressed the crowd. "Let us go back to the village and spread this joyful news."

The villagers' happy voices carried across the lake long after they had disappeared into the trees, such a contrast to their angry arrival earlier in the day.

A lone figure remained on the shore. Onora's mother had not gone back to town with others. Bressa checked the tree line to make sure no one lurked in the shadows before getting her boat out of hiding to retrieve her.

Onora stared at one large rock in particular and called out, "Ian, they have all gone. You can come out." Ian emerged from his hiding place in a niche at the back of the rock and swam to the island. Onora waded in and helped him to his feet. She hugged him as hard as she could. "Ian, thank you, a thousand times thank you!" He didn't respond, and she noticed his utter exhaustion when he couldn't even lift his arms to hug her back. He shivered violently, and Onora told him to lean on her as they made their way to

Bressa's house. "We'll have you warm in no time," she promised, although the worry in her voice betrayed her confident words.

———⚬❀⚬———

M om closed the book with a small thud. "Wow, I'd forgotten what it felt like to see a story unfold that way!"

"Does Onora's story end there?" I asked.

"No, there's more. You understand by now that she's pregnant, right?"

"Yeah, I figured that out before Ian came right out and said it. Wouldn't she have been in big trouble back then for being pregnant before getting married?"

"Not as much as you'd think. When young people were betrothed in the hand-fasting ceremony, they lived as married people for a year and a day until they formalized their vows. Obviously, there was a good chance a baby could be conceived during the year. Sometimes people would go their separate ways when the year was over, but most didn't."

"That's an interesting way of doing things. Sort of a trial marriage, huh?"

"I guess that's a good way to describe it."

I put the book gently back in its protective box. I had to get to homework even though I felt emotional wrung out. I sighed. "Time to study, unfortunately."

Mom patted my hand and headed out the door.

I was only half-kidding when I called after her. "Mom, if all the stories are like this, I'm afraid I'm going to die of heart failure before I ever finish."

She was too far into the hallway for me to hear her clearly, but I thought she said, "Some of them are worse."

I should have asked her to repeat herself, but I wasn't sure I wanted to know.

Chapter Eight

When I opened my locker after lunch a note fell out.

Can't wait for tonight.
Do you want a ride home from school? – T

I cracked a huge smile which earned me a quizzical look from Jess. She was way too nosy for her own good and snatched the note out of my hands. I was afraid she was going to read it out loud. I didn't want my date with Tyler broadcast to everyone within earshot. Actually, I did but I wasn't sure Tyler would like that. Plus, who knew if we'd have more than one date. I didn't need everyone wondering what happened if we didn't go out again after tonight.

Jess handed back the note and said, "I am so excited for you. We should plan a double-date."

"What if he doesn't like me enough for a second date?"

"Don't worry. It seems like he really likes you. I'm sure it's going to work out." Jess gave me a little sideways hug as Jason walked toward us. "Having a boyfriend is fantastic. You'll see." She giggled and grabbed Jason's hand before heading to their next class.

I stood there, thinking please shoot me if I start giggling like that.

My date with Tyler was making me nervous. I was excited and scared at the same time. What if our date was a disaster? What if we didn't know what to say to each other? What if my mom found out? I struggled to stay calm through my next classes. I thought I was doing okay until my nervous pencil tapping caused some minor irritation in Geometry. The day inched slowly forward.

My composure completely disappeared when I finally saw Tyler and an impossibly wide grin stretched across my face. He reciprocated with an equally big smile which made me flip-flop inside. There wasn't time to say more than "hi" before we walked into class.

I had finished the portrait of Mom. Miss Sienna needed to give me a grade before I could take it home, so Mom's face was there – watching me. I felt guilty about lying to her.

Unfortunately, this class continued the day's slow-motion torture, even though I could watch Tyler's gorgeous face concentrating while he worked. I tried not to stare.

We were starting on a new project that needed to include a traditional ethnic theme, and I hadn't settled on an idea. The examples tacked to the board included American Indian and African designs which were bold and wonderful, but none of them were sparking my own idea. I started randomly sketching on my pad.

I wasn't really thinking too much about what I was doing until Moriah peeked over and said, "I love it. Is it Irish?"

I had drawn an intricate Celtic knot design. It was similar to the one in my ancestor's book.

"Yes, I guess so," I answered, not wanting to give any more details.

Finally the bell rang, and Tyler and I joined the throng in the hallway.

"Boy, am I glad that's over. Longest class of my life – I swear." Tyler said.

"I know. Right? Are you psyched for the game tonight?"

"Yeah. It's only Middleburg. We really shouldn't have any trouble winning, but you never know." He tilted his head closer to mine and said in a lower voice, "To be honest, I am more excited for our date."

Then, I did something I can hardly believe. Something so terrible, I am sure I turned a thousand shades of red.

I giggled.

Tyler didn't react, so it couldn't have been that bad, but I lapsed into silence, berating myself for sounding so idiotic.

We were nearly out the door when someone called my name.

"Miss Quinn, Miss Quinn." Mrs. Martin, the school secretary, called to me as she ran down the hall flapping an envelope in the air.

"Oh, I am glad I caught up with you, dear. We're saving on postage and are handing these out instead. You must have a grade change from last semester. So here you go. Have a good weekend, both of you."

"Thanks." I tore into the envelope, completely destroying it to get to the new report card inside. There it was!

"Check it out!" I said to Tyler, pointing to the amended grade. "He gave me an A after all."

"Way to go!" Tyler swung me around in a big hug.

I was out of breath when he put me down. I didn't imagine I'd ever think this way, but the hug was way more exciting than the A.

When Tyler dropped me off, I was lucky, *again,* that Mom wasn't looking out a window. She was busy back in the kitchen.

"Look what I have." I handed over my grade change with a flourish.

She took the paper and scanned it quickly. "Brigit, I knew you could do it. Did he say anything when he gave this to you?"

"No, it was sent through the office. I have no idea what he's thinking, but I'm very glad he raised my grade."

"Well, I can see how happy this has made you."

I couldn't tell her that what she saw was really the anticipation of my date with Tyler.

It was a little eerie when her next question mirrored where my thoughts had been. "So it's my turn to drive you girls tonight, right?"

"Only on the way there. We'll be over at Moriah's after the pizza, and her dad said he'd drive us home." I inwardly cringed as I made my Big Lie even bigger. I was going to be in huge trouble if she figured this out.

Mom didn't ask any more questions about the evening before she dropped us off in front of school, telling us to have a good time. The game was excellent. Our team won, and Tyler played great. I'm sure the whole team did, but I was only paying attention to Tyler. He looked at me once from the bench after his third foul, and I could have sworn he winked. I would have winked back – that is – if I could. Ever since I was little and tried to wink, it always looked like a painful squint. Mom couldn't do it either. We had some sort of genetic miscue.

As we left the bleachers and shuffled to the doors Jess squeezed my arm. "Have a great time tonight."

Moriah waved, and then they were gone. I was left standing alone in the hall, unsure of where to wait for Tyler. It would be at least a half hour before he came out of the locker room. I couldn't just stand around like some groupie. That would be too embarrassing. I should have asked Moriah or Jess where they thought I should wait.

I stalled for time by walking slowly to my locker to get my coat and circled back around near the boy's locker room. I was glad to see that the opposing team was already done with their showers and heading for the bus. In the hall a few parents and friends waited for players. I stayed apart from the group, leaned up against the wall, and tried to look relaxed.

A few players trickled out and then the rest of the team exited nearly all at once. In the chaos of their departure, Tyler didn't see me. I didn't want to shout down the hall and walked toward him. I could tell he was searching the crowd as people dispersed. His shoulders slumped, and even though he had his back to me and was at least ten feet away, I heard him ask. "Where is she?"

No one near him paid any attention to what he said, but Tyler's sad posture made me shove my self-consciousness aside and shout, "Here I am."

Everyone in the hall turned my way, including Tyler. He closed the distance and grabbed my hand.

I was embarrassed my shout had gotten so much attention. "Sorry, I answered you so loudly. I didn't want you to think I'd gone."

Tyler looked at me funny. "Answered what?"

I knew I heard him ask where I was. Maybe he didn't want to admit that he'd been upset for a minute when he didn't see me right away. "Forget it," I said.

"I'm glad you're here." He was more intense than I expected.

"I wouldn't stand you up."

We walked to his jeep, and I realized I didn't know his plans for the night. I'd been so excited I'd forgotten to ask until now. "So, where are we going?"

"I've got a really special place I want to show you. It's a couple miles out of town, but I think you'll like it."

"Okay." I didn't really know what else to say. It was very quiet in the car. The radio was off, but that was fine with me. Somehow the silence was good – comfortable even.

Tyler must not have felt the need to talk either. After a minute or two, he reached over to hold my hand. It was nice. It was more than nice! The way his thumb lightly rubbed against my skin sent tingles up my arm.

He slowed down. I glanced up and saw we were about to turn down a private driveway. It was very snowy, and even though there were tire tracks leading in and out, we were definitely in a secluded spot.

I didn't want to panic but this seemed like the road to some make-out spot in the woods. I certainly hoped he didn't think I was going to be an easy score. I really liked him, but if that's what he thought about me, it was very insulting. Not that maybe someday we wouldn't be like that with each other, but this was a *first* date!

Tyler must have noticed my tenseness because he asked what was wrong.

I took a deep breath before I began. "Tyler, I don't know what you're thinking, but I'm really not – I mean, it's cliché and all to say it – but I'm really not the kind of girl to do this on a first date."

He looked at me confused for a moment and then began laughing. "Is that what you're thinking?"

"Yeah. We're on a dark lane leading into the woods. How stupid do you think I am?" I was getting mad that he was laughing.

"Wait a minute. You'll see."

It wasn't like I had a choice here. We were in the middle of nowhere. Where was I going to go?

Like Tyler said, in a minute we rounded a curve, and in the glow of the yard light up ahead stood a gorgeous white Victorian farm house with scrolling gingerbread trim and a red barn. There were lights on in the house.

"This is my grandmother's house," Tyler said proudly.

"You've brought me to visit your grandmother?" I was confused. I hadn't been on many (okay any) first dates, but a visit to his grandmother seemed like a strange choice to me. It was a better choice than him dragging me to a secluded woodland parking spot, but still, I didn't get it.

Tyler laughed again. "We're actually going to go in there," he said, pointing at the barn. "First, I need to tell Gran we're here so she doesn't wonder what's going on. You don't have to come in if you don't want to."

I didn't want to be rude, so I went with him. Tyler did a quick knock and walked in. "Hey, Gran, it's me, Tyler. I've brought a friend with me."

An older woman rose gracefully from her chair in the living room and came toward us. She did not look like a typical grandma to me. She was wearing black yoga pants and a red knit top with wide sleeves. Her long gray hair hung down her back nearly to her hips. Bright blue reading glasses dangled from a multi-color beaded chain around her neck.

"It's so good to see you, Tyler. Who have you brought to meet me?" she asked.

"Gran, this is Brigit Quinn, one of my friends from school. We have art class together, and I thought I might take her into the studio for a little while. Is that okay with you?"

She reached out to shake my hand, but instead of letting go, she continued to hold it between hers. "Brigit Quinn," she said. "You must be Celeste's daughter."

"Yeah, I am. You know my mom?"

"I've known your mom since she was a little girl, although I haven't seen her in some time. Your grandmother and I were friends before you were born. We had great fun trying out new recipes, even if they didn't always turn out the way we hoped." She laughed a little as she remembered and added in a more somber tone, "It's been many years, but even now I miss her."

I tried to pull my hand back at that point, but she held firm, looking at me intently.

"You have your mother's face, but your eyes come from your father."

"Well, that's what my mom says, but I wouldn't know exactly. I've never met him. He's from Ireland." I didn't know why I'd divulge this kind of personal information to someone I just met, but there it was, spilling out of my mouth like we were old friends.

"Right, of course. I'd forgotten about all that." Her voice seemed to take on an edgy quality like she felt uncomfortable at having mentioned my father in the first place. This time when I went to pull away, she relinquished her grip.

"So is it okay, Gran, if we head to the studio for a while?" Tyler repeated.

"Of course, it's really as much yours as mine these days," she answered. "But, you must be hungry. Let me get you some cherry pie to take with you."

Even though she did not look like a grandmother, she definitely had the normal grandmotherly instinct to feed everyone who came within range. And despite her strange intensity, I found her quite fascinating. She slid two pieces of pie onto the same plate and handed it to Tyler along with forks.

"It was nice meeting you," I said, following Tyler to the door.

"I'm glad to have met you, too." Then, quiet enough so Tyler could not hear, she leaned in and added, "He's never brought anyone else here before. You must be special."

Tyler and I crunched through the snow to the barn and went up a set of wooden stairs to a side entrance. He held the door open with his free hand, and I walked in, waiting for him to get the light.

When he flipped the switch I was stunned by what I saw. The room was amazing – it was huge. The entire loft of the barn had been turned into a studio. There were paintings everywhere, on easels, hanging on the walls, leaning against each other in the corners.

"Look at all this art. Is this all yours?" I asked.

"No, Gran is an artist, too. We share the space."

Whimsical metal sculptures of winged faeries and mischievous elves perched on beams and hung from the ceiling. There was a large window built into the other side of the barn as well as a row of skylights in the roof. Right now they only reflected the room back to us, but during the day I imagined they'd let in an incredible amount of light.

There was so much to take in, I hadn't moved from my spot about two steps inside the door. Tyler had gone to a small kitchenette off to the side to set down the pie. An old cast-iron stove hugged one wall with a couch and chair nearby. Tyler bent down to light a fire in the stove.

"Is that how you heat this place? I'm surprised it can do the job."

"No. Gran actually installed central heating when she renovated, but I like the stove for extra warmth. Come and sit." He motioned to the couch.

It really wasn't too cold, but the stove's heat would feel good. I sat down on the couch while Tyler remained standing.

"I can make something to drink like hot cocoa or tea. I think there's juice in the fridge."

"I'd really love some hot cocoa if it isn't a big deal."

"Not at all. I'll make some for myself, too."

He put the mugs in the microwave and sat down next to me. "So what do you think?"

"This place is great. Are you here a lot?"

"As often as I can be. My dad gets a little irritated when I'm out here too much because he wants me to be at the gym. I like playing basketball, but my art is so much more than a hobby. It's who I am. Can you understand that?"

"Yes, totally. So your dad hasn't changed his mind at all about art school?"

"No, he even said he was forbidding me to go there the other night. I know he's worried about paying for the half of tuition not covered by the scholarship, but I think I can find loans and grants to make it work. It's hard to argue against the free ride to Penn State for basketball, but I don't love basketball the same way Dad does. I know what I want. I just wish he'd listen to me."

The timer dinged on the microwave, and he got up make the cocoa.

"What does your mom say?"

"She keeps telling my dad they need to let me do what I want to do, but he's obviously not listening. He thinks I'll always be broke if I pursue my art." Tyler handed me a mug.

"So how long before you have to decide?"

"Officially, I don't need to sign a letter of intent until April, but the Boston School of Fine Arts needs to know if I'm accepting its offer in a couple of weeks."

"I know it's not much time, but it isn't like it's tomorrow, either. A lot can change in a few days." I felt like adding "I should know" given the revelations in my life this week but decided against it. I couldn't imagine he would react well if I said something like, "You know those rumors about my mom? Well, they're true." Definitely not a good first-date topic.

"How about some of Gran's cherry pie. It's awesome." Tyler sank back onto the couch and offered me a fork.

We sat close to each other, knees touching with the plate balanced between us. As we ate we talked about school and our friends, but then he changed the subject.

"I'm so glad you agreed to go out with me. I've wanted to ask you out all year, but it took me this long to get the courage to try."

"Tyler, I'm only a freshman. I can't believe you'd really be nervous asking me out. You'd have to know I'd say yes."

"Actually, no, I didn't."

I waited for him to elaborate. When he didn't, I finally asked, "What do you mean? It has to be obvious that any freshmen girl would say yes to a date with you."

He began slowly. "I know what you mean that any *typical* freshmen girl might have said yes, but you're so not like the other freshmen girls. You're not like *any* other girl."

I shook my head slightly. He had leaned forward while he was talking and brushed my hair back from my cheek. Cupping my face with his palm he pulled me forward to meet his lips for the most spectacular mind-bending kiss. My lips tingled, and I think I forgot to breathe for a moment.

Tyler pulled back to look at my face, and I took in some much-needed oxygen. "Wow."

"Yeah, wow," he agreed. "That's the way I meant to kiss you after school yesterday."

"Well, I really liked that kiss, too. It's just . . . this one was way, way better."

We both started laughing at my lopsided logic.

Tyler got up and gestured to the other side of the barn. "Can I show you some of my stuff? I've been working on some new ideas."

I walked alongside him as he commented on each piece. His work really was amazing. I loved his abstract paintings and the way different images emerged when I moved a few inches one way or the other. I'd been taking everything in and realized he was staring at me, waiting for a reaction.

"Oh, Tyler," I began, "I don't know what to say. You are truly, truly gifted. I love everything you're doing. I wish I was half as talented."

"Really? You don't think it's too – I don't know – too much? I'm breaking a lot of rules."

"I don't think so, not one bit. Plus, rules were meant to be broken, right? I never heard of Van Gogh or Picasso worrying about that sort of thing."

"I'm so glad you like what I'm doing. I didn't think it would matter this much – your opinion I mean – but it really does. Thank you."

What he said made me incredibly happy, but I was afraid anything I said in response would sound stupid. I smiled up at him and grabbed his hand, pulling him over to a stack of paintings leaning against the wall. "Now, tell me about these," I said, tilting them forward one at a time. "These are very different."

"They're not mine. They're Gran's," he explained.

I couldn't believe what I was seeing. I started to line them up in a row along the wall, so I could look at them all together.

"Whoa," I breathed out quietly. There in front of me were nine paintings nearly identical to the designs in the old book Mom had given me.

"You like them?" Tyler asked. "Gran's always creating Celtic art like this. I'm sure she'd let you have one, if you wanted. I even have one hanging in my room."

I didn't say anything right away, and I must have had a strange expression on my face because Tyler asked if I was okay.

"Yes, I'm fine," I finally answered. "I've seen this sort of thing recently in a book. It took me by surprise to see the designs here. The book is very, very old."

"That would explain it. Gran's a big fan of history, so maybe that's where she got her inspiration."

This coincidence, if that's what it was, along with the other odd happenings of the week was too much to deal with at the moment. In one week my perspective on the world, my life, and everything in it had shifted, tilting slightly out of control. I walked back to the couch and sat down. Suddenly, I was feeling very tired. I glanced at my watch and gasped. "Oh no! It's almost twelve-thirty. I'm past curfew. I was supposed to be home by midnight."

"Are you going to be in huge trouble?" Tyler looked worried.

"It should be okay, as long as I get home soon." I pulled my cell phone out of my coat pocket to see if I'd missed a call from Mom. I hadn't. "I could text or call her, but she might be asleep already. If she is, I don't want to wake her up and make her realize I'm not home."

The ride back into town was as quiet as our trip there. I worried about being late. I sure didn't need Mom staring out the window, waiting for me and seeing Tyler drop me off instead of Moriah's dad. This was getting too complicated.

When we pulled up, I turned to Tyler. "I had a great time tonight. Thank you for showing me your studio."

He leaned across the seat and kissed me goodnight. It was a long, lingering kiss, and I was startled when I heard his words. "I wish this night didn't have to end."

I jerked away from him and stared at this face. It had been Tyler's voice, but that was impossible because his lips had been firmly planted on mine at the time. I had to be hearing things that weren't there. I needed to get out of the car before he could ask me what was wrong. I gave him a quick hug and whispered goodnight before letting go.

"I'll call you tomorrow. Okay?" he asked.

"Definitely okay," I said.

I let myself in the house as quietly as possible and tip-toed up the stairs. Mom's room was dark. When I reached my doorway, I realized I'd been holding my breath and let it out. Sneaking around was not good for the nerves. I latched on to that as the cause of my little episodes, convincing myself that a nervous reaction made me think I heard the mean girl in the hall, Mr. Lintel the other day, and now Tyler tonight. Nerves – that's all it was. Relieved I'd found a semi-acceptable explanation, I climbed into bed without even changing into my pjs.

Chapter Nine

The rise and fall of voices from downstairs filtered into my foggy, just-awakened brain. I thought maybe it was the TV, but then I heard Mom talking. She sounded angry, but I quickly dismissed the thought because she was rarely angry at anyone.

When I walked into the kitchen, I was all set to say a cheery "good morning" to her and whoever was visiting, but the words died in my throat when I saw Tyler's grandma standing stiffly by the back door. How was I going to explain my way out of this one?

"Brigit, say hello to Adele McGrath." Mom had her arms crossed, and she narrowed her eyes at me, looking a little tense. "I'd introduce you, but I understand that you've met."

"Good morning, Mrs. McGrath," I managed to say in a tight voice.

"Hello, Brigit. I was telling your mother about meeting you last night, and what a nice surprise it was that Tyler would bring someone to see his paintings. Your visit made me realize how much I miss your grandmother, so I came to relive old memories a bit with your mother."

"Oh, okay," I choked out.

I was so busted. Beyond busted. I was going to be grounded for life. I turned toward the fridge where I had originally been going for milk to pour on some cereal and decided against it. I wanted to get out of the room as quickly as possible, so I pivoted again and with a jerky movement grabbed a banana from the fruit bowl and tried to vanish through the doorway.

"Brig, don't go too far. We have some things to talk about," Mom called after me.

Her brittle voice made me cringe as I walked down the hall to the living room. Like a condemned prisoner facing her last meal, I sat rigidly in one of the chairs and slowly ate my banana, struggling to swallow each bite around the growing lump in my throat. When I was done, I stared down at the limp peel in my hand. I would normally have thrown it away in the kitchen garbage, but I was avoiding that room and Mom as long as possible. Finally, the back door opened and shut as Mrs. McGrath left.

There was a short pause before Mom shouted, "Brigit Blaise Quinn, come here right now!"

I hurried to the kitchen even though I wanted to run the other way.

"What the heck do you think you are up to? I thought you were with Moriah and Jess last night. Can you imagine how stupid I felt, finding out that wasn't true from Mrs. McGrath of *all* people? Explain please!"

I briefly tried to invent a plausible story, one which didn't involve admitting my Big Lie to her. Maybe I could say I bumped into Tyler at the pizza place, and on the spur of the moment he wanted to show me his paintings, and how I didn't feel it was necessary to call and ask for permission . . .

"Brigit – I – am – waiting," Mom said, overly annunciating each word.

Okay, just tell the truth, I thought, and took a deep breath before plunging forward. "Tyler asked me out earlier this week, and I was so excited I told him yes right away. Later on, I thought you might not let me go 'cause he's a senior, so I decided not to tell you about it." I risked looking at her then but was shocked by her reaction. Her expression was more exasperated than angry. She rolled her eyes at me in disbelief and shook her head back and forth.

"Brigit, I knew you were up to something yesterday. Do not underestimate me, young lady. You know I'm going to have to punish you, right?"

"Yeah, I guess so. I'm – I'm really sorry though. Does it matter that I felt bad about lying?" I didn't think it was too soon to start bargaining for a lenient sentence.

"Well, I guess it's a start. It mostly disappoints me that you felt you couldn't trust me."

"Would you have let me go?"

"I don't know. Look, I have to admit I do not like the idea of you dating a senior – at all. That's a huge age difference. The only thing that makes me slightly less freaked out is that I was friends with Tyler's parents back in high school. I even dated his dad for a little while." She took a deep breath before continuing. "So, I'm guessing they've raised a pretty good kid."

"You dated his dad? That's weird."

"Yes, I suppose that would seem weird to you."

"So would you have let me go?"

"I think I would have, once I'd met him and knew exactly what you were going to do and where you'd be. That's what gets me Brig – I didn't even know where you were."

"I *said* I was sorry."

"Okay, enough for now, we will talk more about this later. Consider yourself grounded for two weeks, and you need to give me some extra time with packing up orders this weekend."

"Fine." I was grateful she wasn't grounding me for longer. I could survive two weeks. I only had to decide what I would tell Tyler when he called later. I was sure he was going to ask me out again, and I wouldn't be able to go.

I spent the next hour hiding in my room and talking with Moriah and Jess. They were dying to know how my date went. I told them I had a great time but moved on to my more catastrophic news about getting caught in my Big Lie. They certainly sympathized with getting grounded, even though neither of them had ever been.

Later, in the kitchen, we had an assembly line going. Mom made a living selling her homemade candles, soaps, and lotions to local stores and through the mail. She was putting the orders and packing slips into boxes, and I was taping them shut and slapping a mailing label on the outside. While we worked in silence, I replayed last night's date in my head, the kissing parts mostly. Then I remembered Mrs. McGrath's paintings.

"Hey, Mom."

"Hmmm?"

"Last night Tyler showed me the old barn his gran turned into an art studio. Besides seeing his work, I saw her paintings, too. She had a whole set that looked like ones in the book. You know, the Celtic knots and stuff."

"It doesn't surprise me she would like old Irish designs. Her last name is McGrath, after all. Were they identical or only similar?"

"I couldn't say without the book there for comparison, but they looked identical to me."

"Probably just a coincidence," she was quick to suggest. Too quick, I thought.

"So Grandma and Mrs. McGrath were friends when you were a kid?"

"Yes, she used to come here, and I remember going to her house a few times. The visits stopped when I was young. It was awkward when I first started dating Toby, Tyler's dad, and he invited me over to his house. By then, of course, I knew why Grandma and Mrs. McGrath were no longer friends."

"What happened?"

"Well, I'd tell you, but I'm sure your grandma will do a better job of it. She put the story down in her section of the book."

"Great. One more story I have to wait to get to."

My cell phone buzzed on the counter, and I looked to see who was calling. "It's Tyler. Can I take a little break?" I asked.

She shut her eyes briefly before responding, "I guess so . . ."

I was already saying hello before she finished. She held up her hand to me and mouthed, "Five minutes."

I nodded back and walked to the living room for some privacy.

"So what are you doing this afternoon?" Tyler asked.

"I'm helping my mom pack up boxes of her soap and stuff for customers."

"Doesn't sound too exciting." He laughed.

"No, it isn't. I'm sort of being punished."

"For missing curfew last night?"

I figured I might as well tell him the whole embarrassing story. "No. My mom wasn't even awake, but I never told her we were going out. Your grandma decided to stop in this morning and mentioned how she met me last night."

There was an uncomfortable silence. Then he asked, "Why didn't you tell her about our date?"

"I thought she might say no because you're a senior."

"Did she flip out?"

"Not completely. Actually, she was amazingly cool about the whole thing. The bad news is I'm grounded for two weeks."

Tyler groaned. "That's awful. I was going to ask you to go to a movie. Are you going to be able to go out with me at all now?" His voice was strained.

"I definitely can't go anywhere but school for two weeks. I hope she'll let us date after that. She did say that she's known your mom and dad for years and figured they have raised a good kid."

Tyler laughed. "Well, there's a point in my favor."

"What's weird is that she told me she used to date your dad."

"Oh, that is kind of weird. Do you think they were serious about each other?"

"Eeeww, I hope not. Don't even go there."

"Yeah, you're right. Better not to think about it."

"Tyler, I'm really sorry I'm grounded. It would have been great to see you again this weekend."

"Wait, your mom said you can't go out, but do you know if you can have visitors? Maybe I could come over tomorrow, and we could hang out and watch TV or something."

"I don't know." I didn't want to push my luck. "She didn't say anything about visitors, but I suppose I can ask."

My desire to see Tyler overrode my fear of asking this favor as I walked back into the kitchen. "Mom, would it be okay if Tyler came over tomorrow afternoon for a little while?"

She tilted her head down and rubbed her temples as though I'd given her a headache. "I'm fine with that, but only because I want the chance to meet him – and talk to him."

That last part had me more than a little worried.

Chapter Ten

Even though I had been through a lot in the past two days, Onora's story had tugged at me the whole time. The real danger she and her friends faced made me realize that getting grounded was nothing in comparison. And the upside to being confined to home was that it gave me plenty of time to continue reading. I entered her story with the verse, and once again the inside of Bressa's little house appeared.

Onora built up the fire and helped Ian remove his wet clothing before wrapping him in a blanket. He sat unsteadily in the chair, and Onora assured him she'd be right back when she went to get the rest of the bedding from the loft. She quickly fashioned two pallets as close to the fire as she dared and gently lowered Ian onto one.

By the time Bressa and her mother came in the door, the fire was blazing, and Onora was trying to warm the still-shivering Ian. She knelt by his side and rubbed his arms and legs as best as she could through the rough wool blanket.

Her mother was cold from the water but did not seem as exhausted as Ian. Seeing the worry on Onora's face, she knelt down next to her and took over rubbing Ian's arms. She spoke quietly to him. "Thank you for your bravery, Ian. You are truly a son of my heart." Ian did not open his eyes but reached out and briefly clasped one of her hands.

"Come, Maureen, you need to get out of these wet clothes." Bressa tugged her into the alcove under the loft. She emerged a few minutes later looking like a gangly girl in one of Bressa's dresses which was much too short. Wrapping up in a blanket, she sat on the other pallet.

"Is he well?" she asked Onora. "He's so pale. He used a lot of strength to save us."

"I believe he only needs warmth and rest to recover from the ordeal."

Onora's mother sat motionless while she spoke, her voice full of awe. "I am stunned he was able to save us all. What an ingenious plan. I was sure I was headed to my death. I felt myself sink to the bottom but then hands grabbed me, and I was tugged along under the water. I was nearly out of breath when Ian hoisted me into the niche in the rock. He held me up until he could cut the ropes. It was all so confusing. The light was dim but I could see the girls clustered together. For a moment I thought we had died and were awaiting judgment in purgatory, but then Ian pushed me up onto the platform with the others. How in the world did you build that platform under the water?"

"It was Bressa's idea, but it took Ian nearly the whole night to get it into place."

"Amazing! I'm not surprised he's exhausted. I'm sure we would have drowned if we hadn't had a place to stand. At the end there was barely room for all of us, and Ian gave up his space and hung onto the rock. He explained what we were to do, and, at the right time he helped Kira to the shallow water. Then he guided the rest of us back until we could touch the bottom and walk to shore."

"I'm incredibly grateful it worked." Onora shuddered. "It was unbearable watching your fear. I felt like I was betraying each one of you. I should have listened to you about Father Banan. I didn't believe our neighbors would join him against us."

"It is not your fault. I did not trust the man, but I never believed he would try to kill us. I only forbade you to go to the ceremony because I didn't want you to draw his wrath, now that you have a babe to protect."

"I can never return to the village. I will never see my friends again. Do you think you shall go back?" Onora asked her mother.

"It would not feel right to live there now."

From her seat at the table Bressa was quick with her invitation. "You may stay here as long as you like. I would be happy for the company. I have been lonely between your visits."

"Thank you, dear Bressa. A more loyal friend there never was." Onora's mother sighed. "I am quite tired now." She burrowed into the covers and turned her back to the fire.

"He looks better, does he not?" Onora asked Bressa.

"Yes, his pallor is gone, and he seems to be in a deep sleep," Bressa answered, walking to her bed. "We will see what tomorrow brings." Her voice was tinged with anxiety.

Onora snuggled under the covers with Ian. He was very warm, and it wasn't long before she closed her eyes and fell asleep beside him.

Some hours later, but well before dawn, Onora was woken abruptly by Ian's coughing. She sat up to comfort him, but he wasn't really awake. Once his coughing ceased, Onora laid down with her cheek pressed against his back. From this position his raspy breathing was unmistakable, and if possible, he felt even hotter than when the fire was blazing. "Oh, Ian, please be well," Onora whispered to herself and drifted back to sleep.

Ian's second bout of coughing was much worse and woke everyone. It was obvious he was quite ill. Bressa got up and gathered ingredients for a medicinal tea. It smelled foul but she assured Onora that it would ease his breathing.

Helping Ian into a sitting position, Onora noticed that although his eyes were open they were glassy and unfocused. "Ian, Bressa has made you some tea." He understood and reached out to take the cup in his unsteady hands. Onora helped him bring it to his mouth. He drank some and sputtered and coughed. He tried a bit more before collapsing back onto the blankets. Onora handed the tea back to Bressa with a fearful look.

All day long Ian mostly slept in between great fits of coughing. They took turns giving him tea and broth when he was able to sip. Each time they touched him, it seemed he was even hotter than before.

Night came, and Onora sent Bressa and her mother off to bed. She promised to wake them if she needed help. For now, Ian was asleep, and her only chore was to keep a warm cloth on his chest. As each cloth cooled she exchanged it for one that was steeping in a pungent mixture of chamomile and goldenseal next to the fire. It didn't seem to be helping, but both her mother and Bressa assured her it was an effective remedy.

She dozed off in her chair after a bit and was awakened by Ian whispering her name. She immediately knelt down by his side, relieved that he seemed better. He remained hot to the touch, she realized when she held his hand, but his gaze was clear, and he spoke very plainly.

"I love you, Onora, with all my heart." As he paused to take a ragged breath, Onora told him she loved him, too. He continued in his solemn whisper. "I can see how things will be. The babe you carry will be a girl. You must name her Aileen. She will be a great beauty and very clever. Promise me you will name her thus." A small smile came to his lips as if he had truly seen his lovely child-to-be.

"Yes, Ian, I promise, but we shall name her together when she is born."

"If only that were true . . ." More coughing interrupted him.

"Ian, you are scaring me. What are you saying?" Onora's voice was near hysteria.

"I must go. I'm sorry . . ." Onora could barely hear his last words, but they struck her as if he had shouted them.

"No, no, no," She wailed in agony. "Bressa, help me!" Onora could see that Ian's chest continued to rise and fall. There was still time to save him, and she called out again.

When Bressa knelt next to Ian, Onora clawed desperately at her and shouted, "Do something. Save him! He thinks he is dying, and I know not what to do."

Her mother grabbed at Onora's frantic arms, saying, "Shhh, shhh."

Bressa's voice cracked with grief. "I'm sorry. There's no more I can do. I thought by keeping you and Ian here on the island when you wanted to leave, I could stop the terrible disaster the embers had shown me. I should have known I couldn't change fate. Death is still coming."

The three women cried and listened to Ian's uneven breathing. Each coarse breath he drew was louder than the last and accompanied by a slight moan. Many seconds would pass as they waited for his next breath. Finally, there were no more.

Onora collapsed against her mother, howling like an injured animal. Her mother rocked her back and forth. Eventually her sobs quieted into sorrowful hiccups. The three of them stayed where they were on the floor next to Ian for a long time. Onora moved first. She stared across at Bressa and said in a hateful tone, "You betrayed me, old witch. What good is your magic if you won't use it for the ones you love?"

Bressa reached out to her, but Onora fled out the door. She ran through the trees onto the slope leading down to the shore and collapsed there on the grass. She lay on her back wishing herself dead while the sky tinged with the inappropriately cheerful colors of daybreak.

Eventually, her mother came to get her and helped her back to the house. She could smell the rosemary and knew Ian's body had been washed and prepared for burial. He was wrapped in cloth and only his face was showing.

"It is time, Onora," her mother said to her gently.

Feeling oddly detached from her body, Onora stepped forward, touched her lips to Ian's forehead and pulled the cloth over his face. With tears streaming down her cheeks, she took the threaded needle her mother handed her and made a few coarse stitches to hold the fabric in place. She avoided looking directly at Bressa as they put his body on the litter they had created from two tree branches and a blanket, and with much effort they made their way to the other side of the island. Onora was startled to see that a shallow grave had been dug and a pile of stones was sitting next to it. She realized she must have lain in the grass for a long time while her mother and Bressa had made these preparations.

They put Ian in the grave and covered him first with the dirt and then with the stones. When they were done, they joined hands and Bressa began to speak:

"Ian, son of the earth,
Our beloved.
We send you on your way
Back to whence you came
To live in the dew on the leaf
In the dust on the air
In the bird in the sky.
We will keep your memory
And when our time here is done
The spirits will unite us once more."

Onora and her mother answered, "Make it so."

Bressa pulled a small packet out of her pocket and tentatively held it out. Onora took it from her automatically and opened it. She could smell more rosemary. She tipped the contents in her hand and made a fist crushing the dried leaves. She held her fist out in front of her, opened her hand and let the leaves float down onto the stones in a final farewell.

Nearly the whole summer had passed, and Onora's belly now strained the seams of her dress. The rest of her was too thin, giving her a strange bird-like appearance. She walked around the island listlessly and hardly ate at meal times.

Onora's mother and Bressa worried about her. They tried to tempt her appetite with a multitude of treats. "For the baby," they'd coax, and she'd try to swallow a few more bites. She simply wasn't hungry. Her guilt was making her ill. She no longer blamed Bressa for Ian's death and had apologized for the accusations she had hurled her way. In truth, she blamed herself. She had saved her friends and mother but sacrificed her future. Her Ian. She found no comfort in the thought that Ian would live on in the babe she carried. The baby didn't seem real to her. She wanted Ian. She needed Ian.

Bressa tried to make Onora understand that they could not have saved him. With as little detail as possible, she described the vision she had seen showing Ian's death if he and Onora left the island. "That's why I insisted you stay. I tried to alter the path of destiny by keeping you here, but death came in a different way."

Bressa's words did not ease Onora's guilt, and she remained nearly paralyzed with sorrow, never thinking to ask Bressa if there had been more to her vision.

Her mother tried to help as well. She suggested that Onora needed a way to express her grief. She left for a day on her mission to a neighboring village in the opposite direction of their old home. She returned by nightfall with a rectangular package wrapped in a piece of soft wool.

Onora opened it and found a thick book with a heavy brown leather cover. She could tell by the smell that it was freshly made, the leather so smooth under her fingers. She flipped through the pages and found them completely blank. She looked at her mother questioningly. This was an extravagance to be sure. Paper was very valuable and quite rare here where few could read or write. Onora knew the book had cost them much of their meager savings.

"I thought you might like to write about your life, as you remember it now, before it becomes all blurry around the edges. It would be a worthy way to pass the time until the baby arrives."

"Thank you, Mother," Onora replied. She wrapped the book back up and set it on one of the shelves.

Each day she took it down, unwrapped it, and touched the blank pages, all the while thinking of Ian.

"Have you decided what to write?" her mother finally asked one day.

"I am not sure my story is important enough for these fine pages."

"You are the only one who can tell it, Onora. Write it in honor of Ian so your daughter can read it when she is old enough."

"Is there not a danger in putting down the truth, Mother? It could be used as evidence against us all. Could it not?"

"Silly girl, have you forgotten some of your first lessons? Surely you remember the way to hide your story from those who would do us harm."

The next day Onora did not put the book back on the shelf after her daily ritual. She laid it carefully on the rough table next to the supplies she had assembled. She picked up the quill, dipped it in the ink pot and paused over the empty page. She began by writing,

Onora Quinn
The Nineteenth Day of September
In the Year Thirteen Hundred Twenty-four

She wrote for nearly the entire day and again the next day and the next. The scritch-scratch of the quill against the page was the only sound in the little house. Bressa and her mother believed her diligence was a great sign she was feeling better and they worked outdoors as much as possible so as not to disrupt her progress. It was near time for the baby to be born, and they hoped she would have the energy to care for the infant once it arrived.

At the end of the third day of writing, her mother approached the table. "How does the writing fare?"

"It has truly gone much faster than I anticipated. I am nearly done with what I had hoped to put down on these pages. Only a few more hours."

"Are you feeling well? The time for the baby grows near, does it not?"

"Yes, it must be. I am very large, but I haven't felt any pains." Onora hugged the roundness of her belly.

"You must be tired. Why don't you stop for the night? You can start fresh in the morning."

Onora agreed that she was a bit tired and put everything away. She even managed to eat more than her usual two or three mouthfuls at supper. The older women exchanged optimistic looks, lingering at the table after the meal was finished.

"Tomorrow is Mabon," Bressa said. "Did either of you remember?"

"Day of equal light and equal dark, time for winter's chilling bark." Onora sang the little child's tune, startling the older women. They laughed when they overcame their surprise and Onora joined in. She hadn't laughed in so long the sound seemed unnatural to her and she quickly stopped.

After a moment, Bressa continued, "Maybe we could have a small celebration to give thanks for our harvest. I will make a special meal, and we could eat outdoors in the sunshine on the grass."

"That would be very nice. Thank you, Bressa," Onora's mother answered.

Onora gave a great yawn when she got up from her chair. "I'm sorry. I must be more tired than I thought."

She waddled to her bed in the far corner of the room. She had not been able to navigate the ladder to the loft for some weeks. She unbraided her hair but was so fatigued she didn't even bother to change into her nightdress and was asleep within minutes.

When Bressa awoke at dawn, Onora was already bent over her book at the table. "Oh, Onora, how long have you been at this?" she asked. "It is barely morn."

"I'm not certain, but when I awoke it was light enough for me to see the page. I thought I had best finish."

"Let me get the fire going again. There's a chill in the air. You should have stayed under the covers."

"I'm plenty warm. It was the child who woke me. I have had some pains." She noticed the worried look on Bressa's face and quickly added. "Only a few and not very painful, I'm sure it will be a long while."

"You should be in bed."

"I will finish this first." Onora continued to write, stopping only briefly when a pain clutched her belly. Bressa and her mother rushed to her side each time, but she ignored their questions and waved them away. It was nearly noon when she finally put down her quill. "I've finished all I can for now. Later I will write in the baby's name and birth date, which may very well be today."

She finally accepted their help and leaned on them as they guided her back to bed.

The pains became sharper and sharper as the hours passed, but Onora seemed no closer to delivering the baby. The older women exchanged worried looks. Bressa felt Onora's belly and realized the baby was not in a good position.

"The babe is breech," she whispered to Onora's mother. "She may never give birth this way. We'll have to turn the child to give them both a chance."

They were as gentle as possible, but Onora still screamed in agony as they attempted to turn the baby. Finally, in one swooping motion the baby seemed to slide into position. By this time, Onora was exhausted. They encouraged her as best they could through the final steps.

"Your baby is almost here. Onora, just a few pushes."

The older women exchanged relieved but exhausted looks when they heard the first hearty cry. As Ian had predicted on his deathbed, the child was a girl, and she was named Aileen, the bringer of light, as he had requested.

When the baby was placed in her waiting arms, Onora touched her finger to the baby's pudgy cheeks and rosebud mouth. "A Stóirín – my darling," she sighed and closed her eyes.

It seemed as though she had fallen asleep after her long ordeal until they saw the growing stain of red on the bed.

Weeks later, Onora's mother, Maureen, sat awkwardly at the table, bent over the book. The basket next to her shook as the baby inside kicked and cooed, little fists waving in the air. She completed the final line, and held her hands over the book while she said the spell, sealing the pages from prying eyes. When she was done she held the baby close, breathing in the smell of her sweet skin.

Bressa came up to her and put an arm on her shoulder, looking down at the baby in her arms. "Sweet, sweet baby," she crooned. "I only wish . . ." Bressa did not finish her thought.

Maureen turned to her with tears in her eyes. "I truly believe she died the day Ian did. She only remained here long enough to give the child life."

"I thought I could keep the whole terrible vision from coming true. If they had left the island that day, both of them would have died. I never told her that."

"She didn't need to know. It wouldn't have changed anything," Maureen consoled.

"I thought I could protect them, but I failed."

"Bressa, some things are beyond our power. You did not fail. This child would have died before drawing her first breath without you. Look at this precious baby. This *is not* failure!"

When they hugged each other, the child between them protested with a little squeak, and they laughed through their tears.

—∞—

I was crying as well. I hadn't expected Onora to die. This book made me too sad. I rested my hands on the page in an attempt to stop them from shaking. I was stunned when something new appeared. I read the words.

Onora Quinn
Born the Twenty-fourth Day of January
In the Year Thirteen Hundred Seven

Died the Twenty-second Day of September
In the Year Thirteen Hundred Twenty-four

Aileen Quinn
Born the Twenty-second Day of September
In the Year Thirteen Hundred Twenty-four

I slammed the book shut, put it back in the box, and snapped the latch closed.

CHAPTER ELEVEN

My miserable mood hung around until Sunday morning when I shrugged it off in anticipation of Tyler's visit. I hoped Mom wouldn't interrogate him too badly. I was sure he'd be able to handle any questions Mom threw his way, but I wasn't sure I wouldn't die of embarrassment in the process.

I debated about what to wear. I had plenty of time because we didn't attend church. We never had. Most kids my age complained about going and thought I was lucky Mom hadn't forced any kind of religion on me. If they only knew.

I settled on my favorite jeans and blue sweater and spent the rest of my time doing things I rarely did, applying make-up and styling my hair. I wanted to look great.

My grandmother's necklace was my finishing touch, and I was fastening the clasp when the bell rang. In my hurry, I thumped loudly down the stairs and slid to a stop with the rug bunched up under my feet. I quickly pushed it back in place, reaching for the doorknob at the same time, when Mom called from the kitchen, "Gosh, Brigit, calm down!"

I cringed, hoping Tyler hadn't heard her admonishment, and swung the door wide. "Hi!" I said, annoyed that my voice sounded so chirpy.

"Hi." He stepped inside and looked around for Mom before giving me a quick hug. "I'm glad to see you," he whispered. He smelled so good, a combination of the outdoors and cologne. Not overpowering, just right.

Tyler slid out of his tennis shoes and hung his letter jacket on the coat tree, the medals clinking against each other. I led him down the hall to the kitchen. "Come on in and meet my mom."

Mom got up from the table and reached out her hand to shake Tyler's. "It's nice to meet you, Tyler. Are you hungry? I made some cinnamon rolls."

"Nice to meet you, too. Wow, those smell great. I'd love one."

Tyler sat at the table while I grabbed the milk from the fridge and poured us each a big glass.

"Your gran came for a visit yesterday morning. I was very surprised to see her after so many years. She seems to be doing well."

"Yeah, she's as busy as ever with her art and all. She even took a welding class last year so she could make some metal sculptures."

"I didn't realize those were hers," I said, thinking back to the whimsical creations I saw in the barn. "I have a hard time picturing her with a blow torch."

Tyler laughed. "She's really something. We get along well, I guess, because we share a love of art." You could tell they had a special bond by the warm way he talked about her. He added, "I'm sure I'd never win an argument with her. She's tougher than my dad."

"I believe that," Mom agreed. "So what are your parents doing these days? I see them here and there but haven't really talked with them in ages. We were all friends back high school."

"My mom works part-time at the library, and my dad's running the construction business."

While they talked I picked my roll apart and popped the pieces into my mouth, grateful for something to keep my nervous hands busy. Under the table my leg bounced up and down, betraying my antsy-ness to be done with this conversation. My heart skipped a beat when Tyler laid his hand on my jittery knee. His touch steadied me a bit, and I focused in on Mom's voice.

"Business must be good. I see the McGrath Construction trucks everywhere. So, is that what you'll be doing after graduation? Going into the family business?"

"I work there during the summer, but I'm definitely going to college. I've been offered a full ride to play basketball at Penn State, but I've also been offered a partial scholarship to the Boston School of Fine Arts. My dad is not happy about the idea of art school."

"Oh, my! That's quite amazing — two scholarship offers. Why does your dad have a problem with art school?"

"Well, even with the partial scholarship, the tuition is expensive. He pointed that out right away. He doesn't believe I'll ever be able to make a living from my art." Tyler shrugged.

Mom tilted her head and almost apologetically said, "He has a point. It is a risk, but sometimes you have to follow your heart."

"Try telling that to my dad."

There was a lull in the conversation. Mom took a sip of her coffee.

I figured we were done with the interrogation and got up to go. "We're going to watch a movie in the living room."

"Wait a minute, please." She motioned for me to sit back down. "We're not done."

Oh boy, here it comes. I fought the urge to crawl under the table.

She addressed Tyler specifically. "I'm going to come right out and say it. I'm surprised that a senior would want to date a freshman."

Tyler began to interject. "But, Ms. Quinn, I . . ."

"Wait — let me finish. As I said, I'm surprised, but I can see that you and Brigit have things in common. I am not totally against the idea of you two dating, but there are going to be some rules. There'll be no going out on school nights. You can go out one night on the weekend, provided I know where you are going to be, and your curfew is midnight. There will be no more sneaking around and lying to me."

I sat there, somewhat stunned, waiting for her to add something more to her list of rules. When she didn't, I jumped up and gave her a big hug. "Thanks, Mom." I was grateful but wary and wanted to make my escape as quickly as possible.

Tyler and I were almost to the living room when she called after us. "You're still grounded for the next two weeks."

"I know." I rolled my eyes, but I wasn't really that annoyed. How could I be, when a moment ago she had given me a huge amount of freedom?

I flipped through channels and, not finding any movies that we wanted to watch, settled for reruns of an old sitcom. Mostly, the TV was on for background noise so we could talk without being self-conscious about Mom listening. I liked how our legs touched as we sat together on the couch with our feet up on the ottoman. Tyler rested his hand on my thigh, sending a jolt zinging all the way up my legs.

"You look really nice. I like that necklace." He leaned in for a closer look. "I saw you wearing it at school the other day, and I was going to say something."

"It was one of my birthday presents this week. Mom gave it to me. It was my grandmother's."

"That's cool. What else did you get?"

"Oh, my God, I can't believe I forgot to tell you. I got a plane ticket to Ireland! Mom always goes for a week at the beginning of May, and this year she bought me a ticket to go with her."

"Awesome! That will be a great trip. That's one thing I'm going to do when I'm older – travel. I've hardly been outside of New England, only on the class trip to D.C. last year."

"I'm the same way. Mom traveled some before she had me, but we don't go anywhere much now. She only takes this once-a-year trip."

"When did you say you were going again?"

"It's the last week of April and into the first week of May. Let me check the exact dates." I walked over to the desk where the itinerary was sitting. "Yeah, that's right." I read from the ticket, "Departing April 28 and returning May 8."

"Oh, no." He sounded upset.

"What's wrong?" I asked, sitting back down.

"You're going to be gone for prom, and I really wanted us to go together."

"Tyler, your senior prom!" I felt terrible. I'd always imagined going to prom and with Tyler as my date it would have been a fantasy come true.

"Brigit, it's okay, really." He softly touched my cheek. "It would be dumb to turn down a trip to Ireland for a dance."

"But, it's prom." I truly wanted to pout. How could my luck be so bad? Two things I'd wanted forever happening at the same time? Life was so unfair!

We managed to enjoy the rest of the afternoon, talking about everything. I was amazed at how comfortable I was with him. When he left, I drifted into the kitchen where Mom had spent her afternoon.

"So, can I come out now?" she teased me. "Did you have a nice visit?"

I laughed at the term. Visit sounded so old-fashioned, like old ladies gabbing over tea. I answered anyway. "Yeah, I did."

"You were definitely talking up a storm in there. You really like him, don't you?"

My answer was written all over my face as I blushed.

She chose to ignore my embarrassment and got up to rummage in the fridge for leftovers. "What are you hungry for? We've got some spaghetti and a little . . ."

"Oh, you are never going to believe this!" I interrupted her inventory when I remembered the whole prom-trip conflict. "I've got the worst luck! Prom is the Saturday we are in Ireland!"

"So a trip to Ireland is bad luck, huh?" She was being deliberately obtuse.

"You know what I mean. It would have been really cool to go to prom, especially with Tyler. It isn't like I'm not excited to go to Ireland. I just want to do both."

"Life is never fair." Mom used that overly-wise tone that drove me nuts, but her comment made me think of Tyler's college predicament.

"No kidding. Tyler's dream has been to go to art school and his dad is practically forbidding it. If he turns down the basketball scholarship, I'm not sure they're ever going to speak to each other again."

"Is it really that bad?" Mom asked.

"I think it is. His mom wants him to make his own decision, but he can hardly talk to his dad about it. I wish there were something I could do to help."

Suddenly, I had an idea. It meant acknowledging that my mom might be able to do *things* that other people couldn't do – *things* I'd been trying not to think about. For Tyler I was willing to put aside my uneasiness.

"Mom, you know how the other day, it seemed like the necklace helped me get through the situation with Mr. Lintel?"

"Hmm-hmm." She put the leftovers on the counter and turned to me. "You know I won't tell you more about that until you've finished reading the book."

"I know, and I'm not asking for an explanation, but I *know* you had something to do with it. I wonder if you could – um – maybe do something like that to help Tyler with his dad?"

She pursed her lips and looked at me through squinted eyes. I stared back.

Finally, she said, "Our Tuatha heritage teaches us that most of the time we shouldn't meddle in other people's lives. The outcome is difficult to predict. I'm not saying no. Just let me think about it."

She returned to foraging in the fridge, and I stood there somewhat stunned, realizing she had just admitted that she could do something most other people wouldn't dream was possible.

CHAPTER TWELVE

As soon as I found Moriah and Jess at school, I shared my big news. "You're not going to believe how things turned out this weekend with my mom. She said I can date Tyler as long as I follow a bunch of rules about curfew and stuff."

"Oh my God, I can't believe it! Now we can double-date," Jess squealed, jumping up and down.

"Wait, you're grounded, right?" Moriah wore a confused expression.

"Yeah, so technically I can't go out until my two weeks are up, but I didn't expect Mom to be so cool about it. Yesterday, when Tyler was over, she totally interrogated him and then listed out the rules. It was so embarrassing!"

"I would have died if my mom had done something like that to Jason," Jess said.

"Tyler was allowed to come over yesterday?" Moriah asked.

"Yeah, she said she wanted to meet him. He stayed all afternoon, and we hung out and watched TV and talked." By then it was time to get to class. "See you both later," I said.

Jess answered, but Moriah didn't say anything back. She slammed her locker hard and stomped off. I raised my eyebrows questioningly at Jess, and she shrugged her shoulders in return.

A few hours later, I slid into my place next to Jess at our lunch table. "Where's Moriah?"

"I don't know. She was in class with me right before lunch. Maybe she's in the bathroom." Jess didn't seem very concerned about it and dug into her mac and cheese.

It didn't make sense. Moriah always sat with us at lunch, even if she wasn't eating. I hoped she was okay and used the last bit of my lunch period to check the nearest bathrooms and the library. No Moriah. I even stopped in the nurse's office. She wasn't there either. I gave up and went back to my locker to check my phone, thinking she had probably sent a text. But my battery was completely dead. I'd forgotten to charge it *again*.

Hours later I was relieved to find Moriah in her regular spot in art class.

"Moriah, why weren't you at lunch? Are you okay?"

Moriah looked at me coolly. "I'm surprised you even noticed I was gone."

"What are you talking about? Of course, I noticed." I tried to tease her out of her mood. It didn't work.

"Are you mad at me for something?" I finally asked.

"Gee, I don't know. I called you like ten times yesterday, and you didn't call me back. I guess you were too *busy.*"

"What are you talking about? You called me? I didn't get any messages." Then I remembered my dead phone and slapped my forehead. "Oh, no, Moriah, I forgot to charge it."

Moriah didn't respond. She kept her head down, working on her sketch.

I didn't get her little tantrum. She knew I forgot to charge my phone all the time. Finally, I couldn't take it anymore and whispered, "Moriah, I was not avoiding your calls. I didn't even know you called. I didn't even look at my phone yesterday."

She sighed. "That's the problem. You were too busy with Tyler to even think about letting me know what was going on."

I couldn't believe she was mad at me. I didn't have anything to apologize for, but I gave it a try anyway. "I'm sorry my phone was dead. I'm sorry I didn't fill you in yesterday. After Tyler left, I had a ton of homework to finish, and then I went to bed early."

"Fine." Her voice was still angry. She was obviously *not* fine.

I ignored her for the rest of class. It wasn't my problem if she didn't want to accept my apology. At the end of the hour, I packed up and started walking out without talking to her, but she grabbed my arm.

"Brig, I'm sorry I got . . . oh, forget it!" She abruptly turned and stomped out into the hall.

I didn't know Tyler had come up behind me until he said, "What was that all about?"

"I really don't know. She's mad at me for not calling her yesterday. She said she called me a bunch of times, but my phone was dead." I shrugged my shoulders. "She'll get over it."

He leaned in and said, "I've got to run to practice, but I was wondering if I can come over later?"

He smelled so darn good – again. "Um, that'd be – I think – okay. Call me first in case my mom says no." I was barely able to stumble through my answer. All I could think was kiss me, kiss me, kiss me. I didn't care that we were in the middle of the art room. I didn't care that people would see. No one was paying attention to us anyway, right? A quick glance around the room made me realize how wrong I was. Plenty of people were packing up and sneaking looks at us. The kiss would have to wait. I settled for a hug, and we went our separate ways.

Jess and Moriah weren't in the hall as I rushed to get my books. Stepping outside, I couldn't believe it! Moriah's mom was pulling away from the curb. Luckily, Jess saw me and must have said something because the car lurched to a stop. Jess threw open the door and yelled, "Hurry up!" I jumped in quickly.

Mrs. Gilbert seemed a little upset. "Sorry, Brigit. Moriah said you were getting a ride from someone else."

"No worries . . ." I said. Moriah didn't say anything and stared straight ahead the whole way to my house. Jess tried to ask what was up under her breath, but I shook my head at her, and she let it drop.

It was a relief to get out of the tension-filled car. I knew I should call Moriah to sort things out, but I was irritated she tried to abandon me. The more I thought about it, I decided *she* should be apologizing to *me*.

Walking in the front door, I could immediately smell that Mom was making soap. Some of her recipes were a little pungent while they were being made, but this one smelled nice. I sniffed the air again and was able to identify lavender, the other scents still a mystery.

When I walked into the kitchen, I was stunned by what I was seeing. Mom was at the stove, holding a letter in one hand. The other hand twirled in the air above a large pot while a tall wooden spoon mimicked the motion of her hand and stirred the soap mixture all on its own. My backpack slid to the floor with a thud, startling Mom.

"Oh, Brigit. You're home. You scared me."

"What are you doing?" I swirled my hand in the air just like she was.

"This? It's nothing."

"No – no it's not *nothing*. Have you always been able to do that?"

"I guess so. I don't have to, if it bothers you that much."

"It – it just surprised me. That's all."

"Honestly, I was so busy reading that I didn't even notice I was doing it."

I sighed. My life was just too weird these days.

"What are you reading? Is it bad news or something?"

"No, really good news. It's from my friend Anya. We'll be staying at her house in Ireland. Their son is a couple years older than you. There'll be other kids at the Beltane festival the same age, so it should be fun for you."

"I hope I can finish reading the book in time."

"I don't think you are going to have any trouble with that."

I started to rummage around in the cupboard for a snack and remembered what I wanted to ask her when I first walked in. "Is it okay if Tyler comes over tonight?"

"I'm not wild about that on a school night. If you have your homework done beforehand, and he only stays a couple hours, I guess it would be alright."

"Thanks, Mom." I ran over and gave her a big hug.

She hugged me with her free arm. She was now stirring the soap the *normal* way and lifted the spoon out to inspect how the soap dripped back into the pot. "This is ready to go. Give me a hand with the molds, Brigit. Can you move empty ones over as I need them?"

"Sure thing." It didn't take long before we had a table full of cooling soap. I pressed a small sprig of dried lavender into the top of each bar and stood back to admire my work for a minute. The lavender reminded me of our wild summer garden and how much I had wanted a regular lawn like the neighbors when I was little, but Mom always said that all plants were beautiful, and the ones I hated were important ingredients in her secret recipes.

My stomach rumbled, returning me to the present. I spied a plate of cookies on the back of the counter. "Oh, yum, I didn't see these before," I said, reaching for one.

"No, not those!" Mom screamed at me.

"God, calm down. You didn't have to yell. Are you saving them for something?"

"Yes, I made them earlier for Tyler, so I guess it's a good thing he's coming over later."

I didn't get it. "You – made cookies – for Tyler?"

"Yes, for Tyler and his parents."

"That's nice, but why would you . . ." my voice trailed off as another thought entered my head. "This wouldn't be a *special* recipe, would it?"

Mom's reply was flat and noncommittal, "I don't know what you're talking about. Just make sure Tyler knows he should share them with his parents."

She'd obviously done something and I shrieked, hugging her for the second time, "You're the best magical mom in the whole world."

When I released my grip, she laughed and repeated her denial. "I told you, I don't know what you're talking about."

CHAPTER THIRTEEN

I rushed through my homework so I'd be done by the time Tyler arrived, but was disappointed when he could only stay an hour. He'd forgotten he needed to study for a physics test. That wasn't anything I could help him with. At least the cookies were on the way to his house, safely sealed under two layers of plastic wrap. I wasn't taking any chances that he might dig into them on the way home. He promised to share them with his parents, and I had my fingers crossed that things would work out. Mom was definitely up to something.

With time on my hands, my thoughts drifted back to the Moriah situation. It was so wrong for her to be mad at me. I had done nothing to deserve it. I nearly dialed her number so we could settle the whole thing but called Jess instead, filling her in on Moriah's rant in art class.

"You know this reminds me of about a month ago," Jess said, "when Moriah got all freaky with me for like a day. It was around the time I started dating Jason."

"I had no idea." I felt bad I was so unobservant. "Why didn't you say anything to me?"

"Well, it was over so fast. Moriah apologized right away. I'm guessing she'll call you tonight or talk to you tomorrow. I mean, both of us have gotten a boyfriend at the same time practically. She's probably feeling left out."

"I guess that makes sense. I'm mad she tried to ditch me at school, though."

"That was kind of nasty, but the look on your face when you walked out the door was sooo funny!" Jess giggled.

"Thanks a lot!"

"Hey, don't be mad at me. I stopped the car for you."

I sarcastically thanked her again for her *extreme* kindness. She was still giggling when I said goodbye.

I needed something to occupy the rest of my night. The book, safely ensconced in its box on my desk, beckoned to me. Thinking about poor Ian and Onora . . . and little baby Aileen, who would never know her parents, made me start sniffling again. I knew I needed to continue reading, but I was afraid the rest of the stories would be as sad as Onora's. My phone rang, saving me from the book.

"Hello." My voice was thick with unshed tears.

"Brig, is that you?" Moriah asked. "You sound funny. Oh my God, are you crying?"

"No – not really."

"I'm so sorry. I've been such an idiot." She clearly thought I sounded sad because of what happened between us earlier. "I don't know why I got so mad about everything. It was so stupid. Can you forget about it and pretend today never happened?"

I was irritated, but I decided to put her out of her misery. "Yeah, sure. I mean if you can't act like an idiot with one of your oldest friends, then who can you be an idiot with?" We both laughed.

"Thanks, Brigit. You really are a great friend."

Remembering Jess' guess that Moriah was feeling left out because of our new "dating" status, I thought I'd try to smooth things over even more. "You know, it's been ages since we've had a real girls' night. I'm still grounded, but maybe my mom would let me have you and Jess over on Friday night. She usually approves of anything involving serious girl-bonding time."

"Count me in. It's just what I need!" Moriah was starting to sound like herself. "Let me text Jess and see if she's busy."

Jess answered "yes" to my girls' night idea right away.

We talked for a while longer but gave up when Moriah couldn't get her little brother to quit screaming into the phone. I wasn't sure she could hear me but before hanging up I shouted, "I'll let you know in the morning if my mom says it's okay." I rubbed my ringing ear and thought that maybe being an only child did have its good points.

Mom was at the desk in the living room writing a letter. I strategically waited for her to put the pen down before asking about the possible overnight. "Mom, I know I'm grounded, but is there any chance you'd let Moriah and Jess sleep over on Friday night?"

"This Friday is our Imbolc celebration, remember? *I* think it would be a nice change to invite friends to our little celebration. It's up to you."

"Oh, I didn't realize Friday was February 1 already." Imbolc celebrated my name-sake, the Fire Goddess Brigid, and I was a little hesitant to include my friends in one of our rituals. "Uh . . . I guess it would be okay. I bet they'd like making the Brigid Crosses. Do you think the candles and stuff will weird them out?"

"If they haven't been weirded-out by me yet, I don't think this will do it."

I laughed a little. "You're right."

The next morning, I was excited to give the news to Moriah and Jess that our girls' night was definitely on.

"I hope you don't mind, but my mom reminded me that Friday night is Imbolc Eve. It's sort of an early spring celebration that coincides with Brigid's Day."

"Uh, okay," Moriah said with a shrug.

"Ooh, what do you do? Do we need to bring anything special with us?" Jess sounded way more excited than Moriah.

I was a little embarrassed to be explaining all this in the car with Moriah's mom, who was listening with interest. "No, you don't need to bring anything. My mom makes some special recipes. Nothing weird. You'll like the cakes, and we decorate the windowsills – light some candles. And we make these little Brigid Crosses out of straw," I added as my voice trailed off. My description of our annual event seemed kind of lame, and I looked at my friends faces expectantly.

Before either of them could respond, Moriah's mom spoke with what sounded like relief. "Seems like fun, girls."

"Well, I'm not real crafty, but I'll give it a try," Jess said.

Moriah piped in then with less conviction than Jess. "Sure, it could be fun."

I tried to reassure them that I wouldn't let our holiday put a damper on our normal sleep-over activities. "It's no big deal, if we decide not to do the Imbolc stuff. My mom won't care." In truth, I had no idea how disappointed Mom would be, but felt I should offer a way out so they didn't get stuck doing things they didn't want to do.

On the way to my locker, I detoured through the senior hallway, searching for Tyler, curious to see if there'd been any changes at his house since there'd been plenty of time for cookie-eating last night. I wasn't sure how long it might take for whatever Mom did to work, but I was very curious.

Tyler wasn't near his locker, and I wasn't going to hang out there, so I headed back the other direction. I was busy navigating through the other students and didn't notice him until he grabbed my arm to catch my attention. "Hey, Brig, I was at your locker looking for you."

"Me, too! I mean – I was at *your* locker looking for *you*. I wanted to see how your night went."

"It was fine, boring. I got my studying done for the test. I'm as ready as I'm going to be."

"So, umm, how were the cookies?" I was in too much of a hurry for subtleties.

"The cookies were great! Be sure to thank your mom for me again."

"Have you been able to talk to your dad about school at all?" I pressed on, hoping for some progress, even just a smidgen.

"Nah, I'm not going to bring it up. We'd only end up fighting. I'm hoping my mom will be able to talk to him. Gran even came over for a while, and I know she was going to try to help. I got out of the kitchen while they were talking. I didn't want to get into another argument."

I was disappointed that the cookies hadn't seemed to do anything. Maybe Mom hadn't done anything after all.

When I got home, I immediately heard the raised voices in the kitchen. What the heck? I let my bag slide quietly to the floor and listened.

"Celeste, what were you thinking meddling like this? Your mother would not approve. We all know how *she* felt about interfering in other people's lives. I couldn't believe it when I bit into that cookie. At first I thought maybe Brigit had been trying to help Tyler, but I realized she's too young for that kind of recipe."

The agitated voice belonged to Tyler's gran, and when Mom responded her voice was controlled, but I could tell she was very angry. "Adele, I don't know what you're talking about. I'm sure that anything you are imagining about my baking just isn't possible, now is it?"

"Your denial is admirable, but you have to remember that your mother and I spent a lot of time together. I know many of her secrets."

"That may be, Adele, but I also know you never learned the most important thing, *harm no one*."

There was silence in the kitchen for a moment, and, when my mother continued her tone was even icier than before. "You didn't know my mother told me about what you had done. Didn't you understand the power you were toying with or were you so arrogant you thought you could control it? The Rule of Three is ironclad – that which you do, good or bad, comes back to you threefold. I feel sorry you've paid such a deep price over the years, but you should have known better."

There was more silence, and I was almost holding my breath trying to stay quiet so I could continue to eavesdrop. Mrs. McGrath's voice sounded incredibly tired when she said, "My heartache has been . . ." Her last sentence trailed off as she began to weep.

My mother's voice was softer now. "Adele, your worry about the cookies is unfounded. Please know all my recipe can possibly do is give a gentle push or plant a mild suggestion for people to see things from each other's point of view. No harm done."

When their voices grew too low for me to catch anything that was being said, I decided to make my presence known and slammed the door, pretending I had just come in.

"Hi, Brigit." Mom called out to me like nothing had been going on.

"Hi," I said and walked back into the kitchen and greeted Tyler's gran, too.

"Hello, Brigit," she responded and stood to put on her coat. "So how are things going with you and my grandson?"

"Um, fine." I shrugged, unsure of how to answer.

"Thanks for taking the time to see me today, Celeste," Adele said and added, "Who knows? Maybe, I'll get what I wanted all those years ago after all." She tilted her head toward me and walked out the door.

Mom shook her head as if to erase the strangeness of the moment before turning to me. "I heard you when you came in – the first time. Thank you for not interrupting us, although I'm guessing it was more out of curiosity than politeness that you waited in the hallway. So now you know about the cookies."

"I figured you did something special with them."

"It wasn't much really, but I felt like I should give it a try." She shrugged.

I hadn't really understood everything they were arguing about and figured this was my only chance to find out. "What's up with Tyler's gran? How could she know there was something special in the cookies, and what was all of that about the Rule of Three and something she did?"

"Oh, Brig," Mom sighed, "there was a small misunderstanding about the cookies, but the rest is a long story and one that you'll get to read about –"

"I know, I know! In the book!" I was really getting irritated with having to wait for the book to "reveal" its secrets.

"Be patient. You'll get to it soon enough when you read Grandma's section." She deliberately changed the subject and asked, "So, how much homework do you have? I hope not too much because I need some help cleaning!"

"You sure know how to spoil an evening," I complained.

"Yes, that's me. Everyone thinks I'm a big party-pooper today."

"Yuck, what a dumb saying. Swear you'll never say that in front of my friends."

She held up her right hand. "I do solemnly swear to never use the term party-pooper in front of my daughter's friends so as to avoid her untimely death from embarrassment."

I groaned in frustration and tried to get out of the kitchen before she issued any specific orders, but I wasn't fast enough.

"Here, catch," she said, throwing a dust cloth my way. "Start by getting rid of some of the dust in your room. You know we always clean the house for Imbolc."

"Yay, me!" I shook the dust cloth like a cheerleader as I left but hesitated in the doorway when Mom sank into a chair and cradled her head in her hands. Something was wrong, but I trusted my instincts not to bother her.

Chapter Fourteen

I straightened my nightstand and reorganized my bookshelf, avoiding any actual cleaning. But I knew there was no getting out of it and eventually picked up the cloth. Lightly dusting over my desk, I paused when I got to the box which protected the old book. I traced the design on the lid.

I had to admit that I was curious to see what came next. I wondered how Aileen's life had gone. Maybe her story would be a happy one. I lifted the book out and opened to her page.

Aileen Quinn
The Fourth Day of August
In the Year Thirteen Hundred Thirty-five

Read me now, read me well.
I am steadfast as I tell
Nine of us to reunite
The blessed Goddess' birthright.
So many years have come and gone.
We call out in mournful song
And change it to one of strength.
Revenge is ours at great length.

Together we are intertwined,
Separate lives but of one mind.
See the truth here below.
If you are worthy, make it so.

⚭

"It is such a blessing Onora's friends are together once more and with their daughters. It is more than I ever expected. The girls are good company for Aileen," Bressa said to Onora's mother Maureen as they watched the girls scamper about, singing and playing in the grass.

"Aileen needs to have some fun. She is much too serious, living with such boring old ladies like us." Maureen waved at Aileen as she looked over at them. "It is hard to believe nearly ten summers have passed since we lost Onora and gained our Aileen. She is much taller than the others, isn't she?"

Bressa squinted her old eyes at the girls. "Well, she is a bit older, but Ian was a tall fellow, now wasn't he? She's taking after him."

This happy gathering had been a long time in coming. First one, then another, of Onora's friends had returned to the island to visit with old Bressa and Maureen. The young women were greatly saddened to learn of Ian and Onora's deaths, but took delight in baby Aileen. In the years between, the rest of the eight had married and had children.

Father Banan had been gone from the village for three years, and his departure thankfully ended the hunt for witches within their community. They kept track of his whereabouts and knew he had taken up residence in a village a half-day's walk to the east. Even so, the women were very careful when celebrating the festivals and only did so on the island where they felt completely safe.

It was impossible for them to forget the ordeal they went through and equally impossible to adequately thank Ian and Onora for saving them, but they honored their memories by coming together just as in the old days. Today, they celebrated the grain harvest festival, Lammas, and made small, round loaves of bread while the girls played in the warm August sun.

When the bread was finished baking on the flat stones at the edge of the fire, they all sat down next to Bressa and Maureen. Aileen felt a sharp pang of loneliness as she looked around at the mothers and daughters. Her mother should have been there. When the storytelling began, the first story was always their great rescue from Father Banan and his followers. Aileen did not remember when she first heard this story. She had always known it as if it had been whispered into her cradle. She was proud of her parents' bravery but at times, like now, wished she could change the past and have them with her, even if it meant the death of everyone who had been thrown in the lake that day. She felt a wave of shame, surrounded by those who would be dead and those who would never have been born if her wish came true. It was a horrible thing to want, but if it was possible, she knew she would not hesitate.

Aileen never tired of hearing the tale and listened as the women took turns telling their parts. But, what happened *after* the dramatic rescue was what consumed her the most. A few months before, Aileen was admiring the precious page her mother had written in the book and this time when she read the verse, the edges of her vision blurred. Her mother and father's story began to play out before her eyes and she was captivated.

Only then had she learned what truly happened after the dramatic rescue and how her parents had died. She became obsessed with viewing her parents' story. She disappeared with the book as frequently as she dared. Hiding from Bressa and her grandmother, she watched the story over and over. Her grandmother finally pried the book out of her arms and hid it away. "I'm sorry, I'm sorry. It is for your own good," she had said while Aileen wailed and kicked at her.

Later that night, when they thought she was asleep. Aileen overheard her grandmother say to Bressa, "She is so young. I never thought she'd be able to unlock the spell at her age or I would have hidden the book away."

Bressa and her grandmother talked low together, and Aileen could not make out their words until Bressa said, "Should we begin her instruction? I worry she might not be old enough to respect the power she would gain."

Her grandmother answered. "We ought not to risk it. I think we should wait until the traditional age of fifteen."

Aileen knew what they spoke of. She wasn't stupid. She had seen their special book of notes and recipes. They were talking about magic. What they didn't know was that she had already been able to master some of the easier spells.

As she fell asleep she replayed her parents' story, and, in the days which followed one scene in particular, never left her mind. The final moments of her mother's life were etched into her brain . . . the way her mother touched her newborn cheek and called her darling. The awareness of the deep love she had been oh-so-briefly given made her grieve for something she had never missed before.

The next morning, she visited the sad piles of stones covering her parents' final resting place and felt something shift inside her. She let out a hideous shriek and kicked one of the stones in anger, setting it rolling down the slope. She didn't care! It was not right she didn't have her parents with her. She blamed her mother for not taking better care of herself after her father's death. She blamed Bressa for not being able to heal her father. She blamed her grandmother for teaching her mother the ancient ways in the first place. She blamed Father Banan for his hunt for an evil which didn't exist. Yes, most of all, she blamed Father Banan. She shook with anger and decided someone should make him pay.

She began to plan her revenge that day but was careful to hide her preparations from her grandmother and Bressa. Her plan seemed simple enough to carry out by herself, but she confided in the other girls and asked them to help her draw the Goddess' energy for her mission. In the middle of the night, they joined Aileen at her parents' gravesite.

Grabbing a long piece of red yarn, Aileen twisted it once around each girl's right wrist and then her own – each of them the oldest daughters of the nine women who took part in that fateful Beltane festival ten years past. "We stand here at my parents' graves. We know the story well of Father Banan and how he hurt your mothers and cost my parents their lives. Their unjust deaths must be avenged. We see how your mothers remain fearful. We must make Father Banan pay for his transgressions so it is truly safe for us to always celebrate the seasons of our Mother Earth together. Let us call the energy of the Goddess."

"Maidens all, three times three
Loyal, loyal we shall be.
We pledge an oath to each other
Protect our Circle from evil power.
Prevent that which threatens harm
By casting spells to disarm.
We will avenge what we must,
Relying on our maidens' trust.
Keep the secret we agree
To never speak of this freely.
This bond is forever tight.
Make it so this darkest night."

Aileen said the pledge twice, with each girl chanting the lines after her. By the third time through they were in unison. Then Aileen instructed them to put their right hands out over her parents' graves. The yarn twisted around their wrists pulled taught between them and as they circled the stones marking where her parents' bodies lay, she chanted, "The thread of red seals our promise and gives us strength as we call the Goddess."

The energy swirled in the air like an electrical storm, tingling their skin and blowing their skirts against their legs on what was a windless night. After the third rotation they stopped. Aileen carefully slipped the yarn from their wrists twisting it into a tight coil she placed under a rock at the foot of the graves. The girls slipped back to their mothers as silently as they had left.

They understood the serious tone of their vow and Aileen's need for revenge. What they didn't know was how soon she would put her plan into motion.

At suppertime after everyone had gone back to the village, Aileen talked with her grandmother and Bressa about how she and the other girls pledged to always come together to celebrate the seasons and protect their circle. She omitted the part about seeking revenge against Father Banan. She knew they would disapprove. She couldn't believe that the tenet to "do no harm" actually applied to him, but she couldn't risk being stopped.

"I hope you will always be able to celebrate with them, Aileen. Your mother would have liked that." Her grandmother smiled at her and patted her arm.

Aileen hated being treated like a child, and her words came out more emphatically than she meant them to. "We've pledged an oath to each other. We will not break it!"

"As you get older, you realize that even when we try our hardest to do certain things, sometimes it isn't always possible."

"That won't happen to me or to any of the others. We're stronger than that already, and when we're together we're . . . we're . . . formidable."

"Aileen, I will agree to that, formidable you are." Her grandmother laughed at Aileen's description and Bressa joined in.

Aileen had to stop herself from saying something awful back to them. They were laughing at her like she was a child, not the young woman she really was. Wouldn't they be surprised to know how accomplished she was getting with her spell-making? Of course, she couldn't let them know this, at least not until after her plan had succeeded.

⌘

I chewed on my lip contemplating Aileen's plotting, nervous about the outcome, and when I realized it was after midnight, I was happy to go to bed. Even though Aileen was many generations removed from me, I hated the idea of her doing something bad. I wondered if I would want revenge just as much if I felt someone had caused my mom's death.

Mom was all I had, and thinking of her gone from me – even hypothetically – made my eyes fill with tears. I loved my mom, strange ways and all. I couldn't imagine being without her. What I *could* imagine and often did, was how nice it would have been if my dad were around, too. I fell asleep thinking of my perfect two-parent world.

CHAPTER FIFTEEN

The next day, Tyler came bounding into the art room like an energetic puppy (a really cute one) and pulled Miss Sienna aside to talk with her. Everybody was watching because his excitement was so obvious.

Miss Sienna's voice carried over to me. "That's great! I know you'll love it."

I was incredibly curious about what was going on. Thankfully, Tyler stopped by my table before setting up his own gear. "Hey, gorgeous." He smiled.

"Hey, yourself. Where were you this morning?"

"The most amazing thing happened this morning. Gran was over and she had big news for me. She offered to pay the other half of my art school tuition. With that argument off the table, Dad said that he would try to be open-minded and suggested we visit the campus this weekend. He's not making any promises, but he felt he owed it to me to at least see what the school was like."

"Tyler, that's so awesome! I can't believe it. Your gran's amazing!" I grabbed his arm and practically jumped up and down. The cookies worked – the cookies worked. I couldn't wait to give Mom the news.

Tyler continued. "Yeah, I almost fell over. My mom didn't expect it either. She just sat there with her mouth open."

"Tyler, get going on your project." Miss Sienna shooed him away from me in a good-natured way.

"I'm going. I'm going." He laughed while he walked over to his table.

I went back to my Celtic knot painting. It was going so well I hardly noticed the hour pass and decided to stay after to finish the section I was working on. Miss Sienna didn't mind.

Tyler came over and stood next to me at the easel. "You should show this to Gran when you're done. She'd like it. It reminds me of her paintings, the ones you saw on our first date. Does it mean anything special?"

"No, not that I know. It's from a book I have on family history. Maybe it's sort of like a crest or something. The book didn't say."

"I bet my gran would know. You should show her the book," he said emphatically.

I was startled by the forcefulness of his suggestion. He was obviously still full of adrenalin about art school.

I didn't tell him that the book was a private, family thing. Instead I agreed with him. "I wouldn't doubt it. She seems to know about a lot of things."

Tyler arched his brow questioningly at my comment and paused a beat before he asked, "Do you want a ride home? I've got to head to practice now, but I'll be done by five."

"Yeah, sure that sounds great. If I finish before then, I'll wait by your locker."

He gave me a quick kiss and ran out the door.

At four-thirty Miss Sienna stuck her head out of her office. "Brigit, I'm going to be leaving in a few minutes. Can you please pack up?"

"Sure thing." I washed my brushes, setting them in the holder to dry and put my paints on the shelf. I left the painting on the easel.

When she walked to the door, Miss Sienna passed by my artwork, paused and backed up slowly to take a second look. "Well done, Brigit."

"Thanks." I tilted my head slightly and looked at the painting with her. I thought it could still use some work, but I was glad she liked it.

"I've never had freshmen in advanced art before. I'm glad I took a chance on you and Moriah. You're very talented. I hope you're enjoying the class."

"Miss Sienna, I love it – best part of my day." I couldn't help gushing.

"You're not just saying that because of some of the people you get to see in the class, are you?"

I felt heat creep into my cheeks. I couldn't believe she was teasing me about Tyler. I didn't know what to say.

She noticed my embarrassment and chuckled. "Hey, I'm only kidding. It would be pretty hard not to notice how much you and Tyler like each other. See you tomorrow, Brigit."

I was glad to make my escape. After I gathered my things, I went to the senior hallway and sat by Tyler's locker, waiting for him to finish practice. There were a few other people around, but I was grateful no one seemed to pay attention to me. Unfortunately, my anonymity didn't last long.

A few minutes later, a senior girl came to her locker a few down from Tyler's. I couldn't remember her name, but I knew she was a member of the dance team.

She looked at me disdainfully. "Are you lost?" she asked, flipping her long blonde hair back while she twisted her combination.

"No, I'm waiting for someone."

"You're waiting for someone here? Who?" Her condescending tone made it obvious that I – a lowly freshman – had no business being in *her* hallway.

"Tyler McGrath." I replied automatically and immediately berated myself for answering her. It wasn't any of her business who I was waiting for.

"*Really?*" She clearly did not believe me and bent down to pack her bag.

I watched her progress, silently pleading for Tyler to show up before she was gone. I nearly cheered when he came out of the gym and gave me a big hug she couldn't miss.

I heard her mutter "whatever" before she slammed her locker shut.

"She's probably a slut like her witchy mom."

At first, I thought she was talking under her breath, but I knew with an awful certainty that she hadn't said that out loud. It was happening again! I couldn't blame nervousness this time. Either I heard what she was thinking or I was going crazy. Neither option was good.

"Yo, earth to Brigit, come in Brigit." Tyler waved his hand in front of my face. "Are you okay?"

"Yeah, sure. I – I was only wondering who that was." I recovered my composure and pointed down the hall toward the senior girl.

"That's Carissa Bloom. She's kind of a pain. Why?"

"Just curious, that's all." I knew it would be dumb to tell Tyler how bitchy she'd been. Guys hated that kind of thing. Although, they probably hated psychotic girlfriends who heard voices more.

On the way to my house, Tyler said he was sorry he would be gone all weekend while he and his parents made the trip into Boston together.

"Don't even think of apologizing. This is big – this is huge!" I emphasized how big by waving my arms in the air and added, "Plus, Moriah and Jess are staying over tomorrow night."

He slapped his hand over his heart in mock distress. "Oh, I'm hurt. You didn't want me around anyway?"

"Well, remember when Moriah was so upset earlier this week? I decided a little girl time might help smooth things out. We think she's been feeling left out with both Jess and I . . . y'know . . . dating people." I had almost said "having boyfriends" but stopped because I wasn't really sure I should call Tyler that – yet.

"Ah, girl time. I'm glad I'm going to be far, far away."

We stopped in front of my house, and when he leaned over to give me a quick kiss, I threw caution to the wind and reached up behind his head to stop his retreat. He groaned and our kiss deepened. When our lips finally separated, he stayed close and leaned his forehead against mine. "Brig, you're making me crazy."

"No, you're making *me* crazy." I couldn't stop smiling as I got out.

"I'm sorry I can't come in tonight. I have some stuff I have to get done, since I won't have the weekend for studying. I'll call you later, okay?"

"Sounds good."

I hurried into the house eager to tell Mom the news about Tyler's dad. "Mom, hey Mom, where are you?" I called out, but there was no answer. In the kitchen I noticed that the backdoor was open so she had to be nearby, maybe in the barn. I ran out the back and flung open the big barn door. "Mom, are you in here?"

"Yes, I'm getting the straw ready for the Brigid's Crosses we're making on Friday."

"The cookies worked! Tyler's dad told him this morning that he wants to visit the art school campus this weekend. Tyler's gran offered to cover part of the tuition. How cool is that?"

"I'm so glad for him. It sounds like his dad is at least listening to him now."

"Okay, so I'm dying to know. What did you do to those cookies?" I used my most pleading voice. "Can't you tell me?"

"It's a simple combination of some spices and a little something else. I found it in your grandmother's book. I didn't know if it would work. I'd never used that – ah – recipe before."

"Is that all you're going tell me?"

"Brigit, that's all there is. Look, I'll even show it to you when we get into the house." She sighed and picked up the basket of straw she had been cutting. "Let's go, we've got a lot to do to get ready."

Back in the house I immediately asked, "Can I see it now?"

"Give me a minute." She put the basket down, took off her boots and hung up her cloak. I was surprised when she went to the shelf above the stove and grabbed the normal cookbook she always used. I truly expected her to pull an old book out of a secret hiding place.

She flipped to the page, placed it on the table and said in a terse voice. "Here you go." I immediately sank into a chair and bent over the open book.

Persuasion Cookies
Use any ginger snap or spice cookie recipe and add the following:
1 teaspoon cloves
1 tablespoon flax seed
A pinch of star anise.
Stir ingredients in a deosil direction and repeat this phrase:
I make this treat to open the mind
So those who take a bite may find

An acceptance of a point of view
They no longer will eschew.
Continue to stir but switch directions to widdershins and
add a pinch of dried slippery elm bark while saying:
I add this last ingredient to make (insert name) more tolerant.
Bake as usual.

"What's deosil and widdershins?" I asked.

"Deosil is clockwise and widdershins is counterclockwise."

"So that's all there is to it?" I felt a little deflated.

"What did you expect?"

"I don't know, but I thought it would be more . . . complicated."

"Brigit, it is entirely possible that this recipe did nothing. Tyler's dad might have made this decision without eating any of these. We'll never know, but it made us feel better because at least we tried to help, right?"

I nodded in agreement and handed the book back to her. "I hope this weekend turns out okay for him. He's really excited."

"Let's get some supper so we can finish up a project or two."

Mom always made a big deal out of Imbolc. Mostly, I thought because she hated winter and liked doing something to break up the boredom of the long cold season. I didn't mind her enthusiasm. Decorating the house was kind of fun and the traditional food we ate was yummy. I was still a little worried that my friends might think it was all too weird.

She started her list making when we sat down to eat. "Okay, the cleaning is done, so tonight we need to make the larger Brigid Crosses for the doors, decorate the windowsills, and bake."

"Mom, I'd rather not make the big crosses, you're so much better at it. I'll decorate the windowsills though." That was something I wouldn't mess up.

After dinner, I stayed in the kitchen with her as she began to weave the crosses. I wound lengths of green and white ribbon around willow branches and put white candles in silver holders. Going from room to room, I put the branches on each wide windowsill with a candle in the middle. I was pleased with how pretty everything looked. I finished up in the kitchen, leaving one windowsill empty for the small dishes of water and salt the Goddess Brigid would bless overnight. Mom was done with the larger crosses, and I hung them on the front and back doors before helping her with the baking.

We always made Mom's special braided bread, and as long as I can remember my job was to twist the dough into long loaves. While I did this, Mom mixed the batter for walnut raisin cake, which was her favorite. She'd already finished the traditional lemony, poppy-seed Brigid Cake before I came home. Hopefully, my friends would like one or the other.

The next morning the sky was gray and yucky, and it definitely looked like it was going to snow. The weather report agreed – a storm was on the way.

By lunchtime the snow was coming down fast and didn't look like it would slow down anytime soon. The loudspeaker crackled to life, and a tinny voice announced, "School will be closing at two o'clock today . . ." Shouts of joy erupted, drowning out any further information. Even though we were high schoolers, a snow day made everyone happy. I called Mom on my cell and almost dropped the phone when Tyler hugged me from behind. I told her about the early closing rather abruptly with Tyler continuing to distract me by pulling me through the gym doors. The doors swung shut blocking out the sound and light from the hallway. The only light came from the dim exit signs over the doors.

"What are you up to?" I laughed.

Tyler didn't say anything, and I couldn't see his expression. He grabbed me by my shoulders, pushed me up against the closed bleachers, and leaned his body against mine, kissing me hard. I wrapped my arms around him and kissed back just as deeply. He left my mouth and trailed kisses down my neck. Tyler froze in place when someone entered the far end of the gym and crossed to the opposite doors without seeing us in the dark. He still hadn't said anything and kissed me again, but I pulled back and whispered breathlessly, "Tyler, my mom is going to be out front any minute."

He took a deep breath and hugged me tightly. "Don't forget about me this weekend." His voice was low and serious.

His tone stopped me from making a sarcastic remark about two days being an eternity. Instead, I answered honestly. "I'll miss you."

I waited for him cut across the gym before I stepped back into the hallway. The sudden brightness made me blink. Moriah and Jess noticed my disorientation. Jess pulled me over. "I saw Tyler drag you in there. Were you making out? You're so lucky you didn't get caught." She and Moriah were now laughing.

I didn't like feeling flustered in front of them, so I lifted my nose in the air and adopted my most haughty voice. "I don't know what you're talking about. I was only telling Tyler to have a good weekend."

"I don't believe you," Jess sing-songed to me.

Mom was idling at the curb when we came out. On the way home, our car slid each time she turned a corner. When we finally pulled into our driveway, I jumped out and opened the big barn doors so Mom could put the car away. We kicked through the new snow on the way to back door and dumped all of our stuff on the kitchen floor in a big heap before heading to my room to hang out.

Preparing to be teased about my gym session with Tyler, I shut the door behind us. Jess surprised me by immediately noticing the box with my ancestors' book sitting on my nightstand.

"Brigit, what's this?" Jess pulled it onto her lap as she sat back onto the bed.

"Hey, be careful. It's really old." I was mad at myself for not remembering to slide it under my bed this morning like I had planned. I knew I wasn't supposed to talk about it, so I said as little as possible. "That was another one of my birthday presents. It's a book about our family history. It's really old and boring." I waved my hand dismissively in the air. "I need to read it before our trip." I rolled my eyes in pretend exasperation with the chore I'd been given and reached over. "Let me get it out of our way."

Jess was busy running her fingers over the carving in the lid and ignored my outstretched hands. "I really like the way this feels."

"Let me see," Moriah said, leaning across the bed. She opened the lid before I could stop her. "You weren't kidding when you said this thing was really old."

"How old is it?" Jess asked. "A hundred years?

"Try six," I said.

"What?" She gulped. "Six hundred years old?"

"Yeah. My mom will kill me if I let anything happen to it." I was getting worried that I'd have a hard time getting it away from them.

"Can we take a peek at the pages?" Moriah asked.

"We'll be really careful," Jess added.

There was no hope for it. I was going to have to let them satisfy their curiosity before they'd let me put it away. I reluctantly agreed. "Okay, only if you're very careful."

Moriah and Jess sat side by side on the edge of the bed and slowly lifted the leather cover on the book. They paged through a little bit only stopping to read the dates. Then they flipped to one of the Celtic knot designs.

Moriah gasped when she spotted the gleaming gilt page. "This is like your painting in art class. Is this where you got your idea?"

I nodded my head.

"Oh, what does that say? It is so hard to read the writing." Jess pointed at the verse on Onora's page.

"Is this like a diary?" Moriah asked.

"Sort of. It's more like a collection of stories from our family." I didn't want to be talking about this and hoped they didn't hear the nervousness in my voice.

"It mostly looks like poems to me," Jess said.

Moriah was squinting hard at Onora's page and mouthing the words. "Wait a second! This is a spell! Is this a book of magic?"

"What – no – what would make you think that? Are you crazy?" I really needed to put the book back.

"This *sounds* like a spell to me, Brigit." Moriah was not going to let this go.

"No, really it's like an introduction to her story. See there are a lot of them." I showed them some of the other verses and tried to shut the book.

"But, Brigit, there aren't any stories on the pages – only these spells – er – poems." Moriah exchanged a strange look with Jess.

What could I say? I hated to lie to them, but I really couldn't tell them about the stories that played like a movie for me. They'd never believe it. And, I wasn't sure how to explain my heritage. I was very confused about what it meant for me – for my life. It wasn't something I could share – even with my best friends.

Maybe there was a solution somewhere in the middle. I began hesitantly, "The truth is . . . the truth is that only direct descendants are supposed to read the whole book. It's really not a big deal. They're only boring old stories about my ancestors' lives. Really." I nodded my head at them and reached for the book again.

"Sounds cool to me. I'd love to have a book like this about my relatives," Moriah said, staring at the page.

Mom called up the stairs to us, and I had never been so grateful for an interruption.

"Coming," I said and put the book back into the box, slipping it under the bed where it would be safe. I practically pulled my friends down the stairs with me.

The fire crackled away, making the kitchen toasty warm. Mom suggested we could make the Brigid Crosses before dinner and pointed to the supplies she had set out on the table. I showed my friends how to twist the straw together to make the design. Mine were never as smooth as my mom's, but at least they could get the idea from watching me.

"Why do you make these on Brigid's Day?" Jess asked.

Mom was happy to answer. "They symbolize the old Irish sun wheel and traditionally farmers would put one near the doorway of their home to protect them from evil and want throughout the coming year. They believed in its power to assure a good growing season."

"Our church calendar says today is St. Bridget's Day," Moriah offered.

"Brigid has been around for centuries," Mom went on. "Before Christianity came to Ireland the people there believed in a fire goddess named Brigid. Later on, the church incorporated her into their teachings and made her a saint for the miracles she performed. Brigid's Day is a very old tradition."

I was starting to get nervous that this was going to be a very strange night for my friends. Thankfully, Mom hadn't gone off on her usual rant about how the early church had incorporated pagan symbols into their religion to make it easier to convert people. Jess and Moriah seemed to be enjoying themselves, nimbly twisting away at their crosses. I finished mine and laid it on the table so they could use it as a guide.

"Mom, do you need help with anything?" I asked.

"Sure, why don't you fill up the bowls for the windowsill?"

I got out the small crystal dishes, one for salt and one for water. After I filled them up, I carried them to the windowsill I had left undecorated. I noticed Moriah watching me.

"What's that for?" She asked.

"The salt and water are left out over night to be blessed by the – um – by Brigid." I had paused when I realized it might sound strange to call Brigid the Fire Goddess and skipped the words entirely.

"Oh," Moriah said.

"She blesses the ribbons, too, and throughout the year they are used as sort of a protection against illness. When I was little, my mom used to tie a piece around my wrist when I was sick. You can take a piece home if you want."

"Oh, I remember you telling me something about this once a long time ago. You came back to school after being sick with a ribbon on your wrist, and I asked you about it." Jess said.

"It's nearly dark, Brigit. Why don't you all take turns lighting the candles." Mom handed me the lighter.

We started upstairs, and at the first candle I said the traditional phrase. "Brigid, bless us all year 'round, bless the plants with fertile ground, bless the sky with faithful sun, 'til the growing season's done."

I cringed, realizing how childish that sounded. "I'm sorry. We don't have to say that at every candle if you don't want to. Does it sound weird?"

"No, I like it," Jess said, completely surprising me.

"Me, too," Moriah agreed.

I appreciated their enthusiasm whether it was real or not, just grateful they weren't laughing. We took turns at each candle. By the third time through, they had the blessing memorized. Mom gave them an impressed nod when she heard Moriah and Jess as they lit the last two candles in the kitchen.

She turned out the overhead light. The glow from the fireplace and the candles made the room seem very magical.

"Everything's ready. Come sit down girls. We have lamb chops, green beans, lettuce salad, our famous braided bread, and champ – that's mashed potatoes with butter and green onions mixed in." Her voice was excited as she recited the menu. I didn't blame her. My mouth watered in anticipation. We didn't eat like this very often.

We all ate a lot and saved our dessert for later, just like on my birthday. In the meantime, we helped Mom clean up the kitchen. When we were done, none of us wanted to leave the cozy room. We stayed there and played cards until nearly eleven. Mom even played with us. The night had turned out fine, and my friends didn't seem ready to bolt away from my crazy goddess-loving house.

Of course, when we went up to my room to get ready for bed, we really weren't planning on sleeping right away. We lined up our sleeping bags on my floor and talked for hours.

It was after two when I was sure that Moriah and Jess were really asleep. They hadn't asked about the book again, but it had been in my thoughts all night, and I was anxious to finish Aileen's story. I wriggled out of my sleeping bag, pulled the book from its box, and slid back into my spot without waking them.

CHAPTER SIXTEEN

It was awkward holding the large book while stuffed into a sleeping bag, but I shifted around until I found a comfortable position. I read Aileen's verse again, and her story began were I left off.

Aileen slowly approached the gate in the low stone wall and looked around once more to assure herself that she was truly alone before entering Bressa's herb garden. She had never been allowed inside but often sat on the wall watching Bressa hoe and weed. When she asked the names of the plants, Bressa always answered but warned her in a very serious voice about their danger. "This garden is not for little girls."

Aileen murmured to the memory, "I'm not a little girl anymore," and went straight to the plant she needed, plucking a dozen dark berries off the stem. She admired their deadly beauty before scooping them into the small pottery jar. She jammed the cork in tightly and pocketed her treasure.

Her plan was progressing well. Her grandmother had endorsed her idea to make some extra money selling rowanberry jelly at the village market day. Bressa had eyed her skeptically, but did not interfere with her grandmother's decision. After all, they did need the money to buy things they couldn't make or grow. It was difficult for the older women to make the trip to the nearby village and decided that Aileen was old enough to travel to market day alone.

With four days to go, Aileen had one more batch of jelly to make. The most important batch of all. The rowan trees did not grow on the island. They had been planted years ago near the road approaching Lough Dooras by superstitious folks in an attempt to keep the dreadful island spirits from assaulting passersby. Aileen thought it was a fitting reversal to now use the rowan tree to aid the delivery of something most deadly from the island. She rowed to the shore of the lake and picked the berries she would need.

Her grandmother and Bressa were busy tying up herbs to dry when she returned to the cottage. Bressa glanced at the berries in her basket and smiled. "Another batch? You're turning into quite the merchant."

"After this, I'll have twenty crocks to sell. That should bring us a tidy sum." She pointed to the shelf where the little crocks of jelly were lined up in neat rows like soldiers ready for battle.

She mashed the berries, cooked them in the large pot over the fire, and strained the juice through a piece of linen, leaving the pulpy mixture behind. Boiling the juice with the honey was hot and tiring work. She stirred constantly to prevent the bottom from burning. When it had thickened, she ladled the lovely amber liquid into the crocks. Earlier, as Bressa and her grandmother went back and forth to the garden, Aileen used the intermittent privacy to take the little jar from her pocket and squeeze the deadly juice from the dark berries. With great care she poured the teaspoons of the nearly black liquid into the last crock and gave it a little stir. To be safe, she drew a black x on the bottom of this crock with a piece of charred wood and sealed them all with a thin layer of mutton fat covered with a circular piece of linen, tied on with twine.

On market day Aileen rose much earlier than was necessary and rowed across Lough Dooras with her basket of jelly. On the other shore she walked in the opposite direction of the nearby village, aiming for Fahlan Town, Father Banan's current home.

After hours of walking Aileen reached the hill above the larger town. It was the final day of the week-long fair and market, so Aileen knew there'd be many strangers about, allowing her to blend in. There were tents set up outside the town to house all the visitors and people were opening their stalls to sell their wares. Aileen readjusted the heavy basket on her arm and walked down the hill to sell her jelly.

She was excited by the bustle of the people. Aileen had not often visited the smaller village where the girls lived, and this was a much larger place. The many people walking about, talking and hawking their wares made it a dizzying experience. The stalls held everything from mouthwatering breads and pies to delicate ribbons and lace. There was a man carving tiny animals from wood. It was mesmerizing to watch his skill as he created the face of a small lamb. "Would you like a wee pet to take home?" he asked.

"No thank you, sir. I'm here to sell my jelly," she answered.

Aileen began asking women if they'd like to buy the rowanberry jelly. "Some fine rowanberry jelly, ma'am, to go with your roast meat. 'Tis fresh made and only four pence a crock."

People were friendly, and Aileen was happy the heavy basket was growing lighter at last. She kept touching the special crock she carried to assure herself it was still there. She did not want to sell it by mistake. Finally, Aileen had the one crock left and sat down at the edge of the market to rest and search for Father Banan. She nibbled on some cheese and bread while she waited. She had never seen Father Banan herself, but hoped that she would be able to tell who he was without asking anyone. She did not want to draw attention to herself.

Finally, Aileen observed a tall man striding past some of the stalls a few yards away and heard some of townsfolk greet him warmly.

"Good day to you, Father."

"Good day to you, my son," the tall man replied.

Aileen watched to see which way he went and rose to follow him. Father Banan walked back to the main thoroughfare of the town and entered the inn. Aileen went through the same door a few paces behind him. She paused to let her eyes adjust to the dim interior and saw Father Banan slip through a curtain into another room. She was about follow when she was grabbed roughly by the arm as a man staggered against her. "Hallo, did you come to keep me company?" The man slurred, his nasty breath making Aileen feel ill.

"Let me go!" She shouted and struggled to hold onto the jelly while she wriggled free. The innkeeper took notice and began to shoo Aileen to the door. "You can't be in here. Get back to your parents."

Aileen's heart was beating wildly, but somehow she kept her wits and calmly said, "Sir, I'm on an errand for my parents. I'm to give this rowanberry jelly to Father Banan. I saw him come in here."

The man sighed. "Come with me. He's eating his meal."

Aileen followed him across the bar room, her shoes sticking to the filthy ale-splashed floor with each step. Behind the curtained doorway she was surprised to find a well-lit dining room so very different from the first room. Here the floor and tables were clean, and the customers appeared to be well-mannered, speaking in low tones over their meals. Father Banan sat at one of the tables and was about to dig into a plate of roast lamb and boiled potatoes.

"Someone to see you, Father," the man said and nudged her forward.

Father Banan's dark eyes stared at her, waiting. He didn't seem dangerous, but Aileen knew better.

"Father, I wanted to give you this." She held the crock out to him. "It's fresh rowanberry jelly. I thought it might go well with your roast meat."

"Oh, that is so considerate. Thank you kindly. Indeed, it will go well with my dinner." He took the crock from her and began to untie the twine.

Aileen waited, hoping to see him actually eat some.

"I don't seem to recognize you. Are you visiting the market?"

"Yes, Father. We're here to sell jelly and get some supplies."

"Are you from the area?"

"No, we traveled some distance." Aileen realized she should not risk any further conversation and took her leave. "Good day to you, Father."

The innkeeper ushered her out a different doorway which led to the small walkway on the side of the building. She hovered near the window peeking in and saw Father Banan flick the hardened disk of mutton fat aside and scoop a dollop of jelly onto his meat.

Aileen shrieked with delight, thinking, "That's the end of you – you evil man!" She had not an ounce of regret.

Aileen left immediately for home, her mission accomplished.

As she pulled the boat out of its hiding place and began to row, she could see her grandmother and Bressa waiting to greet her.

"We're so glad to see you back safe. We expected you hours ago, especially after you left so early this morn," her grandmother said. "Whatever have you been doing all this time?"

"I've had a grand adventure today. I decided to take the jelly to the market in Fahlan Town instead of our village. I sold it all." She tipped the empty basket upside down to show them.

"But, Father Banan . . . the danger . . . how could you be so reckless, Aileen?" Her grandmother sputtered.

"True, I saw Father Banan from afar, but he would not know me, and the market was so busy with people from other towns. It was quite safe, I assure you." Aileen's smooth delivery made her lie undetectable.

"Aileen, you could not possibly know that it would be safe. You distressed us greatly. I need to lie down." Her grandmother was rather pale with fatigue etching her face.

Aileen felt a pang of guilt. "I'm sorry. I didn't mean to worry anyone."

Aileen bid her grandmother good night and had her hand on the ladder, ready to make her own escape to the loft, when Bressa said, "Let us sit outside for a moment."

She followed Bressa to the bench in front of the house and reluctantly sat next to her.

"If you think you have me fooled, you are a foolish child indeed." Bressa eyes stared unblinkingly at Aileen. "I know what you have done."

"I – I don't know what you mean." Aileen looked away as she answered.

"Please do not lie to me. Someone picked a number of nightshade berries from my garden, enough berries to fell a grown man. Did you put them in the jelly?"

"I . . . yes . . . I did." Aileen squared her shoulders defiantly and spat out the rest of the story. "I gave it to Father Banan, and I saw him eat it. He will be dead by the morrow. Don't expect me to feel sorry for the evil man. He – he deserved it."

"Oh, Aileen, we've made a terrible mistake in waiting to train you properly." Bressa shook her head and grabbed Aileen's hands. "I'm so sorry that our reluctance to believe you were capable will now cause you much grief."

"What do you mean? I am not grieved. I am glad for what I have done." Aileen was confused by Bressa's dire look.

"No, no you don't understand at all. The first thing we ought to have taught you is, Harm No One."

"But, I know that already. It can't possibly apply to someone evil like Father Banan."

"That's where you are most wrong. It especially applies to those who have done you wrong."

"The second lesson we would have taught you is The Rule of Three: That which you do, good or bad, comes back to you three-fold, that means three times three. I am afraid for you, Aileen, I truly am. To kill someone is a terrible, terrible thing."

Aileen swallowed hard. "I did not know about the Rule of Three, but surely Father Banan's actions . . ." Aileen trailed off as Bressa shook her head in disagreement.

"The rule is ironclad, Aileen. The only hope for you now is that he will only get sick and not die from the poison."

Aileen sat there stunned with worry as the sky darkened and the stars came out. Bressa pulled Aileen into a crushing embrace. "There may be a way to make this right, but for now, we must rest."

Aileen felt like she had barely closed her eyes when she heard Bressa calling up to the loft to wake her. "I've found a recipe – a possible antidote. Hurry! I need your help."

Aileen nearly slid down the ladder in her haste. "What are you saying, Bressa? There's a remedy for the poison?"

"Yes, there is one that may work, but it could be too late. We cannot delay." Bressa pointed to the page in her book. "See here? Now gather these items from the garden and return quickly."

When Aileen reentered the cottage with the leaves and berries the recipe required, her grandmother was sitting at the table. She took the berries from Aileen and pounded them to a pulp with rapid angry strokes, making it plain that Bressa had told her the whole story.

Aileen wanted to lessen her grandmother's ire and somehow explain her actions. "Grandmother," Aileen's voice was tentative, "I didn't know about the Rule of Three. I only wanted to make Father Banan pay." She couldn't believe that what seemed like such a good idea yesterday had turned into such a bad thing today.

"I do not care about Father Banan, but I do care about you, dear one. We cannot risk the harm that may haunt you for seeking this revenge. No matter how much we hate Father Banan, it was wrong to do." She handed the crushed berries to Bressa who dumped them into the pot over the fire.

The older women's expressions remained grim as the antidote was prepared. Finally, the medicine stood alone in the middle of the table. Bressa had poured it into a small bottle and sealed it with both a cork and wax.

Bressa's instructions were to the point. "Aileen, you must leave at once and travel as fast as you are able. When you get to the village, try not to let anyone see you. Father Banan will most assuredly be in his bed in the rectory. You will need to sneak in somehow and avoid whoever is taking care of him. Make sure he drinks this. All of it."

Her grandmother took Aileen's face in her hands. "You must do this. You must make this right. Come back to us as quickly as you can."

Unencumbered by her heavy basket, Aileen was able to travel much faster than the day before. She approached the village most carefully. She was reminded there would be no crowd of shoppers to help her blend in when she saw the bare spots worn in the grass where the market stalls and tents had stood.

The church was easy to spot as it was the tallest building in the village. She circled around to the back without being noticed. The rectory was next door and had a large garden which would provide some protection as she spied on the house. At the moment there was no one about, and she crouched down behind the tall herbs, trying to determine which window might lead to Father Banan's bedroom.

She was about to sneak a little closer when a hand clamped down on her shoulder. A low male voice said, "What child is prowling about my garden?"

Aileen gasped in fear as she recognized the voice. "Father Banan?" She managed to squeak, turning to look at him as she rose from her crouch. He looked remarkably healthy.

"Oh, you are the kind lass who gave me the jelly yesterday. I thought everyone from the market had left."

Aileen tried to come up with a plausible story. "We are leaving soon. My parents are nearly ready to go. I was . . . I was only playing here. I'm sorry to have intruded on your garden." Aileen started to back away from him and hoped he wouldn't see through her blatant lie.

"About the jelly," Father Banan said. "You wouldn't have any more, would you?"

"It was to your liking?" Aileen asked with caution.

"I never got to eat any. Unfortunately, a man who had too much drink upended the entire table, plate and all, before I took even one bite. The jelly crock was smashed to bits."

Aileen was shocked at her good fortune and took a moment to reply, "I am sorry, but we sold it all."

"A pity," Father Banan said.

"Yes, yes, it is. Good day, Father." She could hardly contain her emotions as she ran away.

It was dark when Aileen returned to the island. Her grandmother and Bressa paced at the shore. They were amazed by her tale about the broken crock of jelly and wept with relief.

"That was most fortunate for you, Aileen." Her grandmother sighed.

"We cannot have a mistake such as this happen again," Bressa said. "Tomorrow your lessons begin."

CHAPTER SEVENTEEN

I woke up feeling like I couldn't breathe and immediately shifted the heavy book off my chest. I'd meant to put it away before I fell asleep to avoid answering more of Jess and Moriah's questions. They hadn't woken up yet, so I stowed the book under my bed before tip-toeing to the bathroom. While I was washing my face, I thought I heard Moriah talking. I turned off the water and listened through the door, but her voice wasn't coming from my room. She was inside my head. It was happening again! My knees turned weak, and I sank onto the toilet seat, holding a washcloth against my eyes. Was I going crazy? After hearing that snotty senior girl the other day, I'd thrown out my nervousness theory and tried very hard not to think about it. Now, I had no choice as Moriah's thoughts slipped into my head like she was whispering in my ear.

There's obviously something creepy going on with that book. I think it's full of spells but I never thought her mom could really do magic. Brigit is hiding something big. I know it. I wonder if she's gone downstairs, and I can look at it again.

That made me snap out of it. Real or imagined, I had to act on what I heard. I couldn't let her have more time with the book. There's no way I could explain it to her without telling the truth, and that wasn't possible. I opened the bathroom door and walked with loud footsteps to the bedroom so she'd know I was on my way. When I went back in, she was pretending to be asleep, and I wasn't sure what to do. I wanted to say something. What exactly, I didn't know, but I didn't want to wake Jess by talking. Instead, I decided to hide the book in Mom's room and seek refuge in the kitchen. Moriah's eyes remained closed as I slipped out the door.

Mom was reading the morning paper with her usual cup of tea. "Brigit, I'm surprised to see you up so early. I thought I heard you girls talking quite late. Are you okay?" She scanned my face, and I purposefully tried to make it blank because she was so good at reading my emotions.

"I'm fine. I just couldn't sleep anymore." I wanted to tell her about hearing Moriah and all the other times I had heard people, but then I would have to explain about letting Jess and Moriah see the book. I was afraid she'd be mad at me for that.

"Are you sure you're fine? You three didn't have a fight, did you?"

"No, really – everything's great, except I'm super hungry." I lied *again* and hoped my attempt to change the topic wasn't too obvious.

"I mixed up pancake batter. I can get the griddle going and make some now." Mom turned on the burners under the big griddle we always used on pancake mornings. "I haven't eaten, either," she added.

She was graceful as she poured exactly the right amount to make eight perfect circles. I could never do that. Mine were always warty-looking globs – far from pancake perfection.

We ate together at the table without talking. Mom continued reading the paper when she wasn't glancing at me out of the corner of her eye. I could hear her voice in my head, saying, *There's definitely something bothering Brigit.* My fork fell to my plate with a clatter. Great! Now my mom was part of my mental illness, too!

Startled, Mom put the paper down to stare at me, but I was saved from answering the question she was about to ask – out loud this time – when Jess shouted, "We smell pancakes."

Mom got up to pour another batch onto the griddle, and a few seconds later Moriah and Jess ran into the room. "You can't believe how good those smell upstairs. I thought I was dreaming." Jess sat down next to me.

Moriah sat on the other side of the table and helped herself to some orange juice.

"Did everyone sleep well?" Mom asked.

"Yeah, sure. Once we finally went to bed." Jess giggled.

"How about you, Moriah? Sleep okay?"

Moriah didn't answer, clearly thinking of something else. I guessed what it might be, but at that moment her thoughts were her own.

Jess reached across the table and flicked the back of Moriah's hand with her finger. "Hey, Moriah!"

"Ouch, what was that for?" Moriah rubbed her hand and glared at Jess. When she noticed our amused faces, she realized we'd been talking to her. "Oh, sorry. I guess I'm not completely awake yet."

"What's the plan for the rest of the day? What time do you have to be home?" Mom asked.

"Probably before noon. I have cello practice at one." Jess said.

"That works for me, too," Moriah agreed.

"Well, since it is only nine o'clock, is there any chance if I ask really, really nicely that you girls will shovel the sidewalks?" Mom put on her most hopeful smile.

We moaned and groaned good-naturedly but agreed, and once the pancakes were decimated, we went upstairs to put on warm clothes. I was nearly giddy to have help shoveling for a change.

We squinted against the sparkly whiteness when we opened the door and couldn't believe how high the snow was. "There has to be at least a foot. It's going to take forever," I complained.

We waded through the snow to the barn to get two more shovels and set to work. Okay, it didn't take forever. It only felt like it as our hands and feet grew numb. It should have gone faster, but Moriah kept stopping and leaning on her shovel, acting like she was going to die. Jess and I threw snow at her each time to get her moving. It worked great. By the time we were done, Moriah's coat was polka-dotted with little white puffs of snow marking our direct hits.

She must have been plotting her revenge because when we walked by the snow bank at the end of the driveway, she pushed us into it. She screeched and ran for the door of the house, but we pelted her with as many snowballs as we could before she made it to safety.

After Mom took Moriah and Jess home, I really didn't have much to do. I could finish my homework, but it was only Saturday, and I had the rest of the weekend for that. My thoughts went back to the book. Reading the stories sounded like a much better option for the afternoon. I went into Mom's room to retrieve the book and found her curled up under her down comforter with a magazine.

"Gosh, you look nice and comfy," I said.

"I am enjoying a lazy Saturday afternoon. Care to join me?" She patted the other side of the bed.

"Okay." Before climbing in, I pulled the book from its hiding place under her bed.

Her eyebrows arched up in wonder, and I explained, "I wanted to get it out of the way when Jess and Moriah were here." I didn't mention they had a good look at it before I moved it.

"I finished Aileen's story – you know, Onora's daughter," I finally offered.

"Right. What'd you think of her?" She put down the paper.

"I didn't like her poison-the-priest idea. I was really glad that the crock was broken before he could eat any."

"I agree." Mom nodded and continued, "The Threefold Law is nothing to mess with."

"Is that really true? That whatever you do, good or bad, comes back to you three times three?"

Mom's voice was almost stern when she answered. "Yes, believe it and live by it. Aileen's anger was understandable, and Father Banan was not a good man, but it seemed a stretch to blame him for her mom's death, too. Her dad I understood, but it was common for women to die in childbirth back then. Onora wasn't strong because she simply gave up after Ian died. I always wished she'd been more of a fighter – for Aileen's sake."

"She loved Ian too much to go on without him." I sighed before asking, "Is it really possible to love someone that much – to die from a broken heart?"

"Yes, I think it is. It's very dangerous, very powerful to have a love like that, but it is also a great gift." Her voice wavered a little.

"Did you love my dad like that?"

She sighed and answered, "I thought I did." Her voice cracked. "It's hard to talk about, Brigit. It makes me so sad. I really believed we'd be together forever."

That was more than the standard line she usually offered. I waited for her to continue, but her expression told me the subject was now closed.

I began the next section on Aileen's daughter Loaise. She hadn't written much. She had recorded the dates when her parents had died. Aileen had lived to be forty-five, which seemed young to me, but Mom assured me it was quite old for that time. She recorded her marriage and the births and names of each of her five children.

She described her friendships with the next set of eldest daughters and their celebrations, which became less frequent through the years as people moved a little further apart. The one holiday they always made sure to celebrate together was Beltane or May Day. With the threat of Father Banan now passed, they returned this ritual to its rightful place inside the stone circle at Beltany. I wanted to ask Mom if this was why she and her friends always celebrated the holiday there, but she'd fallen asleep next to me.

I continued to read through the next generation and the next. Turning the page to begin another account, what I saw made me grip the book in shock. In 1456, my ancestor Dervla Quinn had written about hearing others' thoughts. I tried to control my breathing as I reread the verse more slowly.

I am not lost, I am not broken
I hear the words left unspoken
When they pertain to me
And are thought within, most secretly
Sometimes I do not want to know
What people think, but do not show
'Tis my gift, my talent, my vital knack
I have tried and tried to give it back
See my tale here below
If you are worthy, make it so.

*D*ervla stirred the glowing coals with a stick and reached for the last of the wood they had gathered. The flames licked up and flared to life once again. More wood ought to be gathered soon she thought, but she made no move toward the neighboring forest. She couldn't risk disturbing the conversation taking place just inside the trees. She sat back on her heels and continued to listen to their words and their thoughts. It was vital she know their plans so she could make her escape if necessary. When her brothers first walked away to talk, she had murmured to herself, "A few feet will not stop me from knowing what it is you plot." True, they were hidden well from her sight, but their words and thoughts came through perfectly – only because they spoke of her – her future.

Her elder brother, Cormac, was insisting she be taken to the nuns at the abbey the next day. Aiden, her younger brother by less than a year, offered to travel with her to allow Cormac to return home and tend to things there. He did not tell Cormac everything he was thinking, and she easily plucked Aiden's thoughts from the air. In his mind he strangled her with his bare hands and heaved her body over the edge of a tall cliff into the sea. He would tell Cormac she had run away, and he would secretly keep her substantial dowry which would have been given to the church. She was not surprised by his brutal thoughts.

She knew Cormac was frustrated with her, but she feared no real harm from him. He had always been kind, and when their father had died years before, he had stepped in and taken care of her and her mother. Aiden was different, vastly different. From a young age, she learned to avoid being alone with him. His covert, cruel tricks, nasty shoves, and pinches confused her and made her wonder what she had done to incur his wrath. And yet, she had tried to be nice to him. That ceased completely four years ago, when in her fifteenth year, she was confronted with his true evil. His murderous thoughts were the first she had been able to hear. He wanted to kill her. At first she was confused and thought he was speaking aloud. When she realized she was hearing what he was thinking, she kept this to herself for fear her family would think she were daft. Indeed, for a time she thought she was crazy. Desperate for the voices to go away, she tried every healing potion and spell she ever learned and a few she made up. Nothing worked.

It terrified her to see into Aiden's mind. His thoughts were consumed with hate – hate of her and an irrational jealousy of every loving kindness she received from her father, her mother, and even Cormac. It was as though there had been a tally in his head from the day he was born, and he was compelled to equalize every good thing in her life with an act of cruelty. The cold blackness of his thoughts made her realize the madness of his true evil. He was without a soul. In time she became more comfortable with her ability as it allowed her to stay one step ahead of Aiden. She guarded her secret carefully, never revealing it to anyone.

Continuing to listen in, she heard Cormac agree to let Aiden travel on with her alone. She didn't blame him. Aiden always hid his animosity for her from everyone else. There was no way he would let her survive the trip. Any protective spell she could conjure up here at their meager campsite would be no match for his evil plan. She would simply have to be more cunning.

After her mother's recent death, she knew that things would change. She had hoped it wouldn't be so soon. Her mother had only been gone for a week when Cormac had begun to work on finding her a husband. Dervla had never been interested in marriage, and her mother had not pushed the issue. At nineteen she was comfortable with her unmarried status, running the household as she pleased. She had good friends, the eight eldest daughters of her mother's best friends. Three of them lived in close proximity to Dervla, but five had moved away. The fact that they were all married often reminded her that eventually she would need a daughter to carry on the traditions, but she did not want to give up her independence and avoided the discussion of husbands whenever possible. Cormac, however, had endeavored to secure her a good match and tried to soothe her by saying, "There's no way you can be truly happy without a family of your own."

She wished she could have believed he was sincere, but unfortunately she knew his thoughts were focused on his bride-to-be's request for Dervla to be gone so she could run the household herself. Dervla had been given a choice, a ridiculous choice; marry the man her brother found for her or join the nuns at the abbey. She had nothing against the church, but she didn't believe the abbess would appreciate one of her novices practicing the ancient ways in her cell. She reluctantly agreed to the marriage contract.

Her intended was an older, wealthy man whose wife had died in childbirth. He sought a new wife to tend to his and his children's needs. She shuddered now as she relived the moment yesterday when she was presented to him.

Dirty and sore from riding her horse across the rugged terrain of the Blue Stack Mountains, they made the final approach to his home. Dervla had been looking forward to cleaning the grime from her skin before being introduced. Instead, she and her brothers were led directly to the great hall. The room's vast size and the fine tapestries hung on the stone walls confirmed the wealth of her intended. Her steps slowed as she admired the space, and she was roughly pulled forward by Cormac. She stumbled slightly and was embarrassed when she realized that everyone in the hall was watching her. Cormac leaned into her ear and said, "Dervla, don't be shy now. He's waiting for you."

Her slower pace had nothing at all to do with shyness. Annoyed, she impatiently shrugged away her brother's hand and walked boldly to the man at the head of the table. Cormac caught up to her and made the introductions.

"May I present my sister, Dervla?" Cormac asked. The man smiled and reached out for her hand. "Dervla, may I present Dermot McSweeney?" Dervla gave a small curtsy and tried to hide her shock. She had been prepared to meet a paunchy middle-aged man not the handsome, fit person sitting before her. The gray hair at his temples and the wrinkles near his eyes were the only betrayal of his age. He held her hand a bit too tightly as he appraised her, looking up and down her body. She did not like how his look made her feel naked, and when she heard his thoughts, she gasped in disgust. She looked around to be sure she was not hearing another man nearby. It only took a moment to confirm the thoughts were coming from Dermot. Her heart sank. Beneath that gorgeous exterior, he was a lecherous, perverted lout. He squeezed her hand even harder, to the point of pain. She could tell it excited him when she winced, and he gave her butt a pinch in front of everyone. Dervla lost her temper. She yanked her hand free from his grasp, slapped his face, and shouted, "You are disgusting. I will not share a marriage bed with someone so foul." She strode out of the hall and into the yard.

Cormac followed her and pleaded with her to apologize, but she would not. Without revealing her secret she could not explain how ugly Dermot McSweeney was on the inside. To everyone else he looked exceptionally suitable. Her brothers simply shook their heads, believing she had truly lost her mind.

"I won't waste my time trying to make another match for you. Once this story is out, there'll be no man for fifty miles who will have you." Cormac's voice was tinged with sadness, and Dervla wished she could tell him the truth.

Cormac said it was unthinkable to impose on McSweeney's hospitality after Dervla's outburst. They waited in the stable while the horses were watered and fed and then began the trek to the abbey. They had to retrace part of their journey and tomorrow morning they would reach the junction where the road led east back to their home or west along the coast out to the Kilcar Abbey.

Her brothers returned to the campfire, and Cormac unnecessarily explained to her that Aiden would continue the journey with her while he returned home. Dervla only nodded in response and curled up in her blanket. She pretended to sleep while she tried to come up with a plan to get away from Aiden. But getting away from him was only the beginning. She worried about where she would go after that. Home was not an option, and neither were any of the three friends who lived the closest. They might be able to shelter her for a day or two without discovery but no more than that. Her four friends who lived to the south were too far away to be of assistance. That left Isobel who lived to the north. Isobel would surely offer her refuge for a week or two, allowing enough time to plan her next step. To reach Creeslough, Isobel's village, she'd have to go through Glengesh Pass. It would be difficult traveling and would take many days. She hoped she could manage.

She had been thinking the best option for her future would be to live on her own. She wanted to suggest it when Cormac first presented her with the choice of either getting married or joining the convent but knew he would find it unacceptable. Everyone would say it was unacceptable. Women did not live alone and unprotected. Indeed, it could be dangerous, but far less dangerous than living with Dermot McSweeney or her vicious brother.

The next morning they said their farewells at the crossroads, and Dervla held onto Cormac for a moment longer than necessary, afraid she might never see him again. He promised to visit her at the abbey, which made Dervla feel even worse because, of course, she wouldn't be there.

For her own safety, she rode as far behind Aiden as she could, even though there was enough space to ride abreast. They rode all morning and came into the town of Largy around noon and ate their lunch, watching the razorbills flying over Donegal Bay. It seemed very strange to sit here companionably after spending the morning listening to him debate the different ways he might kill her. He kept changing his mind as to which method would be the best. He really wanted to strangle her and throw her off the cliff, but he thought maybe he ought to keep it simple and lure her to the edge and give her a shove. By the time they were ready to resume traveling, he had not yet settled on his method. She'd have to act soon to get away from him, because at their current pace they would reach Kilcar Abbey by sunset.

A few hundred feet outside of Largy, the coast road narrowed to a path along the top of the cliff. She heard him make his decision and knew he was ready. Her fear made it hard for her to concentrate on his thoughts, but she understood enough. He was going to pretend to show her something near the edge. Then he was going to push her off.

A few minutes later, he stopped and called back to her, "Come here and see this enormous nest."

She met his eyes briefly and saw the stark malevolence there. She abruptly turned her horse and kicked him fiercely with her heels. He whinnied in protest but gave in to her command and galloped back toward Largy. She had no intention of going all the way to the town. She couldn't risk asking the townspeople for help. With her luck they'd believe the tale her brother would likely tell of the reluctant sister on her way to the convent. She had seen a side path leading up into the hills a quarter mile back, and when she came to it, she turned sharply up the slope.

With the top of the hill within sight, she urged her poor horse to go faster. Aiden would not be able see which way she went if she could only get to the other side. She was nearly there when she heard his triumphant shout from below. He had seen her. Her heart skipped a beat when she saw he was starting up the hillside. His horse was bigger and had more stamina. Dervla knew she couldn't outrun him. At the crest of the hill, she searched the valley for somewhere to hide and saw a line of trees in the distance. It was an obvious choice, but it would have to do. She raced across the grass.

Within seconds his horse's hooves were pounding into the ground directly behind her, and an uncontrollable keening rose in her throat as she realized she wasn't going to make it. Aiden pulled even and grinned madly before launching himself at her. She tried to swerve out of his grasp, but he yanked hard on her long, dark braid and pulled her to the ground. It was a terrible fall, and when they tumbled to a stop, Aiden was on top of her. She tried to scramble out from under him, but he held her tightly between his knees. He brought his wickedly sharp dagger up high, getting ready to plunge it into her chest. She put her arms up in a feeble defense and closed her eyes tightly. Instead of the pain she expected, she heard a gurgle, and felt a warm splash across her face. Aiden released his grip and toppled over. She opened her eyes and was stunned to see him staring back at her with a knife embedded in his throat. He was not quite dead and clawed weakly at the weapon. Dervla inched away from him, watching the blood pool into his collar. His hands twitched once, twice, and his eyes turned lifeless.

Forever safe from Aiden, she looked for the knife thrower. A large man was striding toward her, his bow at the ready while his eyes scanned the surrounding area. Dervla got to her feet, prepared to flee. When he was near enough, he asked, "Are there others?"

"No." Dervla barely croaked out the single word.

He relaxed his hunter's stance, pulled his dagger from Aiden's throat and wiped it off in the grass before returning it to the sheath on his belt. He did not seem upset by the gruesome sight or the fact that he had just killed a man.

"Who are your people? I shall return you to them," the man offered.

She cleared her throat and answered his second question more clearly. "I am traveling to Creeslough. I have a dear friend there."

His eyes widened at that answer, and he asked, "You travel there alone?" His tone was incredulous.

"I had been traveling with my brother, but now I shall go on alone." Dervla answered with selective honesty.

"That would not be wise. I'll return you to your brother or did this ruffian get him before he chased you down?"

"You misunderstand the situation. This ruffian *was* my brother." She gestured to Aiden's body. The man's expression showed he was clearly shocked by her revelation and Dervla added a hasty explanation. "It is no loss to the world, believe me. He was quite evil."

"Your brother was trying to murder you?" He shook his head in disbelief.

"Yes, we were traveling to Kilcar Abbey, but I knew he plotted to murder me on the way. I tried to get away but I could not outrun him."

"So you've no other family?"

"None that I shall return to. As I said, I have a loyal friend in Creeslough and that is where I shall go." She looked around for her horse which had run off. "I only need to find my horse, and I'll be on my way. I'm sure it will take a few days to get there."

"I cannot let you do that."

"I do not believe I need your permission," she said with as much tact as she could manage.

"It is too dangerous for you to travel alone. It would not be right that I would save you from one villain and then leave you helpless to defend yourself against others you may encounter."

"You imagine a villain awaiting me at every turn? I am quite confident the world is far less dangerous for me now that my brother is dead." Her hand rose to her throat as she gazed upon Aiden's lifeless body. She was quiet for a moment thinking how close she had come to meeting her end. "I'm sorry. I have not thanked you properly. I would surely be dead if you were not so skillful with your knife. I will be forever in your debt." She said these words while continuing to look for her horse.

"Then you owe it to me to not run off and make me worry about your safety." A growing impatience was clear in the man's voice.

Dervla thought she heard him say "Damn foolish woman," and her eyes snapped back to his face. She stared up at him while she tried to read his thoughts but could not tell if he had cursed her out loud. He was large and fierce looking, not at all handsome, but when his dark eyes stared back at her with a surprising kindness, she felt she could trust him. She could detect no deception in his words. He seemed truly worried for her safety.

"I appreciate your concern, but I cannot ask you to endure the hardship of accompanying me and traveling so far from your home."

"I never said I was near my home. Indeed, I live very near Creeslough. Once I've concluded my business here, I shall return there directly. It will be no hardship to travel together."

In all honesty, Dervla preferred not to travel alone, especially when her companion was not planning on murdering her. She had no more points to argue anyway. She examined the man's gruff face for a few moments longer before voicing her decision. "I shall be glad for your company."

Dervla looked once more at her brother's body and the glint of his ring made her remember the other valuables he carried. She knelt down and hastily pulled the knife from his lifeless hand, before removing the ring which had been her father's. From his belt she untied the purse which held her dowry for entering the abbey. She tested the weight of the purse in the palm of her hand and could tell she now had the means to make a new life for herself. With one last look at her brother's face, she flipped the edge of his cloak over him.

"Let's be on our way." She would be relieved to be away from this sight, but as she turned to leave the man's brow furrowed.

"I know your brother was trying to kill you, but we ought to do something to keep the animals from getting to him."

If anyone deserved to be left for the scavengers, it was he, Dervla thought, but she gave in to the propriety the man was suggesting with an audible sigh. "I suppose we should."

"I think there's enough stone in this field to build a cairn over him." The man immediately set to the task of gathering the nearby rocks.

By the time the rocks provided a sufficient burial, the horses had returned and were busy munching on the grass at the edge of the woods. Dervla's waited docilely for her, but her brother's horse was a different story. He shied away every time she neared. The man must have noticed her frustrated chase and made his own stealthy approach, easily snagging the reins.

"Do you have a horse?" Her voice sounded harsh, but he had irritated her with how easily he caught the horse.

"Yes, I left him in the trees when I saw you being chased."

They led the horses into the woods to where his horse waited, its reins slung over a low branch. He gracefully mounted, and she did the same.

"Where were you traveling today?" Dervla asked.

"I am to visit my brother. We will be lucky to arrive before dark."

They rode without speaking until the shadows began to length-en. When they approached a small stream, he abruptly dismounted, jolting her out of her traveling stupor.

"Get down," he ordered gruffly.

Dervla hesitated, unsure of his intentions. Hearing no ill-will in his thoughts, she joined him at the stream where he stood. He pulled out a handkerchief, dipped it into the water and stunned her by scrubbing her face with the damp cloth.

"What – are you – doing?" She asked between his rough swipes across her cheeks and forehead.

"You're covered in blood, and I don't want you to scare the children. Do you have another dress to wear?"

She shuddered as she remembered the warm splatter across her face when the knife hit Aiden and berated herself for not realizing how horrifying she must look. "Yes, I have one other."

"You could change over there." He waved at some nearby shrubs. "My brother's home is in the next valley."

She rummaged in her satchel for her other dress and went off to change. She wasn't sure she'd ever be able to wash the blood out of the one she had been wearing but balled it up and returned it to her bag anyway. Before walking back she undid the cord fastening her unkempt braid and ran her fingers through the knots in her long hair.

"Am I now presentable?" she asked the man.

"I think you will do." The man looked her up and down much like Dermot McSweeney did the day before, but instead of lecherous thoughts, Dervla only sensed the man's warm approval.

"I apologize for not asking your name earlier, but I will need to introduce you to my brother and his wife when we arrive."

"Dervla Quinn." She said.

"Dervla Quinn," he repeated. "I'm pleased to meet you, and my name is Liam O'Donnell." He extended his hand to her and helped her swing onto her horse.

That was the end of their conversation. She followed behind him on the trail and at the top of the next hill she was able to see a small tower house and walled yard in the valley below. As they began their descent, they heard shouts of greeting directed their way.

⸙

I stopped reading, sensing Mom was awake next to me. I closed the book and closed my eyes as well. I needed a minute to absorb what I'd read. I had an ancestor who could hear other people's thoughts but only when the thoughts were about her. Exactly like me. I pinched the bridge of my nose. Maybe I wasn't going crazy.

"Are you okay, Brigit?" she asked.

"I think so."

I didn't say anything else for a minute and neither did Mom. I know she was waiting for me to say more, and I decided there was no reason not to tell her – not anymore. I was not going crazy. I smiled and plunged on with my news. "Mom, do you remember the story of Dervla Quinn? The one who could hear what people were thinking about her, the one with the brother who tried to kill her?"

"Of course. What about her?"

"Do you think that kind of talent could be inherited?" I paused to catch my breath and then spit it all out in one long sentence. "Because for the past few weeks, I've been sure I was going crazy because . . . because sometimes I can hear what people are thinking about me." I chanced a quick look at her to see her reaction.

All color had drained from her face, and I heard her thinking, *Oh my God. She has it. She has the gift.* Her voice was full of concern when she finally spoke. "Oh, honey, you had to be so very, very scared something was wrong with you. Why didn't you say something to me?" She gathered me in for a hug to end all hugs. Then she laughed and answered her own question. "Of course, you didn't say anything because you thought you were losing your mind." She laughed again, and I laughed with her. She pulled back from me and smoothed my hair away from my face. "Can you tell what I'm thinking?"

"Well, at first you were thinking, *She has the gift,* and now you are thinking, *My poor scared baby.*"

"Brigit this *is* such a gift. I'm sure this is a lot to take in. I can't say I know how you feel. I've only read about it. There were two others after Dervla who could do this; her daughter and her great-great granddaughter. We assumed the skill had died out." She was talking so fast, obviously way more excited about this than I was.

"Mom, stop! You're acting like this is a good thing. I hate it! It's awful to hear what people are really thinking."

"You only have to learn how to use it. It's like any skill. You'll get better at manipulating it the more you practice. You should eventually be able to block people out when you want to, sort of like turning a switch on and off. I'm sure there's more about this in Dervla's grimoire." She launched herself off the bed.

"I've heard that word before. That's a book, right? Are you telling me there are more books?" I couldn't possibly take on more reading.

"Oh, yeah, the one you've got is the important one for now. Consider it like a greatest hits collection. You're reading the main story of each woman since Onora, but each of them also kept a daily book or diary called a grimoire. That's where they would have written down the day-to-day stuff, like things they did and new spells they learned." She'd walked to her book-case, fished the key out of a little tin, and unlocked the large glass doors. "Each book is done a little differently. I don't refer to the old ones much anymore. I mainly use your grandmother's and my own, of course. Those I keep in the kitchen. You've seen them."

"Those? I thought they were regular recipe books. Well, almost regu-lar," I amended, remembering the cookies Mom made for Tyler.

"Not quite," She murmured as her fingers trailed along the book spines until she found the one she wanted and pulled it out. She came back to the bed and sat down. "This is Dervla's book, and I know she wrote in here about learning to control her gift." She carefully flipped through the old, dry pages until she came to the right section and read it to me.

I listened carefully. Dervla had learned that concentration and practice were the keys to mastering control of her talent. I started to feel hopeful that I might be able to do it, that is, until Mom read the next part. It took Dervla nearly a year of daily practice to be able to turn the skill on and off at will. Daily practice? I swallowed hard. I hadn't even been able to handle practicing the piano every day. I groaned and collapsed back into the pil-lows pulling the comforter over my head.

"I'm a freak! A big, huge freak!" My voice was muffled but I knew Mom heard me.

She was waiting for me to come up for air, and when I didn't, she pulled back the comforter. "You know you do have another choice. If you don't actively use your gift, it will fade after a few years and eventually disappear."

A wave of sadness came out of nowhere, enveloping me while I di-gested her words. I didn't particularly care for this gift I hadn't asked for, but I wasn't sure I wanted to wish it away, either.

Chapter Eighteen

We agreed that I didn't need to make any decisions about my *gift* right away. Mom wanted me to finish reading the book and enjoy the trip to Ireland first, saying that it might give me a different perspective.

"Relax," she said. "There's plenty of time to decide."

I didn't know why, but her assurances made me cranky. "You're not the one with people's thoughts running through your head." I retreated to my room. This situation was beyond strange. I needed to be alone.

Mom let me be for a while and then came to my room with what I used to believe was only my grandma's recipe book but now knew was so much more. "Brigit," she started tentatively, "I have found something that might help calm the voices. It won't take them away completely, but it might make the thoughts less intrusive. Can I try this with you?"

"Um, yeah, I guess." I had no idea what she had in mind.

She pulled other items out of bag and created a circle on the floor with a thick brown cord. In the middle on top of a small cloth she placed Grandma's book and a piece of rose quartz. Finally, she put four small candles at equal points just inside the cord. She motioned for me to sit inside the circle and handed me the piece of quartz. As she lit the candles she said:

"East, South, West, North
Blessed Goddess we call you forth.
The Circle is cast in our need.
We seek your blessing in mind and deed."

Then she took a deep breath and closed her eyes. I did the same, waiting for what was next as I rubbed my thumb against the cool, smooth surface of the stone. I jumped a little when her fingers made contact with my forehead and she said:

"O, blessed Goddess of the light
We ask your help with our plight.
Assist your daughter Brigit Quinn
To mute the voices coming in.
Let her heart and mind be free.
Take away her anxiety."

As she spoke, her fingers became warmer and warmer against my forehead. The rock in my hand was no longer cool. The warmth felt good, and as she finished a pulse of energy flowed over me in a protective wave.

She pulled away her hands. "How do you feel?"

I stretched my neck left and right. My head felt lighter. "I might feel better." I stared at her, wondering how she had done that. "Freaky," I said.

"I hope it helps. You'll have to see if you notice a difference. I don't know how long it will last, but we can always repeat it if we need to."

I was able to concentrate on my homework for the rest of the afternoon but as evening approached I found myself looking at the clock more frequently. Tyler had promised to let me know how his visit to Boston had gone. I sure hoped he'd have good news.

The house was very quiet and even though I'd been expecting it, I jumped when the doorbell rang and then laughed at how easily I was startled. Getting off the couch, I put my geometry book on the floor and ran to the front door. Tyler's grin was visible through one of the small glass panes flanking the door. I couldn't flip the lock fast enough.

"You look like you've had a very good weekend. How did it go?" I gave him a tight hug.

He pulled back to answer. "It was the best weekend ever. My dad isn't completely convinced, but he liked the school, and said I could make my own decision. I think his exact words were; "I won't stand in your way if this is what you want. I only hope you know what you're doing."

"So you're definitely going to art school?"

"Definitely. I haven't called the coach at Penn State to let him know I'm not taking the basketball scholarship, but I'll do that in the morning before school."

"I missed you." I leaned in and gave him a soft kiss. Tyler was surprised I kissed him right in my front hallway. I laughed at his expression and explained, "My mom isn't home right now."

"Well, in that case . . ." Tyler's voice trailed off as he bent down to continue the kiss.

I reached up and tangled my hands in his hair so he couldn't escape. His mouth felt so incredible. I swayed into him a little unsteady on my feet. Probably a lack of oxygen.

"Whoa. Let's sit down," he said.

We barely stopped kissing on the way into the living room where we collapsed onto the couch. I pulled off his coat and ran my hands across his shoulders and down his biceps while I kissed him again.

"Did I tell you I really missed you?" I asked.

"Yeah, you did and even if you hadn't, I think I would have gotten the message." Tyler surprised me by pulling me onto his lap. "So what did you do this weekend?"

"Moriah and Jess were over on Friday night; otherwise I've only been reading, doing homework, and hanging out with Mom." I omitted the shocking revelation of my newfound gift.

Tyler took in all of my text books and then his eyes rested on my ancestor's book sitting on the coffee table. "Hey, what's this?"

I decided a vague response wouldn't hurt anything. "It's a book of family history. I got that on my birthday, too. I need to read it before our trip to Ireland."

"So what have you learned about your ancestors? You're descended from wolves . . . they're all cannibals?" He laughed at his own joke, but I didn't.

"Yuck. Don't be gross. Let me just say the book isn't as boring as I expected." I nearly laughed at my major, major understatement. I wished I could share what I was learning with him, but I didn't dare.

I was confused and then nervous, when he slid me off his lap and leaned forward to pick up the book. He ran his hands over the smooth, worn, brown leather, and I swore I heard him think very, very faintly, *This is exactly how Gran described it.*

I sucked in my breath involuntarily and stared at him. He was looking intently at the book and hadn't noticed my reaction. Did I really hear that? I purposefully tried to listen in on his thoughts but found my senses deadened. Then I remembered Mom's dull-the-voices – um – chant. I couldn't quite bring myself to call it a spell. Now, I wished we hadn't done that, whatever it was.

My instincts took over, and I pulled the book out of Tyler's hands, surprising him. To explain my abrupt action, I said, "You're so sweet to pretend you're interested in this. I'll put it away now." My acting skills were fairly dismal, but I hoped he bought my line. I practically ran down the hall with the book and put it on the kitchen table. I returned less than fifteen seconds later, and now it was my turn to be startled. Tyler was standing up and putting his coat back on.

"You're leaving already?" I was confused and disappointed.

"I only stopped over for a few minutes. I really should get home."

I stared at him for a moment and finally said, "Okay, I'll see you in school tomorrow." At the door I expected a goodbye kiss, but all I got was a blast of cold air as he hurried to his car.

That was so strange. Why had he left so abruptly? Had I heard his thoughts right? Maybe the spell to quiet the voices had muddled up the messages that could still get through to me. I should tell Mom about this, but I wanted to be sure of what was going on before I mentioned anything. For now, I was incredibly irritated with myself for complaining about the voices so much that Mom had been compelled to help me.

My thoughts kept returning to Tyler's gran and whether she really could know anything about the book. Something was there on the fringe of my memory, bothering me. Then I remembered what she said to Mom the day they argued about the cookies. *"You have to remember that your mother and I spent a lot of time together. I know many of her secrets."*

Tyler's rushed departure made me feel oddly off balanced, and I got to school early the next morning to make sure things were okay between us. I needed to reassure myself there was nothing to the stray thought I caught so faintly from him – if that's truly what it had been.

When I turned down the senior hallway, I heard shouting and a large crash. Everyone was standing in a group, blocking my view. Then Tyler pushed his way through, walking past without even seeing me, his face bloody and his shirt torn. One of the boys shouted after him. "McGrath, you didn't deserve the scholarship anyway. You belong with all the pussy painters."

Snippets of conversation carried down the hall as I hurried after Tyler. "Gave up the Penn State scholarship . . . going to art school instead . . . the coach is going to freak . . . what an idiot!"

Tyler went into the boys' bathroom at the end of the hall, and I hesitated outside. I pushed the door open slightly and called inside. "Tyler, it's Brigit. Are you alone?"

"Yeah, come on in." His voice sounded funny.

I looked down the hall for teachers and, seeing none, slid through the partly open door. Tyler looked awful. Pieces of toilet paper were wadded up in his nostrils to stop the bleeding, and his lip was cut and oozing. He was trying to clean up the front of his shirt with the useless brown paper towels from the dispenser.

"What happened?" I walked over to the row of sinks were he stood.

"Mason decided to prove how worthless I am for not taking the basketball scholarship."

"Well, that was so nice of him." I tried to make light of the situation, but my sarcasm fell flat. "What difference would it make to him anyway?"

"I guess he thinks he might have had a shot at a scholarship. He said I should have gotten out of the way if I wasn't serious and would rather be a pussy painter."

"Oh, yeah, I heard part of that. Well, for a Neanderthal at least his insults are alliterative." My second attempt at humor made Tyler smile, slightly, but he winced with pain. "Here, let me help." I gently dabbed the towels against his lip.

"Do you want me to get an ice pack from the nurse?"

"I'd rather go home and deal with it there, but I can't. I've got a Calculus test today." He sighed and leaned against the sink. "I have a t-shirt in my gym bag. Is it too big a deal to ask you to get it from my locker?"

"I'll be right back." I was happy there was some way I could help. A few guys were hanging around Tyler's locker, but they didn't say anything to me when I grabbed his bag.

When I got back to the bathroom, Tyler had already taken off his trashed shirt. He balled it up and made a free-throw into the garbage can. I stared at his perfect chest, completely distracted. He took the gym bag from my hand, bringing me back down to earth. I checked out his injuries again. Both his nose and his lip had stopped bleeding, but I could tell he was going to be swollen and bruised. "You really need to get an ice pack."

"Yeah, I'll stop by the nurse on the way to my first class."

The bell rang, and I turned to go. "You're really okay?" I asked.

"I'm fine. Now get your butt to class." He gave me hug, and we left the bathroom together, not realizing how that would seem to the kids passing by. The startled faces of a couple of the girls made me glad that I couldn't hear what they were thinking.

I didn't see Tyler again until art class where I found him at his table resting his head on his hands. When I said hi, he sat up. I gasped when I saw how absolutely awful he looked. The ice pack hadn't done much good. His lip was still puffy, and his eye was now purple and nearly swollen shut. I wasn't surprised when Miss Sienna told him to go home early.

"Can't," he said thickly.

"And why not? You're clearly not going to be able to do anything in this condition," Miss Sienna argued.

"I need to go to basketball practice after school."

"I'll let Coach Munroe know that I sent you home to recover."

Tyler ignored her and put his head back down as if it was all too much to deal with.

"Tyler." She drew out his name in way that made it clear he was about to be in big trouble.

"Fine, I'm going." He swung out of his seat, obviously irritated by her intervention.

I touched his arm lightly as he walked by but I didn't say anything.

CHAPTER NINETEEN

A t home, I told Mom what happened to Tyler.

"That's terrible, Brigit. I hope this Mason kid got punished."

"I doubt he got caught. I don't think any teachers saw it happen."

"But, wouldn't it have been obvious he was hit?"

"Oh, it was obvious," I said and cringed, picturing his bruised, swollen face. "I'm sure Tyler was asked about it, but, Mom, it isn't cool rat someone out."

"I suppose not," she said.

I sent Tyler a quick text to see how he was doing and attacked my mountain of homework. By dinnertime I'd made it through geometry and biology after about twenty checks of my cell phone. Tyler still hadn't texted back.

After dinner, I was antsy about Tyler's lack of communication and tried to take my mind off of everything by returning to Dervla's story.

D ervla followed Liam into the walled courtyard and dismounted when he did. Two young boys ran up, shouting, "Uncle Liam, Uncle Liam!" He picked them up, one in each arm, and gave them big hugs. Dervla assumed the man and woman hurrying toward them were Liam's brother and sister-in-law.

The woman glanced briefly at Dervla and began chastising Liam, "We expected you hours ago. We were getting worried."

"I am sorry," Liam answered. "There was an unexpected delay." He put the boys down and beckoned Dervla forward. "Let me introduce a fellow traveler, Dervla Quinn. Dervla, this is my brother Angus and his wife, Effie."

Dervla murmured polite greetings to them. Effie responded, "We're pleased to meet you as well. Were you the unexpected delay?"

The question so surprised Dervla that she had to hold in her laughter, immediately liking Effie's forthrightness. "Yes, I must admit that I did delay your brother's travel. He skillfully saved me from a most unfortunate situation."

"I cannot wait to hear this story." Effie gripped Dervla's arm and pulled her toward the house. "Now, come inside by the fire, and we can have our evening meal."

As she entered the main hall, she was amazed by the warmth of the room. Although the ceilings were quite high, it felt cozy. A fireplace, large enough to walk into, took up the entire back wall. Dark, wooden benches flanked the sides of the room and zigzagged into deep window alcoves. The benches were covered with bright cushions, and the same fabric was draped across the windows to seal out the drafts. Effie gestured to a chair at the table closest to the fire. "Please sit, Dervla. It sounds like it may have been a trying day for you. Would you care for something to drink? We have a fine ale."

"Thank you. I am thirsty." Dervla answered.

Effie poured a cup of ale for Dervla and one for herself. "I'll be back in a moment. Let me tell our cook we are nearly ready for supper."

Effie disappeared through an open archway in the middle of the long wall. Sipping her ale in the comfortable chair, she realized how incredibly tired she was. She hoped she wouldn't embarrass herself by falling asleep before she could eat dinner.

Liam and Angus came in from outside at the same time as Effie returned from the kitchen. She was followed by a cook with a tureen and two servant girls carrying platters. Effie placed a tray with loaves of dark bread in the middle of the table. They took their seats with Angus at one end and Effie at the other.

They had hardly finished saying grace when Effie asked, "Liam, how did you come to be traveling together?"

"I had stopped to rest my horse and noticed this lady being chased by a . . . ah . . . ruffian and I saved her from him. She is traveling to visit a friend in Creeslough, and I have offered her the safety of continuing on with me when I return home."

Dervla was glad he edited the events of the day, as they were not fit for the young ears at the table.

"I dare say there is more to the story than that." Effie commented on the sparse details and acknowledged the reason, by nodding meaningfully toward her boys. "Maybe later we can hear a full account."

Angus changed the subject and began talking about one of their distant neighbors and some exploit of late. Dervla focused on her meal, an incredibly tasty vegetable soup, followed by roast lamb and potatoes. Hearing Angus utter the name Dermot McSweeney made her head swivel up in disbelief, and she began to pay attention to the conversation.

". . . apparently the brother had arranged the marriage contract, but his sister had not met McSweeney. When they were introduced it took only a few minutes before she was slapping his face and vowing never to share his marriage bed. I gather McSweeney was quite insulted and embarrassed." Angus laughed very loudly and Liam joined him.

"Whatever did he do to make the girl dislike him so?" Liam asked.

"No one knows. They only had time enough to greet one another, but her dislike was more than evident." Angus guffawed again. Dervla felt her face getting hot and looked down at her plate to hide her embarrassment.

"I don't blame her. I do not find Dermot McSweeney to be a fine man at all. He may be fair of face, but I have never cared for his company," Effie contributed.

Angry possessiveness flickered in Angus' eyes. "If he's been over friendly with you, Effie, I will skin him alive."

"Oh, calm down. It is nothing like that. I have instincts about him. I do not think he would make a good husband. That is all I meant. I'm glad she didn't marry him, whoever she is." Effie looked over at Dervla. "You know what I mean about that, don't you, Dervla? A woman's intuition is a valuable gift, is it not?"

Dervla did not want to be impolite and raised her head briefly when she answered. "I do agree."

Effie observed Dervla's flushed appearance. "My dear, are you feeling ill? Is it too warm by the fire? Your cheeks are positively blazing."

"No. I am fine. Really I am."

"It has been a long day. I am sure Dervla would like to get some rest," Liam suggested.

Dervla turned to thank him, but the words stuck in her throat when she noticed his strange expression. She didn't understand why he was staring at her so intensely, but it made her uncomfortable, and she was glad to follow Effie out of the room and up the winding staircase.

Upstairs four doors opened into a central hallway, and Effie led her to the one farthest down the hall. Her satchel and the bag from her brother's horse had been placed in the chamber. Dervla's heart raced when she glimpsed her blood-stained dress laid out across a chair. She supposed a servant girl unpacked her things, but she didn't want Effie to see the soiled dress. She stepped in front of the chair to block Effie's view.

She hoped to be left alone immediately. The bed looked so inviting, and she was bone tired, but Effie fussed about turning down the bedclothes and pouring water into the wash basin.

Finally, she said to Dervla, "We will see you on the morrow. Have a good rest." She was nearly out the door when she spied the dress lying there.

"Oh, let me hang up your other dress." Effie crossed to the chair behind Dervla.

"That's not necessary." Dervla said, but Effie had already seen the blood stains.

"My goodness, were you injured today?"

"No, that isn't my blood. It happened when your brother saved me."

"Dear Lord, you must tell me the rest of the tale." Effie sat in the chair still clutching the dress.

Dervla knew she'd have to give at least a slightly longer version than Liam had at the supper table. She sank down onto the edge of the bed and began, "As Liam said, I was being chased, and the man pulled me from my horse and raised his knife above me. I'm sure I was seconds from death, but then Liam threw his dagger and killed my attacker. That's how the blood came to be on me."

Effie looked at her with big eyes. Dervla could tell by her thoughts that she was full of concern and worry. "What a terrible shock. I had no idea that your attacker had gotten so close to you. I am worried that our countryside is full of bandits and so near our home, too."

Dervla knew she should assuage Effie's fears of roving bandits by explaining this wasn't a random assault, but she simply did not have the energy for the drawn-out discussion that would be necessary if she revealed the attacker was her brother.

Effie saw her long, tired blink and apologized. "I'm so sorry I've kept you from your bed. I'll see what we can do with these stains. Maybe we can salvage your dress. I bid you goodnight." Effie carried her dress as she shut the door behind her.

Dervla barely had the energy to wash up before she stripped down to her shift and climbed between the stiff linens. She inhaled their wonderful lavender scent and closed her eyes.

The angle of the sunlight in her chamber told her she had slept quite late. Dervla stretched and groaned at her soreness from the long days of riding and Aiden's attack yesterday. She wished she could call for a bath but resigned herself to using the cold water left in the basin. She was picking up the cloth when there was a knock at her door. A young voice said, "Are you awake, Miss?"

Dervla opened the door a crack and peeped out. A girl stood there with a tray of food.

"I've brought you breakfast."

Dervla opened the door wide, and the girl crossed the floor to place the food on the table near the chair. "The Missus wants to know if you would like a bath."

"I do not wish to be any trouble." Dervla was thrilled by the offer but forced herself to reply politely, knowing what a great effort it was to heat and carry bath water.

"It will be no trouble at all. We expected you would say yes, so the water is already heating. There's a small room off the kitchen which we use for laundry and bathing. It saves us the trouble of carrying water up the narrow stairs. When you're done with breakfast, I'll show you the way."

Dervla realized she'd been standing there in her shift and wrapped her shawl around herself before tucking into the breakfast. She was exceedingly hungry and wondered again at the time of day. "Would you tell me the hour?"

"It must be half past ten by now."

"I have slept far later than I am normally do."

"It is to be expected after your ordeal yesterday." The girl nodded sympathetically. Dervla knew that she must have been the main topic of discussion in the kitchen this morning as the girl prattled on, keeping her company as she ate the warm, brown bread.

"What a terrible thing to have happen to you. It's a good thing Liam came along. He's a trustworthy sort and so strong." The girl gave a little sigh and continued. "He would make a fine husband, indeed. The Missus has been keeping her eye out for the right girl for him."

The girl continued on about the others who lived in and around the little valley, and Dervla only half-listened as she ate, until the girl mentioned Liam again.

"Liam comes to visit once every two or three months. He brings the news of his parents and other relatives from the north. Mister Angus lives so far from where he grew up because this was Effie's family home. She inherited it when her parents died. Are you done, now?" The girl finally asked.

Dervla had finished eating a few minutes before, but had happily sat there, amused by the girl's ability to talk practically without taking a breath. It never hurt to know the local news. It could come in handy, particularly information regarding her traveling companion.

The girl picked up the tray and said, "Follow me."

"Are there men about? Should I dress or may I walk to the kitchen in my robe?"

"The men have gone out. Come as you are."

The girl led her to the kitchen and pointed Dervla to a small doorway. Dervla entered and felt a blast of heat so incredibly soothing she nearly melted on the spot.

Effie stopped talking to a woman who was working over a large tub of laundry and turned to greet her. "Good morn to you, Dervla. You'll be happy to know that Sylvie has worked wonders, and your dress is nearly as good as new. She is forever saving the boys' clothes from the rag bin. Come see for yourself."

Dervla walked over to where her dress was draped across the washboard. The fact that its bodice showed only a hint of the blood stain was nearly a miracle. She reached out, touched the damp fabric and turned to Sylvie. "Thank you for your hard work. I thought it was ruined."

"I think when I give it a regular washing, the last bit will rinse away." Sylvie replied.

"We have the bath ready for you." Effie gestured to the wooden tub sitting near the fireplace. The steam rose invitingly into the air. There was no screen to afford her some privacy from the other women, but she reasoned she needed a bath more than she needed her privacy. She stripped off her shift, sinking into the water with a contented sigh. She counted the days backward and was appalled that her last bath had been seven days prior when she was preparing to meet her bridegroom, the vile McSweeney.

"Your poor back." Effie crooned. "It is covered in bruises. Was that from your attack?"

"I expect so. I was pulled from my horse and landed very hard. This is wonderful." Dervla sighed again.

The girl helped to wash her hair by pouring water over her long tresses until the soap was gone. Dervla felt decidedly better when she was out of the tub and dressed for the day. She went into the great hall and found Effie serving the mid-day meal to the men and boys.

Liam looked up as she entered, and she heard him think, *Who is this beautiful creature?*

Dervla tried desperately to control the blush creeping into her cheeks and failed. He said aloud, "You look well rested and much happier than yesterday. There seems to be a healthy glow in your cheeks." He smiled at her wickedly.

Dervla's hands flew to her face and Liam laughed at her reaction. She recovered enough composure to look directly at him as she responded. "Yes, Effie's kind hospitality has done wonders for me. I am afraid to imagine how disheveled I appeared yesterday if the contrast is so great today. I'm amazed you even stopped to help me."

"I would never withhold assistance from a lady in distress, travel-weary or not." Liam's eyes continued to hold hers.

"For that, I shall be eternally grateful," Dervla answered in all honesty.

"Sit down and join us for a meal," Effie invited.

"I will be happy to keep company with you, but I am quite full from my breakfast. I am sorry I rose so late this morning. I normally do not stay abed so long."

"We understood your fatigue. Think nothing of it." Effie replied.

"So how long will your business keep you in this area, Liam?" Dervla asked.

"Only through the day today, so we can leave early tomorrow if you are able. Do you think you can manage four days of riding and rough sleeping out in the open?"

"I am sure I can." Dervla sounded more confident than she felt, but at least she'd have one more night in a soft bed to help her sore muscles recover.

"I have never asked you the name of the friend you are visiting in Creeslough."

"Her name is Isobel McNamara. She is married to a man by the name of Michael Mooney. Do you know them?"

"What a coincidence. I know him well and count him as one of my loyal friends. How do you know Isobel?"

"Her mother and my mother were friends, and she and I have continued the friendship. We see each other at least once per year for the Beltane celebration." She immediately chided herself for thoughtlessly mentioning this holiday the church had banned and looked at them nervously to gauge their reaction. No one seemed bothered except for Liam who had peculiar look on his face. It wasn't exactly confusion or surprise but a rather odd mixture of the two. She heard the question in his mind.

She must be Tuatha like us. Is it possible she is one of the Circle of Nine? Liam thought.

Dervla gasped at his understanding. It was only in private that they called themselves a circle of nine, but she was sure he was referring to her and the other eight eldest daughters.

Liam looked at her sharply and deliberately sent a thought her way. *Can you hear me, Dervla?*

To have him address her directly in his thoughts seemed inconceivable. Dervla gripped the edge of the table tightly as she began to feel lightheaded. Should she answer him or pretend nothing had happened? Dervla did not know what to do. Then she heard him again.

Please, if you can hear me, give me some sign.

She should ignore him and preserve her secret, but somehow Dervla found herself giving him the slightest nod. She heard him answer back.

Meet me outside after the meal is done.

Dervla couldn't wait for everyone else to finish eating. She excused herself by saying she needed some air. It wasn't a lie. Once outside she drew in a deep breath and tried to stay calm. She did not understand how Liam guessed the truth, and she berated herself for giving up her secret so easily, especially to someone she did not know well at all. She had never told another soul about her gift.

Dervla was pacing when Liam came into the yard a few minutes later.

Her tense posture conveyed her worry, and he sent a soothing thought her way. *Don't worry, your secret is safe with me.*

"Stop that," Dervla said out loud while a question ran in her head. *How can I ever be certain my secret will remain safe with him?*

Liam answered with the thought, *You know why your secret is safe with me.*

"Oh, dear God," Dervla said. "How can it be . . . can you hear my thoughts as I hear yours?"

"Yes, I can, but only when you are thinking of me. I can't hear all your thoughts." As he finished his explanation, he held Dervla's shaking hands in an attempt to steady her.

His touch made her hands tingle, and she tried hard to guard this thought from him. "That's the way it works for me, too. I didn't know anyone else could do this."

"No one else in your family has the gift? In my family, my mother can hear these thoughts as well, but we are the only two.

My brothers and sisters have never been able to do it, although they tried very hard. It annoyed them greatly that I had this advantage." He chuckled at this memory.

Dervla stared at him in amazement. "I have never been able to share the knowledge of my gift with anyone before. It seems very strange to talk about this openly. Do others outside your family know of your gift?"

"No, it did not seem prudent to share these things. Even among friends in the Tuatha we have been very careful. The church would surely seek to condemn us as demons or some such nonsense if our gifts became public knowledge. It is safer if few people know."

Dervla nodded at his good sense. "Yes, I agree. Far safer to keep this quiet. What are we to do now?"

"Well, nothing changes. Tomorrow we leave for Isobel's home. Until then I have much to do." His fierce façade returned, and he strode away from Dervla, leaving her feeling somewhat abandoned.

She did not understand his abrupt departure until the next day. Having left Effie and Angus' home early in the morning, Liam and Dervla rode in near silence much of the day. Even as they ate their mid-day meal, Dervla didn't talk much, trying to control her thoughts. She was becoming incredibly attracted to him and really couldn't afford to let that knowledge loose. As the sun was going down, they rode on, and Dervla battled waves of fatigue, struggling to keep her eyes open. She noticed Liam pulling close to her but didn't know why until he reached one enormous arm around her waist and pulled her onto his horse. He settled her in front of him between his arms as he explained, "Now, if you fall asleep you won't tumble off and kill yourself."

He seemed amused, and Dervla wanted to protest, but she was too tired to do so and relaxed in his arms, leaning back against his chest and breathing deeply. He must have thought she had fallen asleep and let his guard down on his thoughts. He was replaying the moment in the yard yesterday right before his departure. He had left because he couldn't control his thoughts about her – his very affectionate thoughts. Dervla was happy to know he was also attracted to her and wanted to hear more of this. Unfortunately, pretending to be asleep made her so relaxed she did actually fall asleep. It was nearly dark when Liam shook her awake, and they made camp. He built a small fire, and they ate some of the food Effie packed for them.

Liam broke the silence. "I have been wondering about something." He paused to look at her seriously, which made Dervla nervous about what he might ask. "On the first night at my brother's house, Angus was telling a story about his distant neighbor, Dermot McSweeney, and the woman who refused to marry him. You seemed to react rather strongly, but I wasn't sure why. Was that woman you, Dervla?"

She wanted to avoid the whole issue, but she couldn't lie. Hopefully, her answer would not change his opinion of her. She took a deep breath before answering. "Yes, it was." She waited for a change in his expression but his face remained impassive, and she plunged ahead speaking so rapidly that she was almost unintelligible. "I simply couldn't do it. When I heard his vile thoughts about what – about what – he was thinking of doing with me. I couldn't go through with it. My brothers, of course, couldn't understand my refusal. My eldest brother insisted that I join the abbey at Kilcar after that. He said that no one would want to marry me anyway once the story spread. He had my younger brother, Aiden, accompany me on the journey, but Aiden had no intention of actually delivering me to the abbey. He probably would have been happy to kill me for no reason. He was *that* evil. The dowry money was just an extra incentive to him."

Liam was silent for a while and then asked. "So what do you plan to do when you reach Creeslough?"

"I know Isobel will welcome me for a while, but I was planning to find a place to live alone. I have my dowry money now, after all. That should be enough to find a comfortable cottage. I know that it isn't often done, a woman living alone, but it might be best."

She assumed his dismissive grunt meant that he didn't think much of this idea. She tried to hear his thoughts but he was shielding them from her.

They didn't talk anymore as they lay down near the fire to sleep. Sometime in the night Dervla was shivering, and she felt Liam move next to her and wrap his blanket around them both. The divine warmth of his body sent her back to sleep nearly immediately, but first she was flooded with the images in his mind . . . his thoughts of kissing her and touching her and doing so much more.

The next morning they started early, and again, by late afternoon she was nodding off in her saddle. This time he didn't startle her by pulling her across onto his horse but asked her if she'd like to ride with him. She nodded her assent and settled in happily between his arms. She expected she might hear more of his lustful thoughts, but what came to her were not the vivid images she was privy to the night before. Instead, she was enveloped more by a warm feeling than a specific thought. His deep and growing affection cushioned the rest of the day's ride.

That night, as they got ready to bed down near the fire, Liam approached her. "Dervla, you seemed very chilled last night. Would you like to share blankets to stay warm tonight?"

She controlled her growing excitement and nodded solemnly in agreement, replying in an even tone, "I think that would be prudent given the temperature." Sharing his blanket was totally improper, and Dervla knew it. She purposefully did not cloak her unladylike anticipation and nearly laughed when she saw his shock as he accessed her thoughts.

The blankets were hastily arranged, and they lay down next to each other looking up into the starry sky. Neither one said anything. Their fingers intertwined shyly. Dervla enjoyed the closeness but was surprised he had not kissed her. She turned onto her side to face him, and he did the same, cupping her cheek gently with his large hand. His desire plainly showed in his eyes, but he did not bring his lips to hers. Dervla scanned for his thoughts, and a barrage of random numbers seemed to fly at her. She was confused at first and then burst out laughing when she realized Liam, ever the gentleman, was attempting to control himself by doing sums in his head.

Even while she was laughing, she leaned into him and thought very loudly, *Liam please, please kiss me.* He did not refuse her invitation and ceased his addition immediately.

They did not get an early start the next morning but stayed in each other's arms under the warm blankets. Dervla gradually became aware of Liam's thoughts as she awoke. He was thinking about the future, their future. He was picturing them together in front of a large group of people. They were holding hands, and Dervla saw that he was imagining their wedding ceremony. This filled Dervla with more happiness than she ever thought she could feel. She shifted slightly in his arms and whispered a very quiet yes in his ear while she was shouting it in her head. He kissed her deeply but then pulled back and looked down at her sternly. He scolded her for listening to his private thoughts, but he did so with a smile and punctuated it with another kiss.

———— ⦿⦿⦿ ————

T he story ended there, but the names and dates on the page showed me they lived a long life together and were blessed with six children. I hoped that I would be so lucky to find someone who was such a perfect match for me. I thought it might be Tyler, but his strange departure on Sunday had me on edge. I really wanted to talk to him about it, but given his bad day, there was no way I'd bring anything up with him tonight. I sent another text asking how he was, but got no reply. Could he have been hurt worse than I thought?

The next morning he wasn't at school. My deepening worry was obvious to my friends.

"Hey, what's wrong?" Jess asked.

"Tyler's not here. Maybe he's staying home today. I don't know, but I haven't talked to him since art class yesterday, and he's not answering texts."

"Maybe he forgot to charge his phone." Moriah tried to lighten the mood with a joke about our fight the previous week. It didn't help.

"Don't worry. You'll hear from him," Jess said.

I appreciated her perpetual optimism and repeated her words to myself throughout the day when my cell stayed silent, and Tyler was a no-show in art class.

CHAPTER TWENTY

B y the time I walked into my house after school I was going nuts.
"Mom," I shouted when I didn't see her immediately. "Mom, where
are you?"

"Geez, Brigit, I'm right here." Her reply was muffled as she backed out
of the large pantry off the kitchen.

She turned to look at me. "What's wrong?"

"I'm not sure anything's wrong, but Tyler didn't come to school today
and he hasn't texted me or called or anything."

"Have you tried calling his actual home phone?" Mom asked.

"No," I admitted, a little chagrined that I hadn't thought of it. I had to
find the phone book first because I'd never called him at that number. The
phone only rang once before his mom answered, "McGrath's."

"Hi, Mrs. McGrath. This is Brigit. I was wondering if Tyler's around. I
didn't see him at school."

"Oh, sure. He's right here. He stayed home to mend today." Her light
tone assured me he was fine.

In the background I heard Tyler say "Mom" in an exasperated voice
before he came on the line.

"I was hoping you'd call soon." He sounded cheerful. He was definitely
not in the agony I'd imagined all day long.

"What? I texted you like a million times, and you never answered. Are you okay?"

"You did?" He sounded truly puzzled. "Shoot. I don't see my phone anywhere. I must have left it in my car. I've been sleeping most of the day."

I struggled to control my irritation at his lack of communication. "I was worried about you. Are you super swollen?"

"Nah, not really. The swelling has gone down a lot, but I'm still bruised. I would have gone to school today, but Mom wanted me to stay home. I feel a lot better now. Is it okay if I come over for a little while?"

"Let me check."

Mom was hovering in the doorway to the living room, waiting to hear how Tyler was and before I could even ask, she said, "Yes, it's fine if he comes over."

When I hung up, I explained. "He's fine. He's just been sleeping all day and he left his phone in the car."

"Let him know he can stay for dinner if he wants to."

When Tyler arrived a few minutes later, the sight of his poor, discolored face made me cringe. "My God, Tyler. There aren't even names for some of these colors. Does it hurt much?"

"Not too much. Don't I look tough?" He lifted his chin in the air.

Mom gasped when she saw his bruises. "Oh, my. You know I think I have something that might help that heal faster."

"That's okay, Ms. Quinn. Gran is coming over for dinner tonight, and she said she has some magic ointment for me." He said the last part with a little laugh.

A strange expression crossed Mom's face before she said, "Oh, that's good." For a second I thought she was going to say something else, but instead she set down the plate of cookies she'd been carrying and left the room.

Momentarily lost in thought over Mom's reaction, I picked up a cookie and shoved it into my mouth in one bite. I realized too late, this was less than lady-like behavior and mumbled through my full mouth, "Good cookie," before smiling sheepishly at Tyler.

He laughed and wiped a crumb from the corner of my mouth with his thumb. "That's what I love about you. I can't stand the girls who don't eat anything and are so worried about how they look all the time."

I was stunned momentarily for two reasons. First, he had used the word love, and although he hadn't said I love you, this came close. Second, the compliment was nice as long as it wasn't some backdoor way of saying I ate like a pig. "Thanks," I finally said once I had managed to swallow.

I had planned to talk to him about his abrupt departure on Sunday afternoon, but given his recent compliment, it seemed like we were solid with each other. I still wondered if I heard his thoughts right when he was holding the book, but it seemed so far-fetched that I couldn't think of any good way to ask without sounding crazy. I moved on to a different topic. "Did you tell your parents how the fight happened?"

"Most of it. I edited some because I didn't want my mom calling the school and making a big deal about Mason."

"You're staying on the team, right?"

"Definitely. This is the year we have a chance to go to state. I'm not missing that for anything."

We talked for a couple of hours, and then Tyler noticed the time. "Oh, I've got to go. With Gran coming over, Mom will be mad if I'm late for dinner."

I leaned in to give him a kiss but chickened out when I heard Mom coming down the stairs. I hugged him instead and watched through the window as he walked to his car. I felt so much better now that I'd had the chance to talk with him and everything seemed normal between us. I couldn't wait until the end of the week when my grounding would be over, and I'd be able to go to the basketball game. It's not like the last two weeks had been that bad. Really, Mom's version of being grounded wasn't harsh at all. I'm not sure you could even call it being grounded. True, I couldn't go anywhere, but Mom let Tyler come over and even let me have a sleepover.

"Brigit, dinner's ready," Mom called from the kitchen.

We were having some sort of Italian from the garlicky smell in the air, but my mouth began to water when she pulled a homemade pizza out of the oven. Mom's pizza crust was the most amazing thing ever.

"That smells so good. I already know I'm going to eat it too fast and burn my mouth."

She dished up the slices with the cheese oozing and stringing along behind the spatula. I looped some of the cheese around my finger and dropped it in my mouth.

"Brigit, I've been meaning to ask you how you've been feeling since I tried that little – um – thing on Sunday?"

"It really helped. I don't think I've heard anyone's thoughts since."

"What do you mean? You don't *think* you've heard anyone?"

"On Sunday I thought I heard Tyler, but the words were very faint, and I couldn't be sure of them anyway. No big deal."

"Can I ask what you thought you heard, or is it too personal?"

"It's not personal at all. I planned to read more of Dervla's story when I finished my studying on Sunday, so I had the book out on the table in the living room. Tyler picked it up, and I thought I heard him think, *this is exactly how Gran described it.*" I shrugged my shoulders. "Maybe I have a bent antenna. It didn't make sense anyway because Tyler couldn't know anything about our family book. The only thing that was a little weird is that he left sooner than I expected."

Mom stopped in mid-chew as I relayed my story. Her face had the same strange expression as when Tyler mentioned his gran's magic ointment. She finished chewing and swallowed. "Brigit, you know you do have to be careful with that book. Not everyone will think it's normal family history. Some people might understand the power it holds."

"You said you have to be a true descendant to read it."

"That's the way it is supposed to work, but there might be ways around that."

"Now you tell me! Do you mean someone, like one of my friends, could pick it up and see the stories?" The image of Moriah and Jess' hovering over the book popped into my head.

"No. That's not what I mean, but if someone knew . . . um . . . a way to unlock the words, they might be able to read the whole book."

"Who could do that?"

"Well, there are a few who might try." She looked at my expression and touched my hand. "Don't worry about it. I'm only telling you to be cautious. Okay? And don't take it out of the house."

"I wasn't planning to. It's too big to move around anyway."

With Mom's warning hanging in the air, the pizza didn't taste quite as good as it had at first. I finished up and went straight to my room.

The next morning, as I walked up to Tyler he was putting his books in the bottom of his locker with his back to me.

"Hey, gorgeous." I said. I meant to be funny because with Tyler's bruises he wasn't exactly model material at the moment.

Tyler straightened up and smiled at me.

My mouth dropped open as I looked at his face – his nearly perfect face. The purple-red splotches which were so nasty last night were now only faint yellow shadows. I continued to stare.

"Cut it out," he finally said to me. "You're freaking me out."

"No. You're freaking me out," I said, able to speak after all. "What the hell, Tyler? You were so bruised last night. How can you look like this today?"

"I don't know. Really I don't. Gran gave me that ointment I told you about, and I put it on my bruises before bed, and when I woke up – I looked like this. It worked like magic."

My fingers trembled as I gently touched the skin by his eye. No ordinary medical ointment could make bruises fade that fast. Maybe it worked like magic because it *was* magic.

"Wow. I don't know what to say. Amazing."

"Yeah, you gotta love Gran."

Just then Mason came down the hall with some of his buddies. When he caught sight of Tyler's he stutter-stepped right in front of us and stopped. "Hey, wuss. You don't look bad at all. I guess next time I'll have to hit you harder." He was laughing until a deep voice boomed behind him.

"Mason, come with me to the office."

The voice belonged to Mr. Burnett, the biology teacher. Mason had no choice but to obey him.

From across the hall some of the other seniors were laughing, and one of them said to Tyler. "He's so busted. Mr. Burnett heard everything he said about hitting you harder next time, McGrath."

"Well, that was a fun way to start the day," Tyler said as we separated to go to our first classes.

There were a lot of different rumors about Mason's punishment buzzing around school all day. He was either suspended, or arrested, or he got off entirely. No one knew for sure. At the end of the day outside the art room Tyler filled me in.

"He has a three day in-school suspension which by itself isn't that big of a deal, but he'll also miss playing in the game on Friday. That's what's going to bug him the most."

I grabbed Tyler's hand, held it up like a winning prize-fighter, and proclaimed. "We have a winnah. There is justice in the world."

"Knock it off," Tyler said, smiling. He pulled our hands down together but didn't let go of mine as we entered class.

I told Mom about Mason's punishment the minute I got home. "But that's not the biggest news," I continued. "You remember how purple and red and awful Tyler's face was yesterday?"

She nodded in response.

"Would you believe that this morning all of his bruises had faded to that funny yellow color? He said that before bed last night he put his gran's ointment on his face, and when he woke up the bruises were nearly gone."

Mom's raised eyebrows made her forehead crinkle in surprise. "I guess Adele had some very powerful ointment."

"What?" I screeched. "That's all you have to say about it? But, Mom it simply isn't possible to do something like that with normal first aid cream."

"I agree. This was definitely something special."

I stared at her for a moment before I finally spit out the question I'd wanted to ask all along. "Can Adele McGrath do magic?"

Mom stared back at me as if she were debating what to say and swallowed hard before answering, "She used to be quite talented. I don't know if she tries anymore. It's more likely that she picked up the ointment for Tyler from someone else."

Mom's candor nearly sat me on my butt, and I pressed for more information. "Is that all you are going to tell me?"

She sighed and closed her eyes while I waited.

"It's probably more than I should be telling you at this point. Let me ask you this. How close are you to reading grandma's section in the book?"

"I'm generations away. It might be weeks before I get to Grandma's story, especially with all my school work."

"Okay, when you read Grandma's section you'll understand so much more." As she finished her sentence, she must have noticed my exasperated expression and knew I was going to argue with her. She held up her hand preemptively and said, "Look, don't get mad at me. I'm following rules here that I didn't create. You absolutely must read the book in the order that it is written."

"Should I be worried about Adele McGrath?"

"No, I wouldn't think so. Not anymore. She learned her lesson years ago."

CHAPTER TWENTY-ONE

For the next few weeks, I was conflicted. Mom's words about Adele McGrath should have had me rushing back to the book for a non-stop reading session. Instead, I tried to pretend that Mom had never acknowledged the existence of magic in the world – in our world – in *my* world. Truthfully, the idea of something so unpredictable and powerful – potentially inside me – was very scary. I tried to convince myself that I didn't care about this part of my history very much and spent the rest of February and a good chunk of March being Normal Brigit as much as possible. This meant hanging out with Tyler, finishing art projects, writing a couple of papers, and occasionally reading one of my family's stories. Once I was no longer grounded, I'd been able to watch the last basketball games of the season, which unfortunately ended with a heartbreaking two-point loss at sectionals. With no more basketball, Tyler and I had even more time to spend together. We even went on the much-anticipated double date with Jess and Jason.

As spring break approached, I reached my Grandma's story but I was hesitant to start. I wasn't sure what I'd find out and wanted to be able to digest everything without the interference of school. Spring break was the perfect opportunity. Tyler wouldn't even be around because his parents were taking him and his gran on a trip to Florida.

Moriah and Jess would be gone for most of the week, too. I'd have plenty time on my hands.

As the final bell rang on the Friday before break, the din of gleeful student departure was twice as loud as usual. Even our most somber teachers seemed almost cheerful today. Tyler was packed and ready to go to the airport straight from school. I was extremely jealous. It was cold enough that we still needed our winter coats, and I could have used a little beach time myself. It would have done wonders for my pale skin.

I playfully punched Tyler in the arm. "I am so jealous. Winter is never going to end. I'm always freezing cold and in five hours you are going to be in 80 degree weather!"

"Quit being so grouchy. You could have come along," Tyler said and rubbed his hands up and down my arms in an attempt to warm me up.

"It was nice of your parents to invite me, but there's no way Mom would have let me go."

"Maybe next year," Tyler said.

"I wouldn't hold your breath on that one. My mom isn't going like the idea any better when you're a college freshman."

"Yeah. Probably not," Tyler agreed and looked around before closing the distance between us.

He was going to kiss me. "Tyler, no. I don't want a detention," I whispered. Lately the teachers had been enforcing the no-public-display-of-affection rule more strictly.

He did a check of the hall again. "I don't see any teachers. You can relax."

It was easy to let my worry go when he sandwiched me tightly between his body and my locker and lowered his lips to mine. I focused on the glorious feeling of Tyler against my front while doing my best to ignore the locker handle digging into my back. Our long kiss sent zings through my body, and I grabbed his shoulders, responding as though we were somewhere more private. I ignored the comments other students were beginning to send our way and felt a little sad when he ended the kiss.

He didn't seem at all bothered by the attention we were getting and kept his face close to mine. He tucked a strand of hair behind my ear, cupped my chin, and said, "I love you, Brigit Quinn."

For a second I felt like I had no air. I was going to tell him I loved him back, but he didn't give me a chance. He stopped my words with another kiss, and then he nearly sprinted out the door without looking back at all.

I slowly slid down the locker until I was sitting on the floor. That's how Jess found me a minute later.

"Do you feel sick?" Jess asked, squatting down to my level.

"No."

"Why are you down on the floor then?"

"Tyler," I replied with a breathy sigh.

Jess looked around for Tyler. "Um, Brigit, he's not here."

"He left."

Jess was losing her patience with me. "Snap out of it!" she said and clicked her fingers in my face.

"He told me he loved me," I answered with some coherency.

"Really?" Jess let herself rock back on her heels and landed on her butt next to me.

"Wow," she said, nearly as stunned as I was. "Jason and I haven't even said that to each other yet. Did you tell him you love him?"

"No."

"NO? Brigit, that's bad! When someone says they love you, you usually say it back. Unless . . . unless you don't love him. Is that why you didn't say it back?"

"No, no. I do love him. Well, I think I love him. And, I would have said it back but then he kissed me again and practically ran out the door. I was going to say it back. Really." My words sounded feeble.

"Are you sure you love him? Because, if you're not sure, you shouldn't say it back. Maybe that's why you hesitated?"

"I didn't really hesitate, not really. It all happened so fast."

Jess waited while I replayed the scene in my head and realized Tyler could have misinterpreted my slow reaction. "Oh, no, maybe it did seem like I hesitated. Now he's going to spend the entire spring break thinking I don't love him. This is awful."

"Well, you could call him or text him," Jess suggested.

I shook my head. "That doesn't seem right. When you tell someone you love them for the first time, it should be in person. It should make a real memory – a major in-person moment. Don't you think?"

"Well, that's up to you. Make sure you're not hesitating about this because you're not sure if you love him."

"I wish you'd quit saying that. I didn't. . . I mean, I'm not hesitating. I only want to make sure I do this right."

"Okay. Whatever you say." Jess got off the floor and began to pack up.

I turned to get my things and was glad that there was very little I needed from my locker over break. Spring break was really going to be a break.

At home I tried to decide if I should take Jess' advice to either call or text Tyler. I thought I loved him, but Jess was right. I shouldn't use those three little words unless I was sure. I checked my clock. It wouldn't be long before he'd have to turn off his cell phone for the flight anyway. I figured that bought me some time and curled up to take a nap.

My head felt much clearer when I woke up. I already missed Tyler, and it would be nine days before I'd see him again. I felt like such an idiot for my earlier consternation. Of course I loved Tyler. How could I not? He was absolutely perfect. We had a lot of the same interests. We could finish each other's sentences. Obviously, the physical chemistry was great. I had clearly been over thinking things with Jess. Grabbing my cell phone, I began to dial. He was in the middle of his flight, but I thought I could at least leave a message. Not an "I love you" message, because I refused to give in on that being said face to face, but I could tell him I had something to tell him or would that be too weird? I ignored the impulse to hang up and heard Tyler's voice telling me to leave a message.

I took a deep breath before speaking. "Hi, Tyler. It's me, Brigit. Hey, about what you said this afternoon. I . . . ah . . . wanted to tell you something back, but you left so quickly. So because I really want to be with you when I say . . . um. . . what it is that I'm going to say. You'll have to wait until you're back, but I wanted you to know I already miss you. Call me when you have the chance. Bye."

Okay – that *was* officially weird. Hopefully, Tyler didn't think I was certifiably crazy when he got that message. I scooted off my bed and went in search of Mom.

She smiled at me as I entered the kitchen. "Hi there. You ran upstairs so fast when you got home. Is everything okay?"

"Yeah. I'm fine. I took a little nap."

"You're not coming down with anything, are you?"

"No. Really. I'm fine. I know it's pathetic, but I'm already starting to miss Tyler."

"I'm not surprised. You two have been spending so much time together you're bound to miss him this week."

"I suppose." I sat down at the table. "I'm really hungry. What are we having for dinner?"

"I have a little surprise planned. I've been missing our mother-daughter movie nights. We haven't done one in so long. So I bought a ton of junk food and rented some chick flicks and thought we could hang out tonight. How 'bout it?"

"That sounds perfect." I got up to rummage through the grocery bags sitting on the floor. "You weren't kidding about the junk food. Mom, that's more than we could eat in two movie nights."

"Okay, so I went a little overboard. I was hungry when I shopped," she explained sheepishly. "That means we'll have to do this again soon to use up the leftovers."

I ripped open a bag of Doritos and shoved two of them in my mouth at once. "Can we start movie night now?" I mumbled through the chips.

"Sure, I'm done with work for the day. The DVDs are by the TV."

We each grabbed a bunch of snacks and went to the living room.

Two movies and who knows how many calories later, we agreed it had been a lot of fun to hang out together. It was late, and we were tired, but we sat and talked for a while anyway.

When we finally managed to heave our bodies off the couch to go to bed, she gave me a rather long-ish hug. It made me realize I'd been neglectful of her lately. Until that moment, I hadn't really thought about how all the time I'd been spending with Tyler might make her feel. Maybe it wasn't completely bad that Tyler was on vacation.

I checked my phone for messages, cringing a little as I thought about the convoluted message I had left for Tyler. Hopefully, he understood what I meant. I was too tired to worry about it anymore and went to bed.

I awoke to my phone ringing and groggily reached for it, mumbling a sleepy hello.

"Hey, Sleepy-head, wake up. It's after ten."

Tyler's voice had me instantly alert.

"Sorry. I stayed up late watching movies. How're you?"

"I'm good. We're heading to the beach in a few minutes, but I got your voice mail and wanted to call you back."

I inwardly groaned, wondering what he must be thinking about my strange message. "Oh, that. Ignore me. I was rambling."

"No, don't say that. I understood you perfectly."

"You did?" I was amazed he unraveled what I meant.

"Definitely."

"That's good. I was afraid I wasn't making much sense." I didn't know what else to say, and I heard his mom calling his name in the background.

"I've got to go, but I'll talk to you later. Okay?" Tyler asked.

"Sure. Have fun." After hanging up, I sat in my bed for a minute, somewhat in awe of how well Tyler and I understood each other. I debated about going back to sleep, but my stomach growled, making my decision to head to the kitchen an easy one.

I plunked down on one of the kitchen chairs by Mom. "What are you working on?" I asked, taking in all the books she had out on the table.

"Just looking for some different ideas to celebrate Ostara this week," she answered as she marked a page.

"Really? I kind of like what we normally do." Ostara, the spring equinox, was my favorite holiday. I wasn't sure if I liked it best because it was very much like everyone else's Easter celebration, if you ignored the going-to-church part, or because it marked the end of winter. I remembered how in third grade, feeling very smart, I proudly explained to my classmates that the name Easter came from the spring celebration of the Goddess Eostre. Even though this is true, Mom got calls from upset parents. She wasn't mad at me, but I was careful not to share my knowledge of our holidays again.

"We have to color eggs and make hot cross buns. What did you want to change?" I was wary of making any alterations to what I considered a perfect celebration.

"Oh, I don't know. I suppose you were too little to remember, but when Grandma was alive, we would light a bonfire at dawn and then spread the ashes in the garden along with those from the Yule tree. I quit doing it after she died. It made me miss her too badly, and it's something best done with another person. Would you like to revive the tradition?"

"Dawn, huh? How early would that be?" I was hoping she'd drop the idea. Standing around a fire before breakfast didn't sound like a lot of fun.

"Not too early, around six-thirty. You could go back to bed afterward." Her voice was sort of wistful.

When I glanced up, she seemed lost in thought. I tried to muster more enthusiasm. "Sure, that could be kind of neat."

Her gaze focused on me, and she laughed. "Did I hear you correctly? You agreed to get up at dawn with me during spring break?"

"Yeah. I guess I did. Why not?" I smiled back.

"Excellent. It won't be as boring as it sounds."

"We're not changing anything else, right?" I would dig my heels in if she tried to get out of making hot cross buns.

"No, I promise. No other changes." She held her hand over her heart as she spoke. "Oh, there is one other thing."

"What?" I asked worriedly.

"Often when we – the Tuatha, I mean – hold our rituals, we wear special robes. I don't think you've ever seen me wear mine. Since Grandma died, I only wear it at Beltane each year when I'm in Ireland. I have another one though. I haven't worn it since you were born. Grandma made it for my first Beltane festival when I was your age. The fabric is royal blue crushed velvet, and it's embroidered with white and gold threads in a Celtic knot design. It's truly unique. If you decide you like it, you can wear it on Ostara and for Beltane, too."

"I'd love to see it, Mom." I didn't want to commit to wearing it right away. To be honest it seemed a little weird, and I was afraid I'd look like a dork. "Does everyone wear a robe at these festivals?"

"Oh, some do and some don't. The participants always wear them, but those who come to watch don't always change out of their regular clothes. I like wearing mine. Somehow it makes everything more special."

I followed Mom to her room. She knelt down next to the trunk at the foot of her bed and opened it, pulling out a few things before finding what she wanted. She put the box next to me on the bed and said, "Open it."

I lifted the lid and pushed the tissue paper aside to reveal my grandma's handiwork. I wasn't prepared for the sheer beauty of the fabric and embroidery. I pulled it halfway out and held it up to my shoulders, admiring the exquisite design. "Oh, it's wonderful. I can't believe Grandma made this. Can I put it on?"

"Yes, I'd love to see how you look." She reached out to stroke the sleeve, her eyes full of tears she blinked away.

I undid the fancy metal clasps which fastened the front together, slid into it and walked toward the full-length mirror in the corner. I pulled the front shut before I looked up at my image. "Oh." I couldn't believe how unfamiliar I looked. I didn't feel like myself either. I looked older.

"Do you like it?" Mom asked.

"Yes. It's beautiful. It makes me feel a bit strange – not like myself. I don't know." I looked down to admire the stitching again and felt Mom give me a hug from behind.

"You're gorgeous," she said, but her voice was not as close as it should have been with her arms hugging me. Instead, her voice came from the other side of the room. I felt a chill, and my head shot up to gaze into the mirror. For a split-second I locked eyes with the person embracing me, and then she was gone. It had been my grandma. I continued to stare at the mirror, hoping she'd come back.

"Brigit, are you all right? You look like you've seen a ghost."

"Not funny! You could have warned me. I almost had a heart attack." I held my hand against my chest trying to calm my breathing.

"Warned you about what?" Her voice was puzzled, and I could tell her confusion was real.

"You didn't see her. Did you?"

"What are you talking about? Who was I supposed to see, Brigit?"

"Grandma. I saw Grandma in the mirror. She gave me a hug and disappeared."

Mom's mouth opened in disbelief and then she smiled. "Oh, Brigit, that's wonderful. I've felt her presence before, but I've never seen her." Her tears overflowed. Once she had wiped them away, she took my hands and said, "I'm glad she came. It means she approves of you wearing the robe."

She repacked the trunk and shut the lid before she spoke again. "Brigit, it's time you read Grandma's story. Don't put it off much longer. It's important you know the whole story."

Chapter Twenty-Two

L ater that night, I took Mom's advice and opened to my grandma's page. I readjusted the book on my lap and a small piece of white paper fluttered out. I hadn't noticed it before and reached down to pick it up. It was blank on both sides. Not knowing what to make of it, I slipped it under my thumb as I held the book. Mom had made Grandma's story sound so ominous that my fingers shook when I lightly traced the words with my free hand.

Phoebe Minton Quinn
November 2, 1980

I write this with a heavy heart
To see a friend so torn apart,
Blinded by her greedy quest
Unable to see how she's blest.
A pilfering plan, a meddling moment,
To harm none ignored and broken.
She knew the danger very well
But that didn't stop her lustful spell.
Over time she lived the truth

What you send out, comes back to you.
Watch the story I have written
With the power you've been given.

I could see my grandma looking much, much younger. Her long, brown hair was not streaked with the gray I remembered and her face was free of wrinkles. She was writing at the same kitchen table we now used, but she wasn't writing in the book. A small slip of paper was in front of her. A piece of paper very much like – no – exactly like the one under my thumb. I gasped and examined it more carefully. Words were appearing as if someone were writing on it while I held it in the air. I realized it was a list of names – last names.

Quinn
McNamara
Hanratty
Corrigan
Gallagher
McLaughlin
O'Neil
Clery
McGrath

Why was Tyler's last name on this list? I had a thought, an unbelievable thought, and counted the names. There were nine. *The Circle of Nine.* I recognized that a few of the last names were the same as my Mom's friends in Ireland, but I didn't remember ever seeing any letters coming from anyone named McGrath. Why was Tyler's family name on this list? Was his gran part of the Circle? I couldn't believe Mom wouldn't have told me about that.

I read the verse my grandma had written once again. The writing on the small slip of paper faded away and so did my room as the image of my young grandma became stronger and stronger.

*P*hoebe wrote in the book while the memory was fresh, although she wished she could forget the way her friend betrayed her. Only two days had passed since the disastrous Samhain, or New Year, celebration. Phoebe chastised herself for not seeing the signs. Adele had been acting suspiciously for weeks, and it should have been obvious what she was after. But Phoebe wanted to believe the best of everyone and swept away any concerns, ignoring her instincts.

Adele had willingly offered to co-host when Phoebe had declared her plan to have a Samhain celebration. It was to be their first North American gathering, and Phoebe hoped it would be as wonderful as Beltane was each year in Ireland. The invitations had gone out to the Circle of Nine and their families and other members of the Tuatha. For weeks they had planned the food, decorations, and music. As the responses began to pour in, Phoebe and Adele arranged accommodations at the two hotels in town. The final attendance would be nearly a hundred kindred souls.

When they first discussed their plans, Adele said that her farm would be the perfect site for the actual celebration. She was right. Her farm had plenty of space and would afford them privacy from the distrusting eyes of the community. In the final week before Samhain, Adele's farm was busy as tents, tables, and chairs were delivered and set up. And Adele's husband had taken care of the bonfire preparations.

While most of the food would be provided by a caterer, Phoebe decided it would be a special touch if she made some desserts using the old family recipes. The day before the party, Adele joined Phoebe in her kitchen for a cooking marathon, and they were in the middle of a particularly complicated recipe when the telephone rang. It was the school telling Phoebe that Celeste had fallen on the playground and hurt her arm. Could she come at once?

Phoebe rushed out, her only concern for her daughter, and left Adele to finish cooking.

At the nurse's office, Celeste tried to explain through her tears, "Mom, Toby and I were swinging very high, but I've never fallen before. The swing just slipped out from under me." She continued to cry, her arm resting awkwardly on the pillow in her lap.

"It's all right. We all fall down sometimes." Phoebe reassured Celeste with a caress down the back of her long, blonde hair.

After a whispered conversation with the nurse, who suggested the arm might be broken, Phoebe helped Celeste to the car and drove to the emergency room. An x-ray confirmed the break, and before long Celeste was the unhappy owner of a bright white cast.

On the drive home, with the pain killers at work Celeste was much more comfortable. She was starting to get drowsy but managed to repeat, "I really don't know what happened to the swing. It disappeared . . ."

Phoebe carried the groggy Celeste to the door and was startled when it swung open in front of her. "Oh, Adele, I'd forgotten you were here. Thank you for staying. She's got a broken arm. Let me get her settled upstairs."

"Oh, the poor dear," Adele murmured.

A few minutes later, Phoebe came back into the kitchen and was startled by the sight. Nearly every surface was covered with completed recipes. "How in the world did you do all this? I know I was gone for a while, but really, Adele, this is hard to believe. Did you have some help?"

"No. It was only me, but I work fast. I hope everything tastes okay."

"I'm sure everything will taste great." Phoebe reassured her, somewhat distracted as she searched around the kitchen for her special recipe book. She found it propped up on the counter near the stove. "You were able to decipher my handwriting, then?" She closed the book and put it on the shelf with the others, noticing two of them were out of place. She put them back in order without thinking.

"Yes, no problem with that at all. You're too hard on yourself. I find your writing perfectly legible," Adele said, taking off her apron and hanging it on the hook on the back of the door. "I think I remembered to make all the recipes we discussed. I need to get Toby from school. See you tomorrow."

Phoebe walked out the front door and into the yard with her. "Adele, I don't know what I would have done without you today. Thank you. I'll bring all the food over tomorrow and help put the finishing touches on everything."

The next day Celeste's achy arm made her uncooperative, and she refused to drink a cup of Boneset Tea until she was allowed to add a huge dollop of honey. Once it was sweetened to her liking, she drank it down along with a pain reliever from the hospital. Phoebe felt guilty giving the capsule to her. She preferred using homemade pain remedies, but there wasn't time for anything that complicated today. Phoebe again marveled at the amount of food Adele had made in such a short time the day before as she packed the desserts into the car. There was just enough space to for Celeste in the back seat.

Driving up the long, dead-end road, Phoebe was pleased with the sight of the white tents on the large lawn. The grass was still mostly green as the temperatures had not yet dipped low enough to turn everything brown. Phoebe parked next to one of the tents to unload, and, telling Celeste to stay put for a minute, went in search of Adele and her husband for some help.

She was standing on the front porch, about to knock on the door when she heard arguing coming from the barn. The shouting between Adele and her husband masked the crunching sound of Celeste's footsteps as she walked across the gravel yard.

"You are obsessed," Adele's husband shouted. "This is all you talk about. This is all you have ever talked about. You must let this go!"

"I cannot. I must right this wrong. My mother was not the eldest daughter, but she was more devout to the old ways. While she was alive, it pained her daily that she was passed over. She was the true inheritor, not my aunt. Now that my aunt has passed as well, it is the right time to act. I know I can make my cousin Carmen see that I am far better suited to carrying on the traditions than she is."

Adele's husband gave up shouting, and in a low threatening voice, said, "You need to realize what is important in your life. You love this book, this power, more than you love me, more than you love your own son. If you stay on this course, I am finished." He stomped out of the barn.

Phoebe slipped behind one of the large barn doors as he passed, deciding to pretend she hadn't heard any of the argument. After a few moments, she walked into the barn to find Adele sitting on a bale of hay. With forced cheerfulness, Phoebe said, "There you are. I need some help unloading."

"I'll be right there. Give me a minute," Adele replied, her voice still shaking.

"I'm parked right next to the tents when you're ready," Phoebe said.

The argument reminded Phoebe how much Adele had always resented that the line of inheritance for the McGrath family books and the place in the Circle of Nine had gone to her aunt and now to her cousin Carmen, instead of to her own mother and down to her. There was nothing to be done about it, and she thought Adele had long ago come to grips with the situation. She hadn't mentioned it in years, but obviously it continued to bother her greatly. Adele's aunt had recently died and it seemed like she thought Carmen could be persuaded to give up the book and her place in the Circle.

Phoebe didn't believe that would ever happen. She'd known Carmen and Adele their whole lives and wasn't sure who was the more stubborn of the two. Phoebe hoped they wouldn't argue and spoil the celebration.

She wasn't sure why Adele cared so much about the book or the place in the Circle. They never excluded her from their gatherings.

True, she could not step forward as one of the nine, but she was as talented in the old ways as any of them. The lack of inheriting the book hadn't prevented Adele's mother from instructing her well.

It wasn't long before Adele, looking much more composed, crossed the lawn to the waiting car. After unloading the many trays of dessert, Phoebe and Adele went to work, decorating with bundles of corn, pumpkins, and gourds. They set out candles and little bags of candy on each table. Celeste tried to help her mother and Adele, but by late morning her energy was flagging, and Adele took her into the house where she could nap comfortably.

When they were finished, the place was definitely party-ready for the guests who would begin arriving soon.

Celeste came out of the house and let the door slam behind her, making Adele and Phoebe look up. She walked toward them with her normal bouncing energy. She seemed nearly as good as new to her mother. "Adele, if this is how people feel after napping at your house, I'll be coming over more often," Phoebe commented, and turned to greet her energetic daughter. "So, Celeste, has your nap gotten you ready for our big Samhain celebration?"

"I can't wait. There'll be lots and lots of other kids to play with, right? And, I get to stay up as late as I want, right?" Her words rushed out in a jumble of excitement.

"Right. That's what I told you. But you'll have to be careful with your arm so it can heal properly."

"It feels all better now. It doesn't hurt at all." She moved her arm around to demonstrate how good it felt.

"I'm glad, but if it starts to hurt again, you need to tell me," Phoebe cautioned.

"You're on the mend for sure," Adele said. "I need to run into town and get Toby from school. He was so mad when I made him go for a half day." Adele laughed, heading to her car.

Phoebe took one last walk around to be sure everything was in place with Celeste trailing after her.

"Mom, I had the strangest dream."

"You did?" Phoebe wondered guiltily if it had been the pain pill. "What was it about?"

"Adele was in it. She walked around the couch and said things I didn't understand. Then she put her hands on my cast." Celeste was silent for a second or two and shrugged. "I don't remember anything else."

Phoebe's heart jumped. Was it a nine year-old's imagination, or was Adele meddling with something she should have left alone? She forced her voice to remain calm and said, "What an interesting dream."

Phoebe meant to ask Adele about Celeste's strange dream and gauge her reaction, but before Adele returned with Toby, people began arriving and she was swept up in hugs and the joy of seeing family and friends.

Later on, Phoebe caught up with Carmen, "I really need to talk to you privately."

"What's wrong? You seem so serious," Carmen replied.

"I need to warn you. I don't believe Adele has given up her quest for your position in the Circle. I'm afraid she's going to confront you, and I wanted you to be prepared."

Carmen laughed. "You're too late. She already did."

"Really? What did she say?"

"Oh, the usual . . . It is her rightful place, I should renounce my inheritance and bestow it upon her. Of course, I refused."

"Was she furious? I'm surprised I didn't hear her shouting at you," Phoebe commented.

"No. That was the strange thing. Normally, she gets upset and yells, but she was very calm. She told me it was my last chance to do the right thing, and if I didn't, I'd be sorry."

"I'm not sure what she means to do, but I'd be careful. She was very angry when she was talking about this with her husband."

Carmen waved her hand in the air dismissively and said, "I'm not worried. She's always been this way. It's nothing new."

Phoebe wasn't as confident.

Throughout the afternoon, the party continued with games for the children and some of the more playful adults. In one tent, the guests who were musicians started an impromptu concert and others danced and sang along to the music. When darkness had nearly enveloped the yard, the nine women lit the candles on the tables and the torches around the perimeter.

Before eating dinner, Phoebe gathered everyone under the main tent and gave the blessing of thankfulness. "As we end the growing season with our final harvest festival, let us give thanks to the earth for providing such abundance to us. Let us also give thanks for our ability to gather together and celebrate our love and friendship as we welcome the New Year."

Phoebe had caught glimpses of Celeste as she played with the other children. It didn't seem like her arm was bothering her. Mealtime afforded Phoebe the chance to ask her in person. "Celeste, come here," she called across the tent.

"Hi, Mom."

"How's your arm, Honey? I'm worried about you overdoing it." Phoebe touched the injured arm lightly, directly above the cast.

"It doesn't hurt at all since my nap. Maybe I'm a fast healer." She treated Phoebe to her most mischievous grin.

"I'm a little surprised that's all. Are you sure you're telling me the truth?"

"It really doesn't hurt. Can I go back to my friends now? We're having so much fun."

"Sure, but come and tell me if . . ." Phoebe trailed off because Celeste was already gone.

About a half hour before midnight, Phoebe and the other women went into the house to change into their robes for the ceremony.

"Can we change right here in the living room, or is Adele's husband around?" Carmen asked.

"I saw him when we first got here to set up this morning, but I haven't seen him since. What about you?" Phoebe questioned.

"No. Not once," Carmen answered with a shake of her head.

They changed into their robes and left their clothes folded neatly on the sofa. Each of the nine wore a different color, all of them in bright shades except for Carmen. She wore a soft butter yellow, which complemented her black hair very well. They walked single file out the door and back to the gathering.

All conversation stopped when the women reached the middle of the lawn where preparations had been made for the bonfire. Phoebe's quiet incantation held the guests' attention.

"The year is done, we bid farewell
In the past, we will not dwell
The flame of old we lit tonight
Is gone for good, turn out the light"

Phoebe thrust her arms in the air, her palms facing up, and all candles and torches sputtered out. It was a moonless night, and Phoebe's voice, louder now, sounded otherworldly coming out of the darkness.

"The year anew, we welcome you
Goddess, guide us in all we do."

The torch hissed as it sprang to life, illuminating Phoebe's face.

She brought her flame down low and walked in a circle, lighting the kindling at the edges of the bonfire as she went. Back at her starting place, she threw her torch into the middle of the fire and backed away as the flames roared to life.

Phoebe continued, "We celebrate our life and remember those who have gone before us. Let us feel their presence tonight as we honor them with a minute of silence."

Some spent the minute staring into the flames, others reached out to hold hands, and a few bowed their heads in grief. As the minute concluded, Phoebe spoke again, "We make our circle to remind ourselves that our journey is without beginning or end. Our energy is ever present." Like jewels on a bracelet, the nine robed women surrounded the fire. Then a second, larger circle of participants formed and then another and another, until everyone was united in rings around the blazing fire.

Someone started singing, and they all joined in as they continued to rotate. In the blur of joyous faces, Phoebe caught a glimpse of an angry Adele spinning in the circle behind her. On the next revolution Phoebe searched for Adele but couldn't find her.

Nearly an hour later, while Phoebe was resting her tired feet and quenching her thirst with some punch, Celeste came running up. "Mom, Mom come quick! Adele is doing something to Carmen." Others heard Celeste's frightened voice and gathered near as she pulled on her mother's arm and yelled, "She's in the barn. I fell asleep in there, but Carmen's scream woke me up."

As Phoebe rushed after her daughter, she scanned the crowd for a glimpse of Carmen's yellow robe, hoping Celeste had just had another strange dream. There was no sign of her, and Phoebe's chest tightened.

At the barn door, Phoebe harshly whispered to Celeste, "Stay here. Do not come in. Do you understand?" Celeste nodded.

Phoebe slipped through the partly opened door as silently as possible. The slight swish of robes from behind reassured her that at least some of the nine had followed. It was dark inside, but there was a sliver of light coming from the storage room door at the far end of the barn. They heard Adele's voice rising and falling as she chanted an unfamiliar incantation. Her shrill voice screamed, "Carmen McGrath, renounce your place in the Circle and name me your heir!"

"Never! Adele, I demand you let me go. You will never get away with this. There are a hundred people outside." Carmen's words were strong but the warble in her voice betrayed her fear.

"By the time you are missed, it will be too late. You leave me no choice but to force you to do what I ask."

"You can't force me to recite the unbinding spell," Carmen replied in disbelief.

"There is a way." Adele laughed and began the incantation once again.

Phoebe whispered to the other members of the Circle, "We must interrupt now, before she does any real harm." They all nodded in reply, and Phoebe grabbed the latch, but it was locked tight. She rattled it, and Adele cackled. "I've spelled the door. You will not be able to get in."

Phoebe could see this was going to take time – time they didn't have. While the others tried to unravel the locking spell, Phoebe pressed her eye to the crack in the door and was shocked by what the small slit revealed to her. It didn't make any sense at first. Adele, with gloved hands, was struggling to control a hawk she restrained in a net. She held the bird down with one hand, muttered something, and with the other hand plunged a dagger into its chest.

Phoebe gasped. Now she understood. Adele had embraced the dark side to achieve her goals. "She's doing dark magic," Phoebe whispered to the others. In an attempt to distract Adele, she shouted through the door, "Adele, don't do it! Remember the Rule of Three."

"When the power of my ancestors is mine, I won't have to worry about the Rule of Three," Adele shouted back.

"She's gone crazy," Phoebe said. "We have to get in there. Are you having any luck with the door?"

"Give us a few more minutes, and we'll have it," one of the other women replied.

"Carmen may not have a few minutes," Phoebe warned and looked back through the opening. Adele had cast a circle on the floor boards with the hawk's blood which glistened sickly in the flickering candlelight. Carmen was tied to a chair in the center and Adele held the dagger over her. Drips of blood fell on Carmen's head as Adele continued to recite the strange words.

Carmen screamed for their help. "Get me out of here. I do not understand this magic, but I – I can feel it doing something to me. Make her stop."

The others worked more frantically at the lock. Carmen continued to scream as she fought against the ropes binding her to the chair. She lurched to one side to avoid another drip from the dagger and tipped over, upsetting one of the candles. The flame sputtered but didn't go out as the candle rolled into the corner. Adele was in a trance-like state and did not stop chanting even as the loose hay began to burn.

Phoebe was banging on the door now. "Adele! Adele! Untie Carmen, and get out of there. You'll be burned alive."

"Thank Goddess, we've done it," one of the others said, and the door sprang open. They rushed in and dragged Carmen out of the room, chair and all, to get her away from the fire. While the others untied Carmen in the main barn, Phoebe grabbed Adele and pulled her to the door. They all stumbled outside, coughing from the smoke.

Adele shrieked at them. "It was mine, it has always been mine!" With a keening noise she curled into a ball on the grass and fell silent.

The flames were already visible on one end of the barn, and all the guests were shouting to each other. Through the jumble of voices, Phoebe heard a panicked shout. It was Celeste. "Mom, Mom, Toby's in there. He followed you in. I tried to stop him. He hasn't come out."

Others heard Celeste's shout, and even though smoke was pouring out the door, two men bravely ran in to find him.

Adele heard her, too. She stood up, the light from the flames dancing wildly on her face. "What have I done?" Along with everyone else, she waited with her eyes on the doorway.

The sirens of the fire trucks were wailing down the road when the men finally burst from the barn carrying Toby between them. They laid him down on the grass. He wasn't moving, and Adele rushed over. "Is he . . . is he?" She couldn't finish the sentence.

"No. He's breathing, but his legs are burned. He needs an ambulance."

The fire trucks had pulled up by then with an ambulance close behind. The EMTs went quickly to Toby's side and poured saline on his burned legs before loading him into the ambulance. Adele didn't look back as she followed the gurney into the rear of the ambulance.

Phoebe and the other onlookers got out of the way of the firemen and walked back to the tents. The nine women in the Circle were peppered with questions which they avoided answering. They huddled together to discuss what had happened.

"Adele couldn't let it go. I should have watched her more closely," Phoebe said and sat down on one of the rented folding chairs.

"You tried to warn me, Phoebe. It isn't your fault. I didn't believe she was actually dangerous." Carmen's hand was shaking visibly as she dipped a napkin in a cup of water and used it to wipe the hawk's blood from her face.

"This is terrible. What are we going to tell people?" another woman asked.

"We have to tell them the truth," Phoebe said. As she rose to answer questions, a spray of water from a fire hose arched over the lawn to smother the flames of their bonfire. The resulting hiss of steam seemed fitting as Phoebe explained to the deflated crowd how Adele had embraced dark magic to possess something that was never meant to be hers. It was a sad end to their celebration and a terrible way to start a new year. Only a few people were willing to stay after that. Phoebe didn't blame them for wanting to get far away from this bad energy.

She would have gone as well if she hadn't been the only remaining hostess on the premises. Hours later the fire was out but still smoldering when the fire chief approached her and asked, "You're a friend of the owners?"

"Yes," Phoebe replied, although she wasn't sure how true that was anymore.

"Let them know we'll leave one truck here most of the day to watch for flare-ups, and tell them we think this all probably started with a stray spark from that bonfire. Those bonfires are dangerous, you know."

Knowing the real cause, Phoebe was startled by that conclusion, but didn't think it mattered enough to correct him. She believed in the Rule of Three and knew Adele would soon have a lot more trouble coming her way.

Phoebe went into the house to change out of her smoky robe. She peeked in on Celeste and saw she was awake.

"Couldn't sleep?" Phoebe asked.

"I tried. I really did. I can't stop worrying about Toby." Celeste's forehead was crinkled as she thought of her injured friend.

"I know, Honey. After I get changed and the trucks come to pick everything up from the rental company, we'll go see him."

Phoebe set her clothes on the edge of the bed and was unzipping her robe, when she glimpsed herself in the bureau mirror. Her hair was sticking out strangely, and much of her face was smudged with soot. She tried to smooth her frizzy tresses with her hands, but it didn't work. "Oh, my," she said under her breath.

Celeste began to giggle. "You look a little scary."

"I'd better take a quick shower," Phoebe said and headed into the bathroom.

When she was dried off and dressed, Phoebe reached into the cabinet to borrow a hair brush and noticed the shelves seemed empty. At first she thought, Adele had been doing some housecleaning, but then she realized what was missing. There wasn't a single male toiletry item in the entire bathroom. She padded barefoot into the master bedroom and opened a few drawers. Some of them were completely empty, and the others only contained Adele's clothes. It seemed like Adele's husband had made good on this threat.

The familiar phrase went through Phoebe's mind. Obey the Threefold Law you should, three times bad and three times good. Phoebe plopped down on the bed next to Celeste and said, "Adele what have you done?"

"What, Mom?" Celeste asked and sat up.

"Oh, nothing. I was only talking to myself." Phoebe leaned over and gave her daughter a big hug, smelling the pungent odor of her hair. "Maybe you should take a quick shower, too. You smell like smoke."

"I'll get my cast wet." Celeste held up her arm. "I wish I could take it off. It doesn't hurt anymore, and my skin is itchy."

"I'll be right back," Phoebe said and headed for the kitchen.

She returned with a plastic bag which she tied around Celeste's arm. "There. It's not waterproof, but it should keep it dry enough if you're careful."

Phoebe helped Celeste with her shower before going outside to meet the rental company truck. An hour later, they were able to leave for the hospital.

The receptionist at the front desk gave them Toby's room number. Phoebe hadn't known what to expect and was glad they hadn't been directed to the ICU. They rode the elevator up to the fourth floor and walked down the hall, reading the numbers as they went. The door to his room was ajar, and through the gap Phoebe saw Adele sitting in a chair. Phoebe took a deep breath and called out, "Knock, knock."

"Come in," Adele said in a husky voice. Her eyes widened as she saw who was visiting. She cleared her throat before continuing. "I'm surprised to see you."

"We were worried about Toby," Phoebe explained.

"He's doing fine. See for yourself," Adele said and waved toward the bed.

Phoebe and Celeste stepped further into the room and saw a grinning Toby sitting up in bed.

"Toby, we're so happy to see you weren't badly burned," Phoebe said.

"Yeah, it was really scary when the men carried you out of the barn," Celeste chimed in. "Are you okay?"

Toby nodded. "My legs hurt a lot at first, but now it's not so bad."

Phoebe looked to Adele for confirmation. Adele nodded and said, "It looked much worse when they first brought him in, but it seems he was very lucky." Adele looked down at her hands for a moment and cleared her throat again. "Phoebe, can I talk to you in the hall?"

"Sure. Celeste can keep Toby company for a while." Celeste didn't need the prompting. She'd already pulled up a chair.

Adele led the way down the hall to a small sitting area with a few chairs and a large, fake, potted palm. They didn't sit down. Adele stared out the window while she spoke, not meeting Phoebe's gaze.

"I know what I did was horrible. I won't blame anyone for not wanting to talk to me again. I've never really believed in the Rule of Three, but I'm afraid there's truth to it. Toby's been hurt and Tom's left me."

"I know. I noticed his things were gone when we used your bathroom this morning."

"He says he'll visit Toby later, but he doesn't want anything to do with me. Ever again."

"Maybe he'll change his mind," Phoebe said and touched Adele's shoulder.

"Why are you being so nice to me? After everything I did to you, Celeste, everyone." Adele still didn't turn to look at Phoebe.

"What do you mean? What did you do to Celeste?" Phoebe's mouth was set in a thin line.

"I thought you knew." Adele's voice was so quiet Phoebe hardly heard her.

"Adele, what did you do to Celeste?" Phoebe repeated with a sharp pitch to her voice.

"The swing . . . her arm . . ." Adele haltingly began her explanation. "I needed you out of the house so I could search for your grandmother's grimoire. My mother told me your grandmother had written down the spell used to control someone. She included it in her book along with the counter-spell used to reverse it. I needed the spell to make Carmen give me the book."

Phoebe's face flamed red and she advanced on Adele. "You made Celeste have the accident? She broke her arm because of you? She's been in pain for days. You are a monster! And to think I was feeling sorry for you." Phoebe's anger filled the small space. Adele had retreated as far as she could, her back against the wall.

Adele put her hands up as if to ward off Phoebe's wrath, explaining, "Now, that's not entirely true. She was in pain that first day, but when she took the nap in my house, I fixed it."

"What do you mean you fixed it?"

"I healed the bone with a spell. She's fine. If you don't believe me, have it x-rayed again."

"You stay away from us! Far away!" Phoebe snarled and walked down the hall to collect Celeste from Toby's room.

Celeste was upset at their abrupt departure. "Do we have to leave so soon? Toby and I were going to play a game."

"Yes, now!" Phoebe's anger simmered under the surface. Celeste knew something was wrong and quit protesting.

When they entered the elevator, Phoebe was about to push the L for Lobby but instead she pushed 2 for the orthopedic floor. She had to know if Adele was telling the truth. The doctor who set

Celeste's arm reluctantly agreed to take another x-ray and was as shocked as Phoebe that it showed a well-healed break.

"You're an amazing kid," he told Celeste. "It should have taken at least four weeks for your bone to look this good."

"Does that mean I can get this cast off?" Celeste's eager expression made both Phoebe and the doctor laugh.

"I don't see why not, but I'm going to give you a brace to wear for the next two weeks just to be safe."

Phoebe was glad for Celeste as they left the hospital but her anger at Adele prevented her from sharing the joyous mood of her daughter.

Adele's apology letter came two days later but did nothing to change Phoebe's feelings. She professed regret for her actions, saying how she should have been happy with the many blessing the Goddess had given her. Instead, her greed cost her dearly. She lost her husband, her extended family and friends, and nearly lost her son. She hoped that the healing spell she placed on Celeste somewhat atoned for the fact that she caused the injury in the first place. The final line of the letter read: Please forgive me.

Phoebe wished she could, but Adele's actions changed everything. The members of the Tuatha had always been alert to those outsiders who might misunderstand them or view them as dangerous or evil, but a threat from within was unthinkable – until now. Phoebe did not trust Adele and decided to take steps to at least protect the Circle of Nine and their families from dark magic.

After she recorded the story of Adele's betrayal in the family's book, she began to recite her grandmother's counter-spell to keep dark magic from taking control of any of the Circle of Nine or their family members. As she said the words, she wrote the last names of those to be protected on a small slip of white paper. At the end of the spell the paper became blank once again. Phoebe placed it between the pages of the book and shut the cover.

⊷⊶

I was stunned. I would never have believed that Tyler's gran was capable of such a thing. Tyler would be upset to find out what she did so many years ago. I was sure he didn't know. Mom's warnings had already made me wary of Adele, but at least now I knew why I should be careful around her. It seemed to me that she had learned her lesson. In a way, I felt sorry for her. Even though it was her fault, I imagined her life had been very lonely since then.

Before I closed the book for the day, I wanted to take a peek at Mom's writing to savor how close I was to completing my task. Being careful to keep the small blank paper in place, I turned the page, but didn't see what I expected. Instead, I recognized my grandma's writing on this page, too. She made a second entry. No one in the other generations had done this.

January 5, 1989

Her quest has changed, but not her heart.
Knowing right from wrong sets us apart.
A potion brewed to interfere
With others' love most sincere
Cannot work on those protected
By a spell so well crafted.
If she'd known, she might have stopped
Before the intended love was swapped.
You will see this star-crossed story,
If this tome has deemed you worthy.

Nine years had passed since the last time my grandma wrote in the book, and she was looking older — nearly the same now as in my faded memories. Mom looked more like she did now, too. She wasn't a little girl anymore. I smiled, thinking how cool it was that I had the chance to see her and my grandma at different ages and not in the usual family photo album or home movies either. Our *very special family album* no longer freaked me out, and I welcomed the tingle in my fingertips as the scene began to unfold.

"I'm so glad to have you home, even if it's only for a couple more weeks. I miss you when you're away at school." Phoebe sighed, pausing slightly as she folded a shirt and placed it in the dresser.

"I miss you, too. I wish I could come home more often. The airfare would almost be worth it if I saved up enough of my dirty laundry." Celeste laughed as she looked at the large mound of clean clothes on her bed. "Who knew doing laundry was so expensive?"

Celeste sat down and rummaged through the pile until she found her warmest socks. She pulled these on over her first pair.

Phoebe noticed and said, "I could turn up the heat, if your feet are that cold."

"No. I'm fine. Toby invited me to a sledding party at the county park, and he's going to pick me up soon."

"Do you think that's a smart idea? It sounded like he was pretty upset when you told him you thought you should take a break for a while."

"I know he'll try to talk me out of it today, but I'm not changing my mind. It's not like I'm interested in dating someone else. It seems weird to say you're seeing someone that you never, ever see. If I hadn't come home at Thanksgiving, we wouldn't have had any time together in months. He's so busy getting his business started that I can't imagine this semester will be any different. This break could be good for us. I promised him that we'd talk about it again in June and decide what to do. At least then I'll be home for the whole summer." Celeste had finished adding layers as she spoke and was zipping her jacket when Toby rang the bell.

"Will you be home for dinner?" Phoebe asked.

"I think so. I'll call you if a bunch of us decide to get pizza or something."

Celeste had been gone about an hour when an uneasy feeling came over Phoebe. It was like an alarm bell was going off, and she walked anxiously from room to room, trying to figure out why she felt this way. She almost decided to drive out to the sledding hill to make sure Celeste was okay when she was pulled toward her family's book. Now she understood. It had been so long since she put the protection spell in place that she'd nearly forgotten it would alert her if someone tried to use a dark spell against one of the nine or a member of their immediate families. She turned to her page and very carefully picked up the blank slip of paper by its corners as if it were some priceless document.

She stared carefully at the paper and muttered, "Adele, Adele, Adele." On the paper there appeared to be someone moving around like on a tiny TV screen. It was Adele in her kitchen, and she was making hot cocoa. She poured it into a thermos and, before screwing the cap on, pulled a vial out of the cupboard and poured its contents into the cocoa.

"Now, if that doesn't bind those two together forever, nothing will." Adele said right before Toby entered the kitchen. She thrust the thermos out to him. "Here. Take some hot cocoa. It's my special recipe. Make sure to share some with Celeste. You know how much she likes it."

"Sure, Mom. I'll see you later."

From the kitchen window, Adele watched him leave and spoke to herself, "The McGrath family books may be lost to me, but that doesn't mean I'm beat. The Quinn spells will work just as well, and with Celeste as my daughter-in-law, I'll be able to use the book whenever I want."

Phoebe continued to hold the paper as Adele faded away, and a new picture formed. Celeste sat with Toby on a log pulled up close to a small campfire.

"Geez, I'm freezing. It's colder than I thought it would be," Celeste said, leaning in toward the fire.

"Maybe some hot cocoa will warm you up," Toby said as he poured some out of the thermos into the matching cup and handed it to Celeste. "Here, you can have mine."

Toby took a big swig right out of the thermos while Celeste sipped hers from the cup. He got a funny expression on his face and stared at Celeste. "Wow! That's really good." He sounded a little spacey.

"Toby, are you okay?" Celeste asked.

"I'm better than okay. I always am when I'm with you." He grabbed her free hand and stared into her eyes.

"Yeah, okay," Celeste said and looked back at him with mild amusement.

Toby didn't look away when Celeste's friend Gina plopped down on the log next to her. "Hi, Gina, how're you? How was your first semester at NYU?" Celeste asked.

"Brutal. Exams were rough. I'm so glad the semester is over. It's a good thing we have two more weeks off before we have to start it all over again." She gestured to the cup of hot cocoa in Celeste's hand. "Can I have some of that? It's so cold out here."

"Help yourself." Celeste handed the cup to her.

Gina took a drink, and a big smile spread across her face. "That's the most delicious thing I've ever tasted."

"Yeah, it's good. Isn't it? Toby's mom made it. I guess there are some perks to living at home. Right, Toby?" Celeste looked over at him. Toby was no longer staring at her so strangely. He was staring past her at Gina, who was looking back with the same goofy, lopsided grin. Celeste waved her gloved hand in the air between them, but they didn't even blink.

Toby got up, walked past Celeste and sat down next to Gina. They began talking to each other as if no one else existed. Celeste tried to insert herself into the conversation, but it was impossible. It was like she wasn't even there.

Baffled by their behavior, Celeste eventually walked away and hitched a ride back to town with some of the others.

The scene on the paper disappeared, and Phoebe placed it gently back in its place between the pages. She felt terrible for her daughter, thinking of her hurt and confused expression. She waited for Celeste to come home so she could explain what had happened.

Celeste came through the door with an enormous bang as she kicked it shut with her booted foot. She started to rant immediately to her mother. "I'm so mad. If he thinks he can make me jealous by pretending to be interested in someone else, then I don't want him anyway. How stupid does he think I am? And, Gina, we've known each other forever, and she starts flirting with him like I'm not even there. I could have punched both of them, sitting there like love-sick dopes."

Phoebe waited for Celeste to take a breath, and when she did, she was ready. "Stop for a minute and sit down."

"Oooh, I can't. I'm just so mad." Celeste continued her tirade and paced around the kitchen, leaving slushy footprints everywhere.

Phoebe was patient, and eventually Celeste ran out of steam and sat down. "I don't understand, Mom."

"Celeste, this has nothing to do with you." Phoebe stated.

"What – what do you mean? How can this have nothing to do with me?"

"Okay. It has everything to do with you and nothing to do with you at the same time." Phoebe started the story by explaining the spell she had put in place to protect everyone and how it kept Adele's love potion from working on her. As her mother spoke, Celeste's expression went from confusion, to anger, and finally to disbelief.

"Do you mean that Gina and Toby are bound together now?" Celeste's eyes were full of tears. "Can it be reversed?"

Phoebe shrugged. "It might be reversible. Adele would have to do it, but it's very difficult to stop what has been set in motion."

"Can you ask her to do it?" Celeste asked.

Phoebe took a long time answering. "Celeste, are you sure you want me to do that? Only yesterday you told Toby that you should take a break from seeing each other."

"I know that's what I said, but I didn't expect him to start seeing someone else this soon or this way. I haven't even gone back to school yet, and he's practically married to her." Celeste's voice was shrill with hurt.

"Listen to yourself. Shouldn't the first thing out of your mouth have been something about how much you love him and not about feeling rejected? Maybe it would be best if you let Toby go." Phoebe's suggestion was met with an icy stare.

"I thought you'd be on my side." Celeste shoved the chair back angrily and went to her room.

"I am. I've always been," Phoebe whispered as she grabbed her car keys and headed to Adele's. The drive felt very odd to her. She hadn't been to the farm at all in the nine years since the fire at the Samhain celebration. It looked good. She had heard from others that initially Adele had struggled to keep from losing the place, but her finances must have improved because she managed to rebuild the burned-out shell of a barn, incorporating a new art studio into the design. The house was dark, but there were lights visible in the large barn windows. Thanks to Celeste's detailed description, Phoebe knew where to find the stairs to access the studio, but she paused with her hand on the railing. The bad memories of the last time she'd been here flooded back. She took a deep breath and climbed the steps.

Her light knock on the door had Adele calling out, "Toby, is that you?"

"No, Adele. It's Phoebe," she shouted through the closed door.

Adele whipped the door open so fast it made Phoebe jump back a step. "What are you doing here?" she spat out.

It was clear there would be no false pleasantries between the two of them, and Phoebe jumped right to the reason for her visit. "I know about the love potion. Celeste wanted me to come here and ask you to reverse it."

"What do you think I'm trying to do?" Adele waved to the kitchenette where a number of different bottles and bowls were strewn across the countertop. "Why would you want me to reverse it? If you know about the potion, I'm guessing you understand my ultimate goal."

"I do. I didn't come here to ask you to reverse it. I only said that's what Celeste wants. I came here to ask you to leave it as it is.

Gina's a lovely girl, and I think she and Toby will be very happy together."

"You're willing to betray your own daughter?" Adele was stunned.

"Don't talk to me about betrayal, Adele. You're the one who could write a book on that subject."

Adele shrugged and turned back to her preparations at the counter.

"I mean it. Leave it be. Toby's wonderful, but he's not the one for Celeste."

"What if I don't?"

"I'm not giving you a choice. If you reverse this spell, I will find a way to take away your abilities forever."

"That's an idle threat. You would never risk the wrath of the Threefold Law you're so fond of throwing in my face." Adele tried to sound unconcerned but a sliver of nervousness crept into her voice.

"For this, I'm willing to take the risk." Phoebe spun on her heel and left, shutting the door quietly behind her.

———

Adele must have believed my grandma's threat and gave up trying to reverse the spell because Gina and Toby, Tyler's parents, had definitely gotten married later that year. I had noticed the framed wedding invitation hanging on the wall in their house. He was born in 1989, too. I never did the math before and was now realizing Gina must have been pregnant when they got married. Okay, so I knew how their story ended, but I was very curious to hear Mom's take on all of this.

My grandma's inclusion of this second story reawakened my worries about Adele. I was hoping Mom would reassure me that Adele's desire for the Quinn family secrets disappeared back in 1989.

I started to leave my room but turned to retrieve the book, cradling it protectively as I walked downstairs.

CHAPTER TWENTY-THREE

"Hey, Mom," I said as I entered the living room. She was sitting in a chair next to the fireplace, mostly hidden behind the newspaper she was reading.

When she lowered the paper, she spotted what I was carrying and checked the clock on the wall. "Have you been reading this whole time?"

I nodded. "I finished Grandma's entries. Wow! That was a lot to take in. You were such a cute little girl," I teased, deciding not to start with my serious questions right away.

"I'm still cute," she boasted good-naturedly and flipped her long hair behind her shoulder.

I couldn't help laughing. "It was fun to see you as a kid. You were feisty."

"Thank you. I'll take that as a compliment." She smiled widely back at me.

I plunged forward with what had me really worried. "You don't believe Adele wants the Quinn family books anymore, do you? Because it's been a long time – nearly twenty years now – since she put the love potion in the hot chocolate."

She looked at me curiously. "How do you know about the love potion? Grandma didn't write about that."

"Yeah, she did. It was her second entry. I thought it was strange because no one else wrote twice."

Mom's look was anxious and puzzled. "Show me."

I set the book in her lap and opened it. "Here's the first story about
Adele and how she went after Carmen at the Samhain celebration. When I
turned the page I expected to see your story, but there was this second one
from Grandma." I flipped to the next entry to show her.

She examined the page closely and furrowed her brow. "That's so
strange. I had no idea she'd put this in the book. I don't know how I missed
it when I wrote my story later on. I guess I was so upset at the time that I
wasn't paying very close attention."

"Do you want to read it? It tells about the love potion Adele brewed for
you and Toby and how the protection spell kept it from working on you,
but then Gina drank some." I paused to catch my breath. "How long were
you mad at Grandma for what she did? I would have been furious. Did you
really love Toby?" I had a lot more questions than that and would have kept
going, but Mom interrupted.

"Brigit, slow down. I don't understand. *Why* would I have been mad at
Grandma?"

"Well, it would have made me mad . . . y'know . . . how she told Adele
not to reverse the spell?"

"She did what?" She stared at me with a shocked look.

"You didn't know?"

Mom didn't speak. She shook her head to answer my question, pulled
the book closer and began to read the story for herself.

I waited impatiently for her to finish. Near the end of Grandma's second entry she pressed her lips together in an attempt to hold back her tears
but some escaped and dripped onto the page, making puckered blotches on
the paper where they soaked in.

When she was done reading, she sat back in the chair with a sigh
and wiped her face with the edge of her sleeve. I waited for her to say
something.

"I didn't know she did that. I always assumed she asked Adele to reverse the spell, and it hadn't worked. I never asked her specifically what

happened when she went out to Adele's that day. I – I assumed, and then I thanked her for helping me."

I didn't know how to comfort her and silently cursed my Grandma for not telling her the truth as I patted her awkwardly on her back.

"I'm okay, I'm okay," She finally said with a hiccupy sigh. She smiled at me, a forced smile, but a smile nevertheless. "You must be hungry by now. Do you want something to eat?"

"Sure. Let me help." Together we made a simple supper of spinach and cheese omelets, toast, and tea. We didn't talk while we worked. I didn't want to say the wrong thing. There were a lot of questions I wanted to ask, but I was afraid they might upset her more.

When we sat down to eat, Mom said, "Sorry about that." She smiled a real smile this time. "I was so stunned by what Grandma did. All this time I had a different version of what happened in my head. It's upsetting."

She seemed somewhat back to normal, and I couldn't help asking, "Do you think you and Toby would have been married someday?"

"At the time, I thought Toby and I might get married. I wanted that option. I realize now how juvenile it was to ask for a break, but I was jealous of his attentiveness to his business, and I hoped it might jar him into paying more attention to me. Honestly, until I met your father, I thought what I felt for Toby was true love."

I barely waited for her to finish her answer before my next question popped out. "What did you do when it was obvious that Toby and Gina were going to be together?"

She didn't seem annoyed by my prying and answered, "After moping and crying for two weeks, I packed up and went back to school. I avoided coming home for spring break by going to the beach with some girlfriends, and by the time I was home for the summer, they'd already sent out their wedding invitations. Tyler arrived about five months later. It was hard to feel bad about anything after that. I moved on. Eventually, I went to Ireland for a year to study, and that's when I met your dad."

I was suddenly struck by a thought. "Do Toby and Gina know about the potion?"

"I doubt it, and I expect you to never say anything to them or Tyler about this. That kind of information could be devastating. There's no point in telling them."

"I promise I won't say anything. You know what I think?" I asked Mom.

"What?"

"Grandma knew you and Toby weren't right for each other. I think she wanted to give you the chance to find the right person."

"Well, that hasn't worked out so great now has it?" She sounded much more cynical than I had ever heard her before. "I did believe I'd found the perfect man for me, but my judgment was wrong then, too," she added more softly.

I felt bad to hear her talk about my dad that way, and it must have shown in my expression, because when she looked at my face she added, "He *was* amazing in so many ways, Brigit. He was definitely my great love, and I don't regret a moment of the time I spent with him. You'll see. My story's next."

"I can't take any more tonight. I was going to call Tyler, but now I feel funny about talking to him. I know too many secrets about his family. And, now . . . oh, I don't know . . ." I trailed off, scared to put words to what I was thinking.

Mom filled in the thoughts I couldn't speak. "Now you're worried about Tyler. Given what you've learned about Adele, you are wondering if he's dating you because she wanted him to get close to you because you have something she wants."

"I keep remembering the day when he might have been thinking about our book."

"Maybe you heard wrong or maybe Adele simply mentioned it in a conversation. There could be a lot of explanations."

"I've always been surprised that Tyler would want to date someone like me. It would make sense that he's dating me for a specific reason. Adele really might be planning something, and Tyler might be in on it." I imagined myself at the center of a tightly woven plot.

Mom squashed my melodrama immediately. "Stop it. Tyler's dating you for one reason and one reason only. He sees what an absolutely wonderful girl you are. Don't doubt it for a moment."

"You really think so? But —"

"No, buts — if Adele is still obsessed with getting her hands on Quinn family secrets, she's going to be mighty disappointed. Don't forget Grandma's protection spell extends to you, too."

"I've tried to ask Tyler about his family to see if he knows anything about the Tuatha. It doesn't seem like he does. I could ask him more specific questions, but I would rather do that in person. Then I can look at his face when he answers and see his reaction."

"Please be careful not to tell him anything that he shouldn't know."

I nodded in agreement.

"And try not to worry so much." She gave me an encouraging smile. As we did the dishes together, she changed the subject and we talked about our Ostara plans.

"Will you still get up with me for the bonfire at dawn?" She asked.

"I said I would." Inwardly I groaned at the idea, but I wasn't going to disappoint her, especially after her upsetting afternoon.

The two days before Ostara did not go by particularly fast, but they didn't seem to drag, either. We colored our traditional Ostara eggs. This was a labor intensive project as we started by making natural dyes from plants. We used the inner bark of apple tree branches for yellow, onion skins for orange, beets for pink, spinach for light green, and, strangely enough, red cabbage leaves for light blue. We boiled all of these in different pans which made the kitchen positively reek. The eggs were gorgeous when we were done, and I tucked them into the straw nest we always used as a centerpiece this time of year. Pausing to admire them briefly — very briefly — I then pulled on my boots and coat to head outdoors for my next chore.

I'd volunteered to move the wood from the barn to the site Mom chose in the garden for our bonfire. Grateful for the fresh air and the slightly warmer temperatures, I took longer doing this than was absolutely neces-sary. It was nearly dark when I came back in.

Mom had aired out the kitchen, and only the faint stink of cabbage and onion remained. While I'd been out, she had also made the dough for the hot cross buns, and the little mounds were now rising in a pan on the counter. They'd be ready to bake soon and their wonderful aroma would take care of any lingering vegetable smell. I went over to the pan, snitched a piece of dough, and popped it into my mouth. I loved unbaked dough almost as much as the final product.

"I saw that," she called after me as I went up the stairs.

I laughed and asked, "Saw what?"

"You know what."

Still laughing, I went into my room and stretched out across the bed with my head dangling off the other side. I couldn't procrastinate any longer. Tyler had called from Florida yesterday, and I hadn't called him back. I couldn't really believe he was somehow being manipulated by his gran, but that didn't mean I hadn't been thinking a lot about her treachery and the possibility that she was a danger to me or Mom. Ignoring my fear that he might hear something different in my voice, I hit the send button.

He answered right away. "Hi, Brigit! Great timing. I was about to call you."

"How are you?" I asked. "Did you get a tan already?"

"Actually, I got a little sunburned yesterday. So I kept my t-shirt on today."

"Ouch. So what've you been doing?"

"The weather's been great. We've been hanging out on the beach. There's a bunch of other high school kids staying with their families at the resort, so we've been playing volleyball. I took the sea kayak out this morning."

"Sounds like fun." I paused and then added, "I miss you."

"I miss you, too. I wish you were here. It would be a lot more fun if you were along. You must be keeping busy. Didn't you get my message yesterday?"

"Yes, I did. I'm sorry I didn't have a chance to call back. My mom's had me doing a bunch of things to get ready for the holiday." It was easier than I thought to skirt the real reason I'd been avoiding his calls.

"Easter?" Tyler asked. "I didn't think you celebrated Easter."

"No, Ostara's tomorrow. It's the spring equinox," I explained.

"Oh, so what do you do?"

Launching into an explanation of our Ostara traditions, I was happy it didn't feel weird to openly share things about the religion my mother practiced, and I guess, that I practiced, too. Tyler was so non-judgmental that I never worried he'd think my mom was a nut. Maybe his grandma had talked to him about the old ways, after all.

Tyler's only comment was about the bonfire. "That's cool," he said. "It's just too bad you have to get up so early to do it."

"Yeah, I know, but I'm planning to go back to bed afterwards."

We talked for at least an hour, and after we said our goodbyes, I thought how ridiculous I'd been to avoid talking to him. Feeling much happier, I allowed the smell of the fresh hot cross buns to draw me downstairs. Mom had criss-crossed half of them with white icing. I reached for one of those and ate it in four bites while standing at the counter.

"Yum, yum, yum," I mumbled and grabbed a second one.

Mom came back into the kitchen and put two of them on a plate for herself and warned, "Leave the unfrosted ones for tomorrow. I'll reheat them before I put the icing on. I heard you talking to Tyler. Is he having fun?"

"Yeah. Weather's great. He's been playing beach volleyball, and he got sunburned." I summarized our conversation while I poured a glass of milk.

"Sounds like a typical Florida vacation."

"Definitely beats the weather here."

"It's not so bad. It's warming up, and almost all the dirty old snow has melted. It'll be cold in the morning though, even with the bonfire. You'll want to wear clothes under your robe."

I choked, and milk almost came out my nose. "What?" I sputtered. "Are you saying I normally wouldn't be wearing clothes under the robe?"

She laughed. "Oh, did I forget to tell you that part? Sorry. When the weather's nice, most of us don't wear clothes under them."

I'm sure I had a disgusted expression on my face. "And, how do you know what other people *do or do not* wear under their robes?"

She chuckled. "Hmm, wouldn't you like to know?" Mom raised her eyebrows mischievously, but when she realized that I didn't share her amusement, she gave up with an exasperated, "Okay, fine. Most of the women end up getting ready together, and it's kind of hard not to notice."

"Gross," I said.

"Don't knock it until you try it." Mom laughed again.

As I thought ahead to tomorrow, a wave of nervousness came over me. This would be the first time Mom included me in an actual ritual. I was taking an enormous step, one that I wasn't sure I really wanted to take. What if I thought it was stupid or weird or – what if I didn't?

She was perceptive. "There's nothing to be anxious about. It's only a simple ceremony to welcome spring."

"Do I have to do anything?"

"No. I'll cast the circle and say a blessing, and you can answer 'make it so.' Very simple, really," she said.

I couldn't think of anything else to ask and started for my room, calling behind me. "See you at the crack of dawn."

"I'll wake you when it's time to get up."

Before getting ready for bed, I admired the robe my grandma had made for Mom. It was truly gorgeous. I laid it across my chair and traced some of the embroidered Celtic knots with my finger, feeling honored to wear something that was made with such loving hands. I sighed, wishing I felt more confident. Mom's reassurances had not eased my anxiety one bit.

I slept fitfully and kept looking at the clock to see if it was time to get up. Finally, when the sky was beginning to lighten, I gave up and got out of bed. I took off my pjs, and with my brain still foggy I nearly put my robe on right over my underwear. I laughed at how I had nearly embraced tradition accidentally. Wouldn't Mom have been surprised? I slipped into the jeans and sweater I had set out and was fastening the clasps on the robe when Mom came to wake me up.

"You're up. I am impressed." She nodded to emphasize her words. "I'll be ready in a few minutes. See you downstairs."

I waited in the kitchen for her and noticed that she had put kindling and matches and a few other items into a small basket. I recognized the piece of rose quartz and along with it three other stones in blue, dark green, and gold. The final item, a large container of salt, had me puzzled.

"Are you ready?" Mom asked, entering the kitchen with a swish of her robe.

Her excitement was as obvious in her voice as my reticence was in mine when I responded, "I guess so."

I followed her out the door to the center of the garden where I had stacked the bonfire wood. She set the basket on the ground, grabbed the salt container, and sprinkled a large circle around us. Taking the stones, she placed them just inside the ring of salt with yellow in the east, pink in the south, blue in the west, and green in the north, and said:

> *"East, South, West, North*
> *Blessed Goddess we call you forth.*
> *We cast the Circle to greet the power*
> *Of the new season's dawning hour."*

Being careful to keep her robe away she bent down to light the fire. Once the flames began to grow, she said, "Brightest fire, we light thee to welcome the return of the sun's warmth."

As she stood and held my hand the pink tinge of the sky was unmistakable. We raised our free hands toward the heavens, and Mom continued, "As the earth awakens from its slumber, Goddess, we ask for a fruitful growing season so that all may prosper upon your earth. May the rainfall be plentiful, and may the sun's rays be in perfect balance to make it thus."

The air around us began to hum with energy.

"Help us to open ourselves to spiritual growth as the dawn's first rays light our way. We ask these things humbly in the shadow of your power, from the land to the sea to the air and to the sun." Mom raised our clasped hands high and finished by saying, "Make it so."

I repeated, "Make it so." The words flowed from my mouth as though I'd spoken them thousands of times before. The sun sparkled on everything around us and a jolt ran through my entire body. Mom felt it, too. I heard her catch her breath, and she gripped my hand more tightly than before.

The energy in the air next to the bonfire seemed to coalesce into a shimmering wall. For a moment – just a moment – a flickering image of a low stone doorway appeared.

Mom gave a shocked cry and stepped back, releasing my hand. With a loud clap the doorway disappeared, but I knew I had seen it.

"What was that?" I asked. The strange electric feeling remained, making me very aware of every sound, sight, and smell around me. I felt whole and somehow interconnected to everything else at the same time. I breathed in the crisp, fresh morning air and stared into the fire, mesmerized by the dancing rhythm of each flame.

Mom's voice filled my head, *Whether she's chosen her path or not, the path has chosen her. She's the essence of the Tuatha, and her power is true if the portal opened for her.*

I turned to ask her what she meant, but before the question could form on my lips, I realized these had been her private thoughts. Comprehension washed over both of us. My gift had swept back into my life.

This time I would not be afraid.

Chapter Twenty-Four

I did *not* go back to bed after our bonfire ceremony. Instead, I felt surprisingly alert with leftover energy from whatever it was that just happened outside.

While Mom and I prepared a breakfast of scrambled eggs, fruit salad, and another helping of hot cross buns, neither of us said anything about it. Somehow I knew that it'd be better to be patient rather than pepper her with the questions that raced through my mind.

At first I couldn't hear what she was thinking, but then she began to come through loud and clear. She was surprised my ability came back with such a jolt, and she was amazed at the strength of the energy that flowed from me. Her pride was evident, but I caught an undercurrent of worry and maybe even fear. She was debating about whether she should tell me something. I kept catching the same phrase over and over again; *She opened the portal. She opened the portal.*

As soon as we sat down to eat, I could no longer contain myself. "What's a portal, and how did I open it?"

"Brigit, I don't understand how you opened it. I really don't. We're not supposed to open them. As guardians of the old ways, the Circle of Nine has always protected the portals to keep the sacred treasures of the original Tuatha de Danann hidden from those who would use them for evil."

"What – what are you talking about? Sacred Treasures?" I had a vague memory that in the tales of the Tuatha there'd been some enchanted weapons that had special powers, but that'd been fairytale talk. Things like that weren't real. My fork clattered to my plate with the realization that I hadn't thought the Tuatha were real until a few months before either.

"The Sacred Treasures are real?" I asked as my anxiety grew. It had never occurred to me to believe the rest of the tales I'd been told as a child.

Mom nodded and continued, "When the original Tuatha lost the battle to rule Ireland, they were banished to live in the mountains. They took their Sacred Treasures with them and to keep them from falling into the wrong hands, they were sealed away. We have protective spells in place that let us know if anyone attempts to get to them. We renew this protection at each celebration during the year."

"But what's a portal doing here in the United States? Aren't all the treasures hidden in Ireland?"

"Right, but a portal can be opened wherever important ley lines intersect. If a person had enough power, they could summon a portal and transport themselves back to Ireland using these lines of energy. They'd then be on the inside of the portals and able to hunt for the treasures."

"This is unbelievable." I wished I was having a very, very detailed dream but knew that this was just another great Tuatha heritage surprise. "Why isn't any of this in the book?"

Mom touched my hand. "This is one of the first things that you would learn, if you chose the path of the Tuatha. We've never written anything about the portals or the sacred treasures in our books. It's too dangerous even if the book is protected by a spell."

"Has anyone ever gotten through a portal?"

"Some have tried, but our protective wards have always stopped them. Just a few decades ago someone got dangerously close to summoning a portal right here. Ley lines intersect in our back yard, right where you saw the doorway today. Grandma moved here from Ireland to renew the protection and keep watch at this location. She never did find out who was attempting to get in."

"How could I summon a portal if I didn't even know something like that existed? It doesn't make any sense."

Mom didn't respond right away. She seemed to be weighing her words carefully before she spoke. "Even though you only opened the portal for a few seconds, I want you to understand you have something unique – something way beyond your ability to hear others' thoughts. When the rest of us began our training, we learned how skilled we might be with spell-making and other powers. Some of us found we had a natural talent and became quite proficient, and others found they had no talent at all. The rest of us fall somewhere in between. What we experienced today, Brigit, makes me believe you may have a greater power than we can predict at this point. I'm not saying this to pressure you. You need to make your own choice. I simply wanted to put this into perspective. Most of us do not have the hope of this sort of capability." She said this last sentence slowly and with reverence.

Part of me wanted to cover my ears to block out her words, but another part of me welcomed the acknowledgment of what I had begun to suspect. "I understand that I could inherit the same talent as Dervla. I mean, it's been generations, but we know traits can skip generations, right? But how can I have the power to do so much more than you or Grandma or anyone else in our family history?"

She took a deep breath before admitting, "You're only half Quinn, Brigit. You know all about my side of the family, but you don't know anything about your father's family. I'm sorry I've always avoided answering questions about him. The story I put in the book will show you how your father and I met and fell in love, but there's more. I never told you he was a lot like me. His family followed many of the old ways, too." She shuddered as she spoke. "He was special, very special." Her eyes had gotten that far away look again as she spoke. "You'll see soon enough."

"Don't talk about him like he's dead." I couldn't stand it when she referred to him in the past tense when my most secret desire was to meet him someday.

"I'm sorry. I don't mean to make it sound like he is. It still hurts a lot to imagine the life we could have had together if things had been different."

"What things?" I shouted. I tried to hear what she was thinking, but my anger kept me from focusing.

"You need to read my section of the book. I'll answer *anything* you want after that." She swallowed hard while making this promise. She seemed scared.

The air around me had an ominous weight, and I felt an irrational need to hurry upstairs to my room. As I stood to go, she grabbed my arm. "Come and talk to me when you are done."

The tingle of her icy grip on my arm seemed to transfer her nervousness to me, and as I climbed the stairs I absentmindedly massaged the spot to erase the feeling.

Rejecting the comfortable perch of my bed, I sat at my desk where I'd be more alert. I wanted to remember everything. I rubbed my sweaty palms on my jeans and stared down at the worn leather cover of the book. Mom freely shared stories about growing up, but she'd never really talked about herself after a certain point. I realized now that her stories left off when she was exactly my age – the age when Grandma gave her the book. I guessed she'd held back because her life after that age became too intertwined with the Tuatha and her training, which she wasn't allowed to share with me until now.

A deep breath calmed me enough to open to her page.

Celeste Quinn
June 25, 1992

How to do this, how to tell?
I write this now my fear to quell
Of how I fled into the night
Away from what I thought was right,
To save me and one tiny other
From an evil, dark with hunger.
Beware the signs, learn the lesson
You cannot trust every person.
Watch the scene unfold wholly,
If your gift makes you worthy.

✦

*C*eleste was thrilled to start her final semester of college at Ulster University in Derry. She'd already completed nearly all her requirements for a degree in history back home in the States. Her studies in Ireland would take care of the last few credits, and at the end of the term, she'd stay for the summer to study with different members of the Tuatha. Her mom had worked out an apprenticeship with three members of the Circle who lived in the northern part of Ireland – Lauren in Derry, Claire in Donegal, and Fionna on the remote Tory Island.

Right now, she lived with Lauren and her daughter Petra, also a student at Ulster. To celebrate completing their first week of classes Petra dragged Celeste out for a drink at the student pub. The place was full of a boisterous young crowd, and it took a few minutes before they found seats at the bar.

"The bartenders are really busy." Petra scanned the other side of the long bar and waved to catch someone's attention.

"Hello, Petra. Enjoying the end of the week?" the bartender asked.

"Definitely. The first week is always a killer," Petra answered. "Rowan, I'd like you to meet my friend Celeste. She's living with us while she goes to the university and studies with my mom. Celeste, this is Rowan Dunne."

Rowan's eyes lit up as he learned this information. "It's a pleasure to meet you, Celeste."

Celeste stared mutely at the handsome Irishman until Petra nudged her foot. "Oh," she said, "I'm sorry. Nice to meet you, too." Celeste extended her arm across the bar to shake his hand.

When their hands touched a tingle zinged up Celeste's arm. Rowan looked at her with surprise and then brushed it off by saying, "Sorry, so much static electricity this time of year."

Celeste wondered at his explanation but didn't challenge him.

"What can I get you two?" He asked.

"The local ale is really quite good and there's always Guinness if you like it," Petra explained.

Celeste shrugged, "I don't know much about beer. I'll just have whatever you order."

Rowan pulled the tap and filled two glasses for them. "A fine choice for a fine Irish lass and her friend."

"I'm a fine Irish lass, too," she corrected. "I just happen to live in the States."

This made Rowan laugh loudly. "You do have spirit, I'll give you that."

Rowan continued filling glasses up and down the bar. Celeste observed him as he worked and couldn't help admiring the sharp contrast of his light eyes and dark hair. He made small talk with Celeste whenever he wasn't busy.

"Rowan, are you from the area?" Celeste asked.

"No, I'm not. My da' and I moved here in November from County Wexford."

"Are you a student?"

Petra interrupted their exchange. "I should have explained. Rowan has the same sort of apprenticeship you have with the Tuatha."

"Really?" Celeste said. "You're one of us?"

"Not exactly. I was raised in a similar way, but I never had any real training or education. I know there's a lot more to learn."

"Is that why you moved here – to study?"

Rowan appeared embarrassed by the questioning. "In part. Where we lived there weren't many people like us, and there was a misunderstanding after Samhain." He hesitated before continuing. "My da' felt it was best to start over in a new place, a place more accepting of our way of life."

Celeste wondered what kind of misunderstanding would re-quire someone to move the entire length of a country, but she didn't pry. "So you live here in Derry?" Celeste asked, starting to hope they shared the same neighborhood.

"No. We have a small place out in the country near Strabane. Not far actually from Beltany, where your group celebrates Beltane."

"I was there when I was 15, but I don't really know my way around yet. Is it far from here?"

"Not too far. I drive in for work nearly every day."

He leaned over the bar closer to Celeste. "I'll be working tomorrow night, but I have Sunday night free. Would you like to go out for dinner? I promise we won't stay out too late if you have an early start on Monday."

Celeste was surprised by his invitation and even more surprised that she accepted so quickly. "Sure. That'd be great. It'll give me something fun to look forward to after a weekend of studying." She probably shouldn't have been so eager, but she was incredibly attracted to him.

Rowan walked away to serve other customers and once he was out of earshot, Petra said, "Aren't you the lucky one?"

Celeste agreed she was indeed lucky, and wished to herself that it was already Sunday night. "Oh, no," Celeste said suddenly. "Sunday is Imbolc or do you call it Brigid's Day here?"

"Brigid's Day usually," Petra shrugged. "Don't worry about it. Mum isn't planning anything special. Go out and have fun," she encouraged.

On Sunday when Rowan picked her up, Celeste was full of nervous excitement.

"I have a place in mind for dinner, if you don't mind a little drive."

"Sounds fine to me."

As they drove out of town and into the country, they fell into easy conversation for the half hour or so it took to get to their destination which was an enormous, stone building called Magnus Lodge. Inside the entrance hall, a fire was roaring in the big stone fireplace, and a hostess led them to a wood paneled dining room that had a medieval feel with scarred, wide plank floors, exposed stone walls, and iron wall sconces holding dozens of candles.

"This place is really interesting," Celeste whispered to Rowan.

"I'm glad you like it. Wait until you try the food."

He was right. The food was excellent; Celeste thoroughly enjoyed her salad, salmon, and potatoes. Against her better judgment, she let Rowan talk her into ordering dessert with her coffee and now stared at an enormous serving of sticky toffee pudding. "I'll never be able to eat all of this," she groaned but picked up her fork to take a bite. "Oh, that's phenomenal," she proclaimed once she tasted it.

"See." Rowan nodded. "If you can't finish it, I'll help." He smiled at her as he dug into his own serving.

Celeste ended up pushing half of her dessert across the table toward him. "That's it for me."

They continued to trade bits of their life histories, and it seemed natural when Rowan grasped her hand in his. She felt the same jolt of energy as when he'd touched her the night they first met, only this time he didn't try to pretend it was static. He smiled and asked, "So you didn't leave a boyfriend behind in the States?"

His boldness amused Celeste. "No, I don't have a boyfriend back home, and it would make me a not-so-nice person accepting this date with you if I did."

"I suppose so." Rowan agreed. "You're so beautiful that I find it hard to believe that you wouldn't have someone special."

"Nope. I am definitely not dating anyone seriously, at least not yet," she flirted, figuring two could play this game. The blush that reddened his face made her like him even more.

They didn't say anything else for a moment or two, and then Rowan sat up straighter, "I have an idea of a place we might go since it is Imbolc. Do you need to get back, or can you stay out a little later?" he asked.

Celeste hated for the evening to end and happily agreed to anything that would extend their time together.

"So, where are we going?" Celeste asked when they were out on the main road.

"This might seem a bit strange, but trust me."

For some reason Celeste did trust him already, and when he stretched out his hand to her again, she immediately took it. A few minutes later he pulled to the side of the road and parked.

"Are we there?" Celeste asked looking around. It was dark out, but the moon was providing enough light that she could see they were surrounded by farm fields on one side and a small wood on the other.

"It's good you're wearing boots. We have a short walk."

Celeste got out of the car with him and laughed nervously. "This is like every bad horror movie I've ever seen. You know the kind where you want to tell the girl not to go into the forest with someone she just met."

He came around to her side of the car and stood very close to her, his breath warm on her face. "Are you scared of me, Celeste?"

She tilted up so she could see his face clearly. "No, I'm not scared of you. Should I be?"

"I can assure you I'm not harboring any murderous impulses. It's my other desires that might be a worry at the moment." He chuckled but didn't back away.

Celeste reached up to touch his cheek, and he grabbed her hand, kissing the inside of her palm. He lowered his hand but didn't let go of hers until they reached the back of the car. "Let me grab a couple of things first." He opened the trunk and pulled out a lumpy bundle and a plaid blanket.

"Oh, we're definitely entering horror movie territory now," Celeste commented with a wave toward the mysterious bundle.

He laughed and shut the trunk, pointing to the tree-lined side of the road. "The path should be over here somewhere." They walked through the grass and found the path easily enough. It was dark in the woods, but the walkway was well-groomed and covered with gravel. They crunched along without talking and came out on the other side of the trees.

"Oh," Celeste exclaimed. "I know where we are now." The tall hill in front of them was suddenly familiar. "Beltany. You've brought me to Beltany." She jumped up and down, unable to hide her glee. "I love this place."

Rowan smiled at her enthusiasm. "I'm glad you don't think this is strange."

"No. It's perfect." She put her hand back into his, and they climbed to the top. "I was fifteen the last time I was here," she offered. "It's sort of a tradition in the Tuatha to bring your daughters here for Beltane when they turn fifteen."

"So this is a special place for you."

"Yes, definitely." The standing stones were like sentinels in the moonlight, and Celeste walked through them into the shadows they made.

"Come over here." Rowan pulled her along to the altar stone. He laid the blanket out on the flat rock and set his bundle on top. "I thought we might have our own Imbolc ceremony tonight," he said as he untied the bundle and pulled out a bottle of wine and an opener, but no glasses.

"Are we drinking straight from the bottle?" Celeste joked.

"Definitely not; that would be so uncivilized," he said with fake disdain. He hoisted himself up onto the altar, sitting on one side. "Come up here with me." He offered his arm for leverage as she climbed up. They sat facing each other with the wine between them.

"So you planned all this in advance? I mean, you don't go around with bottles of wine in your car, do you?" Celeste asked.

"I wasn't sure if you'd say yes, but I wanted to be prepared in case you did. Is that awful?" Rowan stared at her intently, waiting for her answer.

"No," Celeste finally said. "No, I don't think it's awful. I think it's hopeful. I like that."

He smiled in response and reached into the bundle to pull out the last two items: a single goblet and a ritual dagger or athame, as it was properly called. It surprised Celeste that he had these items with him. This was much more than the continuation of a romantic date. Celeste picked up the goblet examining the strange symbols on it as best she could in the moonlight. She traced one of the symbols with her fingertip, feeling its raised outline.

"Runes," Rowan explained.

"Ah, I've heard of them but I don't know much about them." Celeste said.

Celeste continued to hold the goblet, and Rowan guided her finger to a rune that looked like the "greater than" symbol used in math. "This one's called Ken. It symbolizes fire, knowledge, and passion."

Celeste set down the goblet and stared at him. He opened the wine, and when he began to pour his hand shook, sending some sloshing over the side of the goblet. He laughed at his clumsiness and wiped his hand on the edge of the blanket.

He took a deep breath before dipping the athame into the goblet and held them both up high and said,

"Bless us on this Imbolc Eve.
God and Goddess we believe
That through your power the winter sun
Will gradually heed the season's turn
And warm the fertile soil so
The new seeds planted there will grow.
Grant this quarter change anew,
And bless us in all we do."

Celeste watched him with an odd sort of feeling, probably because she'd never seen a man giving a ceremonial blessing before. When he finished speaking, he set down the athame and took a drink before offering some to her. He didn't let go of the goblet, and she wrapped her hands around his as she tilted it to her lips. His hands felt warmer than she expected them to be in the chilly night air, and the same electric tingle seemed to move between them.

He held her gaze as he leaned in and kissed her tentatively, barely brushing his lips against hers. Celeste deepened the kiss, tasting the wine they shared, and brought her hands up to his shoulders to steady herself. He gently held her face in his hands and kissed each eyelid before pulling back to look at her. "You're wonderful, Celeste."

"I'm not sure what's happening here, but this feels so right – you feel so right." Celeste stared back.

"I know I'm going to sound like some sort of idiot for saying this on our first date." He shook his head. "Promise not to laugh."

When she nodded her assent, he asked, "Do you believe in destiny or fate or anything like that?"

She thought for a moment and answered honestly, hoping Rowan wouldn't be disappointed that she didn't believe in a magical life plan. "I'm not much of a believer in fate. I believe opportunities are placed before you, and you have to decide which path to take. People make their own destiny."

He didn't challenge her answer and offered a toast to "making their own destiny." They shared more kisses – all the while the strange energy crackled between them.

Although she was warm in so many ways, Celeste couldn't help shivering in the chilly air. Rowan noticed and said, "I'm sorry. I should have planned better for the cold. I'll warm you up." He moved everything off of the blanket and wrapped it around her shoulders. He held his hands out over the center of the altar and uttered something in Gaelic that Celeste did not understand. A small fire sparked to life between them.

Celeste was dumfounded. "Rowan, you . . . but there's no wood . . . how did you?" She quit trying to find the right words and stared at him with her mouth open.

He grinned at her expression. "Cool trick, huh?"

Celeste nodded slowly. "Very cool trick."

"My da' taught me that one when I was about thirteen. He was as shocked as you that I got it right on my first try. It comes in handy," he explained, as though it were a perfectly ordinary thing to conjure up a bit of fire without fuel or matches.

Celeste was no stranger to spell-making, but she'd never seen anyone do anything like that. She felt somewhat honored that he would trust her with this knowledge about himself.

"Warming up?" he asked.

"Much better. Thanks," she said.

They sat like that together for a long while until Rowan said, "It is getting late. I should take you home." He repacked the bundle and helped Celeste off the altar stone. He wrapped his arm around her shoulders, holding the blanket in place as they made their way down the path to the car.

It was after midnight when they pulled up in front of her house. They sat in the idling car for a few minutes and said their goodbyes.

"I'll call you this week, and we can make plans to do something. Maybe we can have lunch one day." He leaned across the seat and said intensely, "I hate to say goodnight." His kiss made her just as sorry the evening had to come to an end.

CHAPTER TWENTY-FIVE

*R*owan called as he promised, and they saw each other nearly
every day that week and the week after and the week after
that. They were amazed, as were the people around them, at how
close they became in such a short period of time, spending as much
time together as they could despite Rowan's busy work schedule
and Celeste's demanding course work. They both took a weekly
Tuatha class with Lauren, too. It was interesting but challenging
as Lauren's specialty was healing with botanical ingredients mixed
with a little spell-making. Celeste enjoyed the knowledge she was
gaining, but thought the best part was that she and Rowan were
learning together, although his skills were far more advanced. He
mastered each spell Lauren taught on the first try.

Before she knew it, the semester was half over and it was spring
break, which combined nicely with Ostara, the spring equinox.
Lauren invited all of the Tuatha in the area to join her at a local
park where she led the Ostara ritual at dawn. When Lauren invited
Rowan, he asked if it would be okay if he brought his father. Rowan
explained that his da' would love to participate in a ceremony on
such an important ritual day.

Celeste thought Lauren hesitated before she said, "Of course. Please tell your father he's welcome to join us."

"That will give me the chance to finally meet him," Celeste said.

"You haven't met him?" Lauren asked. "I assumed you would have by now."

Celeste shrugged. "No. Every time I've been to Rowan's house his dad hasn't been home."

They drove to the park through the morning fog and walked into the open space where everyone was gathering. The mist hovered near the ground, obscuring people's feet, making it look as though everyone was floating. Celeste counted eleven members of the Tuatha, including herself, Petra, and Lauren. Celeste wore the robe her mother had made her for her first Beltane festival. She was glad she had brought it. Everyone else was in robes except for Rowan and his father, who were walking toward the group. Celeste was stunned by how closely they resembled each other. They were the same height and build, and their hair was the same wavy, dark brown. When they were close enough, Rowan made introductions.

"Da', allow me to present Celeste. Celeste, meet my father, Malachi Dunne," he said formally.

Celeste smiled and extended her hand. "It is so nice to finally meet you." She noticed one difference immediately. Malachi's eyes were much darker than Rowan's. In fact, they looked nearly black in the faint light. His large hand closed around hers in a tight grip. Celeste fought the desire to wince, keeping the smile frozen on her face.

"So this is the fair Celeste. It is a great pleasure to meet you. Rowan has, of course, told me much about you already." The warmth of Malachi's deep baritone voice did not match the coolness of his gaze. Celeste could not describe the eerie feeling that washed over her, but she knew she did not like the way he stared at her.

Celeste was saved from having to make small talk when Lauren beckoned them over and arranged everyone into a circle. Although there were more women present than men, Lauren tried to distribute the sexes as evenly as possible. Celeste found herself positioned between Rowan and his father.

They took a few steps back, enlarging the circle, and joined hands. As Lauren began the blessing, Celeste felt the familiar jolt of Rowan's energy with her left hand and was relieved Malachi now held her right hand more loosely.

Celeste focused on Lauren's lilting voice as she offered the ritual Ostara blessing. When she was done, the group rotated the circle three times to symbolize the never ending rotation of the wheel of the year. By the last revolution, Celeste felt a dizzy rush. When Rowan and Malachi grabbed her more firmly to keep her upright, a wave of dread descended over her vision like a black cloud. From far away she heard a voice say, *"Ashes, ashes, we all fall down."*

Gradually, the darkness lifted, and she found herself laying on the damp grass with Rowan's concerned face about two inches from hers.

"What am I doing down here?" she asked.

"I think you got a little too dizzy." Rowan was smiling at her indulgently. "Are you okay?"

"I'm fine." Celeste struggled to stand up quickly, annoyed with herself for looking like a foolish child. Everyone was clustered around which embarrassed her even more.

"Let me help you." Rowan offered his hand and pulled her up.

Lauren asked, "Dizzy spell over?"

"I guess that's what it was. Sorry to disrupt everything."

"No need to apologize," Lauren assured her quietly and then addressed the whole group. "Everyone's invited back to our house for breakfast."

They began to disperse, and Celeste turned toward Rowan, who was talking intently with his dad. Their facial expressions appeared serious, almost angry. "Everyone's going back to Lauren's. Are you coming?" Celeste interrupted.

Rowan glanced back at his dad for a moment before answering. "I'm sorry. I need to do something this morning. I'll come over later."

"Are you arguing?" Celeste asked.

"It's nothing. I'll see you later." Rowan dismissed her abruptly.

Confused by this, Celeste hurried to catch up with Lauren and Petra, her robe billowing out behind her as she ran. She slid into the backseat, slightly out of breath.

"I almost left without you. I thought you'd be riding with Rowan," Lauren said.

"Aren't Rowan and Malachi coming over for breakfast?" Petra asked.

"No, I guess not," Celeste replied, disappointed.

Rowan refused to tell her what he'd been arguing about with his dad when she asked that afternoon. He brushed it off saying, "It was nothing, really."

"It seemed like more than that." She frowned at him.

"You worry far too much." He kissed her, distracting her from asking more questions.

Celeste let him have his way and changed topics. "What did you think of the Circle this morning?"

"I thought it was a fine way to begin the season, but I can't wait for Beltane in a few weeks. Da' took me to the festival on Calton Hill in Edinburgh when I was thirteen. It was too big – really overwhelming. I'm looking forward to something smaller and more intimate." His voice dropped low on his last words, and he squeezed Celeste's hand.

She smiled at him but warned, "It's not like we'll be alone. At least a hundred people were there when I went. Lauren mentioned the other day that it's gotten even bigger since then."

"I'm sure we'll be able to find some privacy somewhere," he assured her, rubbing his thumb along the edge of her hand.

"We'll see," she replied in a breezy voice, trying to lighten the conversation.

He smiled and shifted his position on the couch so he was sitting even closer to her. His expression changed. "Celeste, I'm serious. I want to be with you – completely. Beltane would be the perfect time. It's a festival honoring the fertility of the earth after all."

Celeste felt her cheeks turning red and got up to shut the door to the lounge. She sure didn't want Lauren or Petra overhearing this conversation. When she sat back down, she didn't know what to say.

He pushed her hair back from her face and cupped her cheeks, saying, "Celeste, I've fallen in love with you. I want to be with you, always."

His declaration of love wasn't a complete surprise, but Celeste didn't expect to feel such intense elation. A wave of happiness flowed through her, bringing tears to her eyes. She reached up and covered his hands with her own. "I love you, too." With her emotions so close to the surface she bubbled with laughter while the tears streamed down her cheeks. He laughed with her and kissed the joyful tears from her cheeks.

They never finished the conversation about Beltane, and in the coming weeks neither one of them brought it up. Celeste wanted to be with him, but she wanted their first time to be special, and no matter how romantic it sounded, sneaking off into the woods was bound to be – well – less than comfortable. She knew she should say something, but she didn't know how to begin.

Three days before Beltane, Phoebe arrived. Celeste was struck by how much she had missed her mom when they hugged at the airport. No one gave her any grief when she skipped classes the next day. Celeste was glad to have the time to catch up. Everyone else was simply grateful for the extra pair of hands in the kitchen as they prepared food for the festival.

That night Rowan came over for dinner and met her mother for the first time. Celeste had been worried about her mom's opinion of him, but she shouldn't have been.

After he left late in the evening, her mother declared, "Celeste, you've got a winner there. He's quite the gentleman, and I can tell he really loves you." Celeste was startled by the level of emotion on her mom's face. "If you could see how he looks at you." She moved her hand over her heart. "You are one lucky girl," she finally said.

The day of Beltane Eve, April 30, was beautiful and sunny as members of the Tuatha arrived from near and far. Celeste enjoyed watching her mom greet her life-long friends and work with them in tandem as they orbited gracefully around each other, setting up their campsites near the Beltany stone circle. The colorful rows of festive, medieval-style tents immediately transported the scene to a different era.

"Until a few days ago, I didn't even know people replicated these old styles. It's like going back in time," Rowan commented.

"It does make it feel like we are a world away from our modern lives. I love it," Celeste said, sighing and leaning into him.

They pivoted together toward the stone circle. The wood for the bonfire had already been placed in the center of the stones, and nearby lay a long poplar log, stripped of its branches and waiting to become their maypole the next morning. Ribbons would be attached to one end before it was turned upright and slid into the hole in the ground.

Celeste pitched in with the remaining work and, when she was done, Rowan was not around and no one had seen him for some time.

The Circle of Nine congregated in the main tent and changed into their robes. Celeste did the same. When she emerged, Rowan was back, wearing a robe of his own. It was dark blue with very little decoration, only a green line at the hem and cuffs of the wide sleeves. He looked at Celeste smugly. She smiled and voiced her observation. "You're quite proud about something, aren't you?"

"And don't you want to know why?" he asked with an air of mystery in his voice.

"I assume because you are dressed so stunningly for our celebration. You're very handsome," she complimented.

"Thank you," he replied, continuing to look as though he had a secret.

"What are you up to?" Celeste squinted at him. "I can tell you're up to something."

"You'll find out soon enough," he teased.

The sun was nearing the horizon, and Lauren led the column of nine women out of the tent and to the stone circle. The altar stone was magnificent with mounds of white flowering branches draping off the sides. The silver chalice and athame gleamed in the last rays of sunlight. Celeste was reminded of a much more private moment at that altar a few weeks ago and glanced at Rowan.

His eyes sparkled when he looked down at her. "It's a little more crowded than the last time we were here." Rowan held tight to Celeste's hand as everyone squeezed in as close to the altar as possible.

Her mom's face shone with excitement as she stood next to Lauren and the other women. Lauren held the goblet and athame in her hands and, following the tradition of the ages, dipped the dagger into the goblet and began the blessing. The crowd was hushed into silence, listening to every word.

"Goddess of summer, bless the fertile earth
And all her creatures both male and female.
Place the dark days of winter behind us
And let the sun, earth, wind, and water
Combine to give us a bountiful harvest
So that all may live well until Beltane next.
Goddess, grant us unity in love and harmony for all days."

When she was done they answered in unison, "Make it so." The other women in the Circle followed Lauren to the middle of the stones where she lit the bonfire. The women chanted and circled the fire nine times. Leaving Rowan behind, Celeste came forward with other young women to form a larger circle around the nine. Rowan joined the next ring which was all young men. People continued to form circles, alternating between men and women, completely filling the space between the roaring bonfire and the stone perimeter.

As they rotated around the fire, more than one hundred voices blended together in a magnificent anthem honoring this celebration of life. After an hour or so, people would come and go, to eat and rest, but the ritual dance of praise did not stop. The cadence changed as a new chant or song began, but the lilt of harmonious voices created a potent backdrop for the gathering.

Celeste had not taken a break until Rowan pulled her free and into the relative darkness outside the stones. She was breathing heavily, and her face was damp from exertion and the warmth of the fire.

"Thanks. It's time for a break," she gasped out.

"You're gorgeous out there with your hair flying." He hugged her close and whispered in her ear. "I want you . . . I want to be with you always."

She tried pulling back slightly to look at him when she spoke, but he wouldn't let her. He held her close and covered her mouth in a passionate kiss. He'd never kissed her with such wildness, and she forgot what she was going to say.

Without letting go of her, he said, "Come with me."

She knew what he had in mind from their earlier conversation, and she was torn. She wasn't afraid of making this sort of commitment, but she wanted it to be perfect. "Rowan I'm not sure we should . . ."

He cut her off by saying gently, "Please, Celeste, trust me." His voice was pleading but with a layer of excitement that made her wonder what was going on.

Celeste allowed herself to be led away from the stones and encampment. She kept stealing glances at Rowan as they walked, but he said nothing more. After a few minutes they approached a small copse of trees. Rowan held the branches up so she could enter first. The branches dropped back into place behind them, cutting off their visibility from anyone who might wander this way. Celeste gasped in surprise, not sure if what she was seeing was even real. It looked like a fairytale.

The trees sparkled with miniature lights like hundreds of fireflies inhabited the branches. Their glow showcased the most adorable deep purple tent. It was in the medieval style like the others but much, much smaller. Perfect for two people. Two torches flanked the path to the entrance which was decorated with an archway of woven branches and hundreds of spring flowers. She could smell them from where they stood at least ten feet away.

"Oh, Rowan. You did this for me?" Celeste was in awe of the romantic oasis he created.

"Do you like it?"

"Do I like it? I love it. I love you. What a wonderful thing to do." Celeste hugged him with all of her strength.

"I love you. I wanted to make this absolutely perfect."

Celeste thought he was referring to their physical union until he dropped to one knee and took her hands in his. He looked up at her and with his voice husky with emotion asked, "Celeste Quinn, will you marry me?"

Celeste stared at him for a few seconds, completely stunned. Her heart soared at the idea of being his wife, being with him forever. She smiled and answered, "Yes, Rowan, I would be honored to be your wife."

He grabbed her as he got up and spun her around in happiness. Reaching into his pocket, he presented her with a black velvet jewelry box.

Celeste opened it slowly, wanting to savor the moment and gasped again. A beautiful oval diamond surrounded by small rubies glinted in the torch light. The silver band was intricately engraved, and she examined it closely. She recognized the rune symbol Ken which represented passion, but she didn't know the others.

Rowan explained. "This one is Wunjo for the joy you bring me, this one is Yr for the trust we have in each other, and this one is Ing for the family I hope we will someday have." He held her left hand and slid the ring on her finger.

She tilted her hand up, admiring its beauty and said, "Rowan, I couldn't have asked for anything more meaningful."

He began to pull her toward the tent but stopped under the archway of branches. The scent of flowers was heady at this proximity . . . almost overpowering. She didn't understand why they stopped but waited for Rowan to explain.

"Have you heard of hand-fasting?" he asked.

"Yes. It's the traditional pagan engagement, right? I know some people put the ritual into their modern marriage ceremony, too."

Rowan nodded in agreement and touched the ring on her finger. "I know that we are properly engaged, but what would you say to being hand-fasted as well?"

She couldn't believe she was engaged to begin with, and for him to want to add such a personal touch made the whole moment more than she could handle. Tears slid down her cheeks, and she struggled to speak. "That would be . . . really, really special."

Rowan reached into his other pocket and pulled out a fine braided rope made from four different strands of ribbon. They linked left and right hands creating a cross with their arms. The slim rope came to life, sliding from his grip and winding its way around their wrists. Celeste gasped and nearly pulled her hands away in shock.

Rowan wouldn't let go and assured her, "It's okay."

Her heart began to calm as she looked into his eyes, and he continued speaking. "Celeste, this circle represents the infinity of my love for you and my promise to be united with you always.

I've chosen white to symbolize air so that our union will always be filled with spirituality;

Blue for fidelity, so that our union may be steadfast and unbroken;

Red symbolizing fire, so our union may be filled with passion;

And yellow to symbolize the enduring warmth of our love.

I ask the Goddess to bless our union and protect us always."

Celeste's voice was barely a whisper when she sealed the blessing with her words. "Make it so."

Their hands were intertwined with the colorful ribbon and the loose ends knotted themselves together. Celeste was stunned but knew better than to ask how this was possible because, after all, with Rowan's skill, anything seemed possible.

Rowan bent down to kiss her gently, and with their hands still bound by the ribbons of promise, they entered the tent together.

The next morning the song of the birds woke Celeste long before she wanted to be up. A string of lights sparkled above them inside the tent. Celeste sighed with contentment as she turned on her side to look at Rowan. He was sprawled next to her breathing deeply with the blanket covering his lower half.

Celeste couldn't believe it was May Day at Beltany, and she was now an engaged woman. She couldn't wait to show her mom the ring, and tell her how romantic Rowan had been with everything, especially the hand-fasting. Last night, they had carefully slid their hands out of the loop of ribbon, and she had wound it around her wrist three times for safekeeping. Her mom would appreciate that symbolism as much as she had. But first Celeste was up for some morning mischief. She stepped back into the robe she so quickly shed the night before, and stuck her head outside the tent. The torches had long gone out, but the pale light of dawn made its way through the trees so she could see where she stepped. She left the trees, walking a few feet into the meadow and squatted down to gather up plants that were wet with dew. Careful not to shake them dry, she went back into the tent and sat cross-legged next to Rowan.

She leaned over and shook the dew onto his face and suppressed her laughter as he batted at the droplets in his sleep. She did it again, and he sat all the way up, confused by the wetness. She laughed out loud.

"Why is my face all wet?" he asked.

She held up the leaves. "It's the May Day dew. You'll be gorgeous forever now."

Her amusement was contagious, and he laughed as he wiped his face with his hand. "Your turn," He said and lunged for the leaves and shook the remaining droplets onto her face before gathering her into his arms.

They didn't make their reappearance until much later in the morning, when they caused quite a stir as they announced their engagement to Celeste's mother and everyone else within earshot.

"Oh, let me see," her mother crooned and grabbed Celeste's hand to look at the ring.

Celeste described the beautiful setting Rowan created and explained the hand-fasting blessing, holding up her wrist decorated with the braided loop. She did not say anything about the rest of the night, keeping those details to herself.

Petra sighed. "Aren't you the most wonderful romantic? I wish you had a brother."

Celeste's mom gave Rowan a big hug. "Congratulations. I know you'll take good care of her."

"We'll take good care of each other," Celeste corrected and grabbed Rowan's hand.

They looked around for Rowan's dad and found him sitting on the grass with a few others. They shared their good news, and his dad got up to offer his congratulations.

He shook Rowan's hand and pulled him in for a bear hug. Turning to Celeste, Malachi kissed both of her cheeks and said, "I couldn't have hoped for a more wonderful daughter-in-law."

Celeste didn't know what it was about him, but the warmth of his words never matched the coolness she saw in his eyes.

Rowan and Celeste enjoyed the rest of the May Day celebration together, receiving numerous congratulations as news of their engagement made its way around the encampment.

Celeste couldn't believe she was so lucky to have found a man like Rowan – someone who understood her way of life and even excelled at it. She was truly fascinated by the depth of his powers and humbled by a skill level she could never hope to attain herself. She probably should have been disconcerted by his great abilities, but she knew his heart was good.

After Beltane, Celeste's mom stayed a few days before returning to the States. Celeste spent as much time with her as possible, only attending her most essential classes. She would have been happy to skip everything, except exams were approaching, and she didn't like the idea of ending her college career with less than decent grades.

With her mom's plane barely in the air Celeste launched herself into a marathon study session with Petra. Exam week was as brutal as she expected, but the relief of finally being done was worth the hard work. She mailed her transcript to the university back home so they could finalize her degree work and issue her diploma.

All the studying and exams were hard on Rowan, too. Celeste was only able to see him sporadically before she moved to Claire's in Donegal for the next phase of her training. She'd be staying there through June and part of July to learn the history of the Tuatha. She was grateful Donegal was close enough so Rowan could visit as frequently as his work schedule would allow.

As the Summer Solstice approached, Rowan invited her to a celebration his dad was organizing on the coast of the Inishowen Peninsula in the northern part of County Donegal. Celeste agreed immediately, eager to do some exploring of the nearby ancient sites and spend some uninterrupted time with Rowan.

That same week, Celeste realized that in the chaos of moving to Claire's house and her excitement over her engagement, she had lost track of time. She checked and rechecked the calendar, unable to believe she'd missed the date without noticing. Her period was very late.

They'd been careful the night they'd been together, but had thrown caution to the wind that morning after. It had been a risk, but given the commitment they'd just made to marry, she was not as cautious as she would otherwise have been. Celeste needed to be sure and was relieved when she was able to slip down to the chemist shop for a test kit without having to explain herself. She waited the requisite minutes perched on the edge of the tub, staring at the indicator strip which gradually changed to a most definite plus sign.

Celeste was surprised at her reaction as her heart fluttered with the joy she felt to be having a baby with Rowan. She touched the rune symbol for family on her engagement ring, hoping he'd really meant it when he had it engraved. Celeste planned to tell him the minute he arrived to pick her up for the solstice.

Unfortunately, when Rowan pulled into the drive the next day, Malachi was riding with him, and there was no opportunity for a private moment on the trip northward to Inishowen. As they bumped over the narrow roads near their coastal destination, Celeste felt quite sick to her stomach. She didn't know if it could be morning sickness in the middle of the afternoon or if she had spent too much time in the car. She did her best to regain some comfort in the backseat and put her hands over her belly, wondering how long it would be before she started to show. A particularly bad bump jolted her out of her reverie. She looked up and was met by Malachi's cool gaze, which went from her face and down to her hands on her stomach and back again. Celeste assumed he understood the meaning of this motherly gesture because his eyes had at first widened, then narrowed as a sly smile spread across his face. It was beyond creepy, and she looked away. She was angry Rowan was not the first to know and silently seethed for the last few miles of the trip.

She jumped out quickly when they came to a stop. Celeste was glad to distance herself from Malachi and get some fresh air, although it did little to alleviate her nausea.

"Are you okay?" Rowan's concern was immediate.

"I'm a little sick to my stomach. I'm sure I'll be fine if I lie down for a few minutes."

Rowan hurried to set up the tent so she'd have a place to rest. The cliff they were on provided a wonderful view of the sea but was incredibly windy. She held her hair back from her face, noticing Malachi move from person to person. Celeste was surprised to witness these enthusiastic greetings, as she'd only seen Malachi at the Tuatha gatherings where he was a relative newcomer. Here he seemed to be treated with an inexplicable reverence.

When Rowan was done with the tent, Celeste expected they'd have a few moments alone so she could tell him her news, but he didn't stay, explaining, "I'm going down to the beach to help set up for tonight's ceremony."

"Tonight? But the solstice celebration is always at dawn."

"We'll greet the dawn here on top of the cliff, but we celebrate tonight down on the beach. It's a celebration of contrasts – darkness and light, life and death. I'll be back soon."

Celeste wondered what he was talking about. The solstice did celebrate light and life, but she didn't understand his reference to the opposites, particularly his mention of death. Celeste didn't dwell on it for too long, because she nodded off almost immediately.

She slept for hours and awoke groggily when the tent flap was pulled back, recognizing Rowan's build in the dim light.

"There you are," she said warmly.

But the voice that answered her was unmistakably Malachi's. "How are you doing?"

Celeste tensed, becoming instantly awake. His nearness felt invasive. Although his question was innocuous, she was a little scared of him and struggled with her simple reply. "I'm fine. Where is Rowan?"

"He's on the beach. You should join us if you feel up to it," Malachi offered as the perfect host.

"No. I think I'll wait here for Rowan." Celeste did not want to go anywhere with Malachi and wished he'd leave.

A moment passed as he stared at her with his cold eyes, and a hard edge invaded his previously smooth voice. "I know your secret."

"As soon as I have a moment alone with Rowan, I'm going to tell him. Please don't tell him before I do," Celeste begged.

He didn't respond to her plea, but shifted positions, eliminating the space between them. Celeste saw the fanatical gleam in his eyes and tried to shift away, but there was no room to maneuver. "This child will greatly please our lord," he hissed. Placing his hands on her abdomen, he began speaking in a tongue she didn't recognize, intoning the same phrase over and over again. "*Veni ad me in obscuro patre.*"

Paralyzed by the feeling of dread that accompanied his strange words, she stared at his face as it shifted into a hideous demonic mask. "Noooo," she screamed closing her eyes tightly against the revolting sight.

When she dared to look again, he was gone, and the cold sweat of fear beaded on her lip as she attempted to catch her breath. She needed to find Rowan right away and tentatively poked her head out into the night air. The entire campsite appeared deserted, and she listened carefully, hoping to hear some conversation or laughter or anything approaching normalcy. The only noise was the wind whipping against the tents.

Shoving aside her fear, Celeste walked toward the edge of the cliff until she could see the beach below. The bonfire was burning brightly, and the shadows of people flickered in the light. She began her descent down the path and was nearly to the sand before she could hear the voices chanting. She trusted her intuition to remain hidden as she crept closer and the words became clear.

"Power of the demon rise.
We call your darkness from the skies
Of blackest night, of dread intent,
Let us be your implement."

The words of dark magic – forbidden magic – stunned her. This couldn't be right. Celeste frantically looked for Rowan in the group, hoping she wouldn't find him. Everyone looked so much alike with their dark robes and hoods pulled up. She had no choice but to wait and watch.

The group appeared to be following the lead of one tall figure. Celeste thought this must be Malachi given the reverence with which he'd been treated earlier. The chanting stopped, and Malachi seemed to be speaking, but his words were too low for Celeste to discern. The throng pushed in toward him with their arms outstretched. The person in front of Malachi held a chalice, and Malachi held a dagger. In a blur of movement, he grabbed one of the outstretched hands and held it fast while he drew the blade of the dagger across the skin of the open palm. The person screamed in pain, and Celeste could not tear her eyes away as the blood dripped into the cup.

When Malachi had what he needed from the unwitting victim, he pushed the hand away from the rim of the chalice. Those in front of him shifted out of his way so he could approach the edge of the bonfire. In that instant his robe was illuminated by the flames, and Celeste's heart nearly stopped. The robe wasn't black as she thought; it was dark blue with green trim on the sleeves. It was Rowan's robe. The leader wasn't Malachi. It was Rowan. Her Rowan!

Betrayal swamped her soul, and she nearly cried out to him, but fear caused the words to stick in her throat. She couldn't believe she misjudged him so badly. Instinct told her to run. She flew up the path and into the campsite. A sob escaped her as she tore into their tent, looking for her purse. She was scared for herself and for the baby and knew she had to get away. "Damn it! Where is it?" she screeched in her panic.

She hoped she'd left it in the car and ran to where it was parked, wrenching open the door. The bell started dinging, and the light went on like a dangerous beacon. Leaning in, she spied her purse on the floor of the backseat and grabbed it. She was about to flee on foot when the dinging registered with her. It was the sound a car made to let you know your keys were still in the ignition. So far she'd avoided driving on the other side of the road, but she wasn't going to let that hold her back now. Celeste jumped in and spitting gravel behind her, roared down the road.

At first she just drove, not thinking about where she was going, but when she neared the city limits of Derry, she decided Lauren and Petra's house would be the best option. Celeste examined the road signs, trying to remember the way to their house, when an outline of an airplane came into view on the sign in front of her. She changed her mind in an instant and careened across all three lanes to make the airport exit, relieved she always carried her passport and credit card with her. It would be morning before the terminal opened for the day, and she could buy a ticket, so she pulled into long-term parking to wait out her final hours in Ireland.

Celeste knew she was doing the right thing even as she lowered her head to the steering wheel and began to cry. She needed the safety of home. They both did.

Chapter Twenty-Six

I echoed Mom's sobs, mourning the image I had created of my perfect father. The father who I hoped would one day show up like a knight in shining armor and be there for me – forever. He didn't exist, not the way I imagined. My dad was *not* a good person. My grandfather was even worse. I shuddered, reliving the nightmare image of my grandfather's face shifting into demonic form.

And I was their descendant. What did that make *me*?

The only person who could answer that question was Mom, and I was now grateful she asked me to talk to her when I finished. I was surprised to see her sitting tensely on top of her bed. Her worried expression mixed with grim sympathy, and she held open her arms. I threw myself into them. My body wanted to cry with her, but I had no more tears, instead my sadness settled in my throat, making it hard to breath.

Eventually, I disentangled myself. Mom was a mess, and I supposed I was, too. What a pair. I tried to paste a smile on my face, but it wavered as much as my distorted voice. "He seemed so wonderful," I managed to choke out.

Nodding in agreement, she hiccupped, "Yes, yes he was – until he wasn't."

She took a drink of water, and able to talk more clearly, her words began tumbling out. "Even now, I can't believe he was practicing dark magic. He hid it so well. There were no warning signs. Grandma was as stunned as I was when I told her what I'd seen. Malachi had given all of us a strange vibe when we met him, but everyone loved Rowan." She seemed relieved to finally be able to talk freely about him, no longer keeping any secrets.

"You couldn't have known," I whispered. It felt odd to offer her comfort for trusting my dad.

"I'm sorry though, so sorry I didn't give you the kind of father you deserve to have."

Deep down I agreed with her but would never say it out loud. My loss felt too new – too raw. The dad I dreamt up was pretty cool, and it was agonizing to admit my Fantasy Father was so far from the truth. After seeing what he was really like, years of blame began to fall away like leaves off an autumn tree. I felt guilty for the resentment I'd routinely tossed her way. I couldn't find the words to express that to her, but I reached out, saying, "He tricked you. It wasn't your fault." Needing to know the rest of the story, I asked, "Did you see him again after that night?"

"No, I didn't. I expected him to call or come to visit, but he never did. When I got back I wrote him a long letter about what I saw him do that night and how I could not be part of it. I basically set him free if that was the path – the darkness – he planned to follow. I hoped that when he received the letter, he'd make the decision to change his ways. I would have taken him back in an instant if he'd done that, but he never answered the letter." She was getting choked up again.

"I'm sorry," I murmured.

"You don't have to be sorry." She waved in the air dismissively. "It's just hard to believe that it still hurts so much that he didn't even try to win me back."

There was nothing I could say that would fix that.

Mom laughed wryly. "The envelope addressed to him sat on the desk in the hall forever. I was too scared to send it. One day it was gone, and I knew your grandma had gotten sick of looking at it and sent it on for me. I was grateful to her for that."

"What did Grandma say when you came home from Ireland so suddenly?"

"She was worried about me, of course. At first she thought maybe I was overreacting, but when she heard the whole story, she understood."

"Did you tell her you were pregnant with me right away?"

"I didn't have to. She seemed to know the minute I stepped in the door. You were the bright spot for us. We were so excited getting everything ready for you. We went a little crazy buying all those adorable outfits." She smiled sweetly at the memory.

"Weren't you ever afraid?"

"Afraid of what?"

"Afraid – afraid of what I'd be when I was born. Afraid I'd be like them." I was terrified of her answer and purposefully lowered my eyes, watching my fingers pick the stray threads on her comforter.

"Never! Brigit, look at me," she commanded. I couldn't move, but she reached out and nudged my chin up before continuing. "I was never, ever worried then, nor have I been since, that you are anything but a wonderful, good person. You don't inherit something like that. Malachi and your father made a choice to follow the wrong path, and I know you'll never do that."

"It scares me though, the idea that I could carry evil within me somehow," I admitted.

"What they chose to be is frightening, as it should be, but you are too good inside for that. Believe it."

Her reassurance helped a little, and I released a deep, ragged sigh. "Can I see your ring and your hand-fasting ribbon?"

Surprise flickered across her face before she answered, "I would love to show you, but I sent them back in the envelope with the letter."

"You did?" I didn't expect to be so disappointed. Their love story had played out in front of my eyes, but it seemed so unreal. I guess I wanted something tangible to hold – to touch. I leaned back against the pillows, finally relaxing. We were both lost in our thoughts for a few minutes, until I finally said, "So, I'm done with the book."

"Yes, you've read it all."

"Now what?" I asked. "I don't know what comes next." My voice sounded small and hesitant.

"Now you decide what you want to do. Who you want to be."

"Gosh, and I thought it was going to be something difficult."

We laughed together, the levity a life raft on my wave of sadness and self-doubt.

"There's no big rush. Think about whether this path makes sense for you. The trip to Ireland might make a difference one way or the other.

I wasn't sure whether having more time to decide would make it better or worse. "So how come you weren't allowed to share any of this with me until now? It would have made it a lot easier if I'd grown up knowing all of this."

"I don't think I can agree with you on that, Brigit. This path has to be chosen with complete free will. If, from a young age, this was all you'd ever known, would you be able to choose a different way? Although it might seem unfair, it was important to wait until you were old enough to understand the responsibility which comes with the power you will gain. Your basic understanding of the eightfold year and those celebrations was all I was allowed to teach you."

"So does the energy – or whatever it was – I felt this morning mean I'll be able to learn how to cast spells to make things happen?" I felt a growing enthusiasm for the idea of learning how to manipulate the world around me.

She must have noticed my eagerness and tried to temper it with her answer. "Eventually. First, you need to learn how to focus your energy appropriately. Being talented comes with a burden, too. You already know how it feels to hear what people are thinking about you. You'll experience other unnerving situations if you decide to learn the ways of the Tuatha."

My eyes shut as she talked, but I heard every word. When she was finished, I quit fighting my tiredness and slept.

Waking up in Mom's bed after a long nap only added to my disconcerted state. I lay there without moving and thought about how drastically my world had tilted. Finally, I threw back the covers and went to my own room.

The book was sitting on my desk, still open to Mom's page, and next to it was my cell phone. I reached automatically to check for a call from Tyler and stopped myself. Marching back to Mom's room, I asked for Dervla's grimoire so I could read about her training regimen. Tyler would be back in less than two days, and I was hoping that'd be time enough to gain a small amount of control over my ability before then. I needed to hear what he was thinking. I needed to be sure that he was really interested in me, and it wasn't some game his gran dreamt up to get her hands on our secrets. A feeling of guilt hovered briefly at the edge of my conscience as I made this decision, but I reasoned that my talent was no good to me if I didn't use it to protect myself. I decided to be proactive and dialed the phone.

He picked up on the fifth ring when I'd almost given up and had begun mentally composing the message I'd leave on his voice mail.

"Hey, Brig. How are you?"

"I'm good. How about you?"

"We're out on the beach having a volleyball tournament."

"I can let you go so you can get back to the game," I said rather abruptly.

"Are you okay? I miss you like crazy. I wish you were here."

"Really?"

"Yes, really. Why? Did you think being away was going to make me a different person?" He chuckled.

"No, of course not." I tried to laugh, but it came out funny and forced because what I learned this week about his family might actually make him a different person. It was too soon to know.

"I'll be home tomorrow, but it'll be late. I won't see you until school on Monday."

"That's okay," I said, thinking I'd now have one more night to practice.

"I'll see you in . . . let's see . . . 40 hours at my locker."

"It's a date." My attempt at cheerfulness sounded completely false. I threw the phone on my bed and went to find Mom so she could help me with my training.

After an hour or so, I hadn't accomplished much other than giving myself a terrible headache.

"Why is this so hard?" I yelled after I failed yet again to hear the thought Mom was deliberately sending my way.

"I could say something motherly, like anything worthwhile takes some effort or if at first you don't succeed, try, try again." She smiled as she tried to tease me into a good mood.

I grabbed one of the pillows from the couch and threw it at her. She easily caught it, laughing at my temper.

"Hey, don't take it out on me. You're expecting too much of yourself. It took Dervla a year of practice before she had things under control."

"Don't remind me." My voice was deflated as I went to my room to rest my tired brain.

Eventually, I pulled myself out of my stupor and grabbed Dervla's book again. Out of all of my ancestors I felt most connected with her and was curious about her life. I paged through her book, avoiding the training section, and read some of her recipes for healing spells and funny stories she wrote about her children. I gasped as a drawing caught my eye and took a closer look. I couldn't believe it. There was a picture of the amber necklace I'd been given for my birthday with the title: The Necklace of Necessity

The accompanying story explained how fearful Dervla was for her youngest daughter, Evelyn. She was about to be married and move far from home. Evelyn's fiancé was a kind person, but not part of the Tuatha, and because Evelyn had never been a particularly skilled pupil with her training, Dervla worried that some danger would befall her. She gave Evelyn the necklace as a wedding present, but first she had cast a spell that would give its wearer whatever she needed in times of distress.

She recorded the spell in a more elaborate script than she normally used, bestowing a sense of reverence to the page.

Tawny jewel of ancient trees
It's now your task to relieve
Your wearer's distress in times of need.
Provide for her what she requires
To thwart perilous quagmires.
Precious gem, your duty clear

Your power will last from year to year,
And daughters of daughters far from now
Will benefit from this blessed vow.

Now I understood why Mom insisted I wear the necklace on the day of my meeting with Mr. Lintel. After she refused to explain anything to me that day, I'd come to believe she'd intervened with a spell of her own. With everything else going on, I hadn't even thought to ask about it this week when I finished the book. Grateful to now understand the full power of the necklace, I decided to wear it when I saw Tyler.

Entering the school, I alternated between excitement and nervousness. I'd missed Tyler so much. Being away from each other for nine days had been agonizing, but that was only one of many emotions I had during this strange, strange week. I dreaded the possibility of hearing his thoughts and finding out his sincerity was an act. As I approached the senior hallway, I decided to do my best to block his thoughts until we could be alone after school, reasoning that any bad news would be best heard in private.

And there he was with his golden tan skin, more gorgeous than ever. My heart actually skipped a beat. A smile broke across his face, and my grin felt just as big as I hurried toward him. I gave up worrying about looking like a dork and ran the last few feet, flinging myself into his arms. He easily caught me and our pent-up emotions exploded in one amazing kiss, drawing the cheers of the other seniors. We ignored them until someone loudly yelled, "Get a room!" We broke apart laughing. I was surprised that I wasn't embarrassed at all. The world around me had clicked back into place, making everything seem right again. I chastised myself for questioning his feelings for me.

Remembering what he said to me the last time I saw him, I knew what I had to do. My words flew out of my mouth so fast I was a little shocked he even understood them. "You never gave me a chance to say anything when you were saying goodbye, and I've been waiting until we were together again before I told you that . . ." I took a much needed breath before continuing, ". . . I love you."

He grinned back at me and said, "I love you," emphasizing his words with a kiss.

We didn't have nearly enough time together before the bell rang. It would have been a good day to ditch school, but neither one of us was the type to risk it.

After school we ran out to his jeep, eager to be alone to catch up on everything we'd missed during the week apart. Most of our *communication* turned out to be – er – the non-verbal type, and we lost track of time. Noticing we were the only ones left in the lot, I checked the dashboard clock.

"Wow! Do you realize what time it is?"

He followed my gaze and laughed. It was nearly four o'clock. At least forty-five minutes had passed since we left the building. He smiled, slightly embarrassed as he spoke, "Maybe we should get out of here."

"Good idea." I laughed and leaned across the console and rested my head on his shoulder as he drove to my house. My renewed confidence in his feelings for me nearly caused me to drop my plan to listen in on his thoughts. My inner voice was telling me it was pointless, but a remaining sliver of fear urged me to be sure. I gave in to fear and purposefully dropped my blocking technique, but I heard nothing.

Mom welcomed Tyler back and then left us alone. She was moving things around upstairs, so I knew she wouldn't come back in any time soon. I leaned over and kissed him again. He pulled me into his lap without interrupting the kiss, and we didn't move until we heard Mom on the stairs. Sliding apart quickly, we acted like we'd been talking the whole time. I'm guessing she knew that wasn't true, but she ignored my flustered demeanor and graciously asked Tyler to stay for dinner.

With Mom close by in the kitchen, we switched to getting our mega-load of homework out of the way. It was our teachers' way of welcoming us back from spring break. As we studied, I tried to hear what he might be thinking, but nothing came to me. Not a thing. It would have been nice to hear a good thought or two to help cement my confidence in him.

All through dinner, I still heard nothing and wondered if my ability was working right at all. I turned my attention to Mom and caught her worried thought about me getting too serious with Tyler. I didn't need to listen in on that and was startled by how quickly I was able to stop her thoughts from reaching me. Maybe my practice had been worthwhile after all.

It was quiet at the table, too quiet. I'd been concentrating so hard on listening to thoughts that I'd ignored normal conversation. I hastily tried to jump back in.

"Mom, what were you doing upstairs? It was loud."

"I decided I wanted a change so I moved some of my furniture into new places. You'll have to tell me if you like it later."

"Remember how I was always doing that when I was little?"

She laughed. "You were such a restless child. It was a good thing you had small furniture."

After dinner she went back to her rearranging, and we went back to our homework. My test with Mom at dinner proved to me that my ability was working, but I wasn't picking anything up from Tyler. I finished my assignments before he did, and to spur things along, I went to my room, returning with my family's book. I randomly paged through it in front of him and concentrated on hearing his thoughts. Still nothing.

I'd been trying to figure out how to approach him about his gran for days, and when he finished the last of his work, I was ready.

"Tyler, while you were gone, I finished the stories in the book. It was really interesting reading my grandma's story. I hadn't realized what good friends my grandma and your gran were. They have a lot in common. You know, their philosophy of life and all. Has your gran ever talked to you about any of that?" I tried to keep my voice soft and conversational, hoping I didn't sound too inquisitive.

"No, not really. I didn't even know she knew your grandma until I introduced you to her on our first date. We tend to talk mostly about art." He seemed unconcerned with the direction of the conversation. Bored even. I tried to hear the thoughts behind his words but nothing came to me.

Debating about what to ask him next, I put the book back into its protective box. I decided to come right out with it. "Tyler, has your gran ever talked to you about –" An extremely loud crash from upstairs interrupted my question.

A muffled oath from Mom was followed by her shouting, "Brigit, I dropped the big plant in my room, and the pot shattered. I've got dirt everywhere. Can you bring the broom and dustpan up to me, please?"

The timing couldn't have been worse. I needed to get this over with and put my worry about Tyler behind me. As I moved toward the hallway, I pointed at him and said more forcefully than I intended, "Do not move. I'll be right back."

I didn't know if it was my abruptness or his potential guilt, but his voice shook with nervousness. "That's okay. It sounds like you should help your mom, and it's getting late, so I might as well head home."

"This will only take a minute – really." His reaction made me suspicious, and I felt like I was on the verge of learning something horrible.

I retrieved the broom from the hall closet and sprinted up the stairs, practically throwing it into her hands when I reached her room. I turned to go back, but before I stepped into the hallway, a loud boom like a clap of thunder made my ears ring. I was confused. The sound had not been outside as it should have been – the boom had come from downstairs.

"Oh, no!" Mom shouted and pushed past me, running down the steps as fast as she could. I was right behind her. When we got to the bottom, we could see Tyler lying flat on his back with a dazed expression on his face, clutching our family's book. He had his coat on, and the front door was ajar. It was obvious he'd been trying to take the book with him.

"What's going on?" My voice slid off into nothingness as I sank down onto the bottom step.

In a voice too low for Tyler to hear she explained, "I put a spell on the book, Brigit. So it would stun anyone who tried to remove it from this house. He'll be okay in a minute."

Mom assumed I'd be worried about him, but I wasn't feeling that generous. My mind didn't have any room for anything but the betrayal I was feeling.

She helped him into a sitting position as I began to rant. "Tyler, how could you? Your gran put you up to this. Didn't she?" I poked at his chest as I shouted at him.

Tyler moaned, too confused to respond. As the shock wore off, he looked at our angry faces and immediately flopped back down with his arm flung over his face.

"I'm so sorry," he mumbled through his coat sleeve. Now, I finally heard his thoughts, but they were jumbled and hard to decipher.

"C'mon, Tyler. Let me help you up," Mom coaxed and offered him her arm for support. Once he was standing, he asked, "What happened?" He looked from Mom to me and then back to Mom.

She answered his question, phrasing it far better than I would have. "Tyler, we've had trouble with people wanting to steal this book in the past, and that was sort of a protective shield to keep it from being taken out of the house."

He shook his head in disbelief and stuttered, "Pro – pro – protective shield? Like a security system? That was more powerful than any security system I've ever heard about." He continued shaking his head. "I don't get all the fuss about some old book about your family. Why does everyone want it?"

"Well, not everyone Tyler. It's only your gran who has been after it. Did she ask you to get it for her?" I asked.

"She did," Tyler admitted. "I didn't think it'd be such a big deal to borrow it for a little while. She said she only wanted to look at it but because of some big fight she had with your grandma, you would never loan it to her."

Mom snorted at Adele's understated explanation. "That's not quite the truth, but she was right that we would never loan it to her."

I was far less gentle with him than Mom had been. "God, Tyler, didn't you think that was suspicious? Didn't you think to ask why this was such a big deal to her?" I could tell he felt bad, but I was so angry, I wasn't careful with my words at all. "How stupid are you? You know nothing about your gran and the things she's done. She's not the sweet grandma you think she is."

"Brigit, watch what you say," Mom warned.

Tyler shifted his weight back and forth on his feet awkwardly before agreeing, "You're right – you're right. I should have suspected something was up. When she offered to pay the rest of my art school tuition, she asked me to do this favor for her. I had to agree. Without her offer, it would have been way too expensive for me. I told her I didn't like it, but I thought maybe I could borrow the book and put it back before you noticed it was gone. When you said you were done reading the stories, I thought I might be able to sneak out with it tonight. I'm so sorry." Tyler's thoughts were as sincere as his words – but neither lessened my anger.

"Tyler, she's been after this book and others like it for three decades now. She's done terrible things to people to get her hands on them. First, she went after the book her cousin Carmen has and then she came after our books." A thought suddenly occurred to me, "Did she ask you to *borrow* other books from our house?"

Tyler stared down at his feet, and I heard him think, *This is only going to make things worse.* He sighed. "Yes, she did, but I told her I never saw any other old books around like the ones she described and this would be the only one I'd help her with."

I was nearly shouting now, "She asked you to do this for her before you even asked me out! Didn't she!" I didn't give him a chance to answer and kept shouting. "You've been pretending to like me this whole time."

His face paled over my final accusation, and he took a step toward me. "No, Brigit, it's not true. She only asked me to help her after she knew I was going out with you. You've got to believe me."

I tried to read his thoughts, but now it wasn't working. It seemed like whenever I got really upset, my ability failed me. His expression seemed honest, but I was scared to trust him. Finally, I said, "I don't know if I can believe you. I definitely know I can't trust you when you're willing to steal something from me." Tears started running down my cheeks. I'd been holding them back too long to have any hope of stopping them.

"Brigit, I didn't know what to do. I didn't realize this book . . . any books . . . were such a big deal. Really, I didn't. What's in them anyway? Why are they so important?"

Mom said only enough to satisfy but not enough to reveal anything damaging. "They're family secrets and recipes, Tyler. They wouldn't mean anything to the average person, but your gran would understand the power they hold. I'm afraid she wouldn't use the information wisely."

He nodded as though he understood, but his expression remained bewildered. He turned back to me, and his confusion changed into a sort of sad desperation. "Brigit, you have to believe me. I didn't know what I was getting into here. Please." His last word was an anguished cry.

His painful thoughts broke through my angry shield, and made me want to reach out to him. I almost gave in, but my sense of betrayal overrode my desire to believe him. I ordered him out of the house. Out of my life.

Chapter Twenty-Seven

My body felt heavy this morning.

I could barely make my arm move to whap the button on my incessant alarm. There was no way I was going to school. Call it a mental health day. I rolled over and went back to sleep.

To Mom's credit, she let me sleep away my emotional fatigue until about ten o'clock before coming into my room.

"Brigit . . . Brigit . . ."

"Leave me alone."

"Hey, it's time to get up. I called the school and said you were sick, but you can't stay in bed all day. Get up and have something to eat."

I didn't reply, hoping she'd go away.

"Brigit – I'm serious. I expect you downstairs in a few minutes."

As her footsteps retreated down the hall, I reasoned she could still make me go to school late if she felt like it and used all my energy to heave myself out of bed.

I didn't bother getting dressed and shuffled into the kitchen in my pjs, grabbing a yogurt from the fridge. Mom was busy working on filling orders, and, when she finished the current box, she looked over at me.

"I'm giving you one day to mope about this, but tomorrow you go to school." She waited for me to acknowledge her statement.

"Thanks for letting me stay home today. I couldn't face Tyler."

"I understand."

My phone buzzed on the counter somewhere, and Mom grabbed it before I could get to it.

"Hey, what's that doing down here?" I asked.

"Tyler hasn't stopped calling. I moved it so it wouldn't wake you up."

"Oh." I pretended not to care, and with deliberate nonchalance, peeled back the foil on the top of my yogurt.

"Brigit, I totally understand why you're so mad. Heck, I'm mad, too, but I think Tyler was telling the truth last night. I don't believe he had any idea what Adele was really up to."

"I don't disagree," I said flatly, dragging my spoon across the top of the yogurt like it was a delicate archeological dig.

"You don't?"

"Mom, I know he didn't have a clue what Adele wanted with the book, but the thing is . . ." I swallowed hard, trying to keep from crying. ". . . now I know, if the stakes are high enough, he's willing to lie to me. How can I trust him if his honesty's for sale?"

The phone buzzed again in Mom's hand. "He's very persistent. What do you want to do about that?"

"Turn it off."

"You'll probably have to talk to him at some point."

"Not today."

"Fair enough." She nodded and hit the off switch on the phone.

"You know what's really awful?" I asked.

"I'm scared to guess. There's so much to choose from right now."

I groaned and let my head hang over the back of the chair like a rag doll. "I actually told him I loved him yesterday morning. I wish I could take it back."

"Oh, dear." Mom cringed in sympathy as she spoke. "I don't blame you for wanting to take it back, but you couldn't have known the way the day would turn out."

"The worst part is that I still love him, but I don't think I can forgive him. Can you love someone and be so mad that you can't forgive them?"

"Most definitely." She sighed.

I didn't consider it until later, but she was probably thinking about my dad when she answered my question.

I went back to school the next day only because I had to. Mom dropped me off, so I hadn't seen Jess or Moriah since the day before, and I didn't expect them to know anything about Tyler and me. It seemed unlikely he would have confided in either of them. It was going to be obvious we'd broken up, and I knew there'd be a slew of questions I'd have to answer. I debated about what I might say as I approached my locker.

"Hey, Brigit. Are you feeling better?" Jess asked.

"Yeah. I'm fine." I replied without much energy.

"Was it the stomach flu? My brother was puking his guts out the other day, and it was nasty." Moriah backed up a couple of steps, waiting for me to answer.

"No, no. It was nothing like that. To be honest, it was a mental health day." I turned to my locker and stuffed my books inside, knowing I'd set myself up for more questions.

"Why did you need a mental health day?" Moriah asked, leaning in closely now that she knew I wasn't contagious.

Jess was standing just as closely on my other side, and I pivoted around to eliminate the claustrophobic feeling they were giving me. "Tyler and I broke up, and I was really upset, so my mom let me stay home yesterday."

"Oh, no! What happened? I thought things were going so well between you," Jess wailed, touching my arm as she spoke.

Moriah snorted. "My mom would never let me stay home for that. Your mom is so cool."

I ignored her comment and replied to Jess. "I don't really want to talk about it, but I misjudged him. He wasn't the kind of person I thought I was."

"Did he cheat on you when he was on vacation?" Moriah clearly believed this was a possibility. "I'll kick his butt."

Her threat made me laugh. Given the size discrepancy between them, Moriah was not likely to do any damage. "Thanks for the offer, but that's not what happened. Leave it be, okay? I really don't want to talk about it."

"Talking about it will make you feel better," Jess advised and offered her own explanation. "He wanted you to go further than you wanted to, didn't he? It was impossible not to notice the way you were making out in the parking lot. I'm right, aren't I?"

She seemed so proud of herself for figuring it out that I felt almost mean shaking my head and telling her that wasn't it either.

They continued to try to pry it out of me, and I was starting to get annoyed. I imagined their faces if I told them the truth, that Tyler's slightly witchy gran tried to get him to steal our even more witchy family secrets so she could gain power by using magical spells. Right – that would sound very believable. The idea of telling them the truth was so absurd that I began to laugh, but it wasn't a healthy laugh. It was a borderline psychotic, hysterical laugh which startled the other students within hearing distance.

Jess and Moriah stared at me for a few seconds, and then asked me to stop, nicely at first and then more forcefully.

"You're being really weird. It's freaking me out, Brigit. Knock it off," Moriah commanded and grabbed my arm like she might shake the craziness out of me.

They exchanged an uncomfortable look and somehow that made me laugh harder. I simply couldn't get it under control.

Finally, Jess, whose voice was normally soft and kind, nearly shouted in my ear, "You're losing it, and I'm taking you to the nurse. Now."

That did it. I swallowed back my absurd laughter and, except for the occasional giggle slipping out, I was successful. "I'm sorry. I don't know where that came from."

They didn't say anything but looked at me like they were afraid I might do something else. I smiled and shrugged, offering a lame explanation. "Emotional overload, what can I say?"

"That was really, really weird. Don't do that again." Moriah said.

"Yeah," Jess added with a wary look, obviously traumatized by my Bizarre Display.

When the bell rang they seemed relieved they could escape.

My strange outburst had one positive, unintended consequence. They never again asked why Tyler and I broke up, and that was the only good thing about the next four weeks.

My misery made me a bad friend and a bad daughter. Moriah and Jess tried to get me to do fun things with them on the weekends, but I wasn't interested, and when Mom talked about our trip, I was unenthused. Even though it hurt their feelings, I wasn't able to muster any excitement about anything.

Art class was a minefield. Tyler used our only class together as a chance to talk to me. He didn't give up easily, even though I refused to acknowledge him – at all. Tyler-avoidance became a tactical challenge. I pivoted my workspace so I wouldn't accidentally look his way while I was painting. I never walked near him to retrieve supplies. Moriah was kind enough to get things for me when I deemed them too close to Tyler's orbit for comfort. And every day I packed up my project early so I could bolt out the door the second the bell rang. It took three weeks for Tyler to get the message and quit talking to me. My strategy was probably unnecessary now, but I kept at it.

I knew my behavior was juvenile, but I was afraid if I opened the door to Tyler one little bit, I'd end up flinging it wide open and forgiving him. Then we'd get back together, and I'd be setting myself up for getting hurt again. My plan was a painful necessity, and I was sticking to it.

The Monday of prom week was my last day of school before my trip to Ireland. I was relieved I was leaving because there was no way I would have been able to suffer through the rest of the week with everyone's happy prom-planning talk ringing in my ears. "Where are you getting your hair done? Where should we eat? What time are you picking me up? Blah – blah – blah."

My only concession to the prom hoopla was to share in Jess and Moriah's excitement. "Be sure to take lots of pictures. I want to see how gorgeous you two look," I ordered.

I hugged them and tried to sound very sophisticated as I tra-la-la-ed, "I'm off on my grand overseas adventure."

"Bon voyage," Moriah said in a very bad French accent.

"Have a great time," Jess added.

I looked back, waving as I walked down the hall. Jess and Moriah's expressions froze at exactly the same time I bumped into Tyler.

He held onto me for only a moment before I had the presence of mind to step away.

"I wanted to tell you to have a great trip, Brigit." He smiled at me like we'd never broken up. And if that wasn't disconcerting enough, I heard him think as clearly as if he said it out loud, *I miss her so much.*

Forgetting my vow of silence, I was less than eloquent with my reply. "Um – thanks," I said and fled down the hall, wishing his "hug" hadn't felt so very, very good.

As we prepared to land at the Shannon airport in the west of Ireland, for the first time in weeks, I felt something like eagerness or excitement.

Mom might have noticed, I couldn't tell, but she smiled at me and said, "We're going to have a great trip."

My new-found enthusiasm turned to fear after enduring the first few miles of Mom's driving. Her opposite-side driving hadn't improved much since that first wild ride I'd witnessed in the book when she'd been escaping from my dad's dark magic. I gripped the side of my seat and leaned my head to the center of the car as we flew past a low wall which threatened to remove the passenger side mirror.

Mom noticed my terrified expression and burst out laughing. "Brigit, you need to relax. These narrow roads take some getting used to, but I know what I'm doing."

We sped up the highway, passing through Galway, Tuam, and Sligo. As we neared the city of Donegal, we began to catch glimpses of Donegal Bay on our left around the same time we decided we should stop for lunch. Although Mom had only lived in Donegal for a few weeks, she knew her way around, and she turned down a narrow road which dead-ended at the beach. It was nice to stretch our legs and exceptionally nice to dig into the lunch we had picked up along the way. Ham and cheese between slices of brown bread made hefty sandwiches nearly too thick to bite through and packets of potato chips, called crisps here in Ireland, and two bottles of cola made a very satisfying meal.

We soaked up the warm sun after we ate, and I was grateful for the break which gave my food time to digest before returning to the extreme movements of the car. I wouldn't have minded if we stayed there all afternoon, but that wasn't possible.

"How long before we reach Anya's house in Raphoe?" I asked.

"About two hours. It's less than fifty miles from here, but the roads we'll be driving on after we leave the main highway are really small, and I won't be able to go very fast."

"The roads get smaller than the ones we've been on?" She must be kidding.

"Brigit, we've been on main roads so far, but the ones leading to Anya's farm are gravel lanes. It's one car at a time, so if you meet someone you have to pull off a little bit to pass each other." She noticed my disbelief and chastised me. "Where's your sense of adventure? I feel like you're acting like a mother-hen, and we've somehow switched places with each other."

I gave her an exasperated look. I was as adventurous as the next person, but these roads were just so darn small. Could I help it that they freaked me out?

"C'mon." She moved to pack up the wrappers from our picnic. "Anya is expecting us before three o'clock."

I quit my pouting a mile or two down the road. "So Anya lives there with her husband and kids?"

"Kid," she corrected. "Remember I told you about her 17-year-old son. His name's Bodaway."

"Bodaway?" I snorted. "Who names their kid something so weird? Poor guy," I added.

"I'm pretty sure he goes by Bodie," Mom said. "It means fire maker. I remember Anya was so excited about the name when she was pregnant and found out she was having a boy."

"Okaaay. I hope he's not a pyromaniac." I laughed and rolled my eyes. "You do realize that some of your friends are really weird?"

"They're no weirder than me, honey." Her voice was full of laughter as she said again, "No weirder than me."

True to her description, the lanes we drove on at the end of the trip made me hold my breath. At the crest of each little knoll I was sure we would crash into another car barreling the other direction. When we pulled into Anya's driveway, I took a moment to settle my nerves and get out.

Anya had already rushed up to the car, giving Mom a huge hug before turning to me. "So this is Brigit? Oh my, you are as pretty as the pictures your mom has sent."

I smiled and stared at her, feeling awkward and bland as I compared my boring dark-blond hair with the amazing mass of red curls which cascaded down her back. The color did not seem real, but I doubt she dyed it. Mom cleared her throat, giving me the "say something" look.

"Oh, sorry," I said quickly. "Nice to meet you." I attempted to hide my embarrassment by turning toward the trunk for our luggage.

"Oh, leave the bags for now. I'll have one of the fellows bring them in when they get home. Finn has gone to pick Bodie up from school in Letterkenny. They'll be back soon."

I followed Mom through the front door. I expected an old cottage or farmhouse because we were so far out in the country. This modern, airy structure was a surprise. Anya led us back to the kitchen, which had a large sunroom off the side. The glass walls and ceiling let in maximum light, and I immediately spied her easel leaning against the wall. It was a perfect work space. Anya followed my gaze.

"Your mom mentioned that you're an artist, too. I don't have any projects right now, so feel free to use the space and my supplies if the mood strikes you."

This was an incredibly generous offer. Most artists were a little possessive about their work space and even more particular about their supplies. I was skeptical. "You really mean it?"

"Yes, I do. It would be fun to see another artist at work. It gets a little lonely out here at times. I have friends, of course, but the community of people like us is rather small." She waved her hand to encompass the three of us so I wasn't sure which community of people she was referring to, artists or the Tuatha.

"Here the boys are," she said as we all heard the front door open and shut.

A deep voice entered the room a moment before the person it belonged to. "Thank goodness you've arrived." A tall, thin man with a shockingly white head of hair continued on in a teasing tone. "Anya talked of nothing else for days. It's been quite a trial. Celeste, it's so wonderful to see you again. Hard to believe it's been a year already."

When he turned to me, I could see he wasn't nearly as old as I'd first thought. His white hair had thrown off my estimate of his age by a couple of decades at least. He didn't wait for introductions, enveloping me in a bear hug and spinning me around. "Welcome, fair Brigit, welcome to your first May Day celebration. We hope it lives up to your expectations."

"Put the girl down, Finn. You're going to scare her away." Anya snapped the kitchen towel in her husband's direction.

"I didn't scare you, did I?" Finn asked. His eyes twinkled mischievously.

He was so unabashed about his enthusiastic greeting, I had to defend him. "Of course not," I said.

"And this is Bodaway," Anya said and beckoned forward her son, who had stayed a few steps back during his father's energetic greeting. Bodie was tall, but his fiery red hair made him look more like his mom.

"Bodie," he said, correcting his mom automatically. "It's nice to meet you." His smile was warm and friendly, but unlike his father, he greeted me more formally, holding out his hand.

"Nice to meet you, too," I said, shaking his hand.

Finn and Bodie brought our luggage in, and Mom and I got situated in our rooms. We each had our own and shared the bath in between. It was nice to have the extra privacy, and I again appreciated the spaciousness of the house.

Later we enjoyed dinner together, which stretched on longer than I expected as Mom, Finn, and Anya relived old times. Bodie rescued me by suggesting we go watch TV or listen to music. I readily agreed and followed him to a room he called the lounge.

"They'll be up for hours talking like that. I didn't figure you'd want to sit there any more than I did," he explained.

"Thanks. I appreciate that."

"So do you want to watch TV?"

"Not really. Unless there's something you don't want to miss."

He shook his head. "Music, then?" He asked without expecting an answer. "We've got some of everything in here." He waved to a wall full of CDs behind him.

"Whoa. You're not kidding, are you?"

"You choose," he suggested.

I was suddenly self-conscious about my limited knowledge of music. "Pick something you like. I usually rely on my friends to tell me who the new groups are and everything."

He turned on the sound system and pressed play. Traditional Irish music came through the speakers. He laughed and pushed the buttons until he found something more contemporary. "Here, this is a group I like."

We sat there for a few awkward minutes, not speaking. Finally he asked, "Would you like something to drink, some ale or cola or something?"

"A coke would be great, thanks."

He came back with a coke for me and a beer for himself, which made me ask, "Your parents don't mind if you drink?"

"Not as long as I'm not driving anywhere. The drinking age is eighteen but a few pubs don't care so much."

"It's twenty-one in the states, so I've got years and years to wait." There was a lull in our conversation while I struggled with something else to say. "So how many more weeks of school do you have before summer break?" I asked, figuring school was a safe topic.

"We have class until mid-June and exams after that. We'll be off in July and August."

"You have a lot shorter summer break than we do. My last day of class is June 10. So what year are you, sophomore, junior?"

He laughed. "We don't call the years by names like that. I've got one more year to go before I sit for my exams."

"That'd make you a junior in the states. Everyone's really excited about prom this week. Do you have big dances at your school?"

He looked at me confused. "We have some dances, but we call them Deb's nights. Debs for debutantes."

"Oh, no wonder I sound so confusing." I laughed. "I didn't realize there'd be so many differences when we're both speaking English. A prom is what we call our big formal dance. Everyone gets all dressed up. It's a big deal."

I couldn't think of anything else to say for a moment.

Bodie came to the rescue. "It's too bad you're missing it this weekend."

"Yeah, but if I were home, I'd be missing it anyway. My boyfriend and I broke up about a month ago." Suddenly, I was holding back tears in front of this boy I hardly knew.

To his credit, he didn't try to comfort me or say anything. I'd probably stunned him into silence. When I pulled it together, I felt like I owed him an explanation and spewed forth the entire story like I'd never had the chance to do before. With Bodie I didn't have to edit out the parts about my family's book or Tyler's gran and her quest for power. He was Tuatha. He understood the betrayal. He was an exceptionally good listener. I realized I'd been talking for a long time when he set his empty beer bottle on the table. "I'm sorry. This has got to be awful for you, listening to someone you've only just met crying about someone you're never going to meet. I promise not to bring it up again for the entire visit."

"Don't be so self-conscious. Really – I didn't mind."

"Yeah, sure," I said. "I think it is more likely that you are being very, very nice."

"Do you want my opinion?" he asked.

"Um, sure. What's your opinion?"

"He didn't deserve you, and you need to quit wasting energy on him by being so sad."

"Okay, but. . ." I began, but Bodie interrupted.

"No. No excuses. You are going to have a good time while you're here. I challenge you – no – I dare you to have a wonderful time. Beltane will be better than your prom ever would have been."

I sat there surprised at his audacity but realized he was at least partially right. I had to quit my moping and get on with my life. "You're right," I finally said, hoping the conviction I put into my voice would take root in my actions. "I'm going to make Beltane the best night of my life."

I had no idea that it would exceed even my wildest dreams.

Chapter Twenty-Eight

J et lag had thrown off my internal clock, and I woke early to a beautiful day. The house was quiet, and I wasn't surprised no one else was up. Last night, when I went to say goodnight, Mom and Bodie's parents were laughing and talking loudly, their conversation aided by at least two empty bottles of wine I noticed on the counter. I didn't expect them to be up for a while and tried to be quiet as I helped myself to a cup of tea and some toast. I walked to the sunroom to enjoy my solitary breakfast and the wide view of the yard through the glass wall.

Thinking I was the only one awake, I was startled to see someone doing chores near the barn and recognized Bodie when he pivoted to empty a bucket into a pen. I stood up and waved to him, not sure if I'd catch his eye or not. He saw me and waved back as he walked toward the back doorway. He didn't come all the way in, sticking his head through the doorway as he spoke.

"Good morning, Brigit. You're up long before our drunkard parents. I don't know what will ever become of them," he said with mock disdain. "Get some shoes on and come out. I've got something amazing to show you."

I did as instructed and added a sweater over my pajamas before I went out. "What is it?" I asked.

"I'm not going to spoil the surprise for you," he said. "It's in the barn."

Following behind him, I ducked through the low doorway into the darkened interior. My eyes were immediately drawn to the warm glow made by two low-hanging lights in the corner. I approached the pen with Bodie, peeked over the side, and saw the most adorable newborn lambs. Their little faces and legs were black, and their bodies were a brownish gray color. "They're so cute!" I squealed. "Are they twins?"

"Yes, born a couple of hours ago, I'd say."

"Did you know there'd be two?" I asked.

"We usually have a few sets every spring. I thought maybe it was something you'd never seen before."

"I've never seen any this young. There was a petting farm Mom used to take me to when I was little, and I remember feeding the lambs out of my hand, but they were a lot bigger than this," I explained, watching the adorable awkwardness of the newborns as they struggled to stay on their feet.

"Are you going to name them?" I asked.

"No. We only name the lambs if we decide to keep them for breeding stock. It makes it too hard later on." He didn't finish his thought, letting me fill in where he left off.

It took me a second before I nodded and said, "Lamb chops." It wasn't often that I was confronted with the reality of my carnivore status on the food chain, and I felt bad as their bright eyes looked back at me. "They're so sweet. I want to take them home with me."

"I know how you feel, but it can't be helped." He patted my shoulder as he spoke. "I've got a few more chores to finish, and then I'll keep you company in the kitchen."

Back in the house, I was surprised Mom was awake. A few minutes later we were joined by Finn and Anya.

"Aren't you the early bird this morning? Not like the rest of us who drank too much last night." Finn groaned and rubbed the back of his neck.

"Speak for yourself. I feel great," Anya said. "You'd think at your advanced age, you would have learned your lesson by now." She handed him the bottle of aspirin.

Finn sat at the table, nursing his cup of tea. Anya offered to make us all a big Irish breakfast. Once I heard the description of what this meant, I decided to pass on the bacon and sausage, swearing off meat, at least temporarily.

Finished with his chores, Bodie joined us at the table, telling his parents about the twin lambs. After breakfast, we helped pack the tents and other camping gear into the cars. With Beltany only two miles away, we didn't need to leave until mid-afternoon to have our campsites ready before the opening ceremony at sunset.

Since I'd read Mom's story so very recently, it seemed almost as though I had attended a Beltane festival already. Although, I didn't imagine mine would be quite as eventful as my mom's had been with my dad's romantic proposal and their more – er – private activities.

When we were ready to leave, Mom double-checked that I had her old ceremonial robe with me and asked, "Are you going to wear it the traditional way? It'll be warm enough tonight."

I rolled my eyes at her and ignored the question.

"Oh, quit being such a prude," she admonished and laughed. "Are you excited?"

I didn't mind answering that question and said, "Yes, I really am. I know what to expect now, thanks to your story."

"I'm glad. It should be fun. Bodie will introduce you to the other kids your age." She eased our rental car down the small lane, following Bodie and his parents. "You two seem to be getting along well."

It wasn't a direct question but I could tell she wanted to know what I thought of Bodie. "He's really nice, Mom. He told me that I needed to quit moping about Tyler and enjoy the celebration."

She nodded. "Well, he's wise beyond his years."

"I guess so."

Then she smiled slyly at me and added, "And cute, too."

"Mom, knock it off. I'm not in the market for another boyfriend. Plus, even if he's cute and nice and possibly wonderful in many other ways, there's one really big draw-back."

"What's that?" She asked.

"The Atlantic Ocean."

She laughed. "Yes. That does make dating a little difficult," she agreed before making a suggestion. "You can at least enjoy his company while you're here."

"What are you saying?" I asked, perplexed. After seeing numerous Beltane festivals from years past in my family's book, I knew what often went on between men and women on this special night. There's no way she could mean THAT! I tried to sense her intent by reading her thoughts, but didn't get a fix on anything.

She hazarded a glance at me as she navigated down the narrow road, and my expression made her gasp. "What? Oh, no – that's not what I meant! Geez – Brigit! I meant that you should be friends. I didn't mean for it to sound like I thought you should be intimate with him. For goodness sake, that would be the opposite of everything we ever talked about."

In my defense I said, "Sorry. I didn't really think you'd be telling me to have that kind of *fun*, but it *is* Beltane Eve after all. Aren't the couples supposed to go frolicking off into the wood for an evening of pleasure?"

"Not when you're fifteen. There'll be plenty of time to – er – frolic when you're older."

I was embarrassed I'd jumped to the wrong conclusion. I meant to ask her more about the sexual traditions of Beltane before we'd gotten here, not that I was planning to honor the holiday this way. I decided I would save my questions for another time.

We grabbed our things from the car and lugged the borrowed tent between us, following the path up the hill. Not much seemed to have changed from the images in Mom's story.

Pausing to take in the activity at the top of the hill, the traditional tents and the participants dressed in long robes created an air of ancientness at the site. The tall standing stones jutting up from the green turf encircled the pile of wood in the middle, ready to be lit. My heart jumped a little at the thrill. I was here. I was finally here at Beltany!

With Bodie's help, we set up our campsite right next to his. Mom and I went in to change, and I made sure the flap was securely tied together before I took off my street clothes. Mom undressed completely before she slipped her robe on, and for an embarrassing minute I stood there in my underwear debating what to do. "Oh, what the heck," I said and whipped off my bra and panties before putting on my hand-me-down robe.

Mom's expression did not betray her thoughts, and I refused, absolutely refused, to search them out. She opened the flap, and I followed her into the main tent where she joined Anya and the other seven members of the Circle of Nine.

The other women surged forward, and Mom made the introductions. I recognized Petra and Lauren from my mom's story, but there were too many other names for me to remember the rest. The only person I was sure not to forget was another 15-year-old daughter, Ember, who was also attending her first Beltane celebration. We shared a look of confusion with each other and laughed. Ember looked very Irish with deep blue eyes and dark black hair cut into a short spiky style, the kind of style that I always admired but was too scared to try. I liked her immediately.

The tent was chaotic and crowded until the nine women assembled into a line. At that point everyone but me seemed to know what to do and fell into position behind them. I felt lost without Mom and was grateful when Bodie grabbed my hand, pulling me along with the rest of the crowd toward the altar area. I hadn't seen him since we'd left to get dressed and looked at him sideways, admiring how handsome he was in his sage green robe. I was suddenly conscious of my nudity under my robe as the fabric swished against my bare skin. It felt strangely liberating and slightly naughty.

We pressed forward toward the altar as the age-old ceremony began. I couldn't look away from the goblet and athame stretched high into the air as I listened to the words of blessing being reverently intoned for the hushed audience.

At the end of the blessing, I joined together with the other voices and said, "Make it so." Bodie gave my hand a squeeze and pulled me back as we made room for the Circle of Nine to move to the center and light the bonfire. Mom circled the fire nine times with the other women, her long, blonde hair flying out behind her. She was absolutely beautiful. When they'd completed their last circuit, Bodie pushed me forward with the other young women, and I remembered that there would be alternating rings of women and men around the fire. Ember was next to me, and we linked hands with each other and the women on either side of us. More circles assembled behind us until the space between the bonfire and the stones was filled with people. We rotated around the fire, singing and chanting together. The power of our collective energy surged within me. It felt extraordinary. I was no longer the girl with the strange mother who was merely tolerated by others. I belonged here.

I danced and sang until I was hoarse and in desperate need of a drink of water. Leaving the bonfire, I saw Mom with her friends watching me as I approached them; they all smiled in a way which made me think I'd been the topic of conversation.

"We were admiring your energy," Mom explained, confirming my suspicion.

Their observation didn't bother me in the least, and I leaned close to tell her what I thought. "This is incredible," I croaked. "I feel so alive and part of something so . . . so big." Words failed me, much like my voice.

"Go and get something to drink," she urged. "I'll be here when you come back."

As I wound my way through the tents, Bodie grabbed my hand. "Where are you going?"

"Water," I whispered.

"Lost your voice, have you? Water is not really going to help. Come with me."

I followed along behind him to his family's tent and waited while he went in. He came out with a jug and poured a small glass for me. "This should revive your vocal chords."

I should have asked what it was before I upended the cup into my mouth. It burned like fire and tasted the way turpentine smelled. I gagged and coughed uncontrollably. Once I was able to draw a deep breath, my throat remained uncomfortably warm, and I lashed out at Bodie with my normal-strength voice. "Why didn't you warn me? That was vile."

He laughed and pointed out, "You wouldn't have swallowed it if I warned you, and if you haven't noticed, you have your voice back."

I had noticed and reluctantly gave his nasty remedy the credit. "Thanks, but I definitely need some water now and a breath mint. God, what was that?"

"My dad's home-brewed whiskey. It's strictly medicinal." He nodded seriously and handed me a bottle of water.

"Medicinal? More like poisonous. That stuff should only be used externally to sterilize wounds or start fires or something." I took a big drink of the water and sighed with relief.

Bodie and I walked together, skirting the edge of the tent city. I thought we were avoiding the crowd by taking a longer way back to the stones, but we had veered slightly downhill away from everyone.

I was suddenly leery of his intentions, and after the whiskey incident I was less trusting than I'd first been. Backing away from him slightly, I *listened* to him for a moment and was comforted by the absence of any lurid thoughts.

"Where are we going?"

"We're here. Look up at that."

I followed his gesture and saw what he meant. The bonfire created an orangey glow, making the dark stones stand out like cogs in the wheel of some gigantic machine while the pulsing rhythm of the dancers at the center made the whole hilltop come alive with energy.

It was mesmerizing.

Bodie broke our silence. "I saw this the first year and, every year since, I always come down here and watch."

"Thank you. I'll never forget how this looks. Never."

We watched a while longer, and I shivered in the chilly air, now that I was no longer dancing near a roaring fire. I pulled my hood up for warmth, and we began to walk up the hill.

"I should find my mom," I said to him.

He hesitated for a minute. "I promised I'd hang out with some of my friends. You're welcome to come."

"I will in a little while. Where should I look for you?"

"We'll probably be sitting outside one of the tents," he said, starting to walk away. "See you later."

"Definitely," I answered and continued toward the stones. I'd stopped to scan the crowd for Mom when I was suddenly grabbed from behind and spun around.

The hood fell forward over my face, obscuring my vision. I attempted to straighten it and see who had grabbed me. I assumed it was Bodie until an unfamiliar male voice whispered close to my ear, "Celeste, I knew I'd find you here."

How could someone confuse the two of us? We didn't look that much alike, but I guess the robes made it hard to tell the difference. I turned to explain that I was not Celeste, when it hit me. It was the robe causing the confusion – Mom's robe – the one she hadn't worn for fifteen years. Fear rippled through me. Only someone who'd known her from long ago and hadn't seen her since would make this mistake. I tried to pull free. In my struggle, my hood fell back. I froze in place because I was looking straight into a face I'd seen so many times before but never, ever in person.

He looked stunned and said, "You're not Celeste. Where did you get this robe?"

"Celeste is my mother."

The man yanked me closer and, with a nearly insane intensity, stared into my eyes which mirrored the color of his own. I could tell he knew who I was before his words confirmed it. "No, this can't be. She would have told me," he said, loosening his grip on my arm.

I used this chance to flee, searching wildly for Mom as I dodged in and out of groups of people. When I finally found her, my panicked expression must have been obvious, and she closed the distance, asking, "Brigit, what is it?"

The words stuck in my throat, "My – my dad." I took big gulp of air and continued pointing behind me, "My dad – is here."

And suddenly he was right at the end of my outstretched hand. Instinctively, I pulled it away from his potential grasp. I'd dreamt a million possibilities for the moment when I'd first meet my dad, and this wasn't remotely close to any of them.

Time paused as they looked at each other and struggled with what to say. Finally, my dad said, "Celeste."

And Mom responded just as simply. "Rowan."

"Is this my daughter?" He asked, his voice cracking on the final word. "Yes."

His face sagged and sadness filled his eyes. He didn't seem like a powerful follower of dark magic.

"Why would you hide this from me? Why?"

"After what you did? What you are?" Mom looked at me and then back to him. "I gave you a choice to come back to me, but you cared more about your power."

He shook his head in confusion and shouted, "What are you talking about?"

"Rowan, you know! That night at the solstice, I saw what you did on the beach."

Mom noticed that they had drawn the attention of nearly everyone around. The other women in the Circle knew the whole story about Rowan, and concern etched their faces. Anya stepped forward and spoke for the group, asking, "Celeste, do you need our help?"

"No. We'll continue this conversation in private. I'll be perfectly safe in my tent." She indicated Rowan should follow her, and when he began to speak she held up her hand, indicating he should wait.

I followed along behind them and felt bad for my dad when he glanced back at me with such a sad expression. I heard the mantra in his head. *I have a daughter, I have a daughter.*

Outside the tent, Mom turned to me. "Brigit, I need to speak to Rowan alone."

She was right, but it didn't lessen my desire to know what was going on. Walking away from the opening, I sat on the grass alongside the tent wall where I could hear through the fabric.

Dad spoke first. "Celeste, I can't believe you kept this from me all these years. Why would you do such a thing? I would have been a good father." His voice was pleading, and I thought I heard him weeping.

"Rowan, you're acting like I didn't give you a good reason. I explained it all in the letter, when I sent back my engagement ring and our hand-fasting ribbon. Don't you remember?"

"Celeste, I never got a letter. When I came to see you, an older woman was coming out of your house and told me to leave. She gave me the ring and the ribbon and said that you didn't want to be with me anymore."

"What? You came to see me?" There was silence for a moment. "I never knew. Really, I never knew," Mom said. "Who was the woman you talked to? It wasn't my mom, was it?"

"No, it was a different woman. She said she was your aunt."

"Rowan, I don't have an aunt. My mom was an only child."

"Celeste, what does it matter? I got the ring and the ribbon, and I got the message. I didn't stick around to talk to her."

"What did she look like?" Mom asked.

"I don't remember. I was so upset that I didn't pay much attention to her."

"She didn't hand you an envelope with a letter in it?"

"No! I – didn't – get – a – letter." Dad said this slowly like Mom was a small child.

"Rowan, it was so important. All these years I assumed that you understood everything because of that letter, and if you never got it . . ." She started to cry, and their words became low murmurs that I couldn't decipher.

"Celeste, what did the letter say?"

"It explained what I saw that night on the beach. The dark magic I saw you perform. I couldn't expose a child to that. And, I wrote about how your father came into the tent earlier that night and scared me. He knew I was pregnant, and he said things about the baby, using a strange language. His face changed into something hideous. Rowan, I know I wasn't having a nightmare. I went to find you down on the beach, but I stayed hidden in the grass and watched. You were in your robe; you cut someone's hand to make a blood sacrifice into the flames. Dark magic. That's why I ran away."

"Celeste, I wasn't even there at that point. One of the blokes smashed his hand pounding in a tent spike, and I had taken him to the hospital."

"But . . . but your car was still there." Mom's voice was getting quieter and quieter.

"We used someone else's car. I looked in the tent, and you were sleeping so deeply, it didn't seem right to wake you up. My dad said he'd take care of you. I had no idea that you'd be gone when I got back."

"Oh, my God."

"When I couldn't find you and saw that the car was gone, I didn't understand why you would have left. Petra and Lauren were no help, other than to tell me where to find my car. I even drove to Donegal to ask Claire what happened. No one would tell me a thing except that you'd gone home. I waited for you to call or come back, but you never did, so eventually I followed you to America."

"I saw you – in your robe – that night. It was you."

"No, Celeste, it wasn't. My da' must have been wearing it." Rowan's voice was very firm. "He'd been changing, and I was getting more and more worried about what he was doing. He'd surrounded himself with this new group of people. It took most of the summer for me to realize that he'd gotten into things I didn't want to be a part of. When he decided to move again, I didn't go with him. I made a fresh start in Scotland, and I've been living there ever since. I'm only here on business. It's the first time I've come back, and when I realized I'd be here over Beltane, I knew I had to take the chance to see if you were here."

"What have I done? Oh, Rowan, I ruined everything for us. You must hate me." Her sobs were very loud through the tent wall, and I couldn't hear what Dad said in reply.

The reason I'd grown up without him was one big misunderstanding. I was so angry, I was shaking. I gripped the grass in my fists, pulling out huge tufts and cried at the unfairness of it all.

Eventually, Mom's sobs quieted, probably due to the same exhaustion I felt. I'd lain down on the grass but it was getting wet with dew. May Day dew. I dragged my hands through it, remembering that washing your face with it would keep you eternally young. Touching my dewy fingers to my cheeks, I wished that its magical powers extended to erasing actual years from my age. Then I could go back in time and experience growing up with my dad.

It must have been well after midnight, but there were many people up and about. Anya walked by and asked if everything was okay. I assured her it was. I didn't feel comfortable explaining more. This was Mom's story to tell.

Although we spoke in hushed tones, our voices must have carried inside and Mom stuck her head out and told me to come in.

I'd been waiting for this. I wiped my damp hands on the side of my robe and ducked through the entrance, sitting down across from Dad on a sleeping bag. Mom followed me in and sat next to him. The glow from the lantern was very weak, like the battery was losing power, but I used the dim light to examine my dad's face. His hair was speckled with a little gray at the temples, but, other than that, he looked like he did in the picture I'd kept in my room since I was little.

"Hello, Brigit. I'm your dad." He smiled and let out a little nervous laughter. "I guess you already knew that."

Mom launched into an apology, speaking much faster than usual. "Brigit, I have to tell you that I made a terrible mistake. This whole thing was my fault."

I was about to tell them I'd heard everything when Dad began to talk. "Celeste, this was my fault, too. I should have insisted on talking to you in person. If I had, then we . . . we wouldn't have missed out on so many years together."

I expected him to be mad at her. Really, really mad. But when I saw the way he gazed at her as he took some of the blame, I knew he still loved her. Maybe my fairytale dad existed after all.

I interrupted their argument about who was more at fault by coming clean about my eavesdropping. "You don't have to explain anything to me. I heard everything through the tent. I was listening in."

She digested this information for a moment. "Well, I'm not surprised, and I can't get mad at you for doing exactly what I would have done if I'd been left waiting outside. Are you ever going to be able to forgive me for making . . .?"

My dad interrupted her again. "Brigit, can you ever forgive your two idiot parents for making such a big mistake?"

They were so funny together and so obviously right for each other, I began to laugh. I leaned across the small space to give him an enormous hug, and he squeezed me back just as fiercely. "I'm so glad I'm finally able to meet you," I said before releasing my grip and sitting back.

His eyes were brimming with tears, and he said in a near whisper, "I've missed out on so much."

"We'll just have to catch you up." I said. "Will you come back to the States with us?"

He looked at my mom as he spoke, I think to measure her response to his diplomatic answer. "I'd love to come for a visit whenever you're able to have me."

"Rowan, you're welcome anytime. In fact, if you could fly back with us in a few days, that'd be wonderful." Her smile for him was a thousand times more brilliant than any I'd ever seen.

"I'd love to," he replied.

CHAPTER TWENTY-NINE

The Beltane festival would have been a whirlwind of incredible experiences without the addition of my dad, but with his presence, it turned into something glorious. I couldn't stop smiling. Once the sun was up, it seemed nearly everyone came by our tent to celebrate the reunion of our little family.

When Ember asked me to weave flower wreaths for our hair before the maypole ceremony, I hesitated because I didn't want to leave our campsite. I felt like I was living a dream and was a little afraid my dad might disappear before I got back.

"Get out of here and have some fun," Mom encouraged. "You won't have another first Beltane." And, as if she had read my mind, she assured, "He'll be here when you get back. There's no way I'm letting go of him again." She emphasized her words by gripping his bicep tightly with both hands.

I resisted the urge to head back to my parents the entire time we were twisting the flowers together. We were nearly done when the music began and Ember said, "Hurry. They're starting."

A few last twists and I jammed the wreath on my head, running with Ember to join the gaggle of young women standing by the maypole. All the bobbing floral heads made us look like fairies – well, rather large fairies. We each bent down and chose a ribbon from the brightly colored pile and tied it to the ring at the top of the pole. When we were done, the young men heaved the tall tree trunk into place. The singing and music grew louder as more people gathered around and, much like the night before, we joined in song as we circled the pole, our ribbons interlacing in a beautiful pattern. The colorful strips were long to begin with but rapidly shortened, bringing us closer and closer to the pole until we ran out of ribbon. We tied the ends together at the bottom to hold them in place and backed away, joining hands for one last song. Ember took my hand and looked at me with surprise as she felt my energy. When she smiled and gripped my hand tighter, I exhaled in relief, not realizing I'd been holding my breath waiting for her reaction. Even though I couldn't quite make sense of my special powers, I was getting used to the thrum that filled my head as they flickered on and off.

As I spun, I smiled widely when I passed by the blur of my parents' faces. By the time the song was done, we were going so fast that when one girl released her grip, we all went tumbling out of control, laughing as we fell into the grass. I lay there looking up at the sky for a moment until Bodie's face came into view.

He extended his hand to me with a flourish. "Could I be of service to a maiden in distress?" he asked, bowing deeply.

I extended my hand to him and held back my giggles as I said, "Why, yes. You are quite the gentleman to offer your assistance."

"Would you like to eat with us?" he asked, gesturing to his group of friends standing a few feet away. "I think the food's ready."

I nearly said yes but stopped myself to look around for my parents.

Bodie noticed my glance and said, "I'm guessing they might want a little time alone."

I reluctantly agreed and joined his group, not regretting my decision for a minute. The boys were funny and loud, laughing at all of their own horribly rude jokes. Ember and I rolled our eyes at their antics more than once as we ate our meal. Even though some of the food was unfamiliar to me, it was delicious, and I went back for a second slice of lavender herb bread and another Beltane cake. Long after we were done eating, Ember and I hung around with each other until we noticed the first campsites being dismantled.

We both stood up and brushed the grass off our robes. More impulsive than usual, I flung my arms around her in a big hug. Ember laughed and hugged me back.

I let go of her, a little embarrassed by my gregariousness. "It's been such an amazing day, and I'm so glad I met you."

"I know," she laughed. "Me, too. Promise me you'll come next year."

"You couldn't keep me away."

We hugged again before walking toward our separate campsites. I took a deep breath and let it out. My first Beltane was over and it made me a little sad, but as I approached our tent and my dad came into view, that twinge of sadness was eclipsed by an overwhelming sense of contentment.

The rest of our days in Ireland flew by in a haze of happiness. It seemed unreal to think that my dad would be coming back home with us. I hoped that it would be for more than a visit and took it as a good sign that my mom and dad had been sharing the bedroom at Anya and Finn's the last couple of nights. Afraid that I might jinx the possibility, I didn't ask any questions.

The morning of our departure, I went to see the lambs one last time and say goodbye to Bodie out in the barn.

"Hi," I called to him as I approached. "We're leaving soon, and I wanted to say goodbye to the lambs."

"Only the lambs? You aren't going to say goodbye to me, too?"

"No – I meant you, too – of course." His teasing made the blush reach to my cheeks, and I bent down to pet the lambs to hide my embarrassment. I loved the feel of the tight little curls on top of their heads. "I still wish I could take them home with me."

"Ah, we've already talked about that. You can't get too attached to the little buggers."

"I know, I know." I stood up and looked at him now that my cheeks didn't feel so hot. "Thanks for making me feel welcome. If you're ever in the states, you'll have to stay with us so I can return the favor."

"It was my pleasure, Brigit Quinn. I'm going to miss you." With that he stepped forward and grabbed my face with both hands. I gasped as he brought his lips to mine, gently at first and then more forcefully as I responded. A zing ran through my body, and I know I would have gone on kissing him if he hadn't pulled back.

At most, I'd expected a hug or a little peck on the cheek — not this incredible kiss that made me speechless. I backed out of the barn, waving goodbye.

Bodie laughed at my disconcerted state and called after me, "I can't wait until next year."

On the plane ride home, I kept looking over at Dad, making sure he was really with us. My constant checking must have gotten annoying because he leaned toward me and said, "Brigit, I am not a figment of your imagination. I am real, I am here, and I'm not going anywhere. Now, quit staring at me."

We both laughed and Mom joined in, giving my arm a little squeeze of reassurance. That's when I noticed the glint of a ring on her left hand.

"Whoa," I said, grabbing her hand for inspection. "Is that your engagement ring? It's beautiful."

"Yes." Mom beamed at me. "Your dad had it with him."

"He did?" I asked.

"I've carried it with me always," Dad confirmed. "And now, it's back where it belongs."

My parents gave each other a sweet smile and laughed again. After that I was able to settle back into my seat for the remainder of the flight.

I floated through my first day back at school. Moriah and Jess understood why I was acting so giddy. I'd told them all about my dad the minute I'd gotten home from the airport the day before. They still had a million questions for me which I tried to answer as best as I could before school and all through lunch.

At the end of the day I was in a hurry to get home to my mom and DAD, when a stray piece of paper fluttered out of my locker. I grabbed it and was about to shove it back inside when I saw it was a note.

I'm so sorry.
I need to talk to you.
Meet me in the studio at the barn. – Tyler

Oh my God, Tyler hadn't given up yet. I debated about ignoring the note, but the lesson I'd learned from my parents' mistakes made me realize that I had to at least talk things through with him. In the end, I found myself trying to figure out how to get a ride out to his gran's farm.

I spied Jess and Jason walking to the parking lot and ran to catch up. Since Jason had gotten his license a few weeks ago, Jess sometimes rode home with him.

"Jess, Jason," I called. "Could you give me a ride somewhere?"

"Where do you need to go?" Jess asked.

"Out to Tyler's grandmother's farm. Tyler sent me a note asking me to meet him there."

"What? Are you talking to him now?" Jess' tone was incredulous.

"I don't know." I shrugged. "I guess I feel like I should give him a chance to talk to me."

"Yeah, sure," Jason agreed.

I didn't say anything as we drove the few miles out to the farm. I was surprised Tyler would choose his gran's farm as our meeting place, knowing how I felt about her. I hoped she wouldn't be around. When we pulled in, I was glad her car wasn't in the driveway, but I was puzzled when I didn't see Tyler's car.

"He must not be here yet. I'll wait for him. Thanks for the ride."

I was already getting out when Jess suggested they wait with me until Tyler showed up. "What if he doesn't come? You could be stuck out here," Jess pointed out.

"I'm sure he'll be here." I couldn't imagine him sending the note and not showing up.

"Okay, if you're sure," Jess said. "Call me if you need someone to come and get you."

I waved at them and walked toward the wooden staircase on the side of the barn. I debated about sitting on the bottom step to wait, but, wanting to avoid his gran if she came home, I continued up.

At the top I took one more look down the long driveway, hoping I could see Tyler approaching, but there was no sign of him. I sighed and turned the knob.

As expected, the studio was empty, and I resigned myself to waiting. I walked toward the couch, but as I crossed the floor the throw rug under my feet gave out beneath me.

The solid floor I expected wasn't there!

I waved my arms wildly trying to catch my balance, but there was no way I could save myself. I fell through the hole, cracking my head hard as I landed down below. I don't think I blacked out, but it was hard to tell. I lay there for a minute, my head throbbing in agony before pushing myself up with my hands. I screamed as a searing pain shot up my left wrist and quickly cradled that arm against my chest. I looked around. It was hard to see anything with the only light coming from the opening I'd fallen through. I noticed a trap door hanging down and swinging slightly. I'd seen these before on working farms where the hatches were used to move hay down to the animals in the lower level, but why was this one still there after all the renovations?

A ripple of fear ran through me, and I used my good arm to push myself to my feet, where I swayed unsteadily for a moment. I searched for the door I knew must be there, but with the dim lighting I couldn't see it.

As I patted along the walls feeling for a latch, a knob, a door – anything, I fought my growing panic. There had to be a way out. My terror solidified into a cold lump in my chest when I heard a slight rustle and a little laugh coming from the other side of the barn.

"Who's there?" I called out uselessly. I already knew who it was.

I heard another laugh – closer this time – and Tyler's gran became visible as she stood in the square of light coming from above. She was wearing the ceremonial robe I recognized from my grandma's story. "I knew you'd come. Your family is always so trusting."

She cackled again, but it changed into a hideous shriek, echoing off the stone walls. Her wail reminded me of the banshees from a Celtic legend. My throat went dry, when I remembered that the banshees only wail when someone is about to die.

I swallowed and said, "You – you won't get away with this. My friends know I'm here."

"But they don't know I'm here. They think you're meeting Tyler. I can't believe you were so easy to trick with that note."

"If something happens to me, they'll figure it out, and they'll come after you. Let me out of here!"

"You're going to pay for what's been done to me. Your family has stripped me of so much – my true birthright and even my grandson. You know he won't have anything to do with me anymore. What sort of spell do you have him under? What did you do to turn him against me?" She was shouting as loud as she could and it hurt my ears.

"You did that all by yourself. Leave me alone."

"No," she said quietly. "It is time. I made my decision days ago but had to wait for you to return. Did you like your trip to Beltany? I hope so, for it will be your one and only true May Day. You'll never be one of the Circle of Nine when I'm done stripping your powers. Soon they will be mine."

Her quieter voice made me more fearful than her shrill ranting. I trembled, knowing that focused and in control, she was a far greater danger to me. I backed away from her, feeling along the wall for a way out. My heart sank as I bumped into the corner and knew I'd gone as far as I could. I was trapped.

"Adele, I've done nothing to you. Please let me go," I pled.

"*Please let me go*," she mocked. "You sound so sad and pitiful. Poor Brigit Quinn – you're sure not living up to your namesake. It's too bad for you that your mother hasn't started your formal training. I know you can't defend yourself."

I tried to stifle my whimper, wishing I knew a protection spell which would work against her. I sank down, trying to make myself as small as possible.

She lifted her hands and with palms outstretched, began intoning the same words over and over:

"Now I take your power true.

Bind to me what I am due."

A strange light emanated from her hands and a wind began to swirl around us both. It was hard to breathe as something deep inside me was pulled to and fro like a tug-o-war. I had never been sure I wanted any special powers, but Adele's attempt to take them away forever left me feeling so desolate that I knew I couldn't give them up – especially to someone who would use them for evil. I curled into a tighter ball and attempted to create a defensive cocoon around myself. I could not let her win!

Squeezing my eyes shut, I whispered feverishly to myself, "Someone help me, someone help me." Then I remembered the protection spell my grandma had placed on our family. Would it shield me now? It was all I had.

Adele's chants got louder and louder, and I thought it was wishful thinking when I heard someone shout my name, until I saw Tyler's face peering down through the hole in the floor.

"Brigit, we're coming," he shouted.

His interruption did not stop Adele's trance-like intonation, and the tugging inside my chest ached painfully – almost as bad as my throbbing wrist and head.

A few seconds later the door I'd been searching for was flung open with a tremendous force, flooding the dark space with light. Tyler and my dad rushed in. Dad kept his eyes on me, barely glancing at Adele as he held his hand out toward her and shouted,

"Evil crone, you'll get your due.

What you send out comes back to you"

A flash left Dad's hand and hit Adele square in the chest, propelling her backward until she slammed into the far wall of the barn. She crumpled into a heap as Tyler and Dad reached my side. Her grip on me was gone, and I drew a ragged, deep breath as tears of relief began pouring down my face.

"Are you okay? Are you hurt?" Dad asked.

"I'm – I'm okay. My wrist – I think I broke it when I fell through the floor."

They helped me up and out onto the lawn.

"How did you know where to find me?" I asked.

Tyler answered first, "Jason and Jess saw me at the gas station and told me you were waiting here for me."

I turned to Dad. "How did *you* know I needed help? How could you find this place?"

"I knew you needed me and I came," he explained.

"But there's no way –"

"Fatherly intuition, Brigit," he interrupted. "Let's leave it at that," he added quietly with a wink after Tyler turned to walk back toward the barn.

Tyler peered into the darkness for his gran and cried out in disbelief. "She's gone."

Dad ran to look in and asked, "Is there any other way out of here?"

"No. This is the only door. We would have seen her."

We looked at each other, stunned by Adele's escape.

"What should we do?" I asked.

"Let her go. Her powers are gone, at least temporarily. What's important now is that we get you to the hospital." Dad scooped me up and carried me to the car.

Before he shut the door, I looked back at Tyler and called, "Thank you."

"Brigit, you don't have to thank me. It's my fault that all this happened."

"No, it's not. You can't blame yourself for your gran's craziness."

Tyler shrugged awkwardly and stuffed his hands in his front pockets.

"Will you meet us at the hospital? I want to talk to you."

"Are you sure? It can wait until you're feeling better."

"No. I've waited too long already."

On the way to the hospital, Dad called Mom and explained everything. When we pulled up to the ER door, she rushed to me and knelt down.

"Oh, Brigit, your poor face. What a terrible bump. I hope you don't have a concussion." She touched my forehead gingerly.

She helped me inside, saying, "Grandma came through for us again."

"I didn't know if her spell would still work to protect me. Without that spell, I know Adele would have been able to steal my powers. I hated feeling so helpless."

"Yeah. You and me both, kid. I was so freaked out when your dad rushed out the door and then a minute later I felt the tug of the book telling me the protection spell was in use."

It took a while to get an X-ray of my arm and a CAT scan for my possible concussion. Back in the exam room, I asked Mom to have Tyler come in while we waited.

Mom and Dad stepped out to give us some privacy.

"Tyler, thank you so much for coming to the barn."

"You don't have to thank me. I'm just glad you're okay. Well, almost okay," he amended. "What I can't figure out, Brigit, is why you were out there to begin with."

"I thought you sent me a note, but it was really from your gran. She tricked me."

"After all the days I tried to get you to talk to me, are you saying all I had to do was send you a note?" He laughed.

His laugh was contagious, and I joined in before explaining. "No. It's only that I'm not as mad as I was. I thought that if you still wanted to talk, I should give you the chance."

We were quiet for a few seconds, and then Tyler took a deep breath. "Brigit, you have to believe that I asked you out long before Gran approached me about the money for school and the book in your house. I know what I did was wrong, but I didn't understand what she was really up to. I really didn't. I wouldn't have agreed if I'd known."

"I believe you." I didn't need to use my gift to know he was telling me the truth.

"You do?" He stared at me like he was waiting for me to take back what I'd said.

"Yep. I do."

"Wow. I didn't expect you to say that." The relief on his face stayed in place for a moment before being replaced with a look of worry. "I feel responsible for today, though. While you were in Ireland, I finally had the courage to tell Gran that I would never help her do something dishonest again and that I couldn't take her money for college."

"What did she do?"

"She started screaming at me and telling me that she'd been cheated out of her birthright. It was crazy talk, and I interrupted her and said that if some old book was more important to her than the people who love her, then maybe she deserved to be alone."

"Oh, Tyler."

"She screamed at me again and said that maybe she'd have to teach me what it was really like to lose something important." Tyler dropped his head and muttered. "I should have known that she'd come after you. I should have warned you."

"You couldn't have stopped her."

"Maybe not." He slumped down in the chair, putting his hands over his face.

A knock interrupted us, and Mom opened the door a crack to tell us the radiology report was ready before everyone trooped back into the room.

"When the doctor clipped the x-ray of my wrist onto the light box, he turned to me and asked, "Do you want the good news or the bad news first?"

Uugh. I hated this dumb question every time someone asked it. "How about the bad news first," I said, feeling perverse.

"Your wrist is broken in two places." He turned to the x-ray and pointed at two thin lines with the tip of his pen. "We're going to have to cast it, and I'm guessing it will be about six weeks before it's healed."

"Great." I said. "What's the good news?"

"You don't have a concussion, just a nice big bump and a headache."

Two weeks later, I was getting ready for bed, trying to wash my face with one hand so my cast wouldn't get wet, when there was a pounding on the front door.

"What in the world?" Mom muttered as she made her way down the stairs in her nightgown.

When I heard Tyler's voice say, "Ms. Quinn, I'm so sorry to bother you," I flew down the stairs, too.

"Tyler, what's up? It's really late."

"I'm sorry, but there's something I've got to show you – all of you."

By then Dad had come downstairs and ushered us into the living room where we sat down, waiting for Tyler to explain.

"You know that we've been searching for my gran since that day she attacked Brigit. Tonight we were going through her papers, looking for clues as to where she might be. I found something that I think you should see."

He handed a folded piece of paper to my mom, as he continued to explain. "Brigit told me the story about the – er – misunderstanding that kept you two apart all these years."

I looked quickly at my parents, hoping they didn't mind that I divulged such personal information, but their attention was on the paper Mom was unfolding.

"I knew what this was the minute I saw the names on the letter," Tyler finished.

"Your gran had this?" Mom's voice was shaking. "I should have known she was the Mystery Aunt. Who else could it have been?"

"What?" I turned to Tyler in disbelief. "She had the letter? She was the one who gave Dad back the ring and hand-fasting ribbon? She's the reason my parents were kept apart all these years?" A fresh wave of anger toward Adele engulfed me.

"I'm so sorry, Brigit," Tyler murmured.

"I can't believe I didn't recognize her that day in the barn when she was attacking Brigit. I don't understand why she'd even want the letter. Why would she have been here pretending to be your aunt?" Dad asked Mom.

"I don't know, Rowan. It was the day of my baby shower. Even though she wasn't invited, she probably knew about it and assumed the house would be empty. Maybe she thought she could get her hands on the books while we were out."

"I don't get it," Tyler said. "Why would she have wanted to mess up your relationship? What would she have gained by it?"

We sat there silently until Mom said one word, "Revenge."

I instantly knew what she meant. This was Adele's revenge against our family for so many things. My mom and grandma had both stood in the way of her never-ending quest to be part of the Circle – no matter the cost.

Tyler continued to look puzzled, and I realized we were dangerously close to revealing things he shouldn't know. We couldn't divulge the secrets of the Circle of Nine and we certainly couldn't tell him the story about the love potion which had accidentally brought his parents together.

Mom saved the moment, smoothly mixing a lie with the truth. "It was her revenge for not being allowed access to the books. She was very single minded in what she was after."

Thankfully, Tyler didn't question her further.

"Unbelievable," Dad said, shaking his head.

She handed the letter to him. "Here you go, better late than never,"

"Better late than never." Dad agreed, smiling. He leaned over and gave her a huge not-for-public-display kiss.

"Hey – you two. There are other people in this room," I said while Tyler tried not to laugh.

My parents pulled apart and Mom said, "Get used to it."

CHAPTER THIRTY

The day was perfect . . . not because it was the Summer Solstice, and the weather was gorgeous, and school was out, and my cast was off, and Tyler and I were just maybe getting back together. The day had been perfect because I witnessed my parents exchange marriage vows in our wild, overgrown garden.

This time magic was not used to tie the hand-fasting ribbon. My parents asked me to do the honor. My fingers shook so badly that I'd barely been able to complete the knot as my parents said their vows.

Late in the day with the reception winding down, I excused myself from the few remaining guests. There was something I needed to do before the sun set on the most perfect solstice there had ever been.

I shut the door to my bedroom and pulled the book out of its box before carrying it to my desk. Now certain about the path I would follow, I turned to the blank page after my mom's entry and took a deep breath. Careful to use my best handwriting, I touched the pen to the paper and began my story.

Brigit Blaise Quinn
June 21, 2008

GLOSSARY

Beltane – (*BEL-tane*) Another name for the May Day holiday celebrated on May 1 each year. This is one of the eight holidays on the Celtic Wheel of the Year.

Beltany Stone Circle – (*BEL-tan-ee*) A Neolithic stone circle near Raphoe in County Donegal, Ireland, where the Beltane festival is thought to have been celebrated.

Brigid Cross – A cross woven from straw or rushes with four equal arms around a middle square.

Cairn – (*kern*) A heap of stones set up as a landmark, monument, or burial tomb.

Cell – (*sel*) A small room in which a prisoner is locked up or a room where a nun or monk sleeps.

Celtic Wheel of the Year – The Celtic Wheel of the Year depicts the eight holidays traditionally celebrated in the pagan culture. It includes the four Quarter Days that correspond to the solstices and equinoxes (Yule, Ostara, Summer Solstice, and Mabon) and the four Cross-Quarter Days that fall at the midpoint between the Quarter Days (Imbolc, Beltane, Lammas, and Samhain).

Circle of Nine – A group of nine women descended from the mythological Tuatha de Danann who are guardians of the stone circles and keepers of the ancient traditions. Each woman passes her position to her eldest daughter. *(fictional)*

Deosil – (*DEE-o-sil*) To move in a clockwise direction.

Fire Goddess Brigid – Brigid is the daughter of Dagda and one of the Tuatha de Danann in Celtic mythology and is revered as one of the great mothers of the Celtic people, particularly on Imbolc.

Grimoire – (*GRIM-wahr*) A book of magic spells or incantations.

Hand-fasting – Hand-fasting is a historical form of betrothal where the couple would promise themselves to each other for a year and a day. It was viewed as a trial marriage period where the couple could choose to part after the time period had ended.

Imbolc – (*im-BOLG*) An ancient Celtic festival associated with the Fire Goddess Brigid, held on February 2 to mark the beginning of spring.

Lammas – (*lam-UHS*) The August 1 festival, marking the half-way point between the summer solstice and the autumn equinox with the baking of bread from the newly harvested grain. This is one of the eight holidays on the Celtic Wheel of the Year.

Lough – (*Lok or Lokh*) Lake

Lough Dooras – (*Lokh DUHR-as*) A fictional lake in County Donegal, Ireland.

Nightshade – *(NIGHT-shade)* A plant related to the potato, typically having poisonous black or red berries. Several kinds of nightshade have been used in the production of herbal medicines.

Ostara – (*OH-star-ah*) A pagan holiday celebrated on the vernal or spring equinox, which falls between March 20 and March 23 each year.

Rule of Three – A pagan tenet (also called the Threefold Law) states that the energy a person puts out into the world – whether positive or negative – will return to that person multiplied by three.

Rune – (*Roon*) A mark or letter of mysterious or magical significance.

Samhain – (*SAH-vin*) The first holiday or New Year on the Celtic Wheel of the Year, celebrated on October 31. NOTE: The mh letter combination in Gaelic forms a "v" sound, although you will find many pronunciation guides showing *Sow-hen* as correct.

Scrying – (*SCRY-ing*) A form of divination used to discover hidden knowledge of future events by means of a crystal ball or other reflective surface.

Threefold Law – A pagan tenet (also called the Rule of Three) states that the energy a person puts out into the world – whether positive or negative – will return to that person multiplied by three.

Tuatha de Danann – (*THOOA-haw day DAH-nawn*) Tribe or People of the Goddess Danu. One of the four mythological founding tribes of Ireland.

Widdershins - (*WID-er-shenz*) To move in a counterclockwise direction.

Dear Readers,

The journey to publication is a long one and at times you think no one will EVER get to read your story, so it's very special to me that I've been able to share Brigit's story with you. I hope you enjoyed it!

If you are willing to leave a review on Goodreads or on the website of the retailer where you made your purchase, it would be really helpful to me and to other readers.

To keep up with what's happening with my other books or to enjoy some fun stuff inspired by the Circle of Nine World (like an awesome playlist), go to my website at www.ValerieBiel.com. For more frequent updates, 'Like' my author Facebook page at www.facebook.com/ValerieBielBooks or subscribe to my blog at www.ValerieBiel.com/blog.

As you might have guessed, the stories of these remarkable women don't end here. If you want to know more about the lives of Bressa, Onora, Dervla, and Phoebe, pick up a copy of the Novella Collection.

Brigit's story continues on in the final book in the series, which takes her back to Ireland where she teams up with Bodie and Ember as they battle those seeking to destroy The Circle of Nine forever.

Happy Reading!

Valerie

THE BOOKS IN THE CIRCLE OF NINE WORLD
Circle of Nine - *Beltany*
A Kindle 2015 Book Award Finalist
Readers' Favorite Book Award Finalist
B.R.A.G. Medallion Honoree
Gotham Writers' YA Novel Discovery Contest Finalist

CIRCLE OF NINE
Novella Collection

Descended from a legendary Celtic tribe that guards the secrets of the ancient stone circles, the Quinn women have a great responsibility to protect their pagan rituals and way of life. As members of the formidable Circle of Nine, they celebrate the holidays of the year from Yule to Samhain, keeping the traditions alive through the centuries against insurmountable odds. We first met these women in *Circle of Nine – Beltany,* and now a set of three novellas reveals more of their engaging stories.

In *Bressa's Banishment* the power struggle between Father Banan and village healer Bressa Gormley unfolds amidst accusations of treachery, heresy, and murder. Can the Circle protect their trusted healer and the path of the Tuatha against a growing religious fervor?

Dervla's Destiny brings us to medieval Ireland where this beloved character learns of her gifts and fights tremendous loss and betrayal, all the while never giving up on finding the love she deserves.

In *Phoebe's Mission,* when an evil force on a quest for ultimate power threatens the Circle of Nine, Phoebe Quinn must leave Ireland for the first time and travel to the United States to protect their way of life. Along the way, she meets the handsome Macklin Scott, taking her mission, and possibly her future, on a far different course than expected.

CIRCLE OF NINE
Sacred Treasures

"The first time the portal appeared, I didn't understand how I accidentally summoned a doorway from another realm. The second time wasn't a mistake. I was ready and stepped through with a clear vision of my destination and the grim resolve that my mission must succeed." - Brigit Quinn

26625592R00188

Made in the USA
Columbia, SC
18 September 2018